About the author

This is Peter's first novel resulting from an early childhood-fascination with the world of Tolkien and other fantasy adventure. As a somewhat introverted child and teen, drawing maps of invented worlds, playing immersive computer-games and Warhammer boardgames were keen interests, often to exclusion of all else; being in hindsight a sign of his neurodiverse nature. As an adult Peter has rekindled his childhood interest in the wild outdoors, being a lover of the natural world and bushcraft, his latest passion, the ethos of Ray Mears being a guiding force. Simply being in the wild Welsh woods while enjoying a crackling seasoned-oak fire, carving a spoon, fashioning a long bow, or chopping firewood, all accompanied by the sound of a nearby stream, is considered pure heaven. Further inspiration for this book comes from various workshops, including crafting a bow and fashioning arrows in the surroundings of an ancient hillfort, casting a bronze axe in a prehistoric mine and forging a knife from scrap using an open air hand-bellowed forge. Peter loves the modern trend of apocalyptic survival stories in books, games and film; however, he was always searching for a novel which was more in-depth in terms of being part survival tale and almost a practical how-to guide, all this woven around a story of hope rather than what are often quite depressing situations. Such life affirming tales can be found in stories ranging from the classic 'The Swiss Family Robinson' to the 'Clan of the Cave Bear' series, to the 'The Martian' of more recent years. This book aims to pull out the exciting thread of surviving against-the-odds seen there and to expand on it, while weaving this into an interesting tale. The story that follows is that attempt.

Introduction

This tale is set in a world similar to our own, with various Nordic and Celtic influences, at some unspecified 'post-modern' point in the future. Society as we know it has long since vanished and the natural world has more or less fully reasserted itself, leaving a few isolated pockets of human-existence teetering on the verge of extinction. Birth rates are very low and infant mortality very high, the cause unclear, with remaining settlements slowly withering out of existence. The story starts with a group's desperate flight from danger, their hope being to find a new home and safety.

The story is told almost entirely without spoken dialogue, as if it is being recounted around a campfire; a tale of new beginnings, which follows a small group surviving while carving out a new life, and hoping to thrive. This style of storytelling also reflects the author's preferred means of communication as an autistic person. In a world full of verbal communication which is often difficult to correctly interpret, you are to a large extent told what the characters are thinking and feeling.

The story is intrinsically part guide to survival and the basics of homesteading; it also sets out a more positive possibility for a future where rampant and destructive 'modernity' has vanished. With a natural check on the human population, Earth has become a properly functioning ecosystem and is mostly a near Eden, and not a world where humanity does as it wishes with no thought for the consequences.

The intentionally Tolkienesque map that follows highlights the main area in which the story takes place. It is purposefully kept relatively compact, bound by natural topography, with the main valley and other important features artificially-enlarged in scale, but hopefully that gives the reader a chance to immerse themselves in its detail. Readers may recognise influences for some locations, loosely based around the breath-taking landscapes of Snowdonia and beyond, the Author's home in North Wales. Thank you to Tiffany at www.feedthemultiverse.com for creating the wonderful map which follows from my amateurish sketch, I can highly recommend her friendly and professional service.

Dedicated to my daughter Lilly, and in memory of all our amazing adventures in the woods, long may they continue!

Also, a special thank you to Elizabeth my partner for letting us out to play.

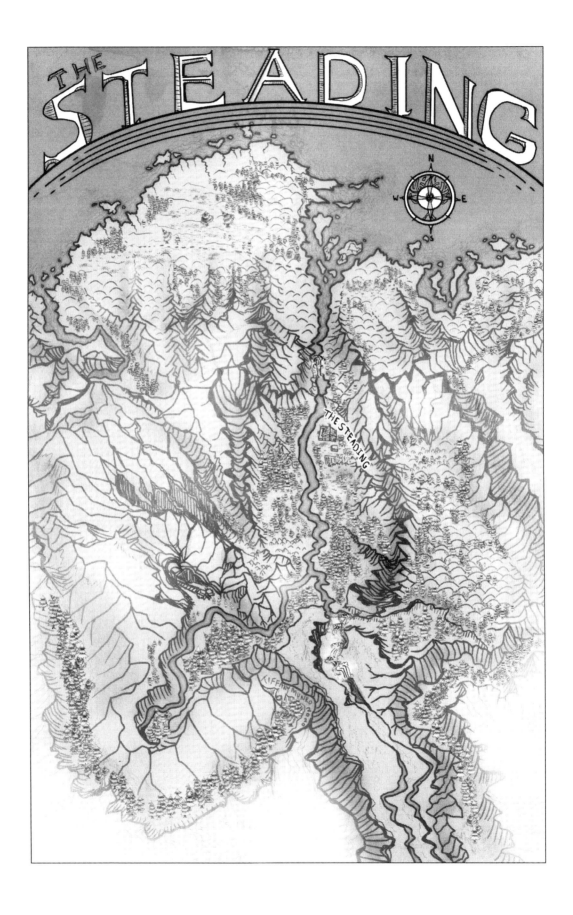

Contents

1 - A journey's end

The high upland-valley was truly isolated, certainly enough at least that you wouldn't find it without serious intent. It was once a coiffured and heavily managed place that those with an abundance of time on their hands had visited for its own sake, particularly the dramatic waterfall at its head and the once well-preserved picturesque and ancient farmstead at its heart. Nonetheless the tamed and suppressed landscape had long since rebounded into something like its wild and primeval state, the interfering human hand now absent. There was huge diversity and abundance of flora and fauna, but the oak and pine predominated; however, these were not your stately parkland-types, but were descended from gnarled and ancient beasts who had hung on to the precipitous valley-sides, where they were previously permitted. This remnant of ancient woodland had long since burst forth from these manacles and scattered its seed across the former lowland pastures of the wide valley, forming a thick forest.

Stillness reigned in the darkening wild-woods, a serene lack of grating noise due to the fact humanity had been long absent. The usual twilight interludes, practically cliché, including blackbirds rustling in the leaves, tawny owls gently hooting, the trickle of streams and the rush of the river were there, but in the background, coming from the very base of the valley, there was something new; humans.

It had been an incredibly arduous journey getting to this point, any bridges, paths and roads that had once existed were washed out or grown over, now that no one was there to repair and maintain. Nonetheless, a battered and much faded vellum-based map had led them here with a promise of a peaceful existence not seen in other parts for many decades. After many wrong turns, due in no small part

1

to the map which was rudimentary at best, they arrived late in the gloaming of the day at the east side of an unpromising V-shaped valley bottom, quite barren except for a few stunted pines which seemed to be clinging onto a precarious existence among the rocky landscape. The entrance to the mountainous upper-valley was essentially a steep-sided gorge thundering with huge amounts of white water, similar to others they had passed on their journey bar its massive size; it was far from welcoming. They had nonetheless pushed on knowing that any respite with a campfire at the valley bottom was likely to advertise their presence for miles around at this altitude, and was best lit well-away from those who might follow. Caution had dictated that they keep in single file for much of the journey to mask their numbers, though modest, including their dogs who were trained to do so at command, but every precaution was needed to keep their potential new home a secret.

The travellers had fled from the eastern lowlands, trekking over many hundreds of leagues, hoping to find a place of safety. On their journey they had passed the odd abandoned settlement, but none in the latter stages. They had mostly shied away from the coast, which tended to offer more hospitable climes and access to abundant food, but would more likely be populated and visited by others, so was risky. As they had approached the relatively inhospitable mountainous-terrain leading to the valley, there was no trace of human life; still though, they had to be extremely cautious.

The leader of the group was as tired and travel worn as the others, scouting a trail as best he could, then stopping to let everyone catch up. His near permanent frown-lines were accentuated by dirt, cheeks hollowed out by meagre sustenance, and long-lank hair in dire need of a wash. As the others passed him he gave them a few words of encouragement, while worriedly observing their troubled and harried look, heads down and despondent, many carrying injuries, though mostly minor. As the last of the ragged party practically staggered past due to pure exhaustion, he quietly sighed and looked again at the map, such as it was, then made his way back to the front, his strong stride showing a confidence he did not feel, intense worry and doubt gnawing at his mind. He was acutely conscious that he had risked everything in deciding on this desperate journey, despite misgivings in the group; it was a gamble and one that might cost all their lives.

The dusky evening was increasingly frigid and snow a distinct possibility, though spring was hopefully on its way in the coming weeks. The mountains were however a fickle beast, sometimes causing a weather front from the north to lift and drop a heavy load of snow, plunging the area into an impenetrable lockdown. However, being relatively close to the warming effect of the sea meant extreme cold was hopefully unusual and tonight was just another of those bone-chilling nights they had come to expect, best kept at bay by keeping their stiff bodies moving and wrapping their cloaks more tightly about them to ward off the biting gusts of wind.

With dwindling energy reserves they fought through the increasingly thick low-lying undergrowth of the upper section of the gorge, receiving scratches from clumps of gorse and thick-tangled briars along with lashes from the unyielding stunted-vegetation, leaving them with new sores to add to their already impressive collection. They had long since left the fragmentary remnants of the easier coastal tracks where a motorised vehicle may once have gone. Not that any of them really knew what a car or lorry might have been, the wrecks having long-since rusted to skeletal hulks, the resulting toxic pollutants creating open patches within the undergrowth that often still persisted. The barely perceptible track they initially followed up the mouth of the gorge was once wide and clear, but now was on the verge of disappearing entirely, then did beneath a particularly large rockslide. They struggled on, hoping that another few miles would see them to the possibility of an ancient homestead in the heart of the hidden-upper valley shown on the map, though the increasingly desolate land they travelled into was not promising; their willpower was trickling away. In the back of their minds they had increasing anxiety that the map may have entirely deceived them or had been simply misread; who knew what they might find, perhaps a trap.

The despondent travellers continued the hard slog up the increasingly steep-sided gorge, following a faint game trail here and there, but mostly it was a near impenetrable mass of loose fallen-rock and thick low-level scrub, the gradient necessitating the use of their hands as much as their feet. At times the thunderous river cast virtually everything into a near-freezing opaque mist, making footing treacherous on the slippy scree. Added to this were massive rock falls and so there were some sections where they had to laboriously clamber up and over huge slick boulders, hauling up the not inconsiderable weight of the dogs, their meagre belongings and the small children. Needless to say the effort brought them to the point of collapse; some started to wonder if they had made a grave error as they stood panting trying to recover their breath, the tang of blood sharp in their throats. There was however little point in turning back, they could not run forever and were out of options, so they forced themselves on.

Then, quite suddenly, but with great difficulty, they mounted a wide, near-vertical ridge, off which spilled the great river in deep clefts. Clambering up they left the oppressive confines of the damp, steep-sided gorge, moving into a new landscape where they could at last catch their breath. With this change came a glimmer of optimism and a burst of borrowed energy; they may have found what they had long hoped for. The area immediately broadened out into what was a very wide valley-floor, U-shaped with high valley sides. Clearly the steep ridge they had scrambled over had once been the terminus point of a massive glacier, the meltwater outflow carving the huge gorge and leaving behind a flattened landscape in the valley as it had retreated in the distant past. However, this landscape was not at all evident to the travellers due to a quickly-accumulating mist, making the true extent of the area all but invisible in the deepening night. If they had been able to see properly beyond a few-dozen feet, they would have noted their eventual passage into thick oak-woodland and extensive ancient stands of coppiced hazel that had once fed the charcoal burners of the past, but now ran rampant and wild. The trees did however thin out somewhat within another half mile of the coppice, making the way easier. Then, passing moss-covered tumble-down boundary walls formed of the local dark angular stone, they came to what had been rich pastures, relatively clear of even pioneering saplings. There in the small light of the half-moon, they found what they had come to find, hoping against hope that no one had beaten them to it, hearts thumping in their chests.

The mist-swamped buildings they cautiously approached were however clearly abandoned and appeared disappointingly ramshackle, based on what little they could see in the moonlight. Everything was nearly completely covered in a sea of ivy and other creepers which had long since consumed much of what once was. After some investigation they found a small partially-enclosed stone-built barn which would serve for the night, offering some respite from the biting wind; they could further explore in the morning. The dilapidated barn was very musty, clearly a space used by animals judging by the acrid smell, but there were some dry spots, a palace compared to the rough camps they were now used to. The group collapsed almost as one, all cold, damp and beyond exhausted; they simply wrapped themselves in their woollen blankets and animal skins, then tucked themselves into a corner of the dilapidated building. Despite being damp the wool and skins eventually offered some warmth and as they snuggled up together in a protective cocoon which included the dogs, they fell into the deep sleep of those who had come to the end of an arduous journey, for better or worse.

2 - Arrival

They awoke to a sharp hoar-frost which brought a monochrome look to the valley, of crisp prickly-white and pools of deep shadow. The first inkling of weak-winter light was already apparent from beyond the high valley-walls, enabling a first view of their new home; nonetheless, direct sunlight was still some hours away from fully breaking the craggy backlit mountains to the east. Although the valley was long and wide, the sun was weak and low this time of year, and would not provide direct sunlight until late-morning, then would set early to the west. Though lacking in light in the winter, the valley was a clearly a sheltered place, with only the wind from the direct north being relatively unhindered, protection otherwise being afforded by the enclosing valley walls. Though high in altitude they would thankfully find that the valley had a moderating micro-climate of sorts which meant it avoided much of the harsh mountainous weather and enabled lush growth of vegetation for a good portion of the year.

The land about them sat in the lee of a ridge of smooth hillocks; these offered some protection from the warmth-sapping katabatic wind that sometimes raced down the valley from the high mountain glaciers. The immediate area comprised a relatively flat plateau of thick rich-soil, though heavily vegetated and which would have been submerged by the encroaching woods in not so many years. As the group woke into this new land the cold air caught in their throats, and it was with effort and no few groans that they extricated themselves from their bundled warmth, then stretched their aching limbs with a cracking of fatigued and swollen joints. On emerging from the barn they mostly forgot their discomfort and excitedly noted the vista of the valley and the indistinct shapes of other buildings which they had thought ruins the night before. As they explored they noticed now that it was possibly as though the structures had simply been submerged in a tide of vegetation and hemmed in by pioneering bushes and trees. It was amazing camouflage and the place would not have been obvious from anywhere except very close by; even then the complex of structures could easily have been dismissed as they had done the night before. Investigating this further would however be a task for later, sharp hunger cramps and the need for breakfast trumped their eager curiosity.

Soon a large bright-fire formed from stacked birchwood found in the barn was burning merrily, and a camp kettle was rapidly boiling, despite being filled with nearly frozen water from a nearby watercourse. Next the group produced between them a decent number of foraged mushrooms and berries along with the remnants of dried strips of meat, partially cured and carried with them for many miles, being nearly the last of their supplies. A large blackened cast-iron frying pan, seasoned from uncountable meals, was then set upon the coals. The meat was added with some water to hydrate the tough fibres and before long sizzled in its own fat. A mouth-watering smell soon followed, great anticipation on everyone's faces as they huddled around attempting to warm themselves, but with few words said in an effort to save energy. Coffee was a long distant memory of the elders' ancestors, but the land could provide teas of bountiful variety, with only somewhat less potency for having been dried and stored in their packs. They could though, if they felt inclined, find spruce for their flavoursome needle tips, or the chaga fungus which grew on silver birch to make a more refreshing brew. The dried tea was soon steeping in the kettle and a wholesome faintly citrusy smell of lemon-balm melded with the wood smoke. Once the meat was nearly done and the mushrooms fried off, the remainder of the traveling bannock bread was added to the pan to mop up and absorb the tasty juices, where it lightly browned; the bread was stale and they had to first pick off spots of mould, but nothing was wasted in such lean times.

The meal was meagre but returned a few precious calories that had been burnt with the risky but necessary journey in deep winter. The sustenance would be sorely needed, as the long journey may be over, but there was much work to do. Following cleaning of the precious cast-iron cookware with water and scouring sand, they ate their remaining berries from a shared pot, drank more hot tea and made plans for the coming day, excitement overriding their state of exhaustion, for now.

3 - Unveiling

Merrick was their current leader, though he was all too aware this was a tenuous position, and a somewhat grandiose title among so few. He was generally hesitant to impose his opinion and tried to hear everyone out, then invariably went with the collective will of the group. There were times though when quick decisions needed to be made with a cool head; that was his strength and why he continued to lead by common consent, despite being relatively young and much less experienced than others in the group. Though his decision to lead them to this new home had been contested by some, the escalating dissent of late had now abated, the gamble seemingly worth the risk based on what they had found so far. Still, his confidence was at a low point and he was mindful there was much that could go awry.

It was all too apparent from the air of excited energy that the group were eager to explore the immediate area, not least to see what might remain of the homestead, for that was why they had come. However, Merrick did not want them wasting energy with uncoordinated effort, so none too subtly herded them all to the largest of the buildings with a few quiet words. The large dwelling, for that was what it appeared to be, with the hint of the chimneys apparent now in the clear morning, was agreed to be a sensible place to start. This was done with some initially hesitancy, as who knew what they may find within. Based upon the merest hint of a protrusion in the undergrowth, the nose-like porch was located and stripped of its ivy overcoat after all the surrounding saplings had been hacked back. What they found was beyond expectations, an ancient heavily-studded oak door, set back in a large open-fronted slated porch, where several people could stand with ease. The door was unlocked, but only opened out a finger's width with an alarming screech then was frustratingly stuck, seemingly due to the rusty hinges and encrusted house-martin nests lining the high stone lintel, the hardened mud-like mortar. Following some none-too-gentle coaxing and cajoling, the door swung back out with a fall of dried dust from the disintegrating overhead nests, causing no end of sneezes and a few muttered curses. The accompanying squeal of rusty-metal hinges sounded like a pig being slaughtered, but the thick door stayed whole and would be serviceable. It was an excellent start and boded well, immediately lifting their morale.

The heavy door opened out to reveal a dark stone-slabbed entrance space littered with small leaves and carpeted with dust. They could just about see that the large chamber contained various portals to a number of rooms, with a substantial timber-spindled staircase straight ahead to the pitch-black upper floor. The space was otherwise difficult to assess further being murky and emanating a faint fusty smell, but there was no immediate sign of significant damage or decay. It was in fact as if the building had been occupied and maintained perhaps in the not so distant past, but that was far from clear. Rather than explore the building further it was agreed with a quick discussion that the building needed to be fully exposed, to shed it of the coat of creepers, to inspect for damage, find windows and let the sunlight in. Long gone were the luxury of battery-operated torches, with their now very limited supply of smoky tallow-based tapers best kept for more pressing need.

They spent much of the morning hacking back the vegetation away from around the base of the building and carefully removing the ivy and other creepers from the walls. Their hard work revealed a number of small window-openings that were firmly shuttered within deep recesses, all in surprisingly good condition. On opening the shutters, the exposed windows were grubby and covered in a mass of old cobwebs, but which were soon cleaned down with warm water and rags, letting in the weak winter-light which now poured down from

11

between the mountains. The greyish weathered timber-framed windows were mostly glazed with small glass panes, often cracked, some mended using creamy translucent-horn, hammered to make it thin. They were more than serviceable though, being well protected by the thick oak-shutters for many a year, until their opening that day. Exposing the windows gave the distinct impression that the eyes of the building had been suddenly opened after a long slumber, breathing new life back into the homestead, albeit with an initial dusty sneeze.

Next the extensive thick-slated roof and stone-built chimneys stacks were carefully cleared, utilising a pair of slightly rickety but serviceable ladders found in the barn. Suitable lengths of pliant creepers from the walls and roof were carefully looped up and kept to one side for later re-use, in making basic baskets, cordage and suchlike. Though vegetation still crowded the back yard of the building and would need to be cleared another day, it was plain to see that there had not been too much damage. If anything, the ivy, honeysuckle and other creepers had provided some protection, as well as creating a perfect nesting-site for many birds. A particularly indignant roost of sparrows had made their thoughts known on being disturbed, flying off with much chattering to the other outbuildings to find a new spot. On standing back to survey the building they noted the dark-blue, thick-slated roof was still in decent condition, with just a few partially-slipped slates, already fixed and wedged back in as they had cleared the roof. The walls of yellowy lime-pointed, dark diorite-type granite were intact, as well as the robust chimney stacks still standing at each gable end. There would be some minor repair of the cast iron gutters to do, along with some repointing of the mortar where it had crumbled in places, but they were tasks for another time.

Being more than satisfied that the outside was substantially intact and better than they had hoped for, they all entered the house to explore, though with no little trepidation at what they might find. They passed through the porch and entered the wide entrance-space, noting a great deal more detail with the light pouring in through the door and a trio of windows serving the room, illuminating the many motes of dust in the air and the multitude of thick cobwebs. The children quickly clambered up the creaky timber-staircase at the centre of the shadowy hall, pretending with some bravado that they had not already made tentative exploratory-quests inside, with a muffled scuffle soon following about which rooms they might claim. Everyone else spread into the various downstairs rooms to inspect and assess, though with due caution, some with defensive staffs to hand, though really the worst they might came across was a large rodent. As they moved through the house they cracked open whatever windows they could, letting in fresh air to help get rid of the stale air and musty odour. Although the lime-washed walls were no longer white, or anything close to it, they helped reflect the shafts of weak winter-light, which revealed a series of well-ordered rooms. Rustic furniture, clearly locally crafted from coppiced hazel and hewn oak planks, was welcome to see and looked dry and pretty solid. Everything was coated in years of fine dust, with small paw-prints of the house mouse here and there apparent now as their eyes adjusted to the areas of dim light. As they moved around, the slight hollow-echo of footsteps on parts of the stone slabbed-floor indicated the likelihood of a large cellar and hopefully a cold store.

On entering the large kitchen off to the right-hand side of the entrance hall, they noted a long table of finely crafted elm dominating one end, with a robust cast-iron range at the other end set into the gable. Again, all was incredibly dusty, but orderly, with the slightly-rusty grate free of ashy coals, indicating the previous occupiers hadn't been forced to leave in a hurry. A series of simple wooden cupboards and shelves lined the main internal walls. Within the cupboards there were various-sized jars of what was mostly hand-blown glass and wooden pots, empty and in need of at least a good dusting. Various hand-carved wooden implements found in the drawers were all in decent condition, seemingly coated with beeswax judging by the faint smell and slightly tacky feel. Overhead, dangling from hefty wooden-pegs driven into a great ceiling beam, hung a collection of robust cast-iron cookware, protected in a thick layer of beeswax. The wax had set solid and was coated in dusty grime, but seemed to have preserved the pots and pans from the ravages of damp and rust, though the wax was slightly nibbled here and there by mice. Under a pair of wide windows looking out to the front of the house was a large tank for water and an area for washing and food preparation, all situated upon a huge slate-slab sat up on brick pillars. The orderly condition of the kitchen spoke of great care and an intention to preserve for the future, though clearly the inhabitants could not have known who they were doing it for. A huge amount of cleaning would be needed, to wash away the years the kitchen had lain empty, but already it had a homely and welcoming feel, helped by the fresh air and sun streaming in through the opened windows.

On exploring the rest of this end of the house, they discovered a steep stair entry down to a near pitch-black cellar, and off the rear of the kitchen a series of pantries and other storage rooms, though all empty of the smallest crumb of food. The orderly rooms were filled with containers of all sorts of shapes and sizes, along with domestic paraphernalia of all conceivable use. A large stable-type door off a short hallway at the back of the house opened onto a yard and outbuildings, but which was still full of thick vegetation, so that was left for another day.

The other end of the house comprised one huge living space easily accommodating the group with much room to spare, essentially a high barn-like hall reaching up into the roof space. There was an enormous open fireplace dominating the end gable, stone lined, with an impressive long oak lintel, carved heavily with designs of various complicated knots and stylised mythical beasts. The roof joists were similarly carved with exposed beams forming a cruck-like frame and an upper balcony opposite the gable end, though any details were hard to make out in the squint-inducing gloom. Simple but functional furniture abounded, with various solid side tables, storage units and a series of large high-backed wooden chairs which spoke of long nights spent in comfort. On closer inspection they were once covered in thick blankets and cushions of wool, but which had long-since disintegrated and fallen to the floor, the mice no doubt lending a hand. To both sides of the fireplace stood great stacks of oak, birch and some kindling, perfectly dry and enough for many a warm night. This was a very welcome find and would save time, sparing their dwindling energy reserves in gathering their own. On inspecting inside the slightly-damp chimney void it seemed completely blocked at first sight judging by the near pitch-black, which was disheartening though not unexpected, likely being full of bird nests. However, on climbing up a little way and with further investigation, it was noted through the cobwebs a simple but ingenious blacksmith-forged flap a dozen feet up where the chimney narrowed. With persuasion and screeching of metal the flap was pushed up and bolted out of the way, with a good deal of soot now coating the investigator and the fireplace. Disappointingly all this revealed was another dark space which indicated the jackdaws had probably filled the top with twigs to make their nests, though there was a slight draft of fresh air indicating it may not be as bad as it first appeared. Although they were all warm and slightly sweaty from their various exertions, they knew they could not afford another night in an exhausted and starving state, with just a blanket and some furs to stave off the chill. The house was almost colder than outside, though out of the biting wind; with the temperature rapidly dropping as the day wore on, it could be lethal, especially to the little ones. The first priority was fire, at least in the main hall, but ideally in the kitchen and presumed sleeping areas above that end of the building. It was amazing what a good fire could achieve, its life-giving warmth a blessing beyond pretty much beyond anything else they could conceive to help lift the spirits. If however the chimneys were blocked, they may have some serious problems.

On re-inspecting the cooking range in the kitchen they found another system of flaps to close off the dual chimneys; clearly the previous occupiers were well aware of the nuisance birds could be with their nests and getting into the house. Again disappointingly the chimneys seemed dark and presumably blocked and so couldn't be lit. After considering what to do, it was agreed that this had to be addressed, to avoid a potentially fatal night of cold. Someone would have to climb the roof and inspect the chimneys to see what could be done; hopefully any blockage would be minimal. Sioned was considered the best climber, being young, nimble and the most fearless, but in any event excitedly volunteered, quickly pulling back her long hair and plaiting it into a functional braid as she went out. On inspection of the gables, it was found that climbing up would be simple enough, there being handholds in the stone not previously seen, with a few seemingly solid rungs of iron on the stack itself. Sioned took her stout staff with her to clear any obstructions, strapped to her back with a cord of creeper; ostensibly it was her walking stick but also an excellent defensive weapon with which she was very proficient. She initially used a ladder then nimbly climbed up to the stack with no small trepidation emanating from some of the group, though they needn't have worried, her sure-footedness and confidence making short work of the ascent. On reaching the base of the stacks and climbing up using the iron rungs it soon became apparent that all bar one, the chimney's pots were simply capped with a wired-on slate, with just a small gap left for airflow to help prevent damp. After Sioned called down with the good news, this was remedied on both stacks; those at the bottom of the chimneys inside could then see daylight, calling out with great delight as to the good news. With the uncapped pot, this was, as suspected, filled with nests from the jackdaws, but with judicious application of Sioned's staff, these were broken up and pushed down, falling into what turned out to be an upstairs sleeping area above the kitchen, with a cloud of dust and soot.

Before long everyone was excitedly back inside for the lighting of the fires in the hall and kitchen. The lighting had a ceremony and distinct gravitas in bringing life back to what they were rapidly coming to see as their new home. It was a tense time though, as they knew the chimneys ideally needed to be thoroughly swept, and they could well do without the danger of them catching alight. It was a calculated risk, the likelihood of loss of life from hypothermia more than offsetting the danger of what appeared to be otherwise well-maintained flues.

To start the fires paper-like birch bark was made ready and a piece repeatedly scraped with a knife to produce a patch of oil-rich dust, which then took a spark from flint and steel with a minimum of effort. Added atop this rapidly-burning pile of birch paper, to ensure the fire took hold, they stacked some finely-split fatwood, this being the resinous core of pine tree branches and old roots. This was shortly burning with a scent which evoked a recollection of summer in the pine forest and helped settle some frayed nerves. They added some freshly-curled feathersticks formed by repeatedly shaving into long split wood, then worked through the thinnest twigs and added increasingly-thicker sticks of silver birch. Once the flames were dancing and hungry for more, they started to stack on the thicker split-logs of dry oak into a log cabin-like arrangement which would allow airflow and quickly create the long-lasting hardwood heat and coals so desperately needed. Suddenly a call of alarm from the kitchen had people running; it turned out that on lighting the range fire the chimney had briefly but alarmingly flared as remnants of dust and detritus were burnt off, but this did not last long and only one set of eyebrows was slightly singed. It had hearts racing but on running outside it was clear it was just a modest flare up, with no evidence of flames from the chimney pot. Care would need to be taken with any fire in the upstairs sleeping-area, to remove the last remnants of the nests, in order to avoid a more serious incident, but this should be possible with the much shorter flue.

Returning to the main hall the wide fireplace was aglow and drawing quite well atop the robust raised iron fire basket. Most of the group had their hands to the now intense heat, rotating to warm their backs and luxuriating in the simple pleasure of limbs slowing losing their numb chill. Soon the heat was being absorbed by the surrounding stonework and radiating it back into the room, slowly starting the long thaw of the building and driving out the damp the draughts had not managed to keep at bay. It was a little smoky at first, creating a smoggy atmosphere in the rafters, but that should improve as the chimney warmed and started to pull and draw. Gathered around the fire, taut and knotted-muscles relaxing in the radiant heat, it did a great deal to make them feel at home, with many a furrowed brow starting to ease.

As there was such success with the ground-floor fires they decided to see what could be done with the two smaller fireplaces in the sleeping areas upstairs. For Merrick this was the first time he had used the staircase and seen the upper floor; the wide steps were fairly creaky but seemed reassuringly solid. He also noticed the carvings not fully appreciated before which adorned the spindles and hand rail, over which he ran his callused hands, feeling the flowing patterns and smooth textures of the ancient woodwork. The stairs led up onto a substantial, though dimly-lit landing; straight opposite there was what appeared to be a small bedroom, and to the left a short corridor which led out onto the high balcony above the still-smoky main hall. Merrick noted the substantial hall roof space which could be strung with lines and would be good for drying clothes, meat, herbs, mushrooms and all manner of food for the stores. To the right of the landing another much longer central-corridor linked a series of bedrooms on either side, pools of weak light from each doorway illuminating the hall. There was a decent amount of space in each room, despite being partially-up in the roof so resulting in sloping ceilings, with small windows under the eaves providing light to stave off the dark. There were a series of large sleeping spaces containing basic timber pallets for their sleep rolls and blankets, most of which had been laid out and claims made, though everyone with the exception of Merrick was currently downstairs getting warm. The rooms were otherwise fairly spartan, bar some deep shelves on the internal lime-washed walls, minor damp-patches showing in places on the external gable end, but not unexpected given the house had lain empty for what was likely some considerable time. The small but efficient-looking cast-iron fireplaces only served the two larger rooms at the far end, Merrick supposed the intention being that the open balcony to the main hall and corridor would provide for flow of heat to other rooms, as well as up through the floorboards from the kitchen. On inspecting the fireplaces, it was apparent that they had only short chimneys, being so close to the stack top, and that Sioned had done a good job with her long staff, loosening the worst of the blockage. It was a simple, though mucky job, to use a pliable bough of pine to thoroughly clear away the remaining detritus, then re-use the nest material as kindling to light small fires to test the chimneys. All seemed promising and they drew well, providing a decent heat with only a little smoke, which should abate once warmed up and drawing

19

better. With the good supply of seasoned logs built up by the side of the chimney breasts it should be a comfortably warm night, with a sleep likely better than any the group had seen in a long time.

The house was quickly becoming homely with no idle hands, and the warmth of the fires and their body heat meant it wouldn't be many days before the last vestiges of surface damp had been driven out from the long-empty house. Windows would be left cracked open a little for now to air the building, but come nightfall would be closed and shuttered to reduce draughts. There would also likely be a good population of mice and other rodents to clear out, but they could live with that for now, it was not as if they had any stores of food they could spoil.

Back in the kitchen, a meal was in the process of being made, the smell drawing in most of the group to the long table, its top now scrubbed back to reveal a deep glossy-sheen. Following removal of the protective wax encrusting a substantial lidded iron pot, it had been placed over the large range fire, and was quickly on the go after a few bright flares as the waxy remnants had caught. Though there was little to add from their measly supplies to make even a thin broth, they pulled together the last remnants of the preserved meat, herbs and dried mushrooms, boiled it up, and so their hunger was satiated, though it was far from satisfying. While cleaning the cooks had discovered that there was a brick oven built into the wall, essentially a hollow space abutting the fire with an iron door, but they had little use for it for now, with bread and sweet pastries firmly put out of their minds. Their travelling cooking kit had been unpacked, but it was close at hand Merrick saw; it would be some time before the flight instinct and stress of continuous travel left their troubled minds.

Resting their weary bodies in front of the fire in the great hall, in large wooden chairs made more comfortable with their well-used travelling blankets and heavily-patched cloaks, the group spent the few remaining hours of the day reflecting on just how fortunate they were, starting to slowly relax after many months of near unbearable tension in their flight from the east. With cups of tea raised they gave heartfelt words of thanks to the absent owners who had gone to such lengths to make the place a home for others, which they had taken to simply calling The Steading. Soon all were yawning despite the relatively early hour; with unspoken agreement an early night was clearly needed by all, and not just for the youngest children who had already dozed-off in the adults' arms. In making ready for their eagerly awaited beds they banked the coals of the fires into a sooty pile to preserve some embers for the next day, shuttered the windows then barred and bolted the doors; they slept that night warm and safe for the first time in many moons.

4 - Whiteout

The new day came, though not that you would really know it in the valley; sound was oddly muted and very little stirred in the deep numbing-cold. All was covered in a thick layer of pristine, slightly pinkish white, which continued building as more snow came down in a thick mass from the heavy clouds. The house was silent, excepting some occasional creaks of the ancient structural-timbers, the frame flexing and settling as the weight of the snow gradually increased on the roof, with the occasional soft thump as lumps slid off and hit the ground.

Durian awoke; he was young, hungry and excited for the new adventure ahead, but often roused first. He was a fiercely independent boy, though quickly turning into a young man, and while he had never gravitated towards any particular adoptive parents as some did, he was loved by all the group as a good-natured prankster. While stretching out his stiff wiry-muscles he noticed the slightly eerie quiet, exaggerated by the fact that of late they had woken outdoors to the sound of the birds, ever present in even the winter cold. The snores of the others were only slight, but it seemed that they were content to slumber for a while more, snuggled and warm in their new beds, so he let them be.

Feeling the need to relieve his uncomfortably full bladder, Durian decided to get dressed and venture outside. Over his long johns he clothed in his usual warm winter-garb, including thick-soled high leather-boots, tweed trousers and shirt, woollen jumper and his outer oilskin coat. His clothes were still functional, though heavily patched and becoming quite frayed and threadbare in places; they would need replacement before too long. He pulled his stiff broad-rimmed battered leather hat over his woollen skullcap while going down the creaky stairs, and made ready knitted under-gloves for after he had relieved himself, his over-mittens left inside for now along with his thick cloak. Passing the door to the kitchen, he saw the inquisitive dogs look up so bade them good morning, but the pack quickly snuggled back down by the still-warm range when they saw who it was, used to Durian's early rising. Noting the great iron-hinges had been greased with beeswax he carefully removed the wooden security-bar and silently swung the heavy front-door out into the porch, revealing a large pile of snow which had drifted in through the night, virtually up to the door. With a new flurry of snow came a freezing blast of chilly air, snapping his senses fully to life. This drew his now sharpened attention out onto the incredibly beautiful vista of the snowy valley beyond, partially revealed in a slight break in the heavy fall, making him gasp with delight, the promise of exploration to come filling him with excited anticipation.

Durian was momentarily torn between racing out to explore and going to wake the group to see the spectacle, but with rare foresight he realised that the others may not be too happy with a dawn wakeup call, especially when all were so exhausted. With his decision made, he left the house and waded through the crunching powdery-snow to find a likely spot to relieve himself; during even that brief outing in the sub-zero temperatures he realised that the cosy warmth of the house had been deceiving. Now out in the biting northerly-wind, with the still-falling snowflakes threatening to amalgamate and become a whiteout, he was near certain that they may be forced to hole up inside for some time to come, worrying when food supplies were already virtually spent.

The others awoke to varying degrees of enthusiasm, and some with slight shock at where they were, until their memories flooded back. All had slept well and were feeling somewhat re-energised, but it might be some time before the aches and pains resulting from travelling in the harsh winter had abated. One-by-one all went to go outside to relieve themselves, but they quickly saw that a quick dash was all that was prudent, including the dogs. Thankfully Nineveh had seen to having collected a good store of water the day before, with the well-scrubbed slate-sided tank in the kitchen near full, kept from freezing by the ambient warmth of the fires. That more than sufficed for a bracing strip-wash in the large sink, though the children were certainly unimpressed, having grown used to minimal bathing on the trail, though that was simply through urgent necessity.

Before long all the fires were stoked back to life from their banked ashy-embers, excepting those in the bedrooms which would be relit later if necessary. They would need to get used to the unknown vagaries of heating the house, but they hoped that the natural circulation of rising hot air from the fires downstairs would warm it through, which did in fact turn out to be the case. With the blanket of insulating snow on the roof, this would help keep it at a comfortable temperature, also saving precious fire wood. They calculated that they had enough for several days stacked up inside, maybe a good two-weeks' worth, but they sorely needed to conserve their supplies for now. For this reason most kept various layers on, including woollen hats, leaving off just their outer oilskins and gloves. This kept them cosy, saving precious energy and was positively luxurious compared to the hard trail of just two days before.

Breakfast was a paltry affair, but a few oats, dried mushrooms and shrivelled berries made a thin gruel which at least was piping hot and felt more nourishing than it perhaps was. The dogs begged for any scraps, but also came up short and unsatisfied with what little could be spared. The children knew better than to complain, but their thin drawn faces belied the stark fact that they had lost much weight and were all desperately undernourished.

An impromptu meeting was called around the kitchen table, at which a dozen could easily sit in comfortable carver-chairs, the children squeezing up on a long pew-like bench. Hot lemon balm tea was poured out into large wooden kuksa-type cups which had been found neatly stowed away, the beverage warming their bellies and lifting the spirits with its subtle earthy-taste. The polished cups now warming their hands were clearly the work of a talented artisan, many in the form of dragons and boats, some in natural but beautiful rich burred-wood, and others with delicate decorative chip carvings similar in design to those on most timber surfaces throughout The Steading. For now they were hesitant to use their own travelling kit, and most had kept their bags customarily packed, but out of habit, more than any tangible fear. The dogs soon settled on their favourite feet under the table and kept one eye open for any sign of food, but were used to being disappointed in that respect of late. It was not that they couldn't hunt for themselves, but this time of year they very much depended upon their human masters.

The first topic for discussion was immediate necessities; they had plenty of fuel and a good amount of fresh water, with a decent supply of dried tea, but little else. They may survive for many days, but foraging and hunting as soon as possible was critical, to at least scout out the area and see what might be found before they became too weak. The mere notion of food had bellies painfully grumbling in anticipation and a chorus of hearty agreement followed the proposition. As usual Sioned was the first to volunteer for a hunting party, knowing with little boasting that she was one of the best archers, though sometimes a little impatient and arrogant in her comparative youthfulness. Merrick then put forward his name, though he knew that hunting in the now near whiteout of a snow storm was a little pointless. However he was conscious that there were plenty of preparations to be made for any break in the weather, which was bound to then encourage out local wildlife currently hunkered down. Durian also keenly volunteered, which was widely welcomed as everyone knew his seemingly limitless energy could not be contained for long, despite the fact that he too was clearly verging on starvation. Together they formed the first scouting party, with another to be assembled later that day if conditions looked like they had potential. Anticipation was high and all eagerly looked to the snow-rimmed windows in hope of a break in the seemingly unrelenting snow storm.

5 - Preparation

Though not openly discussed, all knew that hunting in a completely unknown valley was far from ideal, to put it mildly, not least in a whiteout. They took some comfort in the fact that tracking would be made much simpler once the storm stopped and that the contrast of certain animals with the near blank background of snow would assist. At the very least they could get an initial exploratory feel for their new surroundings and start to understand its potential. The hope was that there would be a break in the persistent snow, if only for a few hours, which might encourage animals to break cover and seek food, if indeed they frequented the area and those which did weren't hibernating or in a state of torpor. They would normally take their dogs to assist in the hunt, but the fresh snow cover made this less than ideal as it would soon foul up their feet with encrusting snow and ice. For this trip they decided to leave them at the homestead, to get used to their new surroundings, conserve their strength and to offer some security and protection to the group. They were conscious that the dogs too were extremely undernourished, their ribs pitifully showing on their once-muscly bodies, though they too were in good spirits in their new home.

Preparation for the hunt began by unpacking their bentwood-framed, waxed-leather travel packs and reloading with the necessities for the reconnaissance, with emergency kit in case a night out was needed. Bows were their primary hunting weapons, with spears as back up, and knifes for gutting any kill. Their bows were of varying height and draw strength, depending upon preference and stature, but currently all were wide flatbows of ash, the basic form being relatively simple to make in their skilled hands, but deadly effective. Bowstrings were woven of whatever could be readily found, but at present were simple

Flemish-twist style cords formed of plant fibres, nettle being the most common. Arrows were predominantly goose-feather fletched shafts of hazel, with a mix of powerful broadheads for larger prey and heavier blunted-heads for taking down birds. These were loaded into their protective stiff-leather quivers, with light buckskin-flaps to keep out the elements and prevent accidental loss. They could ideally do with making more arrows, a good number lost on their travels and not easily replaced on the trail; this would however have to wait until the necessary components could be gathered.

Their spears were simply their multi-purpose walking staffs, mostly smoothed yew, on which they could mount a broad-pointed steel head if needed. The fates willing, they would have time in the spring to seek out purpose-made lighter javelin-type shafts for precision throwing. The staffs served multiple purposes, including as a general defensive quarterstaff and as a pole for hanging and carrying any animal they were lucky enough to harvest. In the snow the staffs would be essential for helping feel their way, testing ice, and to stabilise them where needed in deep drifts.

Knifes were mostly made of precious carbon steel, which was now quite rare and were often handed down through families. They could sometimes find the material for forging from the suspension parts of wrecks they found on the former roads and rail tracks, but which were now often stripped of useful materials. The hope was though, in this seemingly unpopulated land, that there may be metals to be found not picked over by others. In terms of their knives, they tended to favour medium-sized multi-purpose full-tang blades, but with quite slender points for aiding precise gutting and skinning. Their small axes would aid proper butchering of large prey, but this would take place nearer home, with initial gutting far enough away so wolves and other predators were not tempted too close to The Steading by all the blood, though the likelihood was low. Any decent skins would be kept for processing and tanning at a more convenient time, simple enough to store in the deep cold where they would freeze. All were conscious that their tools had been less than ideally treated on the trail, rough spots of rust now marring their smooth surfaces, the edges far from their usual mirror-polished razor sharpness. With small whetstones they slowly removed these imperfections and honed the edges to create a fine burr, finally stropping them on their belts, testing the finish by shaving the hairs of the back of their hands which was achieved with ease. That done they applied a light oil to the metal and worked in a thin coating of beeswax to the handles from the small pots they always carried for this purpose, among others, ranging from a lip-balm to an antiseptic. Even the smell of beeswax was enough to cause further pangs of hunger, a reminder of delicious honey and bounty of the summer.

With the important hunting kit checked, they repacked their basic overnight gear, including their thick wool blankets which doubled as a poncho, insulating sheepskin sleep rolls, fire-lighting kit, oilskin tarp, and other basics. They had no plans to stay out overnight, but preparation for the worst was always prudent, not least in the unexplored landscape they hoped soon to be venturing into. With such low bodyfat reserves they would feel the cold more than ever before, and even one night out in a snow storm could well be their last.

The next task was to construct snowshoes which would render trekking through the snow and any thick drifts a much less laborious process, saving invaluable energy. These were simple enough to fashion from scratch if you had the skill of it, with bentwood hazel outers, an inner-mesh of woven creepers in lieu of cordage and sinew, strapped on with tensioned leather-straps borrowed off their backpacks. Their makeshift versions may not last for long, but even at this altitude the snow shouldn't ordinarily endure beyond a month, perhaps two at worst. They would however look at making upgrades in due course, in case deep and long-lasting snow was a common occurrence in the valley.

Water supplies were next on the list and it was good to see that Nineveh and Shuldan had started melting snow over the fires to increase their water supplies. In all likelihood the stream water would be clean enough to drink without boiling, but their sources were not yet verified and the last thing they needed was a stomach bug in their already weakened state. The hunters rinsed and refilled their hardened leather bottles using some of the previously-boiled water, with thanks to the ever-diligent couple. The pair had also started to mentally catalogue and assess all that the kitchen, stores and cellar had to offer, though with no luck with finding anything resembling food. The hunters then took the opportunity to re-wax their leather garments, concentrating on their boots, to ensure a reasonable level of water resistance, using the large tub of seemingly never-emptying beeswax that Shuldan always seemed to have about his person. Nineveh and Shuldan were a handy pair to have about as the group's go-to experts on cooking, food stuff preservation and medicine. However, there was only so much you could do with a handful of oats; all hoped that they would have something else to work with before too long. The worry lines on even this most positive of couples were ever present, their normally rounded faces thin and haggard, moods uncharacteristically lethargic. Being back in a kitchen had though given them common purpose, providing a welcoming place to be, even if the best they could serve was hot tea in front of the range.

All that was then left was for the hunters to bide their time, further honing their blades, tending the fires and staying warm while monitoring the weather for the scouting trip to come, with the tentative hope of fresh meat and full bellies. Despite how fortunate they clearly were in finding The Steading Merrick could not help but brood on their still perilous state, despite all that they had found; without food they would not last long.

6 - Scouting

Just before midday there came a noticeable brightening of the house, then glorious wintry-sunshine started flooding in, with a drop in the biting wind which had been occasionally rattling at the windows. With only a cursory glance outside all knew the time had come to scout and explore, excitement palpable in the air.

The whole group had tried to keep moving that morning, mostly to stay warm, but all decided it would be good to get out and acquire a feel for their surroundings, to collect water and stretch legs seized up with relative inactivity. Foraging might be difficult in the thick blanket of snow, but not impossible, some bushes still holding onto shrivelled berries and suchlike. The world they found was enough to bring out the child in all of them, even Bolin, the quintessential grouchy blacksmith, whose no-nonsense attitude and craggy face was briefly broken by a wide smile and a quick snowball at the kids. The normally wolf-like dogs were acting like puppies when usually they were calm and collected, taking to rolling in the bright fresh snow and playing with the children. Hunger though was enough to focus the mind and the scouting party soon set out with farewells to the others, who would likely be keeping close to the homestead fires. The dogs pined to come with them, but were made to stay and soon returned indoors to warm back up.

As the hunters had some basic idea of the lie of the land around the bottom part of the valley, through which they had previously hiked and could view from the house to some extent, they had already decided to explore up the valley to the south. They proceeded with great care and stealth in the almost eerie winter quiet, their primary aim being to scout the area and get a feel for likely spots to hunt. The going would have been strenuous in the fresh powdery snow but for their makeshift snowshoes spreading their weight, helping make it less of a slog and reducing sweating, which would quickly cool and chill them to the core when they stopped. On setting out they noted the area surrounding the homestead was surprisingly free of larger trees, mostly just the odd colonising silver birch and rowan. This indicated the area must have been managed to an extent at some point, the hope being that there were fertile areas for crops and pasture not too far taken over by nature. The area was a good two dozen acres, divided and bound by walls which had tumbled over here and there, but could be seen partially peeking through the snow, or revealing their presence through linear mounds of amorphous white. Essentially though, it was otherwise featureless in the snow excepting a few small trees and bushes; the thaw would reveal more in due course.

Before they had gone half a mile they came to the limits of what had perhaps once been rougher pasture marked by a set of circular stone-built animal pen enclosures, and met the edge of the more wooded part of the valley. Apart from one large smooth-trunked beech before the sheltering south-ridge, the transition to the woods was otherwise gradual and indicated encroachment of the tree line over many years. The trees were mostly bare and skeletal, excepting the interspersed veteran pines, so the woods still felt open and lent itself to long views in most directions. Looking back towards the house and the smoke lazily rising from the chimneys, they realised that this may have been an area perhaps frequented by deer given its openness, but clearly their sudden presence the day before and the smell of smoke would have made them wary. They tentatively marked the place as a likely spot for a hunting blind for the future, once re-established game trails had been found.

As they came to the deeper woods, with no small amount of trepidation and excitement, they caught distant views of the slopes to each side of the valley, possible without the lush vegetation that would come with spring. Even at a distance they could see the higher precipitous valley-sides were likely impassable and bounded the whole landscape presently in sight. Venturing further into the woods they started to travel parallel to the course of the river in the valley bottom, still flowing relatively freely at its centre but starting to ice up on the edges where it had cracked and reformed in the strong flow. Though the watercourse was obscured at its edges by ice it was clear to see it was wide, some seventy odd feet at a minimum, and must carry great volumes of wild water in peak flow, likely bursting its banks at times and flooding the area in multiple channels. After some miles of strenuous trekking through the woods alongside the river, they heard a low rumble of a waterfall in the far distance at the head of the valley, which must be of some considerable size to still be flowing with such force in the icy conditions. That would be something well worth exploring and tugged at their spirit of exploration, but not today, food was of the utmost priority.

Passing through the miles of thick woods they had seen all manner of tree species, many of which would provide excellent supplies of deadwood for the fires, along with lumber for building. In spring they anticipated an abundance of wild foods, and meat from small game such as birds and squirrels, which would supply them with sustenance if nothing else could be found. With their mouth's watering, their bellies tight and sore, they brought their wandering minds back to the present, the necessities of here and now.

They progressed up the valley, through acre after acre of mixed woodland, full of robins, wrens, tits and winter thrushes going about their business; the area seemingly untouched and wild. It was a fantastically impressive place, full of the promise of resources of which they had but dreamed. Moving on with due stealth and marking areas for future exploration, once the snow had melted and revealed its secrets, they passed into a more lightly wooded area that predominated the upper portion of the valley. With Durian fearlessly leading the way, they then managed to cross to the other side of the river utilising a natural series of boulders, partially iced up and choked with debris, which served to keep them out of the freezing water. They mentally marked the pinch-point as a potential crossing point for the future, the width of the river unlikely allowing many such ways across.

Keeping a watchful eye on the slopes as they hiked upriver towards the head of the valley, they suddenly had a distant glimpse of moving deer on the more windswept areas of the valley sides, where presumably the grass and other forage was less buried under the blanketing snow. They were more or less specks on the hillside at this distance, but the slowly moving herd contrasted with the snow, making them fairly conspicuous, albeit easily mistaken for rocks when still. This was an unexpected stroke of fortune; though it was unlikely they would manage to get close enough to try for a kill, they decided to make an attempt. With waves of adrenaline focussing their tired minds and reinvigorating their exhausted bodies, they began the hunt.

The ever-thinning woods still provided them with some cover, so they spread out and cautiously moved from tree-to-tree, utilising shadow where possible and exploiting the eroded cuts of the streams running down the valley side to progress upslope. They were very fortunate that their alien smell was masked by natural odours built up over many nights in the woods on their long journey, and the lack of a good wash for many weeks. The absence of dogs accompanying them on this occasion was also of benefit, as they would be too similar to the smell of wolves, with even the slightest scent likely to cause the deer to take off. The wind was not in an ideal direction, but it was currently fairly light and generally going to the south following the storm coming from the north, with the deer more up slope to the west. The breeze also gave them some small advantage of muffling sounds resulting from their passage through the snow, the small squeak of the powder subtle yet more than enough to potentially reveal their presence. Even so it seemed as though the rapid thumping of their hearts would give them away if nothing else, though they logically knew this could not be true.

As they grew closer, they couldn't believe their luck so far, with near perfect cover and decent intermittent views to monitor the deer. Approaching the end of the first stage of their stalking they realised they soon would be in a position to think about splitting up and forcing the herd into an ambush. They discussed this with silent hand signals and agreed on an optimal route and possible ambush point. For the remaining several hundred yards they decided to ditch their snowshoes for the final approach, the snow thinner and agility being their friend at this stage. With hands shaking slightly from a combination of the cold while taking off their gloves to string their bows, along with excited anticipation, they removed their snowshoes and backpacks, then stashed them under a conspicuous fallen pine tree. With that done they started their cautious final stage of the stalk, adrenaline levels further spiking, lending them a burst of energy and focus.

Durian had, as planned, ended up further to the south and was approaching a long ridge of snow which would give him some cover, bringing him out ahead of the deer's slow direction of travel. Sioned and Merrick therefore took an approach keeping within the tree line to bring them to the rear of the herd and looked for likely positions where they may funnel back, agreeing a signal for when the time came to take simultaneous shots. There was nothing ideal, but the natural contours, a substantial watercourse, thick snow drifts and the tree line indicated a very likely direction of travel to a chokepoint in the north east. Their plan finalised they took up suitable spots behind some trees to cover several potential routes through this area, while avoiding being directly downwind at any point. Once selected, they knew better than to then change position, tempting fate that the deer may catch sight of them. It would be an incredibly tense wait while Durian made the attempt to get ahead of the herd and drive them back their way. To combat this nervous energy, they employed subtle breathing exercises, knowing that a steady hand and focussed mind would be vital for an accurate killing shot. As they slowly calmed their minds they achieved near perfect stillness of body and mind; this serene state and the drab colour of their clothes attaining a synergy of camouflage that rendered them virtually invisible.

Some twenty minutes later saw Durian crouched low, using the cover he had found and paralleling the herd's direction of travel. He found it easier going as he gained height up from the valley floor and started to see evidence of the sparse dried yellow grass the deer were after, though he was getting breathless with the exertion and contained tension of the stalk. At the end of a covering berm of snow he slowly turned and looked to see if he could check on the others' positions, but it was too distant and they must have been well hidden in the area they had chosen earlier in the tree line. However the natural chokepoint was evident even from that distance and he could judge their likely hiding spots from experience hunting together. He could see it wasn't going to get any better than this, there was no point in waiting any longer.

After a deep calming inhale, which stretched his lungs to near full capacity, he ran out from cover and into the path of the deer. He saw at once that they had almost supernaturally jumped away, seemingly before he was even visible, and started bounding off in the opposite direction. With his heart now hammering Durian ran after them shouting maniacally and trying his best to send them towards the

37

ambush, with a few well-aimed stones he had picked up earlier launched to clatter in the rocks above the herd to further encourage them downslope and towards Sioned and Merrick.

The pair were in prime positions, staggered apart to intercept the potential paths of the deer, but were nonetheless anxious they may not make a kill. In just a few seconds, but which seemed like an age to the pair, the small herd approached, bunching up in their mad dash away from Durian and right into the predicted chokepoint. With initially nothing more than the noise of hooves to alert them to their proximity, Sioned moved first and then Merrick followed just half a second later, leaving their hidden spots, coming to their shooting positions, then letting their best broad-headed arrows fly into the front of the massed herd. Merrick just missed his intended target as Sioned's premature movement in advance of the agreed signal had spooked his mark at the very last fraction of a second, but thankfully Sioned hit hers, centre mass. With a final few spasmodic leaps and twitches, the deer was down as the rest of the herd sprinted off and were lost to sight.

The party could not believe their fortune; a few hours into an unknown hunting ground, and a relatively easy first kill. It was perhaps a sign of how abundant the valley was and how relatively undisturbed it must really be, though no doubt their superb hunting skills and experience hunting together was critical. Running to the deer they saw it was a clean kill, centre chest and nicking its heart or a major artery, which had let it bleed out quick, the scarlet soaking into the pristine snow, the metallic tang palpable in the air. Though not the largest animal, it was substantial and would feed them for some time to come, the hide also being of excellent quality. The bleeding, gutting and field dressing was quickly completed, leaving the warm stomach and intestines but keeping the other organs, including the nutritious heart, liver and kidneys. The deer was in reasonable condition given it was nearing the end of winter, with some decent fat stores still available to it, showing as a white layer beneath the skin and around the exposed organs. The still steaming offal would be found before long by scavengers keen to the scent of the kill, but it was a considerable distance from home thus avoiding enticing in potential predators, where they would be too close for comfort. There were of course uses for the discarded stomach and intestines, as with all parts of the animal, but they were conscious the necessary processing to stop them going rancid and render them usable was not their top priority for now. They would however use all of the rest of the animal, leaving nothing else that could provide nutrition and raw crafting materials.

Having cleaned out the chest cavity as best they could with water from a nearby stream and handfuls of snow, they bound the legs and mounted the kill onto Merrick's staff, being the longest and most robust. With the deer mounted they then cleaned their hands, drying them in the cold snow, though the blood stains would mark their fingers and palms for some days to come. By that point their hands were raw and numb; the warming embrace of their work gloves and later their fur over-mittens being extremely welcome. Finally they cleaned and stowed away their weapons, taking care to unstring the bows, pocket the cords and wrap the precious weapons in soft waterproofed leather sheathes. Their snowshoes and packs were not far away, hidden beneath the fallen pine tree, and the energetic Durian swiftly had them all collected. After a short break to drink some water and chew on a few morsels of dried meat, they started the long slog back, high on the powerful natural drugs coursing in their veins generated by the hunt.

Passing back into the woods proper, they stuck to their previous path; though not necessarily the most direct route, they could not get lost and it was somewhat compacted, making it less exhausting to re-tread their steps. Even with the carcass weighing in at about forty five pounds gutted, rotating it between the three of them helped make the downhill journey pass quickly, within just two or so hour's hard march. They approached the homestead just as the light was starting to fade, happy in the knowledge of the warm welcome they would receive and the ravenous bellies they would fill.

7 - Feasting

On arriving home they lifted the now partially frozen carcass from the pole and hung it in the dilapidated barn from a robust iron hook, ready for further cleaning and processing. Ideally they would leave it to hang in the cellar to mature thus improving the flavour and to let the natural enzymes tenderise the flesh, but hungry bellies would not allow them to wait for a week and the quick kill had meant the lactic acid build-up would be negligible, so not otherwise tainting the meat.

First though they went inside to announce the good news and to deliver the liver, heart and kidneys to the kitchen, so the cooks could get started. As would be expected the group were elated and tightly hugged the hunters and then each other in tears; they hadn't thought they would be able to do much more than a quick scout that day and were resigned to another hungry night. The dogs were beyond pleased with their share of the other offal and some raw meat, which they quickly gulped down, their bellies soon distended despite the meagre portions. The pack then moved to prime positions for warming themselves in front of the fires, with a sleepy eye kept open for any other food that might be on offer, marrow-rich bones soon filling their dreams.

While the hunters took a few minutes to rub life back into their sore shoulders and to drink some hot tea, they could see the others had been industrious that day, including by way of a brace of woodpigeon hung in the kitchen, and evidence of some breasts already cooked, with the remaining carcasses gently simmering down for stock. The younger ones had clearly been busy with their slings and had also managed to forage some early nettle tips and remnants of last year's lemony wood sorrel located beneath a sheltered south-facing ancient hedge line, which would add some greatly needed vitamins to their

41

meal. Another party had found some very early shoots of wild garlic leaves down by the river while exploring, locating them by chance under the snow with the dogs' assistance, primarily because of its smell, potent when crushed even half buried. In addition a good basket full of shrivelled but nutritious hawthorn and rose hips had been harvested where the birds had not picked them clean from the bushes and rough hedge lines. It was some small miracle that less than twenty four hours at their new home had produced such abundance and they felt blessed. Evidently though, without the substantial haul of rich deer meat, it would have been barely enough to tide them over, a day at most, but with it they were good for many days to come.

Nineveh and Shuldan gave the hunters some much needed sustenance with a mouth-watering garlicky pigeon broth, warming them up now that they had cooled down from the long day out in the cold and the sweat of the hard march back. The deer's liver, its tongue and heart went into the frying pan, thinly sliced with some of the garlic, producing wonderfully rich smells within minutes. This was shared out to keep everyone satisfied while waiting for the venison, with titbits given to the dogs which they quickly gobbled up. Scraping the remnants of the soup from their bowls the hunters felt partially satiated and following a final warming by the roaring fire in the main hall, made ready to tackle butchering of the carcass.

Going back outside they noticed the looming darkness which was coming much quicker than they had expected, along with a deepening chill to the wind which bit at any exposed skin. Looking to the north they noticed a weather front coming in fast, pinkish in the setting sun, stunning but likely to produce further snow. They decided that even between them the job of skinning, jointing and portioning the deer would take an hour or two absolute minimum, so they lit some bright pine wood fires just outside the barn to provide light and a modicum of warmth. The skin came away fairly well, though it wasn't the neatest job in the failing light; this they nonetheless kept and later stored away in the cold store off the cellar where it would partially freeze, keeping it ready for preparation into a useable hide. Next they processed down the meat with efficient skill, keeping aside the tendons, hooves, bones and so on for various uses. Durian took what very little remained, that couldn't be fed to the dogs, and disposed of it some distance from the dwelling, a small feast for the scavengers which would find it, likely corvids, red kites and suchlike.

After having lit some smoky tallow tapers they took much of the meat down through the dark cellar to the freshly cleaned cold store built beyond the foundations of the house, dug out into the ground to benefit from the cold that should persist year round several feet down. There they hung the bulk of the venison from the ceiling on hooks where it would keep for some time, potentially completely freezing in due course, though it would likely be eaten sooner than that. Closing the thick door to the stone lined room they made their way back through the main cellar by light of the flickering tapers, up the steep stone steps and back into the warm kitchen, dark but for the soft inviting glow of the range. On the way down they had left a good chunk of shoulder with the cooks which had already been cubed and added to the hearty pigeon stock along with the fatty brains of the deer, the huge cauldron-like pot now lightly bubbling on a low simmer as it would for some hours to come, eventually fully tenderising the meat. Though not the tastiest element of the animal most of its body fat had been added for calories and to render down, with some later scooped off to solidify, which would be stored in the cold pantry for future reuse. The rich hearty smell of the stew was soon mouth-watering, and everyone's bellies were painfully aching in anticipation.

On the way down to the cellar they had also left, on the slate-topped sideboard, two hefty roasting joints of loin and haunch, with the bone left attached for flavour. These were in the process of being spitted and mounted next to the blazing fire in the main hall, being plenty of room each side in the cavernous fire place for such purposes. Each spit was fashioned out of thick shoots of green hazel with a natural cranked handle at one end, and would be turned by the children and whomever was sat nearby. Initially the joints would need to be turned near constantly, but once seared to lock-in the juice they would only then need to be rotated every now and then, with occasional basting from the metal trays collecting the drips below. Now the fire had been going for a day, the chimney was warm and drawing really well, so in addition they added some wetted-down wood chips onto small piles of coals to create a little smoke underneath the joints for added flavour. The smell of the soon sizzling meat immediately caused everyone to freshly salivate, but the earlier pigeon broth and fried liver, heart and tongue kept their more desperate hunger pangs at bay, for now. They were all conscious it had been some time since they had eaten this well and none had any wish to risk abusing their shrivelled stomachs with too much rich food.

The hunters sat in comfortable chairs with their feet up on stools, their bloody hands now clean following a wash with some hot water and having used up the almost the last remnants of their lye based soap. All had started to realise that braving the icy cold of the rivers might be needed soon to remove the grime from their travel-worn bodies and clothes. For now though they all sat in the luxurious warmth, drank hot tea and talked, while the meat slowly cooked and the stew simmered.

The group eagerly spoke of their work during the day; everyone had been very busy, hunting, scouting, foraging, cooking, cleaning, organising and generally settling in. All that they had achieved in spite of their arduous journey, malnutrition, and exhaustion was no small accomplishment and many found themselves with a rare smile upon their weary faces. The best find that day was without doubt a small store of honey found in a box at the back of the cellar, seemingly forgotten, until now. Upon breaking the wax seals the honey was unsurprisingly crystallised and solid, but on gentle rewarming became runnier and was perfectly fine; clearly its antimicrobial properties and ideal storage conditions had stopped it going bad. As a treat all were given a taste in their tea, uplifting their spirits with the sugar rush. Most of the supply was kept for its medicinal properties, as its addition to dressings would stop festering of wounds in many cases, but a small amount was taken for the kitchen, kept on a high shelf for special occasions. The find made them hopeful that bees were prevalent in the area, though they would need to construct hives to gain a reliable supply, albeit harvesting from wild hives was certainly possible. Another job for the future, but one they looked forward to with great delight, such possibilities now more than just a tenuous hope.

Significant amount of work had been done that day in clearing the back paved yard, uncovering from the encroaching undergrowth an L-shaped block of substantial single storey outbuildings which were in need of some repair, but appeared to house former workshops, storage areas, a wood store and bath house. The stored wood was partially damp and some rotten so this was put to one side for the beginnings of a compost pile; nonetheless a decent store was salvageable which would keep them going for some weeks. The roofs of the outbuildings were mostly wooden shingle in dire need of repair and random slabs of poor quality shale; they guessed that any decent slate had been taken for the dwelling roof, to keep that fully watertight. The bath house was perhaps a grand term for what consisted of a pretty rustic stone-slabbed room with a blocked drain in one corner and a pair of ancient cast-iron enamelled baths. They were chipped beyond belief and a rather unnerving shade of yellow where this could be seen beneath the general detritus; they may however serve after a good scrub with wood-ash derived lye and fine sand, with abrasive horsetail plant used to help polish the pitted surface. Further beyond the outbuildings surrounding the courtyard were the remains of two timber outhouses with drop pits beneath, now virtually filled in through windblown debris. New long drops would need to be dug when the earth thawed and once they could procure enough lumber to construct the basic structures. No one could say that was high on the list of priorities when the woods or a bush would serve, but was another important task which was added to the list, their waste being a precious resource in fertilising the hoped for fruit and vegetable beds.

In addition to these buildings were other ramshackle structures perhaps best just being pushed over, well beyond saving, but one stout stone-built and slate-roofed structure remained, set well apart from the others and substantially open on one side by way of a timber screen which had partially rotted away. Initial investigations had revealed an old forge which Bolin had been quick to closely inspect, declaring that it might do, which was high praise indeed from him. It would need a lot of renovation, being submerged inside with wind-blown leaves and other accumulations, but hope was that it could be repaired. Fuel for the forge would be another matter though; high-grade charcoal would need to be produced first and leather bellows fashioned to achieve the correct intense heat, combined with all manner of other repairs. This would have to wait for now until the raw materials could be procured and energy spared from other essential projects, not least food production, but was an unexpected windfall and all agreed that a happy Bolin was a major bonus.

As the group continued to discuss their days work, they reflected that the well set-up farmstead spoke to past self-sufficiency and made it all the more perplexing that the place was not still occupied. The mystery of the previous occupiers, including why they had left in seemingly orderly fashion, with preparations made for long vacancy, was a topic of fierce debate around the fireside each night, ending with a grudging acceptance that this might never become clear. It was however obvious enough why the place had lain undiscovered, the extreme inaccessibility and sheer remoteness being a valuable deterrent to discovery.

Later that evening, after filling up the corners of their groaning stomachs with tender slices of mouth-watering venison cut from the spit, they moved the meat to cool down and then stored it away in the small cold store off the kitchen near the back door. The remnants of the stew was taken from the kitchen fire and stowed away in the pantry; it would do for a few more meals at least and gain in flavour overnight as it infused and tenderised. The dogs paid great attention to every last movement of the food before it was finally secured away, and then settled down for the night snug in front of the kitchen range, content that it was safe and all was well.

8 - Long winter

Over the coming days the snow continued its steady fall, with just a few brief interludes, blanketing and blurring out all features around the homestead and throughout the valley. There were times that a break in the snow storms allowed for transfer of fire wood from the barn, but these were rare and paths had to be laboriously dug through the drifts each time. This confinement did however allow them plenty of time to melt snow, heat water and use the bath house, once it had been cleaned out back to the stone-slabbed floor and the baths laboriously scrubbed with lye and abrasive sooty ashes. Although all had grown used to it on the trail, being cooped up together meant their ripe odour had become almost unbearable and something just had to be done. The bath house had a substantial cast-iron pot-belied stove in one corner, still perfectly functional though heavily oxidised. This allowed for the space to be thawed out and eventually acted like a mild sauna, with the steam from all the hot water sweating out the accumulated dirt from their pores, which was then literally scraped off with a split stick before getting in the bath to scrub themselves with rough rags and charcoal. A bracing roll in the snow afterwards completed the process, though they were pink and raw afterwards, but very clean, being several shades of dirty brown lighter. Even the children agreed that it was a great improvement all round, despite their initial reluctance and running off to hide in their favourite hidey-holes. Finally, everyone's hair was sheared; the final transformation from their formerly grubby lank-locks to neatly trimmed, clean and shiny hair and beards being quite astonishing. All though still tended to long hair tied back, great for extra warmth in the winter and which could be let down in the summer to keep off flies and the sun. The bath house was also perfect as a wash house for their clothes, the grime from the many long miles being vigorously brushed and beaten out, soaked and scrubbed away.

This required several bath fulls of hot water and used pretty much the last of their hard lye-based soap, but which they could replenish in due course. Come spring they could tide themselves over with the sap from horse chestnut leaves, ivy and other plants which gave a half-decent soapy lather in a pinch. Making hard soap would need good quantities of animal fats mixed with lye. Lye was not a problem, obtained from leaching wood ashes, which they could now accumulate over winter. The fats though were just not obtainable in sufficient quantity for now, but hopefully would be abundant once spring came and the animals fattened up. For now any spare fats from harvested carcasses would comprise essential calories to get them and the dogs through the lean times.

Once all the clothes were washed and rinsed, they were wrung through an ancient mangle found in one of the many store rooms, then hung in the rafters of the main hall on lines fashioned from creepers taken off the dwelling on their arrival. With the heat of the fires and their general body heat, the clothes soon started drying through, forming a damp mist in the rafters though soon dissipating. Following the drying, the clothes were stiff and required some working with their hands to loosen and tease apart the fibres, but they eventually softened up and became less itchy with wear. They carried out some repairs as required, but it was plain that new clothes were needed, with hides and wool being added to their wish list. Their transformation though with clean bodies and scrubbed clothes was amazing, the smell of the house drastically improved, losing its dank fuggy odour; even the dogs seemed happier to nuzzle up to them, having also had a good scrub down.

The deer they had taken kept them going for several days, with stews and succulent roast joints near constantly filling the air with tantalising smells. They managed to get out to explore in the few breaks in the weather, though it was hard going and hunting was pretty poor. In the end they decided to chance their luck at a very early start to a stake out a well-used game trail using a makeshift hunting blind constructed the day before which they had heavily camouflaged with snow. This worked superbly and they took two decent-sized deer, which helped fill their bellies for weeks to come. Supplementing the venison they managed to harvest a number of snow hares and numerous wood pigeons, the birds being easy pickings with their lethargy in the cold weather and lack of feeding opportunities.

Being house bound for long stretches, sometimes days at a time, all the nooks and crannies of their home had now been thoroughly explored. The dwelling had also been carefully cleaned and most of the rodents evicted, though that would be an ongoing battle. The children had found many places they could hide and it became the norm that come their bedtime they seemed to suddenly lose a good third of the household, though the giggles often gave them away and the dogs happily helped to sniff them out. Still though the confinement during the snow storms was starting to get wearing and all looked forward to spring which surely was soon on its way.

One of the big jobs, managed over many days, was loading the cold store in the cellar with blocks of ice, this they stacked at the far end which was deepest underground and away from the house. With luck this ice would keep the stone-lined cellar cold well into the summer and improve its ability to keep their food fresh. That they had time and energy to think about such chores spoke to their increasing confidence and indicated a lessening of everyone's anxiety, along with emerging hope for the future. This was reflected in everyone's faces, the worry lines lessening by the day and hollow cheeks filling out with the now regular meals of protein and fats.

The household settled into a relaxed routine, and once all the jobs of the day were done, they made themselves comfortable in the hall and spent time in crafts according to their specialities and general whim, though materials were limited. Basic baskets were woven, made from the creepers taken from the uncovering of the house and bent frames formed from steam-bent hazel whips, these would serve for foraging come spring until they could harvest and prepare willow whips for more refined and durable basket making. Ideally they would need to find some osier type willow, and set up some coppice to harvest it each year, though a long way off being a priority. Some practiced their wood carving, despite there being many implements and utensils already available, but it didn't harm to have more and was enormously therapeutic. Some laboriously prepared meat for longer term preservation, being cut into thin strips, heavily smoked and then further dried in the halls' rafters. Once that was done this was added to the stores in mouse-proof containers and kept as travelling jerky, incredibly hard but long lasting. With the deer hides collected and roughly processed, they had managed to construct some hardened rawhide buckets, the joints being sealed with sticky birch tar. This was a messy job and left hands stained brown, but would be great to speed the process of water collection, including for the gardens they hoped to create. These basic water carriers would do for a season until the forge was up and running to hopefully create more hardwearing versions, if enough metal could be found. If not they could look at creating slatted buckets fashioned from wood, sealed with birch tar and bound in natural cordage though that would require better wood working tools. Irrespective of the fact materials were limited, there were plenty of other useful items that could be made, including birch broomsticks, hazel rakes and suchlike.

They kept to such industrious routines for nearly a full cycle of the moon, all naturally settling into their specialist roles, though everyone tending to take turns as needed with all jobs and the more laborious chores. It was though a fairly lean time as there was seldom plenty to eat with no stores built up from the autumn glut. All looked forward to the end of the winter, eager to explore and make a start in building up their new home. Then, suddenly as they came, the snow storms ceased, a front giving over to bright sunshine, light wind and increasing temperatures. A thaw was in the air and everyone's hearts lightened, spring was at long last on its way.

9 - Spring

It was a glorious but bracing morning, a week after the thaw began, though there were thick patches of snow where it had drifted and good coverings up the shaded valley sides, with the snow line still visible. Green shoots were making a tentative appearance and then quickly surged up in the growing warmth, a profusion of flowers also bursting forth across the meadows and through the woods. The river roared day and night as it drained the huge snowmelt, the crashing of blocks of ice, cobbles and boulders being heard clearly even from some distance, and sounding quite unnerving in the night. They found that during these weeks the river was quite impassable to the western side as it overtopped and thundered down the valley, ferociously gouging itself fresh channels and sweeping away trees, but it was a minor inconvenience in the grand scheme of things.

Refreshing spring greens were collected in ever increasing bulk, adding to what had become quite a monotonous and unbalanced diet of fairly lean protein. From chickweed and saxifrage, to young nettle and hawthorn leaf tips, to sorrel and numerous velvet shank mushrooms, wild garlic ramsons, goosegrass and bittercress. The profusion was a delight, with the fresh vitamins giving them all a boost and adding much needed flavour and variety to their meals. Their skin glowed with the bounty of spring's relative abundance, the fresh clean air filling their lungs, the pure wholesome water cleansing their bodies, and so they all felt healthier than they had in some considerable time.

A great treat was the rising sap of the birch and maple trees which could be collected by drilling small holes into the trunks or reusing those drilled by the local sap-sucking type woodpeckers, then tapped with hollowed out spiles. With collecting buckets, pots and pans they could accumulate a great deal as the watery sap rose, a refreshing

53

drink but most excellent boiled down to form a sugary syrup or a crystallised sugar, a welcome source of sweetness after the long winter. A huge amount of sap was however needed to get it that concentrated, but the host of birch and maple in the woods more than served them in gathering what they needed. The birch sap particularly also had various medicinal purposes, being a great general restorative, a cleanser and general vitamin booster. For some though the most anticipated use was in making a flavoursome sweet wine liqueur, but this would need patience for the brew to mature.

The melting snow also gave them better understanding of their surroundings, partially hidden until now. What they had perceived to be old fields were certainly that at some point in the past, the boundary walls being distinct to various extents. Many though were just linear grassy mounds with scrubby hedges spilling off the top, desperately needing to be cut back and laid over to encourage fresh growth. It would take many years to cultivate all of what had once been, but they had made a start by fashioning tools over the last few weeks, including rudimentary but functional digging sticks, some hazel-made rakes and spades fashioned from cleaved oak boards. They all looked forward to the day when the forge could produce more durable and sharpened metal tools, saving their backs and hands from no small punishment. Their hope was that perhaps that year they may be able to fashion a small plough, but amongst many hurdles that would require finding and taming draught animals, which would not be simple task. In theory it was possible to pull a small plough with just a team of humans, but far from ideal when breaking what was essentially the tangled sod of raw meadow. It was however surprising what could be achieved with just a simple digging stick and the brute force of determined humans determined to achieve a goal.

On one of their first forays following the initial snow melt, at the far end of the now flower-strewn meadow and beneath a great lone copper-beech tree, they came across a series of small grassy mounds, of varying height and age. There were no headstones, but it was clear they were graves, with two of more recent age, though a decade old at the very least judging by the vegetation growth. The oldest grave was barely more than a slight rise in the spring grass that could have been easily missed, with several small mounds that were clearly infant sized, covered in clumps of snowdrops. This would explain where the occupiers of the house had ended up, seemingly reducing in numbers over the years given the different ages of the graves, some several score years old at least. The previous residents must have been too small a group to make the homestead sustainable, though hopefully their new larger group would not meet the same fate and dwindle away so sadly. They theorised that the one person who presumably remained to dig the last grave and to keep the house must have left, possibly the author of the map that had led them there. They never found evidence of a body, though the carrion feeders and other scavengers would soon have seen to that. It was a sad occasion but the group gave thanks to them all, in time using an adjoining area for burying their own, glad to re-continue the tradition binding them to their new home.

With exploration came a deepening understanding of their new world, the valley holding many secrets that it would take years to fully discover. Just north of the homestead they further scouted the vast copses of hazel and more limited areas of sweet chestnut which were currently carpeted with an understorey of delicate bluebells and started the massive task of cutting back with their axes. This created great piles of cut wood and opened up a huge area, but was going to be of massive help in regeneration of the formerly productive coppice stands, being vital for various raw materials. They stacked the wood in sheltered spots for drying and noted the best places to create the charcoal pits and mounds, needing a ready supply of thick grass sod for piling on top to dampen down the flames and control the burns. Further up the valley to the south, past the fields, they explored the now increasingly luminously green woods and came to know the best animal trails. These they marked and formed a series of hunting blinds and elevated shooting platforms throughout the valley which they rotated through, so as not to render any one area sterile through their presence and over use. They gathered the best of the dry deadfall, ash and oak being preferred, and stacked this in the still standing barn for the fires, keeping some for fence posts and suitable trunks for poles and breaking down to crude planks and suchlike. Much of the hardwood remained useable, even after lying on the forest floor for some time, but they would need to store it to dry for that year at least before use on the fires, bar the ash wood which could pretty much burn green if there was the need. For now though there was plentiful supply of hanging deadwood and easy pickings quite close to the homestead, reinforcing their view that the last humans had been gone for some time, perhaps decades they were coming to realise. It was very demanding work and all soon developed increasingly thick protective callouses on their hands and feet, with sore muscles aching each night they didn't realise they had. Despite this the good food they could now gather with relative ease meant they all put on lost weight, most often with wiry muscle. The upshot was that they all began to fill out their clothes once more and regained their vitality lost through the long lean winter and the desperate journey. Health and wellbeing began to soar and despite the long days of backbreaking labour, they found time to explore and enjoy their new found home, roaming further and further with each coming week.

It was with such curiosity that they explored a good proportion of the wild and tangled woods that blanketed the area, and much of the upper reaches of the valley. The profusion of life in what was a high upland valley was very surprising, the elevation normally resulting in a climate that should have been much more hostile and far from the relatively lush environment they were blessed with. To some extent this was a result of the protective enclosing valley sides, but they also found many springs which were warmer than might be expected, certainly compared to the frigid glacier-fed river. Though they weren't any hot springs or other signs of volcanic activity to be found, it indicated that there must be such geothermic activity fairly close to the surface, aiding the fairly temperate microclimate. Clearly though this moderating effect could not overcome the deep winters resulting from the high elevation but given the evidence of less hardy deciduous trees, relatively lush vegetation and the speed of winter's retreat, it boded well for productive seasons to come.

It wasn't long into spring, with the rapid unfurling of leaves, that the woods acquired their glorious dense coats of green and a profusion of flourishing understorey, which at times was almost blindingly saturated with glowing colour. These woods were quickly filled with the sound of newly-arrived migrating birds, including the vocal two-note chiffchaffs followed by the more expressive willow warblers, then later the flashy redstarts and lemony wood warblers, the cumulative sound reaching epic proportions at times early in the morning. They found that some upper parts of the valley remained fairly clear of successional vegetation, providing rough pasture and upland meadows where flowers and heather was profuse. This was seemingly due to grazing by deer, providing some distant but productive hunting grounds. At the very head of the valley they scouted the waterfall which thunderously announced its presence for some distance before it could be glimpsed. Though not easy to access, the paths long since having been eroded away by winter flooding, they managed to find a way to a series of large upper pools created by the thundering falls. The visible drop from the upper part of the cliff was some two hundred and fifty feet, an awesome sight with the thick wide curtain of meltwater thundering down, fed from the upland glaciers; the sound quite literally deafening, causing hours of white noise in the ears if you got close for too long. They looked forward to the summer when it would be possible to swim in the calmer pools below the main falls, but for now it was near freezing and beyond the hardiest of them to even consider, the swift currents and odd block of ice notwithstanding.

Seeing no need to do otherwise they kept to the valley, managing to slowly tease out many of its hidden secrets over the coming weeks, locating resources and generally getting a feel for its character. Accessing the sparsely vegetated upper-valley sides was mostly a futile task as they mainly comprised precipitous cliffs and vast scree slopes, though they were home to a pair of golden eagles, peregrines and at least two raven nesting sites. They eventually managed to scout out east and west passes that were potentially just about accessible, formed of ancient river beds which had created cuts into the valley sides. These contained numerous sheeting streams and treacherously smoothed rocks and so were simply dangerous at present, hence were left for future exploration. The mountains beyond though held promise of possible upland sheep and goats, mountain ponies and further resources of deer, so was high on the list for an expedition. Despite the difficulty for now, the bonus of this inaccessibility was added difficulty of others finding and accessing their valley; this in combination with the unassuming and narrow valley bottom and near impassable canyon made for an upland stronghold. It was becoming less and less surprising that they were the first to find the valley since it was left empty, even with the very sparse population hereabouts. They could not be sure, but they wouldn't be surprised if they were the only humans for some hundred miles or more. On passing through from the distant east they had found that the small pockets of humanity had seemed mostly to stick to the coast and so had given them very wide berth. This location of settlements made perfect sense given the bounty of the sea and mild winters, though they were far from secure, even in bigger groups. However, even these settlements were seemingly non-existent as they came through the lands nearer the valley, but you could never be sure.

All things considered it was a good start to the new season, but ever warming temperatures and a profusion of life meant more hard work to come in reaping the bounty of the valley and starting on all the various projects planned. Still, all felt blessed to be alive.

10 - Bees

As spring burst forth there came an increasing abundance of flowering plants, which delivered an explosion of colour and delicate fragrance in the meadows, helped on by the progressive hacking back and removal of the encroaching tree line. The area was soon humming with the industrious presence of bees and the soft fluttering of early butterflies, building in number as the days grew warmer and the sun gained height above the valley walls. Though perhaps not a task of necessity, all agreed that getting some hives in place would be very welcome to gain honey as a source of nourishment, flavouring and an important medicine for the inevitable cuts, grazes and sore throats that would benefit from its antiseptic properties. The beeswax they could gain also had a multitude of uses, not least for sealing jars come autumn for preserving foodstuffs, used mixed with rendered fat for reproofing and maintaining leather, making candles and so on. It wouldn't be a massive job to sort out some basic hives and needed to be done early in the year to attract in the new swarms and let the colony build reserves for the winter.

A quiet well-drained spot adjoining the meadow was chosen by Nineveh, but not too far from the dwelling in order that she could keep a close eye on them. Here she positioned the hives to face south-east to encourage the bees to start foraging early with first light. The belt of trees to the side helped as a windbreak and provided dappled sunlight to avoid overheating the hives at midday, but would provide enough warmth to wake the colony each morning. To the perimeter Nineveh organised the construction of a chest-high woven hurdle fence made of straight thumb-thick shoots of green hazel to cut down on the wind further and to help keep out inquisitive animals. Next was constructed a basic structure of split oak trunks to make rudimentary shelves, a

60

basic roof covering of simple waney-edge roughly split boards, with a small protective overhang, into which they could site their woven hives, or as they knew them, skeps. It was a pretty rough and ready set up, but they were functional and would serve pending making wood working tools to construct more efficient timber hives to increase productivity and aid harvesting.

Creating the woven skeps was repetitive work, using supple willow withies and grasses, but between Nineveh and the kids they had four made within a couple of long afternoons, albeit with sore hands as a result. It was useful that the children were all involved, learning the art for the future, but it was really just an evolution of basket making they learnt from an early age. Nineveh showed them the intricacies of the skep construction, a key being a tight and thick weave to keep them weather tight. The youngest kids watched but loved doing their own thing with the weaving, making toys and games but all the while learning the craft for the future. The skeps were of pretty basic form, essentially a tall thick-sided basket with a lid, but in due course they would be replaced with more efficient forms made of timber with internal slats for the comb, removable cleaning trays and controllable ventilation. The heavy basket skeps should hopefully last well through the first season, providing somewhere relatively natural and enticing for their first colony, to be later transferred into the proposed timber hives. In the event they failed to naturally attract a colony Nineveh would hunt down a wild nest and transfer the queen and her swarm, though she hoped this would be a last resort as it was far from fool proof, not a pleasant task even with judicious use of smoke to quell the worst of the stings which would inevitably result. Many of the group were though well experienced in such harvesting, the source of sugar being much sought after and not otherwise readily available in such concentration.

They were however incredibly fortunate in that within just one cycle of the moon the first bees started scouting the skeps and it wasn't long before a swarm had moved into its new home. The colony would spend much of the year building their waxy comb and stocking it for winter, but it was hoped that with the abundance and prime conditions hereabouts, there would be a small surplus to harvest before the end of summer. For now though the colony would be left to their productive activity, Nineveh and Shuldan checking up on them occasionally to ensure optimum positioning of the hives and windbreaks.

That done everyone moved their focus back to other tasks, including the backbreaking and humdrum chores of constantly collecting water and firewood. The gruelling work of tilling the soil in the fields was now their main priority, but between them progressed apace turning clods of soil and carefully picking out the weeds. They were all conscious that there was essential need to get planting as soon as they could to make the best of the growing season.

11 - Planting the fields

Though calling what the group had reclaimed 'fields' was somewhat overstating the reality of progress so far, they had managed to turn over and thoroughly de-weed two half-acre plots revealing a rich dark soil, which clearly had been intensively managed for centuries. That the area had lain fallow for some years, with a build-up of leaf mould, droppings from deer, rabbits, birds and so on, boded well for productivity. With crop rotation and harvesting of leaf matter from the woods for mulch, they should achieve decent results, a reward for their literal blood, sweat and tears. Bolin in particular was an absolute beast in the fields, using his great strength from years at the forge to pound the soil into submission. He was clearly eager to get onto sorting out his forge but he well knew food was the utmost priority, so went at the task like a man possessed.

To increase yields they stripped and mounded the topsoil into long beds which concentrated the best soil; this was edged with logs to reduce erosion from the rain. Buried beneath these mounds were numerous rotten logs which would aid water retention and add further organic matter and goodness. These would settle over time as air pockets within them were compressed and the organic matter broke down. The mounds also had the advantage that the slope on one side would receive more sunlight from the south and provide for some screening of the prevailing wind, thus giving the less hardy seedlings a head start compared to a flat bed. The mini microclimates were surprisingly effective and could be used to reduce water loss to the sun to some extent on the shaded side, an issue until the plants were mature enough to start shielding the soil and cutting down on evaporation. Until then it was a laborious process of watering, but made less monotonous with a rota between them all. Working the beds was also made easier with their extra height and would save more than one sore back, pending getting some better long-handled steel-edged tools to aid hoeing of the weeds and suchlike. The elders of the group especially looked forward to that day, their obviously sore and painful backs borne with few grumbles.

Between the group they had brought seeds of many types and traditional varieties, but all known to be hardy and bred to be resistant to pests; it could hardly be otherwise with no manufactured pesticides and fertilisers. The seeds wouldn't produce massively abundant crops and the results may look odd to eyes of their ancestors, for instance the purple tinged carrots, but they would be very nutritious all the same and often more flavoursome. To the inhabitants of The Steading these seeds were some of their most precious resources and the early seedlings were therefore protected day and night in shifts with the dogs' assistance and via a perimeter of low woven hurdles. This produced a good number of rabbits for the pot and the dogs' bellies, and before long the buck-teethed plunderers learned to stay clear of the beds. Slugs and other pests weren't too much of an issue, the abundant local birdlife and hedgehogs soon clearing these up, the advantage of a natural unpolluted ecosystem. It was simple enough though to keep on top of these with a late night check coinciding with when the slugs came out, unceremoniously evicted and disposed of where they would be hoovered up by their natural nocturnal predators.

Several varieties of seed potatoes were the main treasure they had brought with them, though given relative bulk they had only enough for a few short rows. Before planting these had been chitted and halved to increase the starting number. The shrivelled tubers would soon swell, then multiply and many would be saved for replanting through the year, each time being cut in half and planting them out again in generous spacings to gain maximum yield. They hoped by the end of the year they would have some to store for winter eating, but they were mindful of the need to retain a good number for next year's seed. The carbohydrates they would gain from the potatoes would be their main staple crop and near essential for survival if meat was scarce. From experience they knew it wasn't uncommon for a sickness to manifest itself if all they ate was protein, especially meat such as rabbit. Carbohydrates, roughage and vitamins were well understood to be all important for good health, and the vegetables from their expanding plots should provide them with this in time, supplementing their foraging that was now supplying their needs in this respect. Nineveh and Shuldan worked wonders with the plethora of wild greens that were abundant in the area, there was always a fresh salad at the very least with meals to keep everyone's vitamin levels topped up.

Tiny tomato seeds had already been planted indoors by Amaethon using clay fired pots he had discovered in a store shed; these had covered all the sunny window sills of the house for many weeks, eventually filling the house with their sweet green smell. With supporting frames of hazel poles already in place, Rhian and Amaethon planted them out into the beds once the frosts had definitely passed, taking great care with the delicate plants. Knowing that these tomatoes would be some of their most vulnerable crops they had constructed extra waist-high woven hazel hurdles around the areas that needed most protection. With those barriers in place and a multitude of sharpened sticks scattered about, it would give them the best of chances. This year, to avoid loss of any part of this essential crop, they mostly kept the dogs outside until the plants had established, comfortably set up in the nearby barn so they could ward off larger animals and chase away rabbits and suchlike. The relative proximity of the beds to the busy homestead should be added deterrent. Along with hunting of animals nearby, they would keep loss to a minimum, though some was entirely inevitable.

The tomato crop would be very important this year, especially as so much could be planted out from the huge amount of tiny seeds they had brought with them. Much of the crop would be eaten as it matured, but towards the end of the season there would be a massive effort to boil the bulk down and preserve this for sauces, chutneys and stew bases through the winter. The tomato concentrate could be stored in the multitude of glass jars they had inherited on moving in, which after sterilising by boiling them in water, should keep food fresh in the cold store with a wax seal. Come next winter it was hoped to have amassed a large amount of the sweet tasting crop, bringing a taste of summer to the depths of the long months before spring. For the first few years at least the best performing of the tomatoes and other plants would be carefully selected to obtain the most suited strains for their new environment. Amaethon would keep a close eye on the varieties that worked best and select the hardiest, though often ending up with thicker skins and reduced sweetness to cope with the relatively harsh climate of the valley, but this was more than an acceptable trade off.

Other crops included various hardy varieties of carrots, squashes, onions, garlic, peas, beans, and tubers of all sorts. Added around these they planted green fertilisers and nitrogen binders which could be dug in once matured, including clovers and mustard. These natural fertilisers were accompanied by flowers to help prevent pests by attracting in their natural predators and to provide a sacrificial crop, including borage, marigold and nasturtiums. Supplementing these were a number of companion herbs; lavender, chives and mint being particularly helpful near onions and carrots by way of their strong smell deterring pests and attracting in pollinators. To keep down weeds a mulch would be added of leaf matter and suchlike harvested from the woods, further adding to the accumulation of rich organic goodness. Many of the harvested root crops could be stored in the dark cellar on shelves and should help keep them fed through the winter and early spring, until the garden could provide again. Those that could not be stored that way would be variously pickled, boiled, dried or put into the cold store as suited.

The whole group were competent in foraging and food production and as such they had a rota of weed pulling, watering and tending the seedlings. However Amaethon and Rhian generally took the lead and held the greatest store of knowledge, teaching the children as they grew. The children were considered the responsibility of everyone, though some had parents, the relationships were fluid to some extent and all took care of each other as an extended family. Amaethon and Rhian were definitely the soft touch though as the group's beloved grandads and the children knew it. The pair had quickly commandeered an outbuilding which they used as a store and potting area once the roof had been patched up with simple cleaved wooden shingles. It also became their hideaway when the noise of the house became too much, which was all too often; as much as they loved their adoptive grandchildren they could at times create an unholy racket.

Though there were a few heavily worn metal tools found in storage Amaethon and Rhian often pushed for prioritising the making of better tools at their informal meetings with the group, but they all knew the smithy was a long way off being a reality, much to Bolin's constant frustration. The group's grandfathers were loved by all, being the oldest amongst them by a good margin, with dark tanned skin and deep wrinkles, though they were only in their late-fifties. It wasn't that people weren't known to live longer, but that life was unrelentingly harsh and often prematurely curtailed. The Steading however promised stability, a place of comfort to put down roots, hopefully somewhere one could grow old in peace. The elders were normally seen bent over the vegetable beds, working in the earth where they were happiest together, beneath their ever present wide-brimmed straw hats.

Not far from the ever expanding vegetable beds stood an ancient stand of some three dozen apple trees, and two enormous pears; these were clearly ancient and massively overgrown, interspersed with new colonising trees seeking to outcompete them. They should still be productive given the extensive blossom they had seen, but this fruit could prove to be very difficult to harvest at the optimum time given the enormous height at which they now stood. Rhian advised that with help he would be able to tackle this come autumn by hard pruning them back and clearing out the other invading trees; though this would dramatically reduce productivity for the following year, they should still provide a good harvest. Any apples they could take that weren't too ripe would be stored in the cellar on drying racks. Pears generally were more difficult to store so would be eaten as they ripened and preserved where possible, excellent in a sweet birch sap syrup but amazing in a sweet liqueur that Amaethon considered one of his specialities. Nothing would be wasted in terms of any inedible windfall, and worst case scenario could be collected to add to their compost pile, also being a great draw for wildlife, which they could harvest for additional meat. If possible they also hoped to produce a good vat of drinking cider, sweet sparkling perry and a store of cider vinegar, which would be good for pickling purposes, cleaning and general flavouring.

The hard work would persist as they continued to turn over the raw fields to add other beds, but that could be done at a more leisurely pace now the bulk of a crop was established, much to everyone's relief. This would be done on a rota to pick away at the job, but there was great need to construct better tools to speed this up as Bolin was keen to point out when he could, still eager to get his forge sorted out. The hope was that a plough could be fashioned to aid planting of significant fields of staple crops like oats, though they would start planting their limited supply now simply to grow on more stores of seed. Until then making bread and suchlike would be restricted, but by using crops like acorns and some of the abundant rye grass collected on the meadows, they could produce a flour later in the season for flatbreads and suchlike. Many of the group actually preferred the nutty flour of the acorn, which could be collected in great quantities come autumn, along with walnuts, sweet chestnuts, hazelnuts and the like. Nineveh and Shuldan promised them a feast of such treats, honeyed sweetened cakes being a prize that would keep them keen to crack on when their energy flagged.

12 - Herb garden

To the south-west side of The Steading was found a fair-sized walled area, which though entirely overgrown now was probably a productive herb garden at one point. There were straggly remnants of fragrant mint, rosemary and lavender bushes hanging on, and a hedge of various unkempt bay trees, which all needed a good hacking back to promote rejuvenated fresh growth. The cuttings from the bay trees were gathered up, being ideal for freshening the atmosphere in the house but also good as an insect deterrent in the stores. On clearing the invading vegetation that was choking the area of light they hoped that the seed bank lying dormant in the soil would bloom, though they did also have some more unusual varieties of herb seeds that Nineveh always seemed to be collecting on their travels. The thick south-facing garden wall needed to be partially rebuilt in a drystone fashion, but had a solid foundation and was soon functional again, providing an eight-foot windbreak and sun trap which would radiate heat back into the garden. Against this wall they hoped to plant some of the less hardy fruit trees, including sweet cherry, plum and miniature apricots, trained up against it with a south-facing aspect out of the wind. The garden would also serve as an excellent outdoor eating area, being everyone's preferred way of enjoying a leisurely evening meal if at all possible. A large fire pit would eventually be created at the centre of the seating area, being ideal for barbeques and keeping toasty warm into the cooler evenings; hopefully a place for many a relaxed gathering in the years to come. This area they would eventually surround with climbing plants such as transplanted honeysuckle to enjoy its heady scent and to allow its flowers to be plucked for a pleasant hit of its sweet nectar.

With the fields planted the production of herbs was agreed to be the next worthwhile and most pressing project, which would take time to come to fruition and useful production. Herbs would add much needed flavour and variety to their meals but more importantly there were many that could be used for essential medicinal purposes. Along with their medical benefits the herbs would make excellent teas, always warming and invigorating, perfect for energising or aiding relaxation as needed. Ideally as well there was a hope that Rhian and Amaethon could try and grow on some of their more recreational herbs, nothing potent, but many enjoyed the occasional pipe of differently flavoured tabacum at festivals, celebrations and suchlike.

As with the vegetable plots, they had brought seeds with them to stock a herb garden, including chamomile for calming teas, feverfew for aches to valerian for insomnia, opium poppy for high strength painkillers to potent strains of foxglove for its digitalis to treat heart issues, and many many more. A great variety of medicinal plants and fungi they might use were also found in the woods and nearby streams, so they would harvest any they found and propagate those that were suitable for the garden to breed the best strains. In time they should have a good selection, much of which they would harvest to dry in the rafters of the house and then process for use over the winter. This had the added bonus of providing a freshening of the air come winter time when the house-full of people and dogs would create a rather ripe atmosphere at times, despite a weekly bath and daily scrubs at the kitchen sink.

The herb garden was open to all to use but it was the accepted domain of the chief cooks, Nineveh and Shuldan, but whom also tended to treat the sick. Their adopted son Shulvan was fast learning, being a great experimenter, who from a young age had absorbed the ways of the herbalist and was fast becoming the group's go to expert on many medical matters. It was thought his childhood had likely influenced his choices and led him to medicine; they were unsure what had befallen Shulvan but his adoptive parents had found him alone in the ruins of a village they had come across several years previous, bloody and clearly traumatised. He was a quiet child, but with doting parents, who had been unable to have children, he soon fledged into the caring young man he now was, though prone to brooding and self-doubt. Shulvan and Sioned had at first seemed a less than natural fit, being extremes of personality in some ways, but they had been a couple for some time now and moderated each other's tendencies to introspection and rashness alike. Indication was of a baby on the way, given Sioned's more than apparent and growing belly on her wiry frame, but they left it to them to announce the news when they felt ready.

The herb garden soon flourished under the care of the small family unit, producing flavouring for an abundance of delicious meals and much needed medicine, for ailments from small cuts to major fevers. Much was eventually harvested and stores of cooking herbs hung from the kitchen rafters in bunches to dry, creating a wonderful aroma. The various medicinal herbs were preserved according to learned traditions and experiments, some simply dried, some preserved in oil and others boiled to extract concentrated tinctures; these were placed high out of the dogs and children's way, some being potently toxic and lethal in high concentrations.

Setting up the herb garden was another important job done, vital for their long term survival and comfort, being mindful it would take time to come to full fruition, perhaps years. In the meantime there was an abundance of plants and fungi to harvest in the landscape around them, more than enough for most ailments and plenty for teas and flavourings. With the setting up of the herb garden complete, thoughts turned to other important projects, the list long and time ever short despite the advantage of lengthening days.

13 - Harvest of the sea

Though their valley was bountiful, many yearned for the flavourful taste of the sea as a change to more gamey meats of the valley. There was plentiful fishing to be had in the wide valley river, and within the oxbow lakes and pools it left as it shifted course, but the more delicate freshwater fish and the abundant crayfish were not a patch on the variety that could be had from the sea. An expedition for fish and to gather essential salt for flavouring and crucial preservation of meat for the winter was therefore called for at the breakfast table one morning and unanimously agreed. A big factor which also helped swing the proposal in its favour was Merrick's wish to scout out the western side of the river down on the plains, to make sure there were no surprises lurking in that direction and to assess its potential for hunting and other resources.

It would be a significant undertaking, with the sea at least several dozen miles distant as the crow flies over some potentially tough and unknown terrain. The actual distance was not at all clear but the sea could sometimes be distantly made out from high vantage points by the sparkle of reflected light on the water and occasionally its ozone laden odour was detectable in a hot spell with a strong following wind. They decided for security to take most of the group, with Merrick as usual to lead the expedition. The youngest children were to stay at The Steading, to be looked after by the very capable Sioned and her partner Shulvan for the duration of the trip. The expedition was likely to take three weeks or more with the fishing, smoking and salt making being very time consuming. The dogs would be left at The Steading for security; there were few, man or beast, who would not fear the pack, whose members had now grown massive and muscular with their regular diet of rich meat and huge amounts of exercise. Though they could be ferocious at need, they were incredibly well trained and were extremely gentle with the children, patiently putting up with all sorts, accepting the little ones as naughty puppies and all as their pack.

With great efficiency the group gathered various supplies, including dried meat, teas and some of the early baby root vegetables for their outward trip. They hoped to travel light and fast with just two or three overnight stops and would have little time to pause for hunting and foraging, hoping to spend maximum time at the coast and to bring back as much as they could carry on their backs. Initially they would leave very early morning, crossing the river at a shallow ford to the western side, to exit the valley under relative cover of darkness, minimising chance of detection and revealing their home. This might have been considered risky if not for their now more intimate knowledge of the way down the easier west side of the entrance gorge, but which was still nothing more than a barely controlled descent following a line of least resistance.

Minds made up they spent a long day in excited preparation, finishing off nets previously almost complete in more idle hours, along with long woven thin lines and barbed hooks carved from bone and scarce slivers of stainless steel. These lines and nets were mostly made from thin nettle cordage, surprisingly robust but time consuming to craft, reinforced and interwoven with deer tendon fibre where needed. Travelling packs were loaded with extra sleeping kit and spare clothes; they knew days spent in the sea could be exhausting with the cold of the oceanic water and the salt stiffening their clothes. They also packed old tarps, which had seen better days, but would be perfect for making tripod-mounted smoking frames for the fish, though they would need to make other bark covered frames as well for the bulk of processing that they had planned.

It was after a less than promising night of swirling wind and light misty rain that they left the Steading, Merrick cautiously leading the way, but it would at least mask their leaving the valley, making it all the more unlikely they would be detected. The group cautiously descended the upper boulder strewn gorge and left the mouth of the lower canyon before the first light of day, damp but staying warm with a good pace down the upper slopes of the conifer dotted hills. The party were some miles across the more lightly wooded slopes beyond, moving parallel to the river system, before they felt the first warming rays of sun occasionally making its way through the heavy scudding clouds. Once they were a good distance away they relaxed the pace, readjusted the straps of their heavy packs and settled into a steady mile busting rhythm, muscle memory soon kicking in from their long winter journey. It was only really Rhian and Amaethon who had any real issue getting into the stride of things, but they gritted their teeth and pushed through the aches and pains that their more advanced years and tough lives inevitably troubled them with.

As they had found on their journey to The Steading, there wasn't even a suggestion of other humans being present, at most a faint track showing possible passage on rare occasion, though they were more than likely just game trails. As they had descended through the wooded upper slopes of the hills down to the milder lower altitude of the more open plains, there was an increasing abundance of game and the odd auroch-like cow, a descendent of the highland type cattle, which had reverted back to a much wilder and more massive state. These were considered too difficult to tackle now and the small amount of the sectioned carcass they could carry would weigh them down on the long journey, the precious hide also wasted for want of time to prepare and tan the skin. The massive beasts would however make for fine hunting on another trip, or possibly they might be captured, if

76

not too aggressive, and taken home to create a herd, though only if smaller specimens could be found, perhaps some calves.

Also, while travelling through the increasingly open rolling plains, the younger ones spied out with their better eyesight pony-sized horses, though they were completely wild beasts in highly protective fractious groups and would be nigh on impossible to split up and capture. For now, they were content to plan for scouting the wild moors above the valley to attempt to locate any upland-type, robust ponies that would better suit their needs being already adapted for the cold winters of the valley; that is assuming there were any animals to find. Returning to the plains to capture the horses was however kept on the back burner as a solid Plan B, both to use as potential beasts of burden but also as a possible alternate source of meat.

Travelling the seemingly endless miles of the open plains they marvelled at the abundance of flora and fauna and the profusion of vivid flowers, blooming bushes and sweet fragrances which were released in concentrated clouds as they brushed past. There were also a good variety of aromatic herbs which Nineveh and Shuldan picked to liven up their rather bland travelling rations, the pair also additionally collecting seeds to add to the variety in the garden. It was a region that would have made for fertile farmland, but offered no chance of concealment nor security, so would remain wild plains. They would re-visit to hunt, but this time they kept more or less parallel to the more densely wooded hinterland of their river, dubbed Rhuø, meaning roar in the old tongue. Progress was swift across the landscape of gentle grassy hills and small copses, the group stopping just twice overnight along the way, though they were very long, increasingly warm and exhausting days. To hide their presence at camp they employed an underground fire pit system, cleverly arranged to include a separate chimney vent to increase oxygen flow to the base of the fire and reduce smoke. These were kept small but intense and used to heat water and quickly boil a stew, then extinguished with water and soil. The nights were mild enough to do without the warmth of a camp fire and they wanted to travel with little attention and no trace, albeit there was unlikely anybody to see them for dozens of miles or more in any direction. The nights were however a little unnerving at times, the fires normally doing the job of keeping away inquisitive animals. Nonetheless, the size of the group meant it very unlikely they would be attacked; most predators looking for easier meals on the abundant plains, their fear of humans still engrained into their genes. Still, the younger ones of the group were understandably nervous but stories and songs lulled them into sleep before long.

With the new, already sweltering, day they began to notice the river Rhuø was acquiring an ever more sedate and estuarine characteristic, eventually spreading out into a series of smaller channels, creating shifting islands and vast muddy intertidal tracts supporting a host of wading birds and other wildlife. The change in the river necessitated a more north-westerly direction of travel for many miles where they skirted vast tracts of reed bed filled with wildlife, but by late afternoon they became increasingly aware of the sea by its tangy smell and the distant booming of crashing waves. The approach was dominated by a more sandy and arid landscape for some miles, turning to dunes after a while, with sea buckthorn and marram grass predominating. The landscape was also dotted with small copses of stunted pine huddled out of the wind in lee of the larger, more stable dune systems. The deadfall from the gnarled and ancient pines would provide good supplies of fuel for campfires and helping to boil down sea water for salt. They would need less resinous fuel than pine for smoking the fish, as the astringent taste would taint the delicate flesh, but there were abundant supplies of alder and other water loving trees not too far away on the grassier machair type and tidal habitat abutting the estuary. In addition there would hopefully be lots of dead brush and other woods washed up high and dry on the beach, meaning they should not have to range too far.

Moving through the final strip of dunes and brackish slacks, disturbing the odd bird on the nest as they went, including a small colony of terns, they came to the beach which was mainly sand and pebbles, with some areas of raised bedrock creating pools at lower tides. The beach was rich in birdlife, the shoreline hosting many gulls, the rockier parts home to numerous feeding turnstones and ringed plovers, groups of roosting oystercatchers, redshanks and other waders patiently awaiting the turn of the tide. A good way up the coast they noted a rocky peninsula of substantial length, which to the keen eyed of the group looked as though it could be cut off at high tide, but provided a potentially excellent vantage point for fishing deeper waters. With all now damp with sweat from the journey under the still scorching sun, most divested themselves of their packs, kicked off their boots, peeled off their clothes and dived into the refreshingly cold water. Once cooled they joined the others paddling their sore feet at the water's edge, luxuriating in its cooling effect with the pebbles and sand gently massaging away their aches from the long journey. Some of the more energetic then took the chance to walk the shoreline, sun on their backs, picking up interesting stones and shells, including the prized miniature cowries with which they would make delicate necklaces and use to adorn their clothes. In just that short time they had already seen one large pod of around twenty bottlenose dolphins, indicating the fecundity of the area, besides being a joy to watch, leaping above the water and generally frolicking in the waves.

After a decent rest they spent the remainder of the day carefully exploring, stacking dry wood and noting the best fishing spots, often denoted by fishing terns, diving gannets and frenzied groups of gulls.

It was welcome to note a complete absence of any human activity on the beach and beyond, including no felled trees, or waste middens, nor sign of camp sites betrayed by old fire rings. Sitting on the beach that evening they gorged on the abundance of shellfish, crabmeat, numerous mackerel and a massive lobster which had been found by Durian in a short diving trip. The salty tastes of the sea were superb, contrasting sharply with the robust gamier tastes of the meat they had gotten used to in the valley. As they consumed the small feast they discussed the super abundance of fish just off shore around the reefs and also at the mouth of the nearest river channel, which would be ideal for stringing across their nets to catch the fish bound up in the tidal flows. After a short pause to let their meal settle they all then moved to set up their traveling tarps in a grassy copse of pine nestled within the dune slacks, and risked a large warming fire that night, comfortable that they were safe and well shielded by the dunes and trees. With the abundance of tinder-dry oil-rich pine needles and flammable sub surface roots, they knew better than to build a fire directly atop the ground so they had first dug out a good sized area to then line with stone and created a low wall around it. Finally they added a thick layer of clean sand which formed a great basal layer. This would save any inadvertent underground fires and should make covering up the area simpler in order to leave no trace when they left. Another great feature of the large stones edging the fire place was that they could absorb and then radiate back out heat for much of the night, it even being possible to use smaller stones to pre heat their beds if needs be, though it was unlikely to get cold enough to warrant the bother.

The next day began early with a delightful breakfast of delicious sea bass fried on their small cast-iron travelling pans. Nineveh and Shuldan had done themselves proud with the meal, subtly flavoured with a few herbs and a crispy batter encasing chunks of the delicate moist fish. With full belies the whole group were soon busy setting out nets on the estuary channels and using hooked lines in the deeper water from various rocky spits. The waters were found to be bountiful, though rather cold being oceanic, but it wasn't long before they were pulling fish after fish from the water, including mackerel, bass, pollock, various flatfish and wrasse. To preserve the best of the fish the smokers were rapidly set up and once the fish was gutted and each pre-soaked in briny water, they were ready to be hung on wooden racks at about chest height above the smoky fires, initially covered over in their old tarps to help capture and concentrate the smoke. The smell was distinctive, from the initial tang of the briny saltiness and the sharp wood smoke, turning to a mellower but richer smell as the fish dried and cured in the smoke. Later, once the numbers of fish caught increased and they needed more smokers, they would peel bark from freshly felled trees, creating large sections they could use to cover substantial frames. The fires were fed with driftwood and moist wood chips of green alder found in the delta, with a limited supply of air to keep the smoke coming, the thicker the better to saturate the flesh of the fish. This was a fairly delicate process which needed constant tending by at least a couple of people but done right it would impregnate the flesh of the fish, preserving it and giving superb flavour. The smokers were kept going for many days and nights at a time, building a good supply of preserved fish of all types which they finally left to further air dry under separate covers made of the snedded pine boughs trimmed off the felled trees. There had to be an unceasing watch as there was great interest from the local birdlife, but a few thefts by gulls was not the end of the world.

The process of slowly cooking, smoking and dehydration was a superb way of preserving the fish, it would keep the bacteria at bay and in conjunction with their natural saltiness, initial soaking in brine, then light salting, would ensure they kept for their journey home and for months afterwards in the cool of the cellar. The smoking also imparted the most tremendous sweet taste which would contrast well with their more gamey and robustly flavoured meat sources in the valley. It was a long winded process but there was no rush, better to get the preservation perfect than risk the wasted effort for the sake of another day or two.

While they were catching and smoking the fish, they were also producing crystallised salt flakes, though this was a much longer process, but well worth the great effort. To start they dammed sea water into the uppermost rocky pools at high tide, plugged with stones and clay to seal the gaps, and so allowing its slow evaporation in the strong sun and subsequent formation of strong brine. During this process they turned to the estuary for more clays which they used to form basic pots and trays, fired to form vessels they could then use over fires to further simmer down the brine collecting in the pools. The children found this messy chore of collecting muddy clays especially to their liking, the squelch between their fingers, the formation of random grotesque figures and eyebrow raising sculptures of great delight.

The whole process of making the salt was laborious but it was a precious resource as a preservative and not least for flavouring. So, with dreams of succulent meals to come and a guarantee of food preserved through winter, they amassed as much as they could. The crystallised salt was kept in fairly solid compressed blocks within larger clay pots, collecting many pounds over their stay. While processing the fish and salt they made stiff, woven reed and willow baskets to aid transport home; along with their normal baggage, all would be expected to carry several pounds of salt along with the packed fish, but thankfully that was much lighter. It was a happy time though, everyone keeping busy and productive, aided by fantastic regular meals, the sun warm on their bodies and the light sea breeze keeping them cool.

After many more days of making salt and preserving the fish they began to reach the limit of what they could carry, so they brought a halt to the fishing and gorged on the excess while waiting for the final batches of salt to crystallise and thoroughly dry. With most of the final jobs for the trip home complete, there was in theory much free time on their hands, though it was rare anyone was completely idle, with clothes and equipment to make and mend, crafting projects to complete and so on. However, the children clearly had way too much energy to be kept cooped up around camp and their exuberance was spilling over into play fights as games escalated into fiercely fought competitions, with a few bruises and black eyes the result. Arwyn, Merrick's partner, tactfully suggested it may be a good time to take the children on an 'adventure', and volunteered herself and Merrick to herd the young ones away for a night or two. The other adults were clearly relieved at the offer, quickly getting some light packs sorted for the short trip. The children were initially hesitant knowing they had a long tedious trip home soon and wanting to avoid walking anywhere they didn't have to. Arwyn and Merrick were not the types to force anyone into anything they clearly didn't want to do, but as they discussed between them their plans, in clear earshot of the kids, they soon became interested, speaking of their ideas to visit the sea bird colonies up the coast, do some egg collecting, cliff diving and lazy camps. Once the ringleaders of the children showed interest, Durian being a principal instigator, it wasn't long before the rest of the group were raring to go. With little point leaving it until the next day, their bags already packed by the adults, the motley group were soon setting off north, keen for an adventure.

Arwyn and Merrick soon lost sight of the young ones, though their high-pitched screams of delight every now and then showed they were off in the right direction. The way along the coast was already pretty well known and everyone knew the plan was to make for the peninsular just a couple of hours steady stroll north. It was another glorious day, the sun hot but the sea breeze keeping them cool, making the walk pleasant and easy going. The group mostly kept to the beach, sticking to the harder pebbly ridge to avoid wasting energy, but Arwyn and Merrick could see from their footprints that the children had been wandering and running back and forth between the sea line and the dunes, in little doubt that they would be suitably exhausted by the end of the day, the yielding and shifting sand a massive sapper of even youthful energy.

As the couple walked they kept an eye on the tideline, spotting the odd interesting shell and curious stone, some of which they pocketed but mostly just casually examined and returned. In their time at the coast many of the group had taken to adorning their clothes with interesting little shells, the tiny cowries a notable favourite. As they walked Arwyn tinkled with the tiny sound of the shells gently clinking on her loose shirt, the shiny treasures softly glowing in the sun. They were a handsome pair, happy in each other's company, silent for the most part, content to enjoy the peace and knowing that it may not last long once they caught up with the children. It was another hour or so later that they met up with the kids, who had stopped just before the peninsular, waiting for the tide to recede so they could cross the submerged causeway, which kept their destination an island for most of the time. Clearly they had burnt off a great deal of energy as most were just happily snoozing in the shade of some stunted pine trees on a rocky bluff above the beach. Those who still had some energy were messing about in the surf, though with a much less boisterous attitude than back at camp. It would be possibly an hour or so before they could contemplate using the causeway, so they took the opportunity to fuel up on some of the supplies they had brought with them, comprising various lightly smoked fish and fresh mussels some of the more enterprising children had gathered up from the exposed pools and then cooked over a small fire, gently steamed with thyme and bay leaves. Having finished lunch most took the opportunity to rest, laid out in the sun on the grassy bluff, listening to the abundant bird song and the waves breaking onto the gravelly beach.

Before long though they judged the tide had receded to a level they could safely wade across, the middle appearing no deeper than the knees of the smallest child. Prudence though led them to use their walking staffs for support, which turned out to be just as well given the current was still fairly strong at the mid-point. Merrick and Arwyn ended up giving the littlest a piggy back for part of the way when they started struggling, not wanting any mishaps albeit even the smallest were strong swimmers. As best they could judge the tides at the causeway it was only likely to be this shallow for a perhaps an hour at a time, being close to the high spring tides, but they should be fine for the next day or two, excepting perhaps an unseasonal storm causing a surge in levels. The high pressure weather of late showed little sign of changing so they judged they would be safe, but at worst may have to hole up for a day or two. Taking it steady they crossed in thirty minutes or so, taking their time at the other end to dry off and get their rope-made beach sandals comfortably strapped back on. These they had constructed from corded grasses on their second day at the coast, their boots impractical and bare feet being risky on some of the barnacle covered rocks. The makeshift sandals were already near the end of their useful lives and many of the children just hadn't bothered with them, but as they were leaving soon they could simply be buried to leave no trace, breaking down before long.

When they had arrived at the coast there had been potential plans to use the peninsular for fishing in the deeper waters, but it just hadn't been necessary with such abundance in the estuary and easy fishing from the shore and the various rocky outcrops, so for most of them this was the first time on the island. Merrick and Arwyn had previously visited on a trip to scout the coast but hadn't ventured far along the island, just enough to check for signs of human habitation, but finding none. So it was for all an adventure and a chance to explore, knowing that the island may not have seen humans for many years. First though the priority was to find a comfortable sheltered spot for a camp, ideally with fresh water and some firewood. The group set out, initially climbing over the rocky intertidal area and coming up onto the top of some small cliffs of ancient volcanic rock pock-marked with lichens and stunted grasses. This afforded a view down the long half-island, half-peninsular which stretched off into the far distance. As had already been seen on their approach the south-eastern edge of the island was mostly comprised of sandy bays and inlets set into a fairly gently sloping series of rocky volcanic outcrops, but which sharply contrasted with the more northerly-facing exposed side, of high jagged cliffs and what they guessed would be rocky, mainly inaccessible beaches. Clearly the more southerly-facing sheltered edge would be best for a camp. The steep grassy slope up to the northerly-facing high rocky cliffs were teeming with birdlife, nesting on the cliffs themselves and no doubt with puffins, petrels and suchlike burrowed away in the short-cropped turf at the cliff tops, the insect-rich habitat also much favoured by the numerous red-billed choughs hereabouts.

The centre of the island was a mix of brackish slacks and scrub with intervening wide areas of tough hardy grasses and bracken. These areas too were teeming with birdlife, mainly nesting gulls, but also various coastal warblers in the thicker vegetation, clacking stonechats in the isolated bushes and flighty pipits on the more open ground. From one side to the other the bird-rich island was just a quarter mile wide at the thinnest edge nearer land, ballooning out in the centre to a mile or so and thinning back out again to a distant blunted tip some four miles distant. The centre point of the island seemed the most likely to contain fresh water springs running out of the higher cliffs and with firewood more likely to be in abundance, so more by instinct than anything, the group headed in that direction, the children keen to be the first to find an ideal spot to set up the camp.

The reason for the close-cropped grass soon became clear, with large numbers of plump rabbits in abundance at the centre of the island ranging right up to the apex of the high cliffs. They seemed to have little fear of humans, but they were clearly wary of the large gulls and skuas which patrolled the area, the young rabbits being a prize morsel given the fights that erupted whenever a coney was successfully taken by the squabbling noisy birds. As the group moved along the island they skirted brackish pools and small ponds of water, some clearly less saline than others given the plants that grew in those that preferred the freshwater, including some edible lilies and reedmace whose starchy rhizomes or roots were worth harvesting. It was at one of these pools that they discovered the first of the freshwater springs they would come across on the trip, and which would turn out to be the largest, so anchoring them to this approximate spot for their camp. The pool that it fed was not much larger than a modest pond but was perfect for having a wash to get rid of the build-up of salts from their bodies and clothes. Near this pool were a few low-lying alders and willows, stunted in the wind, but with the dead alder particularly providing some half decent firewood where it hadn't fallen to the floor, fairly quick burning but with bright orange flames and easy to light if dry.

In the lee of the scrubby trees, they chose a good-sized flat spot of the close-trimmed turf and set up their tarps and bed rolls. The nights were warm, especially in comparison to what they were used to in their valley, but they would collect a good deal of wood to keep them cosy through the night, knowing that a damp sea breeze could soon give a chill. With the chores sorted the children scarpered to explore the area, gravitating to the nearby sandy cove. The inlet was superbly sheltered, forming a near circular bay protected from the force of the open sea by a pair of jutting horn-like barriers of basalt, also perfect for rock jumping from into the deeper water. The sun had done its work that day, with the clear water warm and inviting, and was quickly filled with children who had abandoned their clothes as they ran in, previous tiredness forgotten.

Merrick and Arwyn were not far behind the children, finishing up the last of the camp tasks and stowing away their gear, putting the food out of the sun and then splitting and stacking up the fire wood. As they strolled to the bay, they too had stripped off their sweaty clothes, though more sensibly soaping them up and rinsing them through in a stream and hanging them in a bush out of the sand to dry. Without comment, and making sure the children saw, they proceeded to slowly pick up the children's clothes, theatrically shake them free of sand and hang them up; led by Durian, the children were soon sheepishly sorting out their own clothes, chastised without any harsh words needed, though with no few cheeky grins Merrick and Arwyn chose not to see. Clothes properly sorted the group made their way into the wonderfully warm waters, their brown and freckled bodies soon washed free of the grime and sweat from their exertions of the day. Many chose to just float on the surface, suspended in the warmest upper layer of the water, muscles relaxing with the small waves slowly lapping over them, their long hair surrounding them in a halo. Those that still had energy to spare went diving into the rockier spots deeper into the small bay, finding with the low tide that they could easily access the prime hideaways of good sized crabs which they snatched up and dispatched ready for their supper. These they hid away in cool shaded pools higher up the shore, weighed down and covered over with flat stones to avoid theft by the ever-present gulls gliding overhead.

Sometime later the adults first and later the kids reluctantly left the water, rinsing themselves off in a small freshwater stream and taking up positions on warm rocks to lie and dry their naked bodies. As they sunbathed in the late afternoon sun many took a chance for a quick nap, just their heads covered with a shirt, their lean muscular bodies luxuriating in the heat. By early evening, with the temperature starting to drop and stomachs beginning to complain, they gathered up their things, pulled on their loose shorts, then wandered back to the camp.

During the afternoon they had been foraging for edible seaweed, mainly kelp, laver and pepper dulse, and had amassed a good number of crabs and shellfish. As the group walked the short way back to the camp they also harvested some of the abundant rock samphire and sea beets, amassing easily between them what they would need for a good meal. With the smoked and salted fish they had brought along they would have more than enough to satiate them all, though nothing complicated with most of the ingredients just chucked into a big camp pot for a simple seafood soup. It was a pretty quick meal to prep and cook, everyone's bowls filled within the hour and all going back for extra helpings. Feeling contently stuffed, most were happy to just lie back and absorb the rest of the evening's sun sheltered from the breeze in the lee of the bushes, the efforts of the days travel and play having finally depleted the excess of the children's energy. They spent the evening digesting their food and nibbling on the various treats their parents had loaded into their packs, speaking of the day to come, most content to simply repeat the day at the sheltered beach, but all looking forward to egg collecting, seeing the puffins and perhaps catching some rabbits. As the glowing-red evening sun set the temperature soon dropped, so all piled on some extra layers and got wrapped up in their bedrolls, warm and cosy with the radiating glow of the fire. With everyone tired and already dozy, Arwyn and Merrick gently coaxed them into sleep with a harmony of soft singing and gentle humming, accompanied by the soft white noise of the surf in the background and the distant sounds of the seabirds as they settled down for the night.

The children slept in much later than usual, well past the break of day and awoke to the smell of eggs being fried. Merrick had woken early that morning and had collected a good two dozen, mostly from the gulls. It was a somewhat risky business as the gulls could be understandably pretty vicious in protecting their nests, but there was a knack to it in making sure you held a leafy branch above you which they invariably attacked rather than your delicate scalp. Merrick had taken care to only take one or two eggs from each nest, not wishing to denude them completely, leaving at least one. In conjunction with Merrick's egg collecting, Arwyn had been busy fishing in the deeper waters off the rocks, having taken a good few fish within just shy of an hour. The resulting white fish omelettes were superb with some freshly blanched greens, the natural taste of the sea bird eggs being fishy in any case and the high protein content setting them up nicely for the day. After their wooden dishes were scraped and scoured with abrasive horsetail plant, Arwyn and Merrick said to the kids that they could do as they wished that morning as they were going to go and explore the island, though any were welcome to join them if they liked. They agreed to meet up after midday to visit the sea bird colony on the north cliffs, to hopefully see the puffins, check out some unusual eggs, then to later hunt rabbits with their slings. In the end the kids decided they would take it easy, feeling weary after the intense day before, having gone about three times as far as the adults on their meandering trip there and with not having stopped since their arrival. With a wry smile at a mission accomplished in having finally worn out the children,

Arwyn and Merrick set out for a relaxed day exploring the area, leaving the kids free to do as they pleased, knowing the eldest would keep them more or less in line if any ructions broke out.

The couple set out with little intention but to see what they could discover, collecting any edibles they might find as they travelled and stowing them into a simple freshly-woven basket made of reeds and willow. Though there were no paths as such, the presence of so many rabbits, clearly in a boom year, meant the way was easy enough, the close-cropped grass providing a soft and pleasant surface which meant they could keep their eyes off their immediate surroundings and walk barefoot much of the time. Forgetting for the time being their responsibilities, they ambled along, happy in the warm sun on their exposed backs and bare legs, eventually stripping off completely as it got hotter as the morning progressed. In a couple of hours rambling along they reached the end of the island, noting as they did the remnants of a few buildings now mostly subsumed into the vegetation. There was however a rather odd tumbledown tower on the high point at the headland, its purpose unknown but it made for an interesting end point to look back along the island and out to sea, revealing a number of offshore islands in the distance. Below the tower was a large beach, dunes at the back with intermittent marram grass, graduating down to a shingle beach and a little sand. It led out in a more northerly direction so the waves here were more active, breaking onto the beach and the headland. The two of them spent a pleasant hour or so wading at the cool water's edge, then rested while they snacked on some travelling jerky and dried berries, happy to spend some time alone in each other's company, soaking up the sun.

At about midday Merrick and Arwyn met up with the kids, to start on their egg hunt. They would only take those eggs that they would eat, and would not denude any nests completely, but as the birds were super abundant, they had little concern that their presence would be anything more than a minor annoyance. Surrounded by nervous choughs initially, which were feeding on insects on the southerly facing grassy slopes, they moved to the cliff top and came to the burrows of the puffins and petrels. The petrels were of course only active here at night, so for now they only saw the puffins, but what a sight they were, a few hundred at least currently spread across the high cliffs. The children were very excited to see the extremely cute birds with their multi-coloured comical bills, not previously having had such close contact, which here was practically so they could touch them, as unconcerned as they were about humans. Their eggs could be located by getting down and putting in a hand and most of the arm into their long burrows, but it was a little unnerving doing so, and not wanting to unnecessarily disturb too many on the nest, they only attempted a few nests and returned the single eggs they found. They were pretty unremarkable bar at one nest where they found an egg with unusual striated patterns, a small jewel all were eager to see before it was replaced. In addition to the puffins there were a host of birds upon the cliffs themselves, many being just within reach at the very top on the stepped-like rock formation of the cliffs. The most interesting were the guillemots which didn't have a nest as such but laid their egg precariously on small ledges. The eggs could easily roll around at times, but ingeniously had evolved to have one pointed end which meant they would roll only in a small circle, saving them from a long drop. Like the puffins the guillemots had just one egg per nest, but these were often a bright turquoise, amazing to look at. Again they all had a close look at an egg brought up by Merrick who had leaned over to pluck one from a ledge, but soon had it replaced. The thousands of birds on the cliffs including the guillemots, razorbills, shags and fulmars were of course less than impressed with this invasion of their territory and 'borrowing' of their eggs, but once the visitors had moved away from the cliff top and set themselves up to view the cliffs from further back, the host soon settled and returned to their nests. Without doubt the main aspect of the day that the children would find hard to forget, beyond the noise, was the smell, the thousands of birds and their guano being incredibly overpowering, a pretty noxious blend with potent ammonia being strongest of all which almost sent some into sensory overload at first. This was however pretty much soon forgotten as the noisy spectacle of the cliffs enthralled them all, the comings and goings of the birds at random, cutting across each other's flight path, but with no sign of any collisions; it was truly astounding.

As they were considering leaving the incredible spectacle, stomachs starting to remind them they still had their supper to see to, they felt a change come over the seabird colony, a sudden shift and nervous energy palpable in the air. Their first instinct was to search the skies for aerial predators but that failed to yield the normal deadly peregrine that might cause upset. Then in the distance they saw the obvious reason for the cacophony of anxious alarm calls, a pod of orcas coming from the north. The pod was large, some fifteen at least based upon the number of dorsal fins as they cut through the water, their blow holes jetting out occasional blasts of water as they surfaced. Those birds previously in the water diving for fish had sharply exited, perhaps not in much danger but clearly unhappy with the approach. The pod showed little interest in the birds and seemed intent to push towards the cliffs, the precipice being replicated as a deep drop under water to unknown depth. Birds and cetaceans alike knew that the area provided for a rich upwelling of fish, shrimp and small squid, exploited normally by the birds and part of the reason for the massive colony.

As they watched the pod it became clear that their focus of attention was an enormous shoal of herring moving in front of them, the predators seeking to herd and surround their prey, while pushing it

93

hard against the cliffs. As they concentrated the mass of fish into a writhing ball they took it in turns to dart in and slap the edge of the shoal with their powerful tails, stunning the fish a dozen or so at a time and allowing them to eat their fill. The sight was awe inspiring, the vantage point above giving them a view of the hunt that ordinarily would be lost in a distant melee of fins and white water. They watched the scene unfold for a good twenty minutes, the pod eventually swimming back out to deeper water to the north, with some leaping into the air and slapping their tails on the surface, seemingly happy with the success of their hunt. As the pod left, the bird colony settled back down to its normal noisy business, but with a huge number of gulls taking the opportunity to clean up the remnants of the dead herring missed by the orcas.

As they climbed down from the cliff edge, most were still in silent awe, overloaded with the intensity of the spectacle. Ambling down the hill they eventually started excitedly talking, the orcas being the main highlight of conversation, for many their first sighting. As they moved further down from the high cliffs and the excitement ebbed a little, Arwyn and Merrick pulled out their slings and a selection of rounded pebbles they had carefully chosen earlier that day from the beach. The kids soon cottoned on that rabbit hunting was next, becoming quiet as they walked, and within just a few minutes all had their slings out and loaded, ready to pick out a good spot. Even the youngest knew their best chance was to spread out, hide and wait silently; the rabbits would soon be tempted back out by the rich turf and could then be picked off. The children spread out across several hundred yards of the vast rabbit warrens that pocked the grassy slope, most using bushes and large tussocks as cover, with a fair degree of success. All the kids were competent with slings, being used to hunting rabbits from a very young age, relatively easy pickings when they were as numerous and blasé as here, unused to human predators. Within an hour or so of hunting

94

in this fashion they managed to dispatch more than they really needed, but it would do no harm to just take the richest pickings of the animals' meat and give the rest to the gulls, making barely a dent in the booming population.

As the children had been hunting, Merrick and Arwyn had also been busy, finding more of the tiny onions and leek-like plants they had located earlier for their dinner. A good number were needed for a decent meal as they were miniature specimens though incredibly flavoursome, but with what they had gathered on their walk that morning, their foraging basket was pretty full and contained more than enough to bulk out the rabbit stew. The children had already dressed the rabbits by their return, taking the more succulent meat, waiting ready for the pot with a number of legs to be roasted on skewers as a starter. Again, there was no messing about with the main meal and everything was chucked in, with just some pemmican for a fatty stock to grease the pan, a good amount of salt, and a few of the herbs they had gathered on their travels to boost the flavour, mainly thyme and some bay leaves. To add some much-needed carbohydrates to refuel a good number of foraged pig nuts were added, similar to carrots in taste. The plant was a chore to harvest but between them a good number could be harvested from a patch in the grassy centre of the island without denuding the stock for future regrowth.

As the meal was going to be slow cooked for a good few hours to tenderise the rabbit, the children picked the meat off the roasted rabbit legs, munched on some other snacks and left for the beach, a late afternoon of rock diving on the cards. Merrick and Arwyn were happy to keep an eye on the simmering stew, enjoying more of the relative quiet while the kids happily burnt off what was left of their energy. After about two hours the stew was near perfect and to top it off a number of eggs were cracked onto the surface of the simmering liquid to gently poach. Again these were gulls eggs, being a decent size, with only half the clutch ever taken from each nest, meaning a sustainable harvest was possible. While Merrick had collected these, Arwyn had made some tiny dumplings as well from the last of their precious flour collected from early rye grass, bulked out with some of the starchy rhizomes of the abundant lilies and reedmace from the pond. It was a token part of the meal, but with a few herbs and salt, made for a pleasant energy boosting carbohydrate addition to their supper. As they finished second and third helpings the groans of satisfaction showed that all thought the meal was superb as they happily scraped out their bowls with their spoons, then licked them clean. Being protein heavy everyone was stuffed and it took an hour before they could contemplate moving to sort out the washing up, but with that done they could rest in the knowledge of chores done, bar the obligatory face wash and teeth scrub later on.

The contented group sat up late into the night, telling each other stories, watching the starry night sky and singing songs of the past. Many of their songs were simple aural histories, though some spoke of ages more distant, heroes battling mythic winged beasts, great voyages on the sea to lands where all was ice and other tales which had lost their meaning but sounded well on the tongue. It was a contented group that slowly dropped off, soft snores soon the only sound in the darkness.

The group woke early the next day, ate fried fish and eggs for breakfast and quickly had their things packed and ready for the off, the children keen to see their parents and their extended family, though none would admit they had missed them. The journey back to the main camp was a much less energetic affair, the children content to keep with the adults, all taking it easy, picking up interesting shells, harvesting unusual plants, collecting herbs and inspecting other flotsam that had washed up on the strandline. In addition to the usual shells, they found more unusual stones with quartz lines, with sea glass and shark's teeth being coveted prizes, especially those with convenient holes ready for a leather cord to make necklaces and bracelets.

By the time the travellers had returned it was early afternoon, the main camp being visible from some distance due to the small plume of smoke from the cooking fire. All of the camp, but the parents particularly, were happy to see their return and glad the children were content and much more relaxed. While the children had been away the remainder of the group had been busy and it was clear to see they were pretty much ready for the off, everything that could be packed neatly squared away and much of the camp cleared, close to leaving no trace.

That evening they took their last chance to gorge on the various delicacies of the sea, a particularly lush series of large lobsters as the centrepiece, but accompanied by a host of shellfish, freshwater shrimp tails, mackerel and scallops. This was complemented by freshly foraged marsh samphire, sea beets, kale and suchlike. Washed down with great volumes of subtly flavoured teas and a nip of birch sap liqueur, the meal was a delight and would set them up for the start of their long journey home. As night descended and the children fell asleep in their parent's arms, there were many thanks given to Arwyn and Merrick for the great job they had done. The pair shrugged off the praise having greatly enjoyed the trip, but thankful that it had given the group a chance to lower stress levels and sort out the final preparations.

The next day came, bright but with a cooler breeze than they had so far experienced; nonetheless this they greatly welcomed as it would help make the trip home more comfortable, for that day at least. As they loaded up, the stronger adults opted to mainly carry the many pounds of salt, with the bear-like Bolin carrying at least twice his share with apparent ease. Others took on the lighter but bulkier dried and lightly salted fish, loaded into baskets hung between poles which they could comfortably carry between two. This was certainly the lighter load, but would likely still result in some sore shoulders after a full day travelling, so they made sure to pad the ends of the poles with soft sheepskins from their sleep mats. It would take much longer to get home up into the mountains, laden as they were with this haul and all their baggage, but they planned to take their time with an easy pace, though with cold camps as they neared home.

Some four uneventful but long days after setting out from the coast they made the approach to their valley, shoulders sore but buoyed by the prospect of a hot bath. They were careful to move with stealth as they negotiated their way up the tricky entrance gorge, but come late afternoon, with the sun setting over the mountains, they finally arrived at the farmstead, very tired but happy to be home. Those that had stayed behind, namely the youngest children and their caretakers Sioned and Shulvan, were absolutely delighted to see them all, racing out to meet them on the first alarm calls of the dogs. They soon had a celebratory feast made and the home fires roaring for the tired travellers, wryly commenting that they needed a soapy bath as a priority, the smell of fish and sweat a ripe combination.

They took the time to stow away their treasures into the stores, with the salt pots left near the fire in the main hall for a few days to ensure they were thoroughly dry. Some were later broken open and the salt crushed to add to the pantry stores, with the rest kept safe for later use in the dry cellar. It was welcome to see that the young children and their caretakers had been busy, with two brace each of pigeon and hares hanging in the cold store, the majority of a fresh deer carcass, as well as various baskets of mushrooms and fresh greens from the forest and vegetable gardens in the pantry. Evidently they had not gone hungry, but none had expected otherwise, Sioned being a superb hunter and all more than competent foragers, including the youngest.

It had been a successful trip, but the journey back was tiring beyond belief; they agreed it would need to be a rare treat for now with such effort. As they discussed the expedition, first in the steamy bath house and later in comfortable chairs in the main hall, they gave thought to ways to make the journey more manageable for the future, thinking that canoes would be of great use in transporting back a greater amount, though a laborious undertaking to construct and could only be used to travel part way. Horses or ponies were thought to be of greater potential, being beasts of burden often used for such purposes and whom could potentially navigate the entire way. With this labour saving it might be possible to mount more expeditions to the sea, as well as enabling various other possibilities.

Sitting in front of a roaring fire in the hall, giving out presents of shells, sea glass and all the other treasures they have found to those that had stayed home, they were soon excitedly planning their next expedition. Their next trip was likely to explore the uplands above the valley where they hoped to scout out other supplies of meat to avoid denuding local resources, and perhaps, with fortune favouring them, by locating animals they could domesticate as beasts of burden. For now though they settled back, warm, clean and well fed, content to be home and comfortable. As they relaxed into their cushioned chairs they spoke of plans for the coming days, mainly catching up with chores and preparations to be made for future projects and expeditions. It was a cheerful and merry atmosphere once more in The Steading with everyone home and safe, but before long came the yawns and so, one-by-one, they left for their beds, soon sleeping the deep and content sleep of those happy to be home.

14 - Narrow escape

Their first summer at The Steading was near perfection, everywhere you looked the fecundity of nature spilled forth, sometimes unforgiving, but that was the way of life's endless cycle of death and rebirth. Much of the community's time was spent tending to their fields, hunting, trapping and fishing, but mostly done at a fairly relaxed pace. The weather was sublime, with warm temperatures and regular light rains which resulted in verdant growth and a promise of good yields from the crops. The valley air was more wholesome than any they remembered and lifted the spirits, a mix of pine, earthy tones and sweet heathers off the mountains. In combination with the incredibly clean water and the nourishing plentiful food, they felt invigorated and this leant them the energy to achieve nearly any task with the minimum of fatigue.

It was though hard work and there were many grazes, cuts and minor ailments as you might expect, but all were tended to expertly by Shulvan, the cooks' son, who increasingly became the first port of call for any such issues, but with backup from his parents. That was until one day, while working in the kitchen, he heard his name being called in a tone of sheer unadulterated panic, with one of the children, Seren, suddenly rushing in, breathless and clearly in a major state of distress. In calming the pale youngster down, Shulvan eventually managed to get from her that while playing, Durian had slipped on some rocks and bashed his head. As the child started to gain back her breath she went on to say that Durian was unconscious and looked in a really bad way, his deep head wound bleeding badly, spurting until someone had wisely pressed a shirt on the wound to partially stem the flow. Nineveh and Shuldan were out that day, otherwise Shulvan would have instantly called on their experience and expertise, but knowing they were likely still far out in the woods collecting herbs and mushrooms, he was left with no option but to grab his medicine bag and run to the patient, though knowing it may be a forlorn hope because serious head wounds were often lethal.

Shulvan and Seren swiftly exited the kitchen leaving the house by the back door and ran through the rear yard, passing the vegetable beds and hitting the meadows at an impressive speed, adrenaline giving them both a boost. Seren led the way, heading out the top of the meadow and into the trees, briefly following the main path up the valley and then turning towards the river. After a while of crashing through the undergrowth, their faces and bodies whipped by the stunted saplings and their shins torn by brambles, they came upon the group of children gathered around the prone form of Durian. It was plain to see what had happened, the rock behind him mossy and slick from the mist off a nearby waterfall, a small scuff on the boulder showing where he had slipped and fallen hitting his head below. There was a sickly-sweet metallic tang in the air which did not bode well, indicating a significant loss of blood, despite the staunching efforts with the makeshift compress. Even the birds hereabout were silent as if already in mourning for the child, reflecting the shocked faces of the children, uncharacteristically mute and still.

Shulvan quickly took stock of Durian, checking for his pulse and signs of breathing, which were erratic and shallow respectively but thankfully still at least present. His vitals checked, he then began examining the obvious head wound on the side of his head; it was deep and had bled profusely but was just starting to clot and though looked horrendous, was to the trained eye to be expected with such an injury. He was however very worried at his ashen colour and lack of responsiveness to his name. After washing his hands in a special mix of herb-infused soapy water, he then used a clean pad to dab away the blood from around the wound, necessary to inspect it, though causing fresh blood to ooze. It was indeed nasty, the bone slightly depressed with a good two inches of skull exposed under the loose flap of skin. Pinching this together, with help from the braver of the children, he took a needle and expertly stitched the skin together then bound it with a fresh absorbent pad and bandage, further staunching the blood loss and covering over the bone. Durian was lucky this was not a wound on a tighter part of the scalp and that there was no skin loss, which would be an altogether trickier, if not impossible proposition to repair. Despite what must have been a fair amount of pain from the wound and the stitches, Durian had not woken nor were his pupils reacting to light, and so Shulvan decided it would be best to take the boy back to the house, given that even in a best case scenario it may take some time for him to come around. Before attempting this he made a thorough check of the boy for any other injuries, but could find none, beyond some developing bruises. This was not to say though that there would not be some injury of the bones or swelling not immediately obvious, so he took great care to keep him as still as possible for now, this would need to be checked again when he regained consciousness. A stretcher would be needed to move the boy, but first Shulvan immobilised his neck, achieved using a stiff bone-ribbed leather collar carried in the medicine bag for just such an eventuality, completed only just a few weeks before. That done he instructed the kids to cut two stout poles, which they made into a stretcher using various clothing and cordage lashed between them. With Durian gently positioned on the stretcher Shulvan then made sure his head, neck and spine would move as little as possible. It was not ideal but would do if they moved with care keeping him flat.

With Durian carefully secured Shulvan took one end of the stretcher and two of the largest children took the other. With the remainder of the children going ahead and bashing down the vegetation, they moved with reasonable speed through the trees, though all were soon sweating and shaking with the exertion and stress. On the way back they came across others of the group who had heard the alarm calls and seen the mad dash of the pair, but had lost them in their haste; they came running when they saw the boy, a pair of them carefully taking over the makeshift stretcher and continuing the steady march back to the house. On arriving Shulvan instructed them to head for the main hall where a long low side table would suffice to lay Durian down. This he instructed they do atop some blankets, while calling others to boil some water and find some clean bandages from the stores.

Bringing Durian inside, out of the damp and cold forest floor, had led to some small improvement, his colour now better, but getting him warm was key at this stage with the blood loss. With him laid on the blankets, they brought some of the sheep fleeces to cover him over, after having removed his muddy boots and trousers. Shulvan again checked his pulse and breathing which had settled somewhat to a steadier rhythm, though he was still unresponsive. Between them they first washed their hands then cleaned his face of blood while Shulvan prepared a fresh bandage to cover the wound, following application of a light poultice of yarrow over the stitches to help stop festering. With that done there was not a great deal more they could do, but to anxiously wait.

The day passed with little noticeable improvement, but thankfully no obvious worsening bar some swelling. Come mid-afternoon Nineveh and Shuldan returned, immediately sensing the mood on entering the building and moving quickly to the main hall. With Shulvan's concise explanation of events they scrubbed their hands then went to check on the patient. Lifting the bandage they made positive noises, noting the superb stitching of the puckered wound and the extensive bruising

103

and swelling which now obscured the skull depression. Covering the wound they gave small nods to Shulvan and confirmed his initial suspicion of trauma likely having led to swelling around the brain, but which they thought could subside given time, the bone hopefully knitting together in due course. Their only additional suggestion was a mix of restorative and calming herbs to burn nearby, though this was as much to relax the others of the group as for any benefit of the patient.

The afternoon slowly turned to evening, which sluggishly led to midnight, with no change in the patient excepting a small improvement in his erratic pulse and a deepening of his breathing. This was though a positive sign and slightly calmed frayed nerves, though anything could still happen. Shulvan and his parents decided it would be best to leave Durian that night downstairs and so made up a comfortable chair and took it in shifts to monitor him. It took some time to get everyone else to bed, but they assured them that Durian's best chance at recovery was peace and quiet, his potentially being able to sense their stress even in his unconscious state. It was a long nerve-wracking night and none slept properly, but as dawn approached most fell into an exhausted stupor, their light snores giving them away.

It was early morning as Durian slowly and very groggily half-opened his eyes, confusedly sensing that he was indoors, and on slightly turning his head seeing a lightly wheezing Nineveh besides him, her head fallen forward in a doze. He soon regretted the small motion of his head, feeling a sudden pounding and dull ache with a flickering of random colours in his vision. Next he vaguely noticed the bandage wrapped about his skull, though it was initially sensed as nothing more than a tightness until his shaking hand went to it feeling the slightly rough fabric and thick dressing pad for what it was. Again he regretted the movement with an acute wave of nausea coming over him and his hand limply falling back down, bringing with it a waft of antiseptic herbs. Exhausted and now delirious with just those small acts, his eyelids closed and he passed out.

When next he awoke, he noticed that it must be evening, though of what day he had no idea. His head was still throbbing but he felt much stronger than before and the random flickering colours and nausea had vanished. Shulvan was quick to notice the movement and went to Durian, calmly checking his vitals, but with the boy begging him to explain what had happened. With Shulvan's checks complete, he turned to the boy, briefly met his eyes and then explained what had happened, saying that he had been very lucky indeed it had not been a fatal accident. Durian's face drained of what little colour he had at that point, bringing on a mild shaking as his words sank in. While Durian absorbed this they methodically checked his body more thoroughly, looking for sore spots and possible fractures. Shulvan judged that he may have cracked his ribs and possibly fractured his shoulder in the fall, but that these should heal with time once bound up and assisted with compresses of comfrey. He then made him take sips of water with a little poppy extract for the pain and meadowsweet for the inflammation, explaining they had managed to get him to take some fluid during the times he was half-awake but delirious, however, he was still very dehydrated.

Shulvan then called out to the others he knew were anxiously waiting in the kitchen that all was well, and that Durian could have visitors. Slowly the group entered in twos and threes, clearly distressed, and it was then that Durian realised how lucky he had been simply based on their reactions and pale faces, relieved but evidently exhausted from lack of sleep over what must have been several days. Though Durian didn't have parents in the group like some, he was dearly loved by all and he could see that in their eyes, plainly beyond happy to see him alive. All warmly praised Shulvan on his expert care, though he shrugged it off as if with his typical modesty. There was though little doubt that he was their accepted medicine man from that day forth, the saving of a precious young life an act with special meaning.

It took several weeks for Durian to recover his strength enough to undertake even light chores, though he eventually seemed no worse for wear bar some slight hearing loss on one side, the resilience of his youth being a major factor in his healing. He and the children were though from that day forth more careful in their games, some of their carefree joy suppressed by their scare, an experience no one wanted to repeat. Durian's impressive hairless pink scar and depression to the side of his skull showing through his hair a times was though a constant reminder of the precariousness of their existence, if in fact they needed one.

15 - Exploration

The midsummer solstice passed quickly and before long they started to feel a subtle change in the cooling weather. It had been a glorious growing season, but it brought to the forefront of their minds that winter came early to this part of the world, with the first birds already preparing to migrate. The screaming swifts were among the first to depart, their presence nesting in the eaves with the swallows and house martins soon missed. With such changes they became keenly aware that the passes to the uplands above the high valley sides would soon become treacherous again, once it grew rainy and cooler. Though they didn't keep to a calendar as such, Amaethon kept tally of the passing days by adding each as a notch to his staff. Midsummer was approximately known by keeping an eye on a permanent yardstick he had installed in the herb garden, monitoring the shadow of the sun with a series of stones, noting the shortest and a return to lengthening shadows. In time this would become a permanent feature set up on the pasture, a tall central stone and series of concentric solid oak posts inscribed with a system of carvings marking the passing seasons and important events of each year.

With the advancing seasons they all felt the excited anticipation of another journey, though this would be undertaken with much fewer of the group than the trip to the coast, being primarily one of exploration, but with a hope that they could bring back perhaps some goats, sheep and maybe a pony or two. In the end they decided to increase the likelihood of success, and to expand the area of exploration, by forming two parties, Merrick to head up one to the west, and the other Nineveh and Shuldan, the near inseparable pair, to the east.

Within a day of finally deciding on the trip they had quickly packed, including supplies for about a week or so, lasting longer if they hunted as well, if this was indeed possible to any significant extent at the higher elevation. They also took with them a good supply of root vegetables, with which they hoped they could tempt any animals and make them more pliant and receptive to the rope harnesses they would hopefully use to lead them home. Nineveh took her medicine kit with her, with a few special herbs that could in theory be used to calm recalcitrant animals; they may not be needed, but were better to have than not. While they could do without sheep and goats, they were desperate for beasts of burden, the perhaps forlorn hope being that hardy mountain ponies would be found.

They started out on a fine late-summer's day which was incredibly fresh and bright, and almost immediately went their separate ways to the previously tentatively explored high passes to each side of the valley. Merrick crossed the river with his small group and headed for the pass nearer the valley head. Nineveh and Shuldan headed to the much nearer eastern pass, not too far from The Steading. Both parties had considerable difficulty with the climbs, but now that it was drier there was no major hindrance beyond the epic nature of the boulder strewn gullies. So taking great care, they slowly picked their way up, marking easier paths with small cairns for future reference.

To the east, some two thousand strenuous feet climb above their valley, the party would find a rolling grassy landscape, a few stunted trees leading off into the far distance, with a massive glaciated mountain range to the south. The deep river leading to their valley above the waterfall was the natural boundary between the two parties' exploratory areas, perilous to cross at this elevation, swelled by multiple swift watercourses and as likely as not to sweep them away.

For Merrick's party to the west, it was a much harder initial ascent of some three thousand odd feet, which was then met with multiple blind summits, leading them to an inhospitable rocky terrain. There was only sparse scrubby vegetation on the numerous precipitous slopes and deep gullies, but which was likely ideal for hardy mountain goats. Making progress across the area was arduous and spirit sapping, an endless slog to ever higher elevation, but they were determined. As it was mainly an exploratory undertaking the two parties had agreed to walk for two days at least if possible, to assess the way ahead to the east and west, so this they did, albeit distance covered as the crow flies would be very different.

Nineveh and Shuldan's party made very good progress over the first day, moving through a grassy landscape, though denuded, with abundant heathers and small copses of stunted trees. It was filled with birdlife, with numerous red-billed chough picking insects from the turf, flighty pipits, larks on the wing and all manner of other species, indicating the fecundity of the upland landscape. On the second day of travel they quickly came up against sheer cliffs and steep rocky slopes that wouldn't allow them to proceed further without great effort and no small risk. To the north they knew from their trip here that this upland was not easily accessible, with great scree slopes, topped with steep cliffs and numerous hanging waterfalls spilling off the top, which were likely to dissuade most. Essentially this was a substantial isolated upland plateau of mostly poor grassland and heathers, with many small streams and modest scrubby bushes. There were some patches of trees, but these were mostly stunted rowans and birches which leaned away from the prevailing wind which came from the north-west. The area was however rich in ground-nesting birds, grouse particularly, which they took with their slings as they exploded from the heather, making for a welcome meal as they planned their next course of action. They hadn't yet seen any larger animals, but the area seemed promising as they had come across much deer dung, though now desiccated and odourless, so this indicated their presence at some point at least in the not too distant past. They decided it would be worth trekking to the higher ground of the south, as it was possible the herds had moved on from what was now an overgrazed area, to somewhere which could be potentially relatively lush. As they sat around the campfire and digested lunch, it was theorised that the animals had likely followed the retreating snow line through the season, being at its minimum now in the late summer. The landscape was in essence that left behind by a long retreating glacier, the hillocks formed from dropped gravelly moraine, scraped bedrock and erratically placed boulders, with just a thin veneer of soil and vegetation accumulated over the mere blip of geological time. The glaciers still loomed on the higher mountains to the south and provided a constant stream of meltwater, saturating the land and providing the rivers with vast volumes of fresh water. It was a formidable barrier to anyone from the south, essentially creating an impassable upland ice cap which had to be skirted via the surrounding lowlands nearer the coast.

The eastern party made their way over the undulating post-glacial landscape and progressed southwards, gradually climbing and gaining altitude towards the distant mountains and glaciers, which were most often shrouded in thin cloud. The way was not easy, with an increasing number of streams to be forded, some of which seemed to disappear then reappear at will. Finding their way through the convoluted topography meant a great deal of concentration was needed on what was in front of them, and so, mounting a ridge two days later, they were surprised to come upon a flatter area, but still full of streams which fed down from the edge of the glacier higher up. It was abundantly clear to see that they were crossing the remains of a freshly retreating glacial landscape, and that meant it was fairly open and only so far populated with grasses, sedge, a few dwarf birch and suchlike. The air was fresh and cool, they presumed from the proximity to the glaciers, exhilarating though akin to a cold late autumn. It was though a paradise for the herbivores which they now saw in considerable number in the form of deer, the grasses here being much more abundant through less grazing. From their vantage point they could also see to the west and were glad they had come east, avoiding what was a much more mountainous and inhospitable landscape.

Merrick's group were doing their best to travel west and explore for the promised two days; they were sweaty and sore and whenever they had chance to look back, wished they had chosen the easier east plateau, but pressed on nonetheless. They had found birds to hunt called dotterel, a mountainous species, thinner and smaller than grouse but still tasty and capable of being caught in numbers as they were present in tame groups. In addition they had located some ptarmigan, a more robust bird, being a relative of the lower altitude red grouse. Their camps had been exposed and any fires limited with the sparse vegetation hereabouts, but they knew how to stay comfortable enough with multiple layers and low-profile shelters in the more sheltered spots.

Early in the trip they had unexpectedly come across a distant herd of goats, who were trotting about the slopes as if showing off, but none more recently as they slowly climbed to greater altitude. Finally on the eve of the second day, and with little to show for their efforts, they stopped and surveyed the landscape before them, essentially more of the same stretching off into the distance with a backdrop of an imposing snow-covered mountain range looming on the horizon. They reasoned it might possibly be passable with great effort in milder times of the year, but was far from hospitable to travellers who could use the coastal route with ease, with the far mountain range running north-south being perhaps an impassable obstacle. It was possible there was a valley or small dale further on, the prospect making future exploration worthwhile, but no sign of such had been seen from the highest vantage points.

With relief the western team therefore decided to start heading back to relocate the herd of goats and see if they could tame some to take home. They were under little illusion how hard taming a recalcitrant mountain goat would be, but their supply of root vegetables to bribe them would certainly help, though another trip may be required. They spent the next day finding the most hospitable part of the landscape they could, veering a little to the south to cover new ground. However they simply found more of the same and decided enough was enough. Moving towards the area where they had previously located the herd, they found them still present, and little more than half a day from the western pass to their valley. It was frustrating that they had expended so much energy to end up back where they started, but at least they knew their western boundary was very likely secure by way of its extreme inhospitability.

Merrick suggested a halt, which was to general relief of all agreed; they made a more substantial camp than previously, in a relatively flat area between two ridges where they had caught sight of the goats on their way through two days previous. There was a fast-flowing stream providing fresh water within fifty yards enabling a bracing but much needed wash, to everyone's relief. This site proved to be a good decision because almost immediately they saw the herd again, who seemed to have little fear of these visitors in their domain, if anything being inquisitive and fearlessly investigating them before long. While the weary group were setting up camp for the night they set out some of the root vegetables nearby to see if this could tempt them in.

In the morning they saw that the vegetables had gone with not a morsel remaining; the animals responsible were not far away, seemingly even more inquisitive than before. The group spent the day in relative relaxation, doing little that might spook the animals, and so tried to gain their trust and get them used to their presence. The next few days were spent in this way, and the goats seemed more and more accepting of them, coming quite close on occasion, their musky smell hard to ignore when they did. On the next day, while making breakfast, they were surprised by the goat they had dubbed Dion, who wandered into camp and started grubbing around in their bags, without a care in the world. They thought he was likely the leader, as the others held back, but seemed to go where he led, eventually following his example. Merrick was careful in his movements, and slowly moved to the bag of vegetables they had brought, now not far from empty, removed a small carrot and offered it to Dion. The goat hesitated just a second and took the carrot, which was quickly chomped, then he started rooting about looking for more. In this way Merrick managed to gain the old billy goat's trust; he later succeeded in loosely looping a halter over his head while still feeding him the remainder of the vegetables. Eventually the goat cottoned onto the fact he was haltered and kicked up an almighty stink at the serious affront, giving everyone the evil eye and bad temperedly stomping about. This did not last long, and he allowed the halter to be picked up again, while being fed tasty morsels all the while, seemingly satisfied that his point had been made.

The rest of the herd were less than impressed and kept their distance, but could seemingly sense no harm was meant. After a while Merrick had managed to lead the goat around, though Dion did so with some disdain. On moving a little distance from the camp he noticed the other goats seemed happy to follow. On reflection this was all too easy and should not have been possible with truly wild goats; their suspicion was that this herd must have been the descendants of the previous occupier's herd at The Steading. Perhaps only a few generations had meant little time to revert to their fully wild state; it may also mean they kept some of their more domesticated genes, hopefully favouring milk and accelerated wool production, which would be ideal.

With little point in now remaining at this camp, the group packed up, Dion and Merrick leading their now swollen band to the valley pass, on a mission which in the end may have been the easier of the two.

Nineveh and Shuldan's group were starting to wonder what they had let themselves in for, the area they explored was vast and difficult to negotiate, a myriad of streams and islands of grass. It was at times quite unpleasant with clouds of biting insects in the swampier areas; it must have been hellish mid-summer, but they soon learned to give those areas wide berth. There were however many small deer in the area offering plentiful hunting opportunities, their subtle odour often apparent, but they had yet to see much else in the way of larger wildlife. The only spark of excitement was one day finding some pony-sized hoof marks in some soft turf, so they could finally be sure they were on the right track. They spent two days in this way, with very little luck, no sightings and rapidly diminishing patience. Once they thought they heard the snort of a pony, but this was brief and distant, the sound caught in a rare moment of calm when the wind dropped right back, only to recommence its persistent flow down from the glaciers and mountains.

Though not openly discussed the eastern expedition were starting to lose heart and felt it might be best to turn back, but gave it one final half day; they were glad they did. Over just the next rise they came upon a herd of stocky mountain ponies, though with barely a look at each other the beasts quickly trotted off and out of sight. The moment of elation for the group was dashed by their rapid departure, but it at least gave them something to follow. They approached the next rise with more caution, climbing on their bellies to the crest of the small hillock, where they again caught sight of the shaggy beasts in the next

114

dip. There were nearly two dozen including the young, of various colours but tending to a thick dark brown coat with the odd dark grey. They were quite unkempt looking animals, their manes long and dishevelled, but clearly all were in great health, evidently thriving in their natural environment. The herd had quickly settled back down to grazing, though some were plainly on the lookout and in protective stances with the young to the centre of the herd. Nineveh assessed the situation and spoke in hushed tones, saying that rather than spook them further and play chase across the plains, she would attempt a less orthodox approach.

The group retreated back down the slope and they found their baskets of vegetables picking out the carrots. Nineveh then retrieved from her ever-present hip pouch a series of dried herbs, including powdered valerian, chamomile and raspberry leaf, with just a touch of crushed opium poppy seed. This she wetted and added as a crushed paste into a hole cut into the vegetables, applying what would typically have put a grown man into a contented sleep. It was a subtle art in getting the quantities correct and only Nineveh was really experienced enough to get this right, but she erred on the side of caution. Most of the group had meanwhile retreated further and let Nineveh take the drug-laced vegetables to the top of the hillock, where she carefully placed them in full view. Happy the herd would at least see these tasty morsels and possibly investigate in due course, she carefully backed off and went back to the group.

Some hours passed with no sign of any interest, but they kept their quiet vigil, allowing the ponies time. The evening passed into night and they awoke the next day to see the vegetables untouched, which was perhaps not surprising given that they were alien objects, but it was disheartening all the same. They retrieved half of the vegetables and left watchers to monitor the remainder. The others went further afield and found another likely spot on a small ridge. From that vantage point they could see that while the ponies had not ventured far, they may need coaxing back towards the spots they had prepared. This they did over the next few hours, with the slowest of flanking movements, gentling coaxing the herd and getting them used to their presence, showing they meant no harm.

It was several hours later that saw the group of ponies mainly hunkered down, but the watchers observed what seemed to be the vague interest of one or two in the food. They waited, and waited, then with a disdainful flick of its head, a pony approached the pile nearest Nineveh, followed by another now eager to investigate the tempting treats. It was not that they would really know what the vegetables were, having subsisted on grass for generations, but their curiosity kicked in. They nosed the unfamiliar objects but clearly could sense they were food; with a flick of their manes, both ponies took some food, found it to their liking and then quickly chomped down the whole pile. With a quick snuffle at the ground to hoover up any remaining morsels they left with a snort and re-joined the herd.

It didn't seem long, though it was an hour or more, before the two ponies who had taken the food were dragging behind the others; they were certainly less frisky and showed minimal fear. Making sure of the animals' continued docility, the bulk of the group kept their distance and Nineveh approached, everyone's hearts beating fast in anticipation. The majority of the herd bolted soon after she drew near, but the two partially sedated animals seemed fairly content, and continued grazing. They appeared a little apprehensive as Nineveh came closer, who was still aiming to first let them get used to her presence and odd odour, but the closest pony seemed fairly happy to let her walk around nearby. Not wanting to tempt fate, she left it at that for the day, and withdrew to the camp.

The next day they found the herd again, not far away, and so reset the original pile of laced vegetables in their view. They hoped today the same animals would realise the food was good, and no harm would come to them. This proved to be the case and within the hour they had the pair sedated and calm, so again approached. Careful not to spook them Nineveh eventually managed to hand feed the pair some more of the carrots and succeeded in gently stroking the beasts, who protested only a little. She decided that while a risk it would be worth trying the halter, so gently, while feeding the first pony more of the small succulent carrots, she gained their trust and slipped the rope on. These she let drape on their necks, getting them used to the weight. It was only once she had done this and stepped back that she allowed herself a deep breath, what seemed like the first for some time. After some hours the drugs had seemed to wear off, but the constant feeding and stroking had put them at relative ease. Nineveh showed her special touch with the animals, exuding calm and patience, and so with the most gentle of contact she took the halters and led the beasts just a few paces away from the herd while hand feeding and stroking them, then stopped. This she repeated through the day, but come nightfall she let them loose to spend time with their herd, though leaving the simple halters attached.

Slowly over the days that followed Nineveh managed to get the two ponies who had taken the vegetables more tolerant of her, then the group. The herd could sense her calmness in the way she moved and her soft tones setting them at ease which let her eventually walk among them. In time they managed to peg the tamest pair down on long ropes between the two groups overnight and then one day they left the herd behind, with surprisingly limited protests. Nineveh had continued to use a little of her calming herbs, but eventually she found it was unnecessary and they followed her of their own free will, seemingly bonded.

With their mission accomplished the group wasn't long in making their way back to The Steading, in no rush, and in time came back to the pass into the valley. During this journey it seemed the ponies had come to more or less accept them as their new herd, and though not as accepting as the goats had been, the long process of taming was bearing fruit.

Arriving home they came first upon the herd of goats, loose upon the pasture; clearly that expedition had been successful. Two children had been left to watch them, but they needed little attention it would seem. The multitude of useful products they could now make from their milk, including cheese and proper soap, their wool for super fine and tremendously warm clothing, and eventually their meat, would be very welcome.

On approaching The Steading they had become quite the joyous band; away for much longer than they had anticipated, which had caused concern with those who remained, but those worries soon evaporated. The ponies were however far from impressed and kept close to Nineveh, whinnying and snorting in their discomfort, but she quickly had them away from the group and into a sheltered corner of the barn, which would offer some seclusion. She gently but firmly warned the others off when they approached and eventually had the ponies settled in, making them a basic pen out of the wind. Nineveh would sleep next to them that night, though she insisted her pallet be brought out with proper bedding and a tarp set up to cut the breeze. The night promised to be mild, under cover and with the benefit of proper food; without doubt this was a vast improvement on their extended trip in the exposed uplands.

Much congratulations was offered to both parties, and that night they ate a hearty venison and vegetable stew, artfully flavoured now Shuldan was home to execute his signature dish. The ponies were treated to more root vegetables and soon settled down, with their mistress Nineveh keeping a close eye. The goats were later herded from the pasture and brought down to an area near the barn, where they were safely corralled into a substantial new post and rail made enclosure, watched over by the dogs. Really their missions to explore and find these animals could not have gone much better in the end, excepting the extended time it took. Additionally they knew their borders were more or less secure and that the beasts would render their lives easier and more comfortable. Though the animals would remain half wild for some time, it was clear they still carried genes which rendered them amenable to humans and it was not many weeks before they were at ease in their relatively comfortable domesticated life.

16 - Charcoal making

Bolin had been in an increasingly crabby mood of late, grumbling that the forge wouldn't be ready before winter came. Everyone concurred the last thing they needed was an irritable Bolin all the way through a winter cooped up together, so it was agreed their next concerted effort would be to get the forge completed. Fuel was thankfully almost the last outstanding issue, though the only viable option was to make high quality charcoal to attain great enough heat, with any supplies of coal near the surface having long since been mined out by their distant ancestors. They were conscious steel tools were needed to increase food production for the next year, particularly in constructing a plough. Ideally, they needed to get the plough made and the ponies trained to turn over the field before the first frosts, in order to get in a winter planting of oats if at all possible. It was a tall order but would be a fantastic bonus to productivity and food security if they could manage the task.

Early in spring they had cut and stacked a huge amount of hazel and created huge piles of brash, restoring the coppiced area to productive stands and creating much improved habitat. In addition they had also dragged in much dead standing oak and some ash which they had laboriously split down. They would need huge quantities of dry wood to make the high grade charcoal, essential in getting the forge to a high temperature for metal working. It wouldn't be necessary to smelt iron ore, not that they could mine it anyway, as they would organise collection of scrap metal in a trip to the hulks that still dotted the distant highway to the northwest on the rolling plains. The ponies would be invaluable in this transport, and Nineveh was in the process of getting them accustomed first to baskets straddled on their flanks, then other jobs like collection of tree trunks by dragging them out of the forest using leather harnesses, but they seemed to mind the hard work very little, so long as their favourite treats kept coming.

To start thick green turf was cleared from three areas some eighteen feet wide, the sods kept for later to form the outside layer of the special Clamp mound, basically a small wood-filled mini hillock. Pits were then dug to about three feet deep, the base compacted and then filled with thinner wood, progressing up to larger cords, the whole pile being some eight to ten foot above ground to the peak when complete. As little as possible was left in terms of gaps, filling any with smaller wood as needed, a near solid mass being crucial. An open chimney vent was however left in the centre, comprising greenwood stakes set in a loose circle held up with binding cordage, designed to last just long enough to get the burn established. With the three great stacks of wood in place they were covered in soil and then the turf sods to complete the shell of the Clamp mounds; the key being to make sure that no air could enter, except as they wished via vents near the ground. It was a huge amount of work, but like most tasks, one they all took great pride in, also knowing that ultimately the products of the forge would make their lives easier.

Once the Clamps were deemed fit by Bolin, they lit a separate hardwood-based fire and transferred the subsequent long-lasting coals to the bottom of the clamp chimney hole, then loaded it up with more oak and ash, the principle being to create a slow burn in the absence of too much air. What they hoped to achieve was essentially a long cook in an oven, the "roast" as it was known. If it did start to burn too quick, they could reduce the chimney diameter and wet down the outside, closing up any ground level vents as needed. With some minor adjustments the early evening air was soon filled with the smoke from the three Clamps, almost fog like but self-evidently wood smoke

121

from the sweetly acrid aroma evoking a primordial feeling that nothing else could.

It would take some three or four days to fully complete the burns, the key being to quickly cover any cracks in the sod that might open and to carefully control the process, too much air meaning the wood would burn completely, too little resulting in the charcoaling process not being completed. In shifts of two they also had to ensure that the wind was not preferentially pushing air into any one side and burning it too quickly in that part, so moveable woven hurdles were positioned to help control this. The colour of the smoke was the best indicator of how it was getting on, initially being thick and yellowish, then turning white as it became mostly water vapour being driven out, this being ideal.

They took it in turns to monitor the burns, sleeping in shifts nearby in case prompt attention was needed and conscious that a small mistake could render the whole process a failure. You could easily tell who had last been on shift, the smoke permeating their pores and the smell noticeable at no short distance, though not entirely unpleasant. A great deal of washing and scrubbing would result and it may be some time before they expunged the worst of it, though the smoke was excellent at killing off any bugs in their hair and clothing, their blankets and skins all being brought out to receive a good smoking through. The smoke was also excellent for preserving meats hence a great deal was smoked during the process, filling the stores with jerky which would help see them through winter if hunting was poor. It was though a very peaceful, almost therapeutic process, and the biggest risk was falling asleep on the job and losing control of the burn. This was overcome with the use of a one-legged stool, which would provide a decent seat but as soon as you nodded off, you lost balance and fell in a somewhat drunken manner, coming back awake with a jump. It was amusing to watch, and the children found it hilarious, much to the sitter's initial embarrassment as they were jerked awake.

Once the initial burn was over and the white smoke had acquired just a small blue tinge, the odour now much less, they knew it was almost complete, so the chimney hole was blocked to prevent any further air entering and the whole Clamp mound wetted down to help close off gaps. This initially produced a fair amount of steam, but water kept on being added to cool the outer layer as much as possible, releasing a sizzle and rich earthy smells. Without then completely saturating the stacks they were then left to cool completely, which took many days. Uncovering them too soon may allow a re-ignition which would consume all their hard work, so was best done without haste.

Once the stacks had totally cooled, with Bolin happy all was well, they uncovered each Clamp. Two of the three had produced very good results, the third a little disappointing, with a good amount burnt to smaller than ideal size. Nonetheless, this wasn't a bad result, they still had about half the weight of the original wood in charcoal, which was many cubic feet worth. The results of the third would be mostly kept as finer charcoal suitable for crushing further and adding to the vegetable beds and fields as a soil improver over winter, but it was still possible to save a good amount of larger chunks for the forge.

As there had been relative success they repeated the whole process, knowing that now the ground had hardened and completely dried out beneath the three mounds, almost like a fired clay, it would be better sealed. With their experience of the first burn the results of the second were fantastic and overall they now had several tonnes of very high-grade charcoal, enough to keep Bolin happy for many months of smithing. They also took some of the highest quality charcoal for other purposes; it had a range of medicinal uses, including toxin absorbing capacity, for treating intestinal issues, as a toothpaste, for skin care, including dealing with infections, filtering water, and so on. In addition they had purposefully added some thinner sticks of willow to the burns to create twigs of charcoal which were decent as crude writing and drawing implements. It was an all-round great resource to have at their disposal.

The Clamps would be fine for future use, each burn creating a better basal surface as it compacted and hardened in the heat, so they were closed down with care, covering them with loose soil and turf. The charcoal was then transported up to the forge and placed in the abutting separate storage lean-to in a series of large bins, where it would be kept bone dry and away from stray sparks. This was a big task, but between them and the ponies, with Bolin chivvying them along, it was soon done, though they were all filthy as a result

Following completion of the work, there followed a mountain of washing, not least to try and subdue the worst of the smoky odour, but also from the black carbon deposits they were all now covered in. First though the ponies received a good brush down and were then led into a nearby stream, lathering them up with a mild soap and then scraping them down with stiff brushes. Initially the ponies were not best pleased, but with all the attention afterwards, the grooming out of excess hair and trimming of their manes and tails, they begrudgingly seemed to find the process to their liking. The same could not be said for the children who were all bathed and scraped down until their skin was pink. With that done they also had their shaggy hair shorn, and looked much more presentable as a result. All of the hair was collected, with the stiff tail and mane hair of the ponies used for new brushes, and the remainder thoroughly cleaned and used for various crafts. The children's hair was collected up and used as an effective slug repellent in the vegetable beds, though much would be taken by birds for their nests as a soft lining, being particularly coveted by the diminutive goldcrests that abounded nearby in a copse of larch and pines.

With the ponies and children looking quite respectable the adults all took their turns, luxuriating in the lavender-infused water of the steamy baths and relishing their haircuts and beard trims for those who needed them. The washing of all their clothes was not a chore enjoyed by anyone, but after an initial rinsing in the streams, a soak in warm soapy water of the baths, a good pounding underfoot, a further rinse and a pass through their ancient mangle, it was done. Their long washing lines were then filled for days with the wrung clothes which soon were snapping and cracking in the stiff breeze flowing down the valley.

17 - The forge

Restoring the forge had been an ongoing process since spring, it consumed much resource but soon they hoped the almost soothing rhythmic clang of hammer on steel would fill their ears. It would represent a great achievement and increase their supply of tools, making their lives much easier. Perhaps most importantly Bolin would have less to be grumpy about and give him space to escape the busy house.

The forge bellows had been completed some time ago, and a set of spare parts made as well. They were formed on the basis of a double-bellow system operated one after the other like pistons, to achieve constant air flow, increasing efficiency with less effort. They were relatively simple to make, being formed of two hinged oak boards, bound in pliable leather of the auroch, glued and pinned via cold forged flat headed pins, with small flaps of soft buckskin as air valves. The pipes delivering air to the centre of the forge were made of a metal tube found in the remains of the old hearth; it wasn't ideal, being by now quite thin and virtually rusted through, but would do until Bolin could forge better ones.

Following the success of the charcoal making Bolin proposed and led an expedition to the hulks that dotted the old highway running across the plain to the northwest. The ponies were taken with Nineveh leading, being essential beasts of burden for the weight of the metal sought. The trip would be several days, two each way at least of travel and a few scouting out the choicest metal to forge. As on previous trips they left the valley under the cover of first light, the air damp and close now autumn was nearing. The rocky gorge was a little tricky to navigate but the sure-footed ponies led the way, picking a path without incident. Entering the coniferous forest and moving downslope from the misty mountains they were some distance away from the valley entrance before they would consider any fire for tea, wishing to avoid marking their presence. The route took them north along the western wooded bank of the river Rhuø, where it eventually met the barely apparent remains of a bridge, which had long since collapsed and mostly washed away, the eroded foundations of a few support piers all that remained. From there they went west into the plains following the remnants of the old east-west highway, slowly gaining higher ground to where the river did not flood and erase what had once been. Before long they met the first hulk, which must have been a large vehicle at one point, but now was just a broken chassis, mostly rust and smelling sharp and metallic in the otherwise clean air. Bolin was especially interested in what had once been the suspension parts, including any remaining leaf and coil springs which potentially should yield decent steel, although much was normally rusted away. Nonetheless, at times the rust eventually created a protective layer dramatically reducing the process of decay on larger chunks, but as the years went on it became harder to find good material that hadn't already been scavenged. Fortunately these hulks had not been picked over, certainly not for a very long time and provided for some rich scavenging. To some extent they were fortunate the residues leaching from the hulks into the soil had kept much vegetation at bay, otherwise they would be very difficult to find. They were however an unpleasant reminder of the destruction humans once had on the environment, their pollution and noise thankfully now a distant memory.

Having excavated the chosen wreck from its partial cover of creepers Bolin managed to find the remnants of some huge leaf springs, and having knocked off the worst of the rust, could check their carbon content by the distinct forking sparks produced when struck and he swore also by the smell of the metal. He was satisfied with what he found, and they mounted those to the ponies' packs, strapping them

127

down firmly. This would be excellent steel for making new blades but would be perfect for forming the larger cutting and soil turning parts of the plough. They spent the next few days moving west from wreck to wreck, finding what Bolin would need; in this way they accumulated a fair amount, limited only by what the ponies and Bolin could carry. Bolin for once seemed content, loaded down with his haul, already muttering to himself about his plans and aching to get back as quickly as possible. Their return journey was however slow with the heavy load, but the ponies did an admirable job, bringing them home a few days later.

On arriving back Bolin had his materials squared away in the forge and was readying his workspace with a few final preparations. Without even a night's sleep he had the forge fired up and was testing the metals, by heating and checking the glowing colours, then hammering test sections, most of which he eventually deemed would indeed suit his purposes. The heavy anvil was the most precious of his inherited equipment, which was found at the back of the forge. It had been lovingly stored, though still had required some attention, the rust being sanded off with handfuls of coarse then finer loose sand. The waxy coating and multiple wraps of waxed cloth had though saved it from the worst of the rust, and being dry, was in good working order in a short time. A new anvil would have been next to impossible to make with the limited tools and materials to hand, though he might perhaps have been able to fashion something small with a section of railway track or similar, still occasionally found buried in certain places, often near roads. Bolin had brought with him just one precious hammer head which he had re-handled in straight grained ash, lovingly contoured and shaped, in long anticipation of this day. He had not been able to justify carrying more tools on their long journey here from his old forge, but that did not matter as first he could make tongs, more hammers, punches, files and so on. The joy of the blacksmith was that with one hammer he could craft pretty much whatever he needed, each new tool adding to the possibility of more complex projects. In any event though the forge did still have a few tools left over from the past owner, though they were worse for wear and limited to the basics, indicating at best an amateurish skill level.

He first practiced and got a feel for the new forge by making some new tools, then some basic arrowheads, broadhead style with wicked barbs for the deer hunt needed before winter. As he got the feel for the forge he made more complicated items as his skills and strength came back to him. Buoyed with confidence, though with somewhat sore muscles still unused to the repetitive actions, he decided the next day he could tackle the plough as it was so desperately needed. It wasn't until he looked out of the forge that he saw it was in fact well past midnight and almost a new day in any case, so he banked the forge and made his way back to The Steading, electing to sleep in the main hall that night rather than wake the others in their no doubt deep slumber.

With just a few hours sleep, but raring to go, Bolin had a great breakfast of smoked venison bacon, cheese and flatbread, washed down with a fresh pint of strongly flavoured goat's milk. With barely time for a quick burp and to grab a full water skin, he hurried back up to the forge, with promises in his wake to Nineveh that he would break for lunch.

Bolin knew that much of the plough would be made of timber, but to make this they needed better tools, so first he made a new carpentry set, which was immediately out of the workshop and being used the same day. The frame of the plough would be of smoothed elm, naturally bow shaped and hewn to form the main shaft and secondary elements. The first smithing task undertaken was the manufacture of the coulter, a long heavy blade essentially, which would come first at the front of the plough to cut the sod; it would be subject to great wear,

129

but could be detached and re-forged to restore its shape and sharpness. That part of the plough was really quite simple, essentially made straight with the long cutting edge, but constructed and mounted to allow it to change depths down into the soil. Added behind that was the curved mouldboard designed to lift up and push aside the sod cut by the coulter; that consumed much of the steel but was vital in efficiently turning, aerating and loosening the soil. The other parts were smaller but more intricate, including a small pair of adjustable height wheels to aid travel and stability across the land.

While Bolin tirelessly worked on this project over the next few days, the wooden frame took shape, with the steel parts added as they were finished. At the same time leather harnesses for the ponies were made using thick wool padding on the collar, using much of their supply of brain-tanned leather hides. Replenishment before winter would be vital to give them plenty of materials for the long winter nights crafting other projects. The plough and the harnesses were agreed by all to be things of great beauty; form and function melding seamlessly. Bolin was clearly proud of his work, though not at all boastful, spending all hours refining and sharpening, until at last he was happy. He was very complimentary to the teams producing the frame and leatherwork, as they were to him, an acknowledged master blacksmith. The plough was eventually baptised with generous tumblers of moreish elderberry wine and sweet birch sap liqueur, then christened the "little ripper", an apt name for what they hoped would be a formidable piece of equipment.

18 - Tilling the fields

While the plough being made they undertook the vital concurrent task of training the ponies to pull the contraption. This was a task which would nearly break Nineveh, the now acknowledged pony mistress, even with her legendary patience. In theory it wasn't a difficult task to cut and turn over the soil, but in practice it was an art which took considerable trial and error with ponies new to the plough.

Normally the ponies would have been trained from a young age, so the undertaking was made beyond difficult with this pair, who until recently were wild on the hills. First was getting them used to the full collar and harnesses, though they weren't massively dissimilar to the arrangement of the simpler pack harnesses, but still enough that it took some days of patience and no small amount of bruises to their handler before they became used to them. Nineveh eventually rediscovered the old trick of rubbing a cloth over their bodies to get them to accept the contact of the bulkier harnesses and make them feel at ease with the heavy collar. With the collar and harnesses accepted to some extent and a prodigious number of small carrots for bribes, she took them on increasingly longer walks, leading them quietly with no hurrying by their new bridles. Nineveh enlisted the help of Shuldan who also had a calm demeanour, and between them they continued the lessons with patience beyond most. They managed to teach some basic commands to aid direction and speed, and after a week were content it was time for the full collar, harness and traces. Even this though was hazardous as the pair of ponies were still headstrong and liable to do as they pleased if bored.

Rather than risk the precious plough they first attached the ponies to increasingly large logs to practice pulling; this was a very useful job in itself and they managed over time to start bringing in various hefty trunks to the proposed saw pit, where lumber was to be produced. These trunks could be as much as several hundred pounds to extract by brute force from the undergrowth and to then transport through the woods. With the new padded collars the pair found the job much easier, spreading the load onto their powerful chests and off their wind pipes, much better compared to simple leather harnesses. They also found after some trial and error that a rounded metal skid plate could be strapped to the front of the log, essentially like a big conical bucket, avoiding it digging in and easing its travel. After some days of moving logs, the ponies, buoyed on by a number of treats, became used to the work as a cohesive team, positively enjoying it at times, with excited snorts and tosses of their heads as they were led out each day.

Then came the day of trying the plough in the field some weeks later. The ponies had made great progress with the logs and now responded to verbal commands, but still were of a mind which occasionally involved sudden searches for grass. Attaching the plough was tense but the ponies soon had it moving on just the wheels with the coulter progressively moved down to start limited cutting into the grassy sod. This went quite well to their surprise and within an hour they had completed a short furrow at a decent depth, the hooded crows and a scattering of black-headed gulls soon flying in and picking over the earth for worms and grubs. Over the days and weeks that followed the ponies were introduced to others of the group who learnt the intricate craft of the plough, albeit with some trial and error as none were experts. The extensive fields that resulted were not pretty but it was a start and for now they mainly needed to turn over the soil to let the birds pick out the pests and to allow the winter frosts to break down the soil and kill the more pernicious weeds. It was however a massive leap forward from that spring when they thought back to the backbreaking labour using digging sticks and crude wooden spades. They would however get planted out their increasing supply of oat

132

seed grown on that year, in a small section of the newly turned field, to hopefully get another crop early next summer, to then plant out again as seed for a very late autumn harvest.

During the weeks following completion of the plough Bolin had turned out a treasure trove of useful tools including shovels, spades, hoes, two-person saws, adzes and draw knives, so was quickly out of raw material, using up all the scrap collected on the plains and any metal found spare around The Steading. With winter coming Bolin decided to undertake another trip to forage for more metals, and with the ponies now well trained, this was a simpler operation. As part of this trip a team also hunted the plains on route, the mighty auroch being their goal, for leather and rich beef. This was a great success, with a smaller cow taken providing another food source to supplement their now rich and varied diet, along with its valuable hide for thick leather. All in all it was a very productive several weeks, a massive hurdle overcome in ploughing the fields, setting them up for a significant jump in food production and self-reliance.

19 - The waterfalls

Though most had made a trip up to waterfalls at the head of the valley when foraging, hunting and generally exploring, it was seldom visited for the pure pleasure of swimming in the deep pools and just enjoying being away from the chores of the homestead. Merrick and Arwyn thought it would be good to take the children up to the falls, along with anyone else who fancied a few relaxed days camping out, though the lure of a quiet house was a major attraction for many far too good to miss. In the end all the other adults decided to stay, but that was fine as far as Merrick and Arwyn were concerned, who reassured everyone they were more than happy to give them a break after the long busy summer.

The trip wouldn't need a great deal of gear, nor food, as they hoped that they would be able to fish and hunt at least some hares, ducks and grouse, but ideally a small deer. The days were still quite long and warm, though autumn was plainly just around the corner judging by the cooler air of late and the departure of the last of the migrating birds. They proposed to take plenty of blankets and hides to wrap up in, as it still got cold at night, exacerbated by added damp from the proximity to the mighty waterfall and river.

As would be expected the children were tremendously excited to be going on an adventure and forgetting all about their normal chores, expecting long days playing and swimming in the pools. They knew both Merrick and Arwyn could be a soft touch, so intended to stay up late if they could and tell stories into the night. They all would take their slings for competitions, their bone dice for games and lots of little treats that Nineveh would quietly stash in their packs, including succulent fruit leathers and intensely sweet honeyed cakes.

It was a merry band that set out from The Steading, rambling with no hurry through the nearby fields, the children racing the younger dogs that had tagged along, soon well ahead of Merrick and Arwyn. The children knew the way, being a fairly-well defined series of tracks this close to The Steading, but were mindful to keep in calling distance. The adults were more than happy with this very passive arrangement, leaving them time and peace to enjoy the woods and wildlife, free of the need to be constantly engaged in the various tasks of the farmstead and leadership.

The sun streamed through the tree canopy creating an intensely green, almost ethereal light, with the odd dappled glade where trees had either fallen or been harvested for lumber. These clearings created little havens of woodland flowers and patches of fireweed, eager to race the dozens of saplings that would outcompete them in the years to come. It was still a little early for animals to be focussed on storing away food for the winter and so it meant there were an abundance of young who had little to do but enjoy the mere fact of being alive. The red squirrels were seen in particular scampering here and there, with an energy that reflected the spirited children and dogs darting in and out of the trees with the odd squeal of delight.

They came in time to walk roughly parallel to the river that flowed somewhat sinuously down the centre of the valley and often in multiple channels. This time of the year it was a relatively gentle affair, though never low given that it was fed by meltwater from the glaciers in the high mountains. Following the river was always a delight, with an abundance of fish to be seen in the ponds and pools, minnow, pike and trout especially, occasionally seen with the odd flick of silver and a small splash in the calmer areas. There were also various birds, like the tail flicking and constantly moving grey wagtail, the stately heron and smart but elusive goosander, the bobbing dipper and a plethora of others indicating the healthy state of the ecosystem. The riverside was abutted by various shallow meres and grassy swales created in the areas which flooded in winter and during intense storms. These areas were a delight to paddle in on hot days and it was at one of these meres that they caught up with the children for their mid-day meal. Clearly the children had already been gorging on the sweet treats that Nineveh had provided, so they spent the time and surfeit of energy madly splashing about in the relatively mild water, then briefly sunbathing to dry off. Merrick and Arwyn had a lovely lunch of soft flat bread, tangy goat's cheese, cold meats and sliced tomatoes sprinkled with salt, perfect for a lazy time spent dipping their feet in the refreshing water, keeping an eye on the children and then dozing in the sun.

For the afternoon they knew they would need a livelier pace, as the head of the valley was a decent day's walk overall and they needed to cross the river, though really all that meant was pointing the children in the right direction and ensuring they didn't range too far off track. It was a warm day but the rest and a paddle in the pools at lunch had invigorated them all, so good progress was made over the next few hours, the glorious bird song filled woods a welcome restorative. Nonetheless, as they approached the valley head all were starting to get a little weary and sweaty with their heavy packs, but perked up on hearing the welcome sound of the thundering waterfall, which would offer a cooling respite. On arriving they quickly relieved themselves of their packs in a clearing near the lower pools, stripped and jumped straight in from the steep-sided rocky bank, Durian as always leading the way. The cold water was initially a shock, being straight off the mountains where fed by the glaciers, but was wonderfully refreshing after the long walk in the heat. Following a bracing swim they climbed out and laid on the warm rocks, letting the sun dry them and rewarm their bodies.

With an eye to the lowering sun the adults were conscious that setting up camp was a pressing chore, so after corralling the children they assigned jobs and quickly everyone was industriously setting up tarps, laying out bed rolls, chopping wood and forming a cooking area. With the children engaged in those tasks, Merrick and Arwyn set to getting a big pot of stew on the go. They had brought with them dried meat from the stores which would soften as it rehydrated and added to this they threw in some tangy onions, a couple dozen sweet baby carrots and chopped potatoes; to season they added a good amount of salt and Shuldan's all-purpose spice mix. The children's tasks didn't take long between them so they took off again to play, with the endless energy of youth high on life and no small amount of sweet treats fuelling their mad games.

With the sun starting its slow descent below the tops of the mountains, the children returned, delighted with the lovely smells that awaited them of hearty stew and fresh bread, realising they were all ravenous, their earlier sugar rush having long faded. There was of course plenty to go around and all had second helpings, with the ever-ravenous kids mopping up the gravy from the pot with the remaining bread. After a rinse of the pots in the river and a good scrub with sand, they all laid back around the warming fire letting the food digest, filling up any remaining holes with honeyed cakes and apple-scented camomile tea. As Merrick and Arwyn had earlier predicted it wasn't long before the children were yawning, exhausted after the lengthy walk, which they must have doubled in length with their mad dashing about and their swimming sessions. Though they resisted, one-by-one they nodded off and were left where they lay, some cuddling up to the now exhausted dogs that had tagged along. Merrick and Arwyn would move them later to their bedrolls under the tarps, but for now just covered them up and let them rest the contented sleep of well-fed healthy kids out in the fresh air, warmed by a glowing fire.

The next day was absolutely glorious and promised to be scorching, the air soon oven-like out of the shade, so plans were made to spend the day messing about in the pools and the feeder streams, building dams, fishing, exploring the woods and generally enjoying life. Breakfast comprised a huge mound of fried venison bacon, freshly made flat bread, sweet-baby tomatoes and lashings of rich goat's butter; it would nicely set them all up for a day of adventure, fishing and hunting.

While the children explored the woods that morning, Arwyn and Merrick intended to go hunting with their bows. They would keep an eye out for hares and grouse but their target was a small deer, which should keep them and the dogs going for the remainder of the trip. This would take them a little way down the western side of the valley to an area less visited, but known for its small herds. The hope was, if they were approachable, that they could be back for a late lunch. The pair took the first section at a comfortable jog, keeping just within the cover of the cooler woods which allowed easy monitoring of the more open areas of the valley side. Knowing well the best areas from previous hunting trips, they approached these with stealth as they came to each one, using their acute sense of smell as much as their keen hearing and sight. On approaching the third area, a plume of fresh deer scent was readily apparent so they cautiously approached, their moccasin-shod feet picking out a near-silent path. They knew the area comprised a large sloping meadow, approachable via thicker undergrowth and near ideal for using the bow at range. From their concealed vantage points they could see there were plenty of deer to choose from, but generally they looked for the smaller and weaker who might not make it through the winter, thus improving the gene pool and health of the herd overall. This time there was an obvious target, a young doe who had seemingly seriously damaged a hind leg, with a painful-looking limp potentially contributing to its relatively poor weight gain for this time of the season. With subtle hand signals they discussed and agreed on the target, and with minimum of fuss, carefully stalked, then took the doe, with two heavy arrows hitting it about the chest in quick succession. It wasn't a big job to field-dress the carcass, and they would only take the best meat this time along with the heart and liver, not wishing to properly process the skin, nor laboriously haul the whole thing back to the valley top. It would be a fine feast for the carrion feeders and it wasn't long before they saw some kites and a high golden eagle circling overhead, eager to sample the tasty meat and offal. With the carcass dressed they mounted it onto Merrick's stout walking pole, then between them carried it back to camp at a near jogging pace. The doe was such a size that they could easily mount it on a simple spit over the fire but for ease they would cook it as a pit roast, which could be left with minimal attention needed once set up. With the young tender meat slow-cooked, it would be a fine feast, with plenty left for the next couple of days, even with the tribe of hungry young mouths.

With the hard work of the hunt, hauling back the meat and digging the cooking pit, Merrick and Arwyn were more than ready for a good lunch, but first they joined the kids for a dip in the pools to cool down and to wash themselves and their sweaty clothes. While swimming in the cool waters they were told all about the sling competition earlier on, though it was difficult to understand the complex rules and scoring; it seemed that nearly everyone had won at some point. The afternoon would be given over to generally messing about in the pools and perhaps some fishing, in particular they would dive for some of the succulent crayfish that abounded among the rocks, which would go perfectly with the venison.

As predicted much of the hot afternoon was spent in the pools diving down and making a competition of who could find the most crayfish, easily plucked from the river bed once stones were overturned, though a great number also got away. These were dispatched and stored in a small side-pool to keep them cool and fresh for later, to be cooked on green-hazel skewers over the fire. Towards the end of the day they occasionally got a whiff of the cooking venison, which would taste superb if the rich smell was anything to go by. Starting to feel fatigued after the long day, they spent much of the remaining daylight sunning themselves on the warm smooth rocks at the pool edge, happily dozing in anticipation of the meal to come.

The evening meal was an absolute delight, tender full-flavoured venison contrasting marvellously with the more subtle-tasting crayfish which were toasted over the fire. They also had lovely flatbreads cooked on hot rocks, sprinkled with nutty plantain seeds and smothered in butter; dessert being a plethora of blackberries drizzled with honey and topped with wild mint. It was another superb meal and in no time at all most were laying back happily dozing, some telling stories and others making up inventive games with their bone dice. It was a happy party who eventually turned in to their warm bedrolls and slept the contented sleep of those entirely worn out from simply enjoying life.

Next morning they all awoke early again, having slept splendidly, to smells of a hearty stew and more fresh bread. Merrick and Arwyn said they intended to explore around the base of the waterfall, noting on a late walk the day before what seemed to be caves previously partially hidden, but now exposed with less volume of water coming down the falls. The children were very interested too and it was agreed they would all go to explore before then deciding what to do with the remainder of the day. The main waterfall was a little way up from the swimming pools, but was not a long walk; on-route they very luckily came across a family of otters which they managed to watch for several minutes before they slipped back into a feeder stream and vanished without a trace. Clambering over increasingly huge boulders they came upon the base of the mighty falls, the air saturated with a fine opaque-mist from the thundering cascade of water. It wasn't the easiest climb up, but on a close approach it became apparent that there was what might be a series of small caves not previously seen to one side of the falls, which normally would be completely shrouded in the mist from the waterfall. Accessing the caves wasn't too difficult, with an indistinct path of sorts from the side of the falls leading in. It was almost as if the mist would normally just obscure the caves rather than hinder access and they wondered if it was potentially possible to walk in with care, even with the waterfall in full spate. The group made their way up the indistinct and boulder strewn path, passing various small shallow openings but then came to the mouth of a larger cave, noting that with a decent pace they were far from soaked, as might be expected. Once just inside they found that the cave sloped quickly up, then narrowed to become a long rocky tunnel with some sign of having been worked with tools at certain pinch points, though mostly it seemed a natural formation. It was near pitch-black not far in, though with a faint glow of light at the end which made exploration possible as their eyes adjusted. With some wariness they carefully made their way along the meandering tunnel, feet feeling for any obstacles and a hand kept on the side wall. After several minutes the tunnel ended with no mishaps and brought them out into a wide dry cave, with daylight flooding in at the far end. Approaching the far side of the cave they noted openings out onto the cliff face, some way around from the main falls. There was a natural ledge below the openings, which would shield views of the cave from anything but more distant viewpoints, though it afforded stunning views down the whole valley, its U-shape now very apparent. All were somewhat lost for words; the view was breath-taking and most just sat on the ledge in the glorious sunshine and took in all that they could see, some pointing out features like The Steading appearing as a clearing in the far distance, the narrow valley end, the east and west passes, the upper plateau and in the very far distance a hint of the huge plains beyond.

The group sat on the wide ledge and took in the splendour of the valley for some time; eventually though the more inquisitive among them started to explore the rest of the substantial cave. It was a large airy-space which could accommodate a good number of people, more than swallowing their group with ease, being surprisingly dry, with good ventilation afforded by the multiple openings. It was an excellent hideaway and place of potential retreat in case of any pressing need; none would find this sanctuary without considerable luck, the entrance likely being completely invisible most of the year. They also found the very old remains of a crude fireplace with a chimney hole leading to the outside of the cave. This would have rendered the space very cosy indeed, perhaps even a home and great as a cooking area. As their eyes grew accustomed to the low light, they started to note what were distinct areas in the cave, including a space which was littered with stone chippings and shards, with a couple of broken arrowheads and incomplete spearpoints apparent as they scratched about in the debris. It was unclear how old these workings were but they spoke to habitation and use of the cave by other humans, though likely some ages past. On examining the walls, they also discovered stylised drawings of animals scratched into the rock and the remnants of very faint handprints. It was unclear how old these may be, but they judged some were possibly hundreds of years old if not more ancient. After an hour or so they finished their exploration, agreeing that it would be a good place to stash a few essentials and a supply of fire-wood, in the event it was needed as an emergency shelter or possible retreat if danger arose.

With the caves thoroughly explored the group made their way back down the falls to the camp, where they all fuelled up with sweet tea and bathed in the sun. Talk was of the caves, then their plans for the afternoon; most proposed to take advantage of the sun warmed pools and would go swimming again, while those remaining fancied going fishing and crayfish hunting. Merrick and Arwyn said they would take a long walk skirting the slopes to the side of the falls, up to the less-visited corner of the valley, then down the side and looping round through the woods to the river to pick up the children later on. With plans laid and an agreement to meet later for supper, they all went their separate ways.

Merrick and Arwyn took their time strolling up the river back to the falls then following the valley head west to the less-visited area they hoped to better explore. As they walked gently uphill, they noted an abundance of wildlife, the stonechats making their pebble-knocking sound, the peeps of pipits, the flash of the ring ouzel's smart white breast and all manner of other creatures. Following the head of the valley further around they came to the largest of the valley's feeder rivers, fairly wide in itself, but passable with care this time of year, then coming to an area seldom visited to date. Before long they came across a number of scree slopes, noting in their idle curiosity the odd hand-sized stone which appeared to have been shaped. On looking through the scree and overturning a few rocks they discovered some which were clearly oblong rounded axeheads in various states of completion, some very rough but some in initial stages of polishing. It was further indication, if any were needed, that humans had been present in the valley off and on for many hundreds if not thousands of years, theirs being just the next in a long line. They took a pair of near complete axeheads to show the children and to take home as curiosities; Amaethon they knew would be very interested as he was a keen knapper of stone, often producing new arrowheads for the hunters to supplement their limited supply of steel heads. It might also make a pleasant project for the long winter evenings to mount the axeheads into shafts and display them in the hall. With the axeheads stowed in their packs they followed the valley side further, noting not far from the axe factory the presence of stone circles and various low walls, presumably part of an older settlement at some point. They explored these overgrown ruins, finding a few which retained a drystone roof of sorts, fairly squat with a low entrance, but surprisingly dry inside, though a little acrid with the smell of animal musk. It was a very interesting place to explore and they thought it would make a fine place for the children to visit the next day, to find axeheads of their own and to further explore the settlement.

Merrick and Arwyn continued their walk, now angling back down to the wooded valley-bottom and eventually met the river. They went a good way down the watercourse to ensure there were no stragglers, the children not being all that clear where they would fish in their plans made that morning, but likely much closer to camp. Satisfied that there were no sign of the children having recently passed, they walked up the river side, and in time came upon the anglers. They had managed to catch a few trout, some pike and a good number of crayfish, which would all go very nicely with supper. With excitement they breathlessly told of a monster crayfish at least two foot long, which they had very nearly caught, but had just gotten away, pulling them down into the water with its ferocity. Merrick and Arwyn listened to their tall tale with rapt attention, smiling and gasping in all the right places, much to the children's obvious delight. As they collected their things and continued their tale, the embellishments grew more and more fanciful and then simply outrageous, until at last the children could no longer control their laughter and started to tease the adults for believing them in the first place. This jolly band came upon the upper pools in short time and all agreed a swim with the others in one of the shallower sun-warmed pools would be a perfect end to the afternoon, followed by another hearty supper.

The trip continued with the children visiting the newly-discovered settlement the next day, all delighted with finding their own axes in the scree, exploring the ruins and coming across further intact buildings and underground spaces. There was also the odd upright-stone which clearly had once been decoratively carved, though were now weathered to the point where any design was lost to time. As they explored the beehive-shaped drystone buildings, they noted small cairns and rock-strewn areas in amongst the structures. It was in one such area that an adder was spotted sunbathing, coiled up on top of a sheltered spot, clearly making the most of the mid-day sun. They rarely saw the snakes, though knew they were about from the odd occasion one had been seen, usually as they quickly slithered off when their paths crossed. Though in little real danger the children knew to keep their distance, the adder's poison of little real threat to human life, though better not to tempt fate with a bite. Everyone managed to get a good look at this elusive animal, the better acquainted everyone was, the greater the chance that the unconscious mind would instantly recognise it as a danger. Though difficult to spot, the zig-zag pattern down its back was pretty distinct and gave it a striking appearance when you got your 'eye in'. After putting up with being inspected for several minutes longer than they had expected, it slowly moved off into the thick heather and disappeared from sight.

As it was to be their last full day of the trip, the afternoon was spent back at camp organising their kit, tidying and packing, with the evening meal comprising a gluttonous series of leftovers. They spent the evening staying-up late, gazing at the constellations, the planets and spotting shooting-stars, making up tales of the shapes they could see, of the bear, the archer and mythical beasts. All the while they variously

145

quietly hummed and sang, the young children's reedy-voices a pleasant contrast with the bass of Merrick and Arwyn's mellow contralto. By the time the children had started dozing off, it was getting towards midnight, their mission to stay up really late finally accomplished.

The next morning there were some sleepy heads, but they were soon breakfasted and packed, the camp area being cleared, leaving little trace. With that complete they made their way down the valley at good speed, though the children did not quite have the boundless energy they had exhibited on the way up, being content to trek along telling stories, while looking forward to seeing their parents and the extended family. In due course they arrived back at The Steading, the families happily reuniting, with the parents looking somewhat brighter and more rested than they had in some time, thankful though to see their precious little ones again. The parents couldn't thank Merrick and Arwyn enough for volunteering to look after them all and certainly gained a fair few credits to their already good names.

20 - Winter preparations

As the cooler autumn came, they increased their urgency of the numerous preparations for winter, wanting more than just to survive, aiming for every comfort possible. The green of the woods had soon turned to a kaleidoscope of vivid autumnal colours which showered down in the wind, delightful if not for their heralding the winter to come. With their expanding collection of animals, they would need to store considerably more feed to see them through, so additional hay was gathered and stacked in the now fully-repaired barn. The goats would eat many of their kitchen scraps and would be fine with any of the poorer weedy hay they harvested, the better hay being kept for the more fussy ponies. The animals would be kept on the pasture even with the first snow, as they knew how to look after themselves and to dig down to forage, but to keep them healthy and safe they would bring them to stables they hoped to build, reducing expenditure of energy with warmer quarters out of the wind. The goats would also be kept within the oak woods for a time to let them gorge on the bounty of acorns, then moved to the hazel woods to feed on the glut of fallen nuts, though they would have to ensure this was mixed with other pasture to avoid them getting ill. Many of the hazelnuts would also be harvested and stored, a treat when drizzled with honey, and great crushed and sprinkled into flat breads for added flavour and texture.

Now Bolin had become productive in his forge he had created numerous and quite excellent tools entirely becoming of his master smith status, with considerable time having recently been spent on a large two-person saw. This was a difficult tool to forge, requiring a long flattened piece of metal with the teeth then die-cut with a punch and sharpened with a file. It would have been simple to manufacture with a hot-metal roller, but this was a complicated piece of kit to produce

147

and beyond their resources. Nonetheless the time it took to make the saw was well worth the investment, with everyone taking a turn to help laboriously flatten and smooth the metal with flat sections of grinding stone. The edge was then preferentially heated in the forge and quenched to harden the teeth, allowing a decent sharpness retention on the toothed blades, but overall spring to the wide steel-body. To complete the tool, it was mounted with a pair of smoothed-ash handles at a right angle to the line of the saw, allowing for a person at each end to operate it two-handed. While creating this saw they had finished a great pit abutting the back of the workshop and created a basic shelter from some straight pine trunks, jointed and pegged together, covered with a basic pitched shingle-roof. This allowed for them to work in relative comfort out of the sun and rain, and which avoided the pit becoming a pool. Once seasoned straight-trunks had been pulled in by the ponies they could be rolled atop the pit and wedged firm so each could be worked upon. With one person standing on the trunk and another in the pit below, planks could be created, though not without considerable effort. The job tended to get the person in the pit absolutely covered in sawdust, itching like mad and irritating the lungs if no fabric mask was worn. Given these issues the role was rotated between the sawyers and also kept for those who had committed some minor transgression, usually sleeping-in late.

The lumber they had now started to accumulate was used to construct two long-drop outhouses, all agreeing that this beat the exposed 'bench over a trench', which could get a little ripe and chilly to say the least. The new outhouses were located away from the main buildings, but not too far, as nobody wanted a long trip in the winter. It was though important to keep the outhouses away from any water course and to ensure they wouldn't be flooded. The general area of the old outhouses were though found to be near perfect, a gravelly soil helping keep the area from getting waterlogged, but well away from any water course where water might be drawn. These structures were essentially deep pits shored up with cedar logs with a small shed atop containing a fairly rudimentary seat. They used a little sawdust or grass to help with the composting process and to deaden the smell, but they were surprisingly odour free, except sometimes in high summer. It was though possible to add a small venting chimney from the top of the pit running up the back of the structure to vent the worst of it. On those rare occasions it became unbearable it was sometimes preferable to take a spade and pick a spot in the woods. Generally the long drop was not used for urine as this tended to increase the smell, but there were a thousand bushes for this purpose, though they kept much in a designated bucket to mix with wood ash as a fertiliser. They also kept a decent quantity for leather making, the ash mixed with urine to create lye used for de-hairing and de-fleshing the hides. After about a year the long-drop sheds would be picked up and moved to a new spot and the contents of the hole used as a soil improver on the fields; the pits also made an ideal planting spot for new fruit trees, no resource being wasted.

An abundance of vegetables and fruit was stored for the long winter and early spring, much being variously pickled and boiled, then sealed in sterilised glass-jars and made airtight with wax. The larders and stores were soon bursting, with every space and shelf double-stacked with the bountiful crop. Jams were a particular favourite and a variety were made, including wild blackberry, dandelion petal, raspberry and bilberry, using pectin for setting them to jelly from the numerous wild crab-apple trees growing at the forest edge. With the use of honey and birch syrup the jams were a delight, the intense sweetness a rare treat. That autumn they had found the fruit trees had produced good amounts of fruit, but as expected it was too high up in the overgrown trees to harvest before much had become too ripe for dry storage. Once it has dropped to the ground this overripe fruit was used to make

149

ciders and vinegars in the main, and some fed to the goats and ponies. Any windfall too far gone was taken for the compost pile, though they were often beaten to it by the wasps who drunkenly gorged on the abundant fermenting sugars. Once the fruiting was completely over they cut back the trees very heavily under Rhian's direction, it was a risk doing so, but there were good numbers and it should do them good, encouraging fresh growth and hopefully rejuvenating them. It would cause them to be less productive the first year after, while they recovered from the trauma, but there were many trees in the orchard so this would not matter too much, any complete losses being sustainable, with any fruit then being easier to pick at optimum time. An added bonus of opening up the canopy was that a profusion of wild flowers should bloom below next year, further increasing nectar for the bees and butterflies. The dense fruit-wood timber was kept for carving and special projects, the characterful grain and colour being very sought after by their artisans. Any remnants would be good for handles of smaller tools, with twigs and small whips being excellent for hard wearing baskets. Anything left would be kept for wood chips they could use for smoking meats, giving lovely delicate flavour.

Several hunts had claimed a good number of deer, taken from the system of hunting blinds they had created through the valley. To supplement their supply, they had driven down several herds from the higher plateau to the east; this they probably naturally did anyway to take advantage of the lower pastures in deep winter, but forcing them sooner would be less risky on the slippy gorges, likely saving a good number. They had also located a small family of wild pigs in the west woods, previously unknown, reverting to something like the hairy boars of old. This was a precious and limited resource so they intended to manage them and if possible domesticate the small herd. They did however decide to harvest one of the old sows which seemed to have passed its likely fertile time of life. These meats had replenished their supplies and the wild pork was a welcome change which had excellent flavour, sweetened with the smoke of fruit wood, and served with some apple sauce and tart crab apple jelly. They kept back a good deal of the fat to be used for soap making, as this was still quite scarce despite the supply from the goat's milk. They did have a good supply of plant-based cleansing alternatives, like the leaves of the horse chestnut, though a good hard soap of lye and fat was a better cleaning agent for most tasks.

They had collected and stacked a huge amount of firewood through the year, favouring the dense and long burning oak and ash hardwoods, but also much blackthorn from hedge laying which burnt very nicely to excellent coals. There was such abundance in simply collecting natural deadfall that they seldom took down live trees except when selecting certain especially straight trunks for lumber. Wood stacks had been created throughout the forest, lifting the wood from the ground and letting it air to prevent rot and promote drying. To keep off any rain that dripped through the canopy these were covered with bark stripped from any freshly fallen trees. Done right bark could be stripped in great long rolls, though ideally earlier in the year when sap was rising. Once stripped these could be weighted flat and would dry into substantial sheets, a great material for all manner of jobs.

With the ponies now fully trained, it was a relatively easy task to haul the firewood back to The Steading, at least compared to doing so by hand, though it was still a time-consuming task. Back at base the wood was broken down to one and a half foot lengths, this they achieved fairly easily with new wooden-framed tensioned bowsaws Bolin had been busy churning out. These logs were chopped with new splitting mauls, then neatly stacked in the barn and under simple shelters, reusing the bark sheets where they could. While the wood wasn't perfectly seasoned, it would be mostly okay for burning, with a good amount already several months under cover. Worst come to worst the ash could be burnt when fresh and green but its heat output dramatically improved with even a few months drying. The key was to keep collecting and stacking firewood in a continuous loop which was laborious, but now made much easier with the ponies to assist. By the time winter came they had little space left for more but it never hurt to have reserves in hand, so every conceivable space was filled including against the walls under the wide overhanging-eaves of the house, in the porch, the potting shed and so on. The stacks almost became an art form in themselves, symmetrical rows and freestanding beehive-like arrangements of hard-won split logs; order from the chaos to sustain life. For next year they would look to possibly rebuild an old barn and other stores for increased storage, but first they would need to cut much lumber and churn out many roofing shingles.

In the house the main job was to ensure the chimneys were carefully swept and ready for the long winter and spring. The bedroom fireplaces were relatively easy, being short runs up to the stacks and which hadn't been used much since spring. These could be swept with fresh conifer-boughs, dragged up and down with a rope repeatedly, clearing any soot quite efficiently. The kitchen and main hall chimneys were though in constant use through the year, for cooking and heating of water. They had become quite thick with ash and tarry deposits which could set alight if they weren't swept. To some extent it was possible to climb up the main hall chimney, the smallest of the kids doing a decent job cleaning for a good eight foot up. However for the remainder Bolin again proved his worth, the forge producing stiff wire which was twisted into a thicker core to form the head of the sweep brush. This was attached to series of light but flexible wooden shafts which were screwed together with expertly made connectors. The sweeping was a messy task and resulted in much coughing and sneezing but they took care to collect the deposits as it formed another good fertiliser.

Once the tail end of the vegetable crop had been harvested, excepting the late winter potatoes and overwintering onions, the beds were cleared, and any last seeds stored away, the bare soil then turned over. Charcoal was subsequently worked in, along with all the other improvers they had collected through the year. The tops of the beds were finally mulched with the fallen leaves and decaying bark, which would keep any late weeds suppressed and rot down to improve the soil further.

The next job was to ensure the bees would make it through the winter. Insulation was provided around the now eight occupied hives in the form of dried vegetation and straw. They had been very fortunate in sourcing most of these colonies from the woods, though with no few stings resulting from relocating the hives. In addition two of the colonies had been split after having outgrown their new homes, with another to potentially be split next spring. The hives were then boxed in to greater extent to keep off the wind, and any gaps filled, with added woven hurdle-type panels to assist further and keep away inquisitive animals. Essentially this would create a decent amount of insulation and general protection, mimicking the natural hives found in fissures of trees. That year had produced a very modest surplus of honey and wax, but with nearly all left to help the new colonies build for the next year. Once they were active again, they would be moved from their temporary woven skeps to slatted-timber versions, which would dramatically increase their efficiency and make harvesting much simpler. The new hives would be a complicated carpentry task, with various dovetailed-slats and trays needed. This was a job for the long winter nights and would need Bolin's assistance with the production of various small chisels, rasps, augers and fine-toothed saws.

153

Almost the final task was the completion of the stables for the ponies and goats. Being more or less wild animals they could spend the winter out in the worst of it, capable of course of surviving up on the exposed plateau above the valley, but it would help keep them safe and more comfortable in sheltered stables, but importantly meaning less food would be needed to maintain their body temperature. The ponies would be taken out together to graze as much as they could and to exercise to avoid muscles atrophying, but they had supplies of hay for the worst times, likely early spring when pickings in the valley would be slim and snow cover likely. The stables were built next to the restored barn, being simple affairs constructed of timber posts, scorched around their bases in a bonfire to reduce the chance of rot where they contacted the soil in their post holes. The sides were formed from timber cladding using some of the outer waney-edges of the logs that had been cut for boards, stripped of their bark to reduce insect damage and rot. The roofs were made of cleaved sweet-chestnut shingles, more accurately termed shakes as they were split rather than sawn, overlapping multiple times to keep out the rain. Chestnut was ideal for the shakes, though of very limited supply in the valley, being well outside its normal range, with any trees hardy enough to survive best kept for their autumn crop of sweet chestnuts. Their guess was that the trees must have been intentionally planted several decades ago from seed to take advantage of the food source. However one of the smaller trees had fallen in a storm so was perfect for the task and would soon regrow, already sprouting multiple fresh runners from the base, perfect for eventual coppicing. That winter they hoped to encourage germination of some chestnut seeds by potting them up indoors then planting out late spring following the frosts. A good working coppice would be some decades off but it was a worthwhile project if they could get enough saplings to survive in the sheltered sunny spot they had in mind. The not insubstantial chestnut-shingled roofs of the stables were linked to basic timber troughs which would collect rainwater for the beasts, though it not being far to a number of nearby streams, it would be handy when these potentially dried up in mid-summer.

With all these jobs and many more besides complete, Arwyn suggested it was high time for a feast, to which all eagerly agreed. They chose a brilliant sunny day, chilly out in the wind but with vibrant blue skies, nearly the last of the warmth they would see for many months. A big bonfire was stacked up for later to keep them toasty, though not that they needed it with the powerful tart cider warming them through. They made up a long table from newly-sawn boards on trestles located in a sheltered spot within the herb garden, and set out the bountiful food. The star of the feast was a pit-roasted haunch of auroch, taken a few weeks before, which had been hung in the cellar and was now nicely matured. Early that morning a large fire pit had been created, lined with heat-retaining rocks, into which they added a good deal of hardwood that burnt down to long-lasting coals. Onto the coals they added soaked apple-tree chips, then the meat which was covered with leaves to help keep in moisture, some hot stones and finally capped off with a layer of sod. The meat had slow cooked since early morning and when unearthed was succulent and disintegrated in tender fibrous chunks. It was left to rest, though nibbled near continuously with dollops of wild horseradish sauce and sprinkled with salt, the bulk of the meat later forming the centrepiece to the feast. Added to this they had been cooking various meats and fishes over the fires, with wonderful smells as a result, making every mouth salivate in anticipation. Venison was of course present in abundance, prime cuts of back steaks mounted on small wooden frames to angle next to the fire and was cooked to chosen preference, though most preferred rare and juicy. This was generously salted, bringing out the lovely flavour.

As well as the meats they skewered crayfish onto sticks and cooked these over the fires, turning scarlet as they became ready to eat; these morsels were eaten warm, dribbled over with hot butter made from the goat's milk, slightly tangy and sweet, a lovely complement. They had also rehydrated and desalted some fish that had been in the stores; these were made into a soupy chowder, bringing a taste of the sea and a reminder of their trip earlier that year to the proceedings.

Mushrooms were abundant that year and had been gathered in great quantities by Shuldan and Nineveh, with many dried for the stores, including some for medicines. Fresh rich mushrooms picked that morning were sliced and fried in pans over the fire, some in butter, some in fat kept from the boar. These were excellent with the meats, and accompanied by onions and wild garlic pesto were a dish simple yet wonderful in the open air.

Various bannock-type breads were baked in small cast-iron trays, made of flour processed from the autumn acorns, an oaty flavour combined with various dried fruits and hazelnuts creating a sweet cake-like delight. They were also herbier thinner pita-type breads just cooked on stones forming beautiful pockets for the meats and vegetables. With these breads they served butter and cheese melted over the fire, wonderfully moreish. For those that were not averse to the strong taste, a particular delight was the soft-creamy goat's cheese, the flavours of the valley being readily apparent to the extent that it was almost possible to taste and smell the herbs the goats had gorged on through the year, abundant on the upper meadows. This was quite excellent with a little bramble jam smothered straight onto freshly baked bread, washed down with a tart cider.

Added to these dishes were the last of the late winter vegetables, the prime specimens being stored away, but those left were still lovely, with some fried and others slow cooked over the embers of the fire in thick leaves, imparting smoky-sweet flavours. Some of the vegetables were used for kebabs, with a honey tomato glaze, giving a sweetness that was a real treat. Though they would normally keep back the fruit preserves for the deep winter to take advantage of the scarce vitamins, they had broken out some of the fruit jellies and jams, to be smeared onto the meats and bread. Another treat was the abundance of sweet chestnuts they had harvested, many of which were in stores and a good number eaten as snacks. Today though they were partially cooked in the coals of the fire, shelled and fried-off in butter, with a glaze of honey and a small sprinkle of salt and crushed hazelnuts, very moreish, a real taste of autumn.

In terms of drinks the cider was superb, though young and tart. The crowning glory was the sweet and flavoursome birch and blackberry wine, made earlier that year and just opened. It was potent, almost a liqueur, which they imbibed with relish following the meal, snacking on various favourite nibbles as the feasting of the day came to a close.

They spent the darkening evening hours sat around the bonfire, happy and full, feeding titbits to the dogs, but whom could neither barely move from the excesses of the day. As they lay back, and not for the first time that year, they observed the bats fluttering overhead, likely not too far from their long hibernation. They were in great abundance that night, attracted in by the moths which were compelled to dance above the bonfire, the bats glutinously building up their reserves for the long winter when they would roost in the various outbuildings of The Steading. As the fire burnt down to ashy coals and the night grew cool, they moved indoors to the easy chairs and new feather cushions of the hall, bringing with them what little food they had not consumed. The final chores of the day complete, they each eventually went to bed, satisfied and very sleepy.

21 - Bow making

The household awoke to find they were blessed with another of those normally rare, crisp early-winter days. The clear sky was an amazingly vivid hue of blue, with the sun providing such a lovely warmth, that Merrick and Sioned decided it would be ideal to teach the children bow making. The children could easily make simple bows of essentially a bent branch, but those the hunters used were complicated and refined tools of many different designs. Their hunting bows exerted a great deal of force, some up to sixty or seventy pounds, though today they would make thirty odd pounders the children could learn with, but which were still deadly.

Earlier that year Merrick had been keeping an eye out for suitable timbers for bows, mostly of ash boles unencumbered by any side branches, which had grown straight and true with even growth rings. This wood had been split down to aid drying and then stacked up in one of the store rooms within the house, where it could dry slowly, kept at fairly constant humidity and temperature. This wood would make for excellent bow-staves, to be crafted by the more experienced of the group. With a decent supply of good staves they would have several bows being made at any one time in case of breakages, all but inevitable with wear and tear from constant use. They had also found some straight staves of yew, having near perfect proportions of central heartwood and younger outer sapwood which would create excellent bows, albeit harder to get right than the flatbows they would initially make with the children. However for learning the art of bow making Merrick had chosen some relatively fresh green ash, felled just that week, being much easier to cleave and carve for the children when more moist. The only drawback would be the bows would have to be left to dry after they were finished to reach full strength, but the ease of carving the softer green wood would more than make up for this inconvenience.

They set up their workstations in the warm courtyard of the herb garden, starting the morning with mounds of bacon, fresh flat bread and melted cheese, washed down with chaga tea; while they consumed this meal Sioned explained the basics of what they hoped to achieve that day. To start they selected their raw staves of green ash and Sioned got them thinking about their flatbow designs. The centre part would form the narrower ovoid grip, which would then flare out above and below to a long wide flat section, continuing up for a few hand widths, then tapering back down to a rounded point where the nock slits would be made for the string. Overall the bows would be just a little shorter than the height of the maker, which would dictate its relative strength proportional to the individual user; however, for now they would be left somewhat longer to allow for room in tweaking of the design during the end process of tillering, which they would come to later.

All got down to the initial process of forming the back of the bow, perhaps counterintuitively the forward face, which essentially comprised removing the bark and soft outer cambium layer of the last growth ring, then working back to form a smooth D–shape. Sioned and Merrick would be making new bows at the same time, never doing any harm to have a number of spares. They showed the children how it was important to ensure the back of the bow had a uniform profile, keeping within the one growth ring, to ensure it didn't then peel and split at what would be a weak point, if mistakenly stripping back into another layer. This was achieved mostly by using drawknives, a wide two-handled tool which allowed thin shavings to be easily removed in a pulling fashion. It was however more than possible to use their

159

normal knives, which they did, with the point wedged deep into a thick stick to form the second handle. Once the children had the knack of it, the D-shaped staves were made ready for the outline of the bow to be drawn on its flat front with twigs of charcoal, using flat strips of wood as a guide for the straight lines, though much was done by eye while working with the natural variations of the wood. It was less about the precision of the measurements and more about the proportions, starting with the width of each person's clenched fist for the grip and working out from there. In deciding on the design, they had to ensure that any small pin-knots were central to the bow, leaving extra thickness of wood to avoid a weak spot. With the front on profile complete, they next sketched out the side as a guide, highlighting the areas that would need to be cut out to create the small central bulge of the handgrip, quickly tapering back to the flat long sections of the bow arms.

The forge had provided them with saws which were used to section up the waste elements of the stave into smaller parallel teeth-like chunks, to make it simpler to cut across these to very carefully chip out the surplus wood. With chisels and gouges the bulk of the waste was quickly removed, with the finer work completed with the drawknives. Sioned stressed that they were now at a critical stage and should aim to leave a good thickness of wood for fine adjustments later, especially around any knots or areas with any deformations. With the bulk of the bows now roughed out, they took a break for a mid-morning snack, Nineveh providing hot tea and bread laden with jam to keep up energy and attention levels. While they were eating Merrick started to explain about the most delicate part of the process; tillering. The aim of this process was to slowly remove wood from the arms of the bow to ensure they bent and flexed in a consistent and smooth manner. Merrick cautioned that over-enthusiastic removal of wood could easily lead to a weak point, or hinge, where the bow preferentially bent, causing excess pressure and likely breakage in due course, sometimes catastrophically. Demonstrating the first step of the tillering process he took his bow and braced it on the floor against his foot, resting the tip onto a softwood offcut to keep it out of the dirt; he then quickly flexed the bow, applying just enough pressure to examine the bow arms and marked on the sections which clearly bent less, remaining flatter. With those sections marked he removed a few shavings of wood, then went back to the bracing and flexing, repeating this with patience and skill belying its difficulty. After doing this for some time he managed to bend the bow more as it become thinner and more flexible. Encouraging the youngsters to have a go, he and Sioned took it in turns to show the children the skill.

All of the children did well, initially showing great patience and starting the refining process, though before long they were tired with the intense concentration. At that stage they decided to break for a late lunch of sliced meats, pickles and cheese. Sat in the sun, their energy soon restored, the adults let them go off to play, to loosen sore muscles, unused to the repetitive fine motions of the tools. Within what seemed like only a few minutes to the children, the adults called them back to carry on with the tillering. While they were gone Sioned and Merrick had set up what looked like a very odd set of contraptions, comprising long-boards mounted vertically on a wall, each with a central small shelf of a few inches wide at the top padded in leather. Below the shelf was a simple pulley system attached to a cord with leather cups on each end. Sioned then demonstrated, placing her new bow on the top shelf, being just narrower across than the span of her handle. She then attached the linked leather-cups to each end of the bow forming a loose bowstring across, linked with a further cord to the pulley below. Explaining as she went, she demonstrated that the device would allow them to stand back, using the pulley system to pull the bow down and easily view the two arms bending at the same time, to ensure consistency of flexing, looking to make them as symmetrical as possible. To the children's eyes the bow looked near perfect, but Sioned marked a few points then demounted the bow and proceeded to very finely remove almost imperceptible slivers with her drawknife. She then remounted the bow and seemingly satisfied used the pulley to flex the bow further towards the ground, keeping the motion steady, explaining that holding it static under tension could cause wood fibres to fail and permanently deform. At once the children could see this accentuated any asymmetry and flat spots, being simpler to see where modification was needed. Merrick commented that this was a crucial stage and it needed to be done without hastiness, as one aggressive cut could cause an imbalance that would be hard to correct, or at worst result in a hinge which might deform and fail. It wasn't without great justification that the board was referred to as the torture rack, for bows and bow makers alike.

As the children started the tillering process, there was a sudden crack and a cry of dismay as a bow-tip broke, possibly having been over tensioned on the tillering board. Being a little aggressive with the pulley hadn't helped, but on inspection there was a clear flaw in the wood only exposed in the break, so the failure was almost inevitable. Durian was the unlucky one, initially inconsolable, but soon seeing what had gone wrong, gutting and of limited comfort. Sioned had foreseen the potential mishap for some unlucky soul, and so she had been working on another bow which she offered to Durian for him to finish up, sympathising with him as something all bow makers eventually went through. Durian was however surprisingly circumspect and chose to stick with his original bow, deciding to essentially shorten it by a couple of inches at both ends. With an energy they had come to expect, though with uncharacteristic concentration and determination, he quickly but confidently had the bow reprofiled and was working on the re-tillering within the hour. The failure seemed to spark within him previously unknown maturity and levels of single-minded attentiveness to the task which indicated he may have a found a passion. Merrick and Sioned exchanged a shrewd smile as Durian continued on, long past the others in final tweaks and shavings, eventually producing what was by far the best of the children's efforts, and superficially not that far off Sioned's, which was a thing of functional beauty.

With the tillering complete they created small grooves at each end of the bow for the string to rest within, utilising a thin rounded file usually kept for sharpening small saw teeth. That done they came to making the bowstrings. Merrick and Sioned had already created the fibres from nettles and woven this into a tight waxed-cord, with very little stretch, but still supple. In pairs the children replicated the actions of their teachers and twisted and wove the cord to form a permanent loop to hook over one tip and sit in the grooves. With that completed they took the other end and tied off an adjustable loop, but shorter than the length of the bow to allow it to be bent and the string seated and tensioned. There was some tweaking needed to achieve the necessary fist and outstretched thumb gap between the handle and string, but with some flexing of the bows to loosen them up they all achieved this before too long, with varying degrees of assistance. Satisfied they were about right, to be easily adjusted later on, they all bent and unhooked the string and gently re-bent the bows to straight, to avoid the bows setting into a curved position and losing power, especially likely in their green state.

They would leave the making of arrows for another day, Sioned explaining to the children, whose faces soon dropped, that the craft of bow making was nothing compared to producing a consistent set of straight and true shafts, the plethora of arrowhead types, the craft of fletching, steam bending and straightening the shafts over the fire, and so on. It was only Durian who looked keen and ready to go, but knowing all would want to test fire their new creations, they allowed them some practice shots with an assortment of simple un-fletched hazel shafts. These basic shafts were great for allowing them to get the feel of their bows and didn't matter if they were lost. Sioned cautioned them to use restraint to allow the wood fibres in the bows to settle in, recommending three quarters power or less for now. Only Durian took this to heart, treating his bow with great respect, the others soon pushing the limits, though this would unlikely do them any great harm, beyond possibly a slight reduction in long-term power. Once the initial bedding in was complete they led them over to a small stack of late-cut hay in the meadow and let them take some practice shots with some properly-fletched arrows. Merrick showed them the technique and mechanics of the arrows, advising a relatively quick draw and release, allowing muscle memory to build over time with practice. He explained it was important not to hold the bow for too long under tension as this put unnecessary stress on the fibres of the wood, especially when fresh and green, becoming less of an issue once properly dried.

They continued until the failing light and risk of lost arrows finally caused them to pack up and head back to base. They carefully un-stringed their bows, flexed them back to straight, then stowed them away in the hall, finally going back outside to finish tidying their work stations and to finally clean and oil their tools. With all squared away safely back in the store, the children were taken to the hall and showed how to maintain their bows, using a very light coat of beeswax to create some water repellency and to help avoid the wood fibres drying out too quick and cracking. The wonderful smell of the beeswax soon permeated the hall, mixing with the smell of the roasting meat on the fire and grumbling bellies. Before letting them go for their food Merrick showed them how to properly store their new bows, not being just left like walking sticks in a corner but laid flat and preferably weighted down to stop them deforming as they dried.

The children wolfed down their supper and were yawning before long, so took themselves to bed, tired after the long exhausting day, but still excited to try their new bows again tomorrow. Durian however stayed up late that night, eagerly picking the brains of Sioned and Merrick on relative merits of different woods, bowstrings, fletching, stave selection and so on, until they were yawning themselves. He then moved over to Bolin to discuss with him when he may be able to show him how to forge arrow heads; Durian was an eager audience, and Bolin was keen to share with him all that they knew, promising that he would soon let him come and make his own before long.

Over the months and years that followed Durian showed a deep and lifelong passion in bow designs and experimentation that saw their first laminated bows, formed with glues of his own devising, considerably increasing durability and reliability. He would also spend hours at the forge designing new arrow heads for various applications and would get so bound up in his work, he would still be there until late into the night, on several occasions being chased away by Bolin and sent to bed. In time Durian surpassed the skills of even Sioned and became their master bowyer, producing many fine bows of extraordinary variety. When teaching the next generation his skills, it was always with a wry smile when they came to the torture rack, recalling his dismay at the heart wrenching crack, but never without a spare bow to hand.

22 - The west

As early winter settled in, there came a stable spell of weather which was unusually mild, the warmth of the sun palpable by midday, though still hovering just above freezing by nightfall. As it had remained dry for some weeks it was more akin to a fine late autumn, though it could soon turn for the worse, potentially alternating between a muddy quagmire, sleety snow and thick crunching frost. Rather than waste the opportunity provided by the unseasonal bout of relatively dry conditions, Merrick thought it would be good to settle his lingering doubts about their western border. Although he had explored this way previously that year, the group had only travelled for two days, and though it was exhausting and comprised extremely inhospitable terrain, there was no clear insurmountable obstruction, unlike to the east bound as it was by natural steep-cliffs and impassable glaciated-mountains. They felt confident no surprises were lurking on their eastern and southern border, but the west was an unknown, best resolved if at all possible. Besides the unsecure permeability of their border, it would also be useful to scout out what the landscape might have to offer in terms of resources, beyond the possibility of more goats found previously.

Merrick spoke of his plans to the others around the kitchen table at first breakfast and it was agreed a trip to further explore would be very much worthwhile given the ideal travelling weather. There was a slight risk of an early winter storm trapping them in the uplands, but extreme care would be exercised, the trip undertaken by the most experienced of the group, travelling light and fast. Though otherwise the person best suited to such an expedition, Sioned was now in the later stages of her pregnancy and was unable to travel too far beyond the homestead, much less on a strenuous and risky trip beyond the valley. Merrick and Arwyn would therefore form the exploratory team, being

166

otherwise the two most capable, taking with them the stoutest of their ponies to carry supplies. The hardy mountain pony who would accompany them, affectionately known as Sindri, was already well into his winter coat of thick insulating-hair and his help would be ideal on the scouting trip. The resilient beast was more than used to plodding for hours over harsh terrain; a steady pace being the best they would otherwise manage. The pony would save them the necessity of hunting on the trip as they could load up decent stocks of travelling jerky, cured bacon, salami, energy-dense honeyed-acorn and sweet-chestnut cakes, dehydrated shredded vegetables, fruit leathers and nuts. With meals taken care of this would dramatically speed up exploration, though they would of course take any grouse and suchlike for the pot if the opportunity presented itself. For the pony he would benefit from a good store of oats and some carrots, but it was expected he would find some grazing to tide him over when they rested, Sindri's constitution being more akin to a goat when compared to his lowland cousins.

Though Amaethon sagely advised that he expected the period of fine high-pressure weather to last, the nights would be below freezing at altitude and the ground solid with frost for much of the day, especially once out of the shelter of the valley itself, which also tended to act as a sink for warm air. Full winter garb would be loaded, along with tarpaulins, extra blankets, thick furs, oilskins and their sleep rolls. Sindri may be heavily loaded to start but they knew the main obstacle was progressing up and out of the valley; beyond that were fewer problematic inclines which would become easier as they ran down their heavy food-supplies. In previous discussions the group had reasoned that there must be sheltered areas or routes down to lower altitudes given that the goats lived in the area and seemed to thrive based upon the herds they had seen before, though they also knew goats were adept at negotiating sheer cliffs if needs be, that may be

167

impassable to them. Potentially though there may be other more sheltered refuges like theirs, or at least some areas of lower altitude which may provide for some respite if poor weather struck or they needed more food. Though preparations were all they could be, many felt a sense of trepidation about the trip, there would be some considerable risk with the various unknowns. However, the dangers of leaving an exposed border open to those they knew were roaming the countryside, at least further to the east, was deemed worth the risk. Concern was on everyone's faces as the trio made ready, though all knew they were extremely capable and fully prepared.

With plans set, Merrick, Arwyn and Sindri set out early the next morning, buoyant with a small parting-feast the night before and a hearty breakfast laid on by Nineveh and Shuldan, which should set them up nicely until supper. The air was clear and fresh and they made good time at a near trotting speed on the increasingly well-worn trails nearer the homestead, crossing the relatively-calm river by mid-morning. It was a glorious time of the year with the last of the autumn leaves falling from the trees, catching the light with warm russet colours as they did and crunching as they were crushed under foot. Just before mid-day they were already at the base of the western pass up the valley side and were relieved to see it was still virtually dry, far from the treacherous slippery-sheet of water that could coat the route with a change in the weather. They took it easy progressing up the pass, taking regular breaks but making excellent time with the pony's assistance as he tramped on at a solid pace. By the time they reached the ridge of the pass they were glistening with sweat and down to just a thin wool base-layer, panting slightly, bodies steaming and ready for a break. Finding a place out of the stiffening breeze they removed their heavy packs, peeled off their saturated base layers, and let their sweaty torsos quickly dry before piling fresh dry-layers back on. They had also divested Sindri of his burdens and covered him over in a blanket once he had stopped steaming, giving him a few oats and letting him rest after a good drink from a stream. Using their flint and steel, a bird's nest type bundle of desiccated grass and some of the scrubby heather that was abundant hereabouts, they got a small blaze going, allowing them to heat water for tea and to help them warm back-up after their exertions gaining a few thousand feet of altitude up the steep valley side. Taking in the vista before them they could just make out The Steading, and from this angle also had an excellent view of the waterfall at the head of the valley, up to the glaciated mountains in the far distance. Sipping their lemon balm tea, which was liberally laced with honey, and chewing on some travelling jerky, they spoke of plans for the remainder of the day, energised by the feel good-endorphins released by the strenuous climb. Though there was still a good hour or two of light, they really needed to locate a good sheltered-spot for the night and get set up. Their current location was exposed and ideally they needed to find a natural overhang or depression in a dry gulley to maximise the effectiveness of a fire overnight. The pair agreed that simply using the next hour to scout a good spot would be prudent so they finished their sweet tea, doused then scattered the fire remnants, packed up and started out due west.

They already knew the land was far from hospitable based upon their last exploratory trip this way, so were careful not to be too picky with their camp spot. Mounting the third ridge of the past hour they came to a wider gorge than those previously negotiated, really a small sheltered valley, noting a decent free-running stream at the bottom which would serve better than the more sluggish watercourses they had come across so far. Following this stream, they came to a small waterfall above which was a decent flattish area dotted with the odd large boulder, providing for some cover from the increasingly cold wind. On the sloping south-facing side of the valley there were some small stunted trees in amongst the heathers, including a few greyish bleached skeletal rowans and dwarf birches which would serve for firewood. They made their way to a particularly large boulder, easily twice their height, which provided a good screen on one side to which they could fix their tarpaulins by lodging the ties into cracks secured with wedges of wood. This would hopefully create a decent covered space with room for a fire and a spot for Sindri to hunker down near the entrance.

First they stowed their packs against the boulder and relieved the pony of his considerable load. They gave him a check over, particularly for any stones stuck in his hooves, and then a good brush down, first with handfuls of dried grass then with the stiff brush they had brought. Once satisfied Sindri was well they let him wander to drink his fill and find some forage, there being ample albeit stunted dried-grass hereabouts to keep him busy. The pony seen to, Merrick and Arwyn started to arrange their tarpaulins into a shelter using the boulder as one side and enclosing the other two, utilising their walking staffs and guy lines for supports. At the open end they formed a fireplace with a high back of hard angular rocks to reflect heat and to create a small windbreak. They then built-up other rocks around this to act as additional heat stores which would radiate heat back even as the fire cooled, essential with the quickly plunging temperatures. As always they were careful to avoid any rocks which may have been saturated with water, these being liable to shatter with the expanding effect of the sudden heat on excessive moisture.

Collecting and processing fire wood was the next chore, as it wouldn't be long before the light failed and it would be near pitch black until the moon rose later. There were several dead-standing trees hereabouts, and much was dry so snapping easily and splitting down to a bone-dry core using just their large knives, with judicious application of a weighty log as a baton. In just a half hour they had a good store of firewood which should see them through the night, stacked adjoining the fire so they wouldn't have to move far, and to allow it to dry further in the heat. Utilising bundles of oil-rich birch bark from the dead trees and scraping some dust from the resinous fat-wood they had brought along, they produced some sparks with their flint and steel and rapidly had an intense fire burning, ravenously consuming the dry wood and forming a decent bed of cooking coals in short order. They managed the fire by progressively moving the coals to one side, keeping the other half loaded up with a good stack of logs to produce more. That night they would cook a pair of thick venison steaks they had brought along out of the cold store, the meat well-hung so matured and tender. These they slapped straight onto some fresh coals, quickly searing the outside and sealing in the juices. To go with this they boiled up some of the dehydrated vegetables they had brought with them and toasted some flat bread, which was ready just as the steaks had been rested for a few minutes. With some of Shuldan's all-purpose spice mix the meal was superb, and savoured as they knew any further fresh meat was unlikely to be on the menu anytime soon, bar perhaps if they were lucky with a grouse or mountain hare. They had half-considered taking a goat from the herds they knew lived in the area, but it would be a hassle and a drain of time, unnecessary given their plentiful travelling rations.

With the sunlight now almost completely faded to a faint reddish glow and the temperature quickly plummeting, their pony returned, ate a small carrot handed to him by Arwyn and with the look of a satiated soul, hunkered down in the sheltered lee of the boulder, head tucked into his stomach facing the fire. Sindri's thick winter coat would keep him plenty warm, but he was now well-used to the company of his human masters and kept close to his surrogate herd. Though they would be up and ready to move by first light if possible, it was early yet, the winter sun setting quickly this time of year. Merrick and Arwyn

171

were perfectly comfortable in each other's presence, having no need for constant chat, content to enjoy each other's company, softly humming and singing, observing the stars and allowing themselves to be hypnotised by the fire as it danced and crackled into the night.

A frosty dawn came and they quickly had the fire coaxed fully back into life, having fed it through the night in shifts to keep them warm. Breakfast comprised flat bread, butter, cheese and some of the wonderful honey-glazed bacon Shuldan had recently cured. Washed down with copious amounts of piping hot sweet tea, the robust meal would set them up again for a full day's travel, with snacks of jerky, apples and suchlike to top up energy levels. They gave Sindri a few oats, though noting he had been at the grass already and had taken a good drink, sensing they were making ready for the off. Packing up the camp was a simple affair, leaving no trace as far as they could, burying the ashes and returning the rocks to where they had found them, original side up with the scorched sides beneath. It was obvious enough to a tracker where they had stayed the night, but it wouldn't be noticeable from any distance.

They spent the morning following the small valley to its head, providing them with an approximate desired line-of-travel to the west and gaining further altitude as they did. Near the top they veered up the northern side as it become more of a steep-sided gorge and mounted the more exposed ridge. As expected it led to one of many blind summits they knew they would encounter, but it was somewhat higher than many ridges thereabouts so gave them some perspective on the wider landscape, dotted here and there with patches of snow in shaded areas. As previously scouted earlier that year, they could see the numerous valleys and gullies which abounded hereabouts, most running approximately west to east from the upper reaches of the increasingly precipitous north-south ridge of high mountain peaks further west. The distant ridgeline was certainly far higher in altitude than any they had so far negotiated in their time at the valley, covered with significant accumulations of snow with a hint of what may be glaciers inexorably flowing down from the high passes to the south-west. It was though traversable terrain to at least the vicinity of the main ridge of peaks, but represented a more and more formidable barrier the further south you went. With a short discussion they agreed heading due-west was prudent to take a closer look at the main ridge, to make sure it was impassable and then to veer northwards where the situation was less clear, though the mountain ridge and peaks also looked daunting in that direction.

For that day and the next two they travelled at good pace to the west, gaining altitude steadily and mainly following ridge lines as they progressed, seeing little wildlife bar the odd white mottled hare, a flock of snow bunting and a covey of speckled ptarmigan. By now they were well beyond the limits of their previous slower exploratory journey, and once again were forming the view it was unlikely a way anyone would venture. The inhospitable landscape comprised a multitude of increasingly barren gulleys and ridges, with some limited hardy sedges in the wetter spots, stunted heathers and sparse lichens on the exposed bedrock, essentially an arctic tundra with increasingly larger patches of snow here and there. They could sense the increasing cold almost with every step they took, the ground becoming progressively more frozen, though thankfully the breeze stayed light and wind-chill was negligible, but still well below freezing at times. It was with thanks to their prudent foresight that they had brought their full winter furs, as they were sorely needed.

They were now as far west as they intended to go, right at the foot of the looming vast ridge of high peaks which thrust up-and-out of the more gullied landscape, covered with thick snow which started in earnest maybe just another few hundred feet up. Higher still the mountains were riddled with glaciers of increasing mass as the range rose to the south where they suspected it coalesced to form a near continuous ice cap. As they had suspected it was an impassable obstacle to even the most foolhardy. Seeing no reason to continue further in that direction their attention was turned to the north. From their vantage point on the higher foot of the mountain range they could see the landscape was essentially similar to that they had passed since leaving the valley, comprising gullies and ridges and a small valley every so often, stretching off into the far distance. Their travel plan and rations allowed for at least another two days in that direction, with enough for the return leg, but they could comfortably go further if circumstances dictated, more if they could harvest some meat.

Their journey northward was hastened by sticking to the base of the mountain range, which presented less of an undulating terrain, bar the odd frigid-river and various streams which needed to be crossed. It was at one of these streams, with their attention focussed on keeping as dry as possible, that they left the ravine cut by the watercourse and came up out upon a vista of a much lower plateau stretching off into the distance, still cut by numerous gulleys and gorges, but definitely more hospitable compared to the land thus travelled. Upon this more densely vegetated area they could see specks that were likely herds of the goats which had moved off the highlands for the winter in order to find better forage. In addition there were also loose herds of larger animals, at first sight thought to be deer, though the landscape was likely too harsh in deep winter for such beasts, unless of course they further migrated to lower altitude. As they progressed steeply down onto this plateau they felt a small but welcome warming of the air, perhaps simply a result of a reduction in the frigid breeze from the mountains, but welcome nonetheless. The land was far from verdant, but compared to the landscape they had recently travelled was lush with heathers, blaeberry, sedges, low tufts of dry grass, clumps of lichens and stunted trees, mainly isolated dwarf-birch. It wasn't long before they came upon the first of the long-haired goats who moved off with due caution, but were nonetheless inquisitive, like their now more domesticated brethren. As they continued across the plateau, they acquired a tail of goats following along behind, but whom eventually lost interest as the travellers continued on at a good pace. Their next encounter was with the larger beasts they had spotted previously, being much more wary and keeping a good distance. It was however plain to see that they were herds of reindeer, the first they had seen in this area. The lack of distinctive antlers this time of year no doubt added to their initial confusion as to misidentifying the animals as deer, though they could see the young males still had a small rack of antlers, persisting longer than their elders whom had shed theirs to regrow next summer. Their pelts tended to a whiter shade than the more lowland reindeer, or caribou as they were also known, who tended to inhabit some of the lower-altitude boreal forests, also being on the smaller side in the exposed uplands, but still impressive animals nonetheless. Of particular interest to Merrick and Arwyn were their rich pelts which provided for superbly-insulating clothes, the hairs being hollow which trapped air and heat very efficiently. Though they had no particular plan to hunt and gather furs, this was too good an opportunity to miss as a trip back out this far was unlikely to occur very often. The meat would also be welcome, they knew to be somewhat like the auroch, rich and lean, and less gamey than the deer they were used to.

Neither Merrick nor Arwyn had much experience of hunting the tundra type reindeer, so they decided it would be prudent to set up a camp nearby to enable them to watch the herd and decide on a plan of action. As they had walked the plateau they had already come across a couple of bigger ravines, some fairly dry and it was at one of these they decided to make camp, providing a spot out of the wind with good cover for observing the herd. The ravine was one which was wider than many with a small stream at its base, but which was well on its way to freezing solid. Setting-up camp was still a little awkward as there was little in the way of flat ground but they managed to find a small area where a slide of stones had slumped and formed a more or less level area. On this they set up camp, forming a base layer of springy heather to cushion and insulate them from the rocks, then setting their tarps to form one plough-point type configuration, low to the ground and opening downwind. Ideally they would have avoided a fire to avoid spooking the herd, but it was simply too cold so they selected the driest wood they could and kept it small to minimise the odour and smoke. They had already sorted out the pony who went off to explore the land above the gulley, clearly intrigued by the other animals hereabouts, but they knew Sindri would keep close by given their bond and the prospect of a carrot later that night.

Though they hadn't planned to bathe on the trip due to the cold, they did have to strip wash every now and then, hygiene being important to avoid uncomfortable skin rashes, potentially debilitating sores and suchlike. Before they lost the light they took it in turns to strip and used clean rags and soap to wash the worst of the grime from their bodies, then rinsed out their base layers, which would soon dry in the breeze hung up near the fire. As they did each evening, they swopped their socks over for spares before settling down into their sleeping rolls, hanging the thick garments in the apex of the shelter to dry and air. As with most of their clothes they were wool, very hard wearing and naturally antimicrobial, they did though need darning on occasion, hard-use wearing holes which needing patching up. Chores complete they settled down together and spoke of the hunt to come, discussing strategies and recalling the spoken lore of their ancestors that should assist. Though they fell asleep quick, excited anticipation caused them to wake every now and then through the night, but exhaustion from the past few days pushed them back into deep sleep and dreams of the herd before long.

The next day broke fresh and clear with a stiff breeze whistling above them on the open landscape. They had already made a brief recce and were pleased to see the reindeer had not moved far overnight, still within a mile or so, grazing on what must have been a good spot judging by their focus on the ground and normal proclivity to constantly wander in search of food. Merrick and Arwyn made a robust breakfast, heavy on the protein, and decided to spend that morning at least studying the herd, selecting one or two of the beasts to harvest, ideally those which represented the weakest of the herd so as not to impact negatively on its overall health. They left the pony to his own investigations of the area, squared away the camp and set off with light packs, making sure to mark the ravine at its head with a large cairn of stones so as not to lose track of where they had left their gear.

The morning progressed with the pair carefully stalking the herd, finding that with slow movements they could achieve a fairly close approach, albeit with expected wariness and some posturing by the larger males. They had made their final approach using one the many smaller gulleys hereabouts and had managed to stay out of sight, though one or two slight accidental-noises clearly had the large herd on guard. The approach was though with the wind in their favour, lightly blowing from the herd towards the hunters, avoiding spooking them with their odour. In the end they managed to get so close as to hear on the wind the odd faint but distinctive clicking the beasts made by way of the tendons slipping over bones in their legs, a communication tool used in whiteout conditions to minimise loss of heat via their mouths through vocalised calls. The animals were not the largest, being about four foot maximum at the shoulder, but were

177

still substantial beasts of about three hundred odd pounds. From this distance they could also see that the reindeer were feeding more often than not on the huge abundance of lichens which they knew was a favourite food, as well as the sedges and grasses. The blueberries were pretty much dormant that time of year, but come mid-summer there would be a profusion of the sweet fruit, much loved by the reindeer, the juice also known for its soothing medicinal effects with stomach upsets, though too many berries definitely had the opposite effect.

The hunters' position was near optimal and they now knew patience was key so they decided to hold where they were and hunker down, hoping the herd would progress further in their direction. This allowed them to observe the herd and they began to get a feel for its dynamics and habits. There was an older bull which looked to have seen the peak of its prime, perhaps just that last year, but seemed to be partially marginalised in favour of a more robust looking but clearly younger bull who appeared to hold general dominance over the herd. It may have been just that rutting season that this power balance had changed, but what was important was the clear shift of dominance from the old bull, who had reached the end of his leadership. He would make a great target animal, being out on the periphery of the herd, still the largest animal by some margin, with a very fine pelt, so they kept tabs on him for the next couple of hours, communicating by silent hand signals and moving only to stretch stiff muscles. Bar the herd they saw signs of other wildlife as they waited, including a hunting snowy-owl, an arctic-type fox moulting to white, a fly-over covey of ptarmigan and a number of mottled hares warily grazing. It spoke of a productive ecosystem, utilising what must have been many square hundreds of miles they had access to in these uplands, the vast majority of which they had but touched upon in their trip. They thought it likely there were apex predators they had not yet seen, wolves being very much suited to the terrain, but whom were very unlikely to show themselves unless they so wished.

It was after midday that saw the herd closer than ever to their hiding spot, with the big bull one of the closest animals to their position. By now the sun was also at a near optimum-angle being partially behind them and so providing for a degree of glare in the animal's eyes, which should help keep Merrick and Arwyn obscured unless the hunters broke cover and exposed their silhouette. The wind was also in their favour, having further picked up, blowing their odour and any noise away from the herd.

As they sat and watched, the old bull came closer still, some thirty yards from their position and then kept up a route parallel with the gulley; it seemed a closer approach was unlikely, aware as it was to the spot as a position a predator could lie in ambush. Clearly though what the animal hadn't reckoned with was the ingenuity of humans and a ranged weapon like the bow, the herd not likely having encountered any such foe in perhaps many years. Merrick and Arwyn already had their bows strung and knocked their best arrows, heated and straightened over the fire that morning. Their robust hazel shafts were tipped with a fine cross-tipped broadhead, fresh from Bolin's forge and already proven to be deadly effective against deer in the valley. As they made ready the old bull kept up his parallel track with the gulley and was almost opposite their position, the soft click of his tendons now indicating his position without direct line of sight. With a look at each other, pupils blown-wide with shots of adrenaline coursing through their veins, they nodded to each other and stood, drawing their powerful flat bows of ash as they did.

With practiced fluid motion both let fly their arrows as soon as their torsos cleared the top of the gulley ridge. Though seemingly in slow motion, they saw their arrows quiver in the air as they left the bow and noted the startled look of the animal as the arrows approached and in quick succession both thunked into its belly and vital organs, then passed from sight as they buried themselves into the beast. The animal jerkily moved away from them for just a few yards, with its brain soon registering the clean killing-blows and allowing it to fall to its side with just a few final twitches. In that brief few seconds the rest of the herd had taken off, nosily cantering away into the far distance.

The hunters approached and took the time to bow their heads and thank the beast for providing them with its fine pelt and meat. Their first impression was at the impressive size of the bull, a good third bigger than the smallest of the herd and magnificent even past its prime. Ensuring the kill was clean and final they positioned its chest slightly downhill, opened some veins and let its blood pour into the ground, pumping its chest to ensure it fully drained. Their main purpose in the kill was the pelt so they took care in ensuring this was skilfully skinned without haste. The skin was then washed and quickly scraped in a nearby stream, then folded in on itself and lashed to the pony who had already instinctively made his way to them. They then butchered the animal, taking the best cuts of meat, leaving the lower legs, ribs and head for the lucky scavengers. This still left them with a good amount of prime meat which could keep for many days in the near freezing air temperatures after cooling and cleaning. They would however take their time to preserve most of what they had taken, knowing this would allow them many more days to explore.

They used the pony Sindri to bring the meat back to the camp then went about collecting as much wood as they could, including whatever they might find that was soft and punky. Their aim was to smoke the meat for a good twenty hours for the rest of the day and overnight, reducing moisture, killing bacteria and so ensuring it would last perhaps a good week at least. At the same time, they cut up some thin strips to make some jerky while putting the sectioned haunch onto spits. It was a huge amount of meat but would provide them with meals for the remainder of the trip, extending their time out to perhaps two weeks if needs be, while eating like kings. Even then there may be enough to take back to The Steading, presuming it didn't spoil, though the cold weather should help avoid that. The skin was the prize and so they made sure that this was de-fleshed as much as they could, then hung it to dry and partially freeze overnight in the brisk wind at the top of the ravine. By morning it would be stiff but could still be folded and then allowed to cool to below-freezing temperature, halting the work of the organisms in the decomposition process.

Neither of the hunters slept much that night in making sure the jerky slowly cooked and dried and that the precious skin remained secure on the ridge of the ravine, strung onto the improvised frame they had created. As they spent the night tending to the meat, as it slowly smoked, they managed to create a rough circular stone-wall, concentrating the smoke and screening the worst of the wind that reached them at the bottom of the ravine. Around the hollow cairn they wrapped the oldest of the tarps, so further concentrating the smoke; it wouldn't do the tarp any harm so long as it didn't get too hot, the smoky oil-rich residue of the silver birch adding to its water repellency in any event. As they tended to the meat, they ate slices of the haunch while it slowly roasted and fried off the heart in some fatty pemican, gorging until their bellies were bloated. It was fortunate really that the night air was so cold as it kept them awake till morning, the delicious feast would otherwise have quickly sent them off into a deep sleep.

Come midnight, the smoker pretty much looking after itself, the deep black of the moonless night revealed an unusually clear sky, filled with stars and flashes of meteors, the broad sweep of the Milky Way particularly prominent and glorious. Then with just an initial faint hint of wispy green, they detected to the far horizon a blur of the Northern Lights, building in intensity and eventually creating great swirls of luminous greens, pinks and hints of red. It was a sight they seldom saw; more common they knew in the far north upon the true permafrost-ridden tundra and ice cap beyond. Being so high and cold the atmosphere was incredibly clear and so it was by far the best display either of the couple had been lucky enough to experience, the odd wisp of green on the far horizon the most they had witnessed before. The incredible display continued for nearly an hour, much longer than any they had ever heard of, the lights dancing across the sky in surges and swirls, almost above them at times. Otherworldly in its silence and power, the couple watched in rapt amazement, feeling fortunate indeed to be alive to see such a wondrous display of nature.

As the light of the new day eventually broke and the morning advanced, they took it in turns to get a few hours decent sleep, the majority of the makeshift preservation process done. They were pleased at the extent to which the meat had been impregnated by smoke, thoroughly crusting the surface and penetrating the flesh to about a quarter inch. The jerky was near perfect, dehydrated but still quite soft and great for ensuring it was fine to eat for a week at least without being as jaw breaking as some of the hard tack jerky they sometimes produced, which may last for many months but nearly broke your jaw unless you slowly masticated on it for what seemed like an age.

Once they had broken-down camp, stowed away the now stiff pelt and loaded the preserved meat onto Sindri, they set off to cover more of the plateau. Though the landscape might seem endless and progress slow, they covered nearly twenty-five miles that day, following the line of the mountains to the north-west. It was a beautiful place to be in its own unique way, stark, rugged and inhospitable to mere humans, but all the same the light particularly was incredible, clouds creating huge shadows and permitting sporadic shafts of light which lit up the plateau in great glowing-pools. It made you feel alive and in connection with nature, the smoother surface allowing their eyes to be taken off the ground in front of them in a way that the rocky tundra didn't allow. It would have been a much less pleasant experience in the spring and autumn, the ground sodden and the air thick with endless insects, but the early winter cold thankfully kept these to a minimum.

Before they had even started thinking about making camp they found they had reached the sudden edge of the plateau, essentially a sheer drop-off bounded by cliffs and craggy mountains to the immediate west. It might perhaps have once been the route of a glacier, but had long-since eroded-back the land, presumably forming a huge cascading waterfall as it melted. There remained a few small hanging-waterfalls created by little streams cutting into the thin soil, which occasionally blew back up into arcs of spray as the wind picked up, often forming little rainbows as it did. Below the dried-up falls some thousand feet or so below were great dense pine-woods leading sharply down to a steep-sided fjord many miles away, presumably once the outlet for the vast falls. It was without doubt a foreboding obstacle and bar perhaps perilously scaling the sharp mountainous ridge to the west, could not be passed by anyone sane at this point.

Despite the somewhat stomach-churning vertigo caused by the drop, it was a thoroughly impressive view and they spent the next hour sat simply admiring the splendour of the panorama, catching distant hints of the sparkling sea in the far distance. The fjord particularly was hugely impressive, its steep sides of pillar-like basalt plunging into the vivid blue-green water from its jagged peaks. The day was however wearing on and they could not linger in the exposed spot to camp, so very reluctantly, they pulled themselves away and moved to the north-east following the wide expanse of the former waterfall. Reaching the far side after about half an hour the ground rose sharply to exposed bedrock and a new range of peaks, with their steep impassable-sides dropping down to the pine woods and eventually the fjord. The area was much rockier with only sparse vegetation in comparison to the plateau, marking a return to the more arctic tundra-like upland of the area to the south as the ground rose. There were however a few relatively sheltered corries or armchair-like depressions in the rear of the peaks comprising the rising spine of the boundary down to the fjord, and it was within one of these they found a flat area out of the northerly wind and set up for the night. It was a cold camp with only minimal vegetation to burn which only really sufficed to boil some water, but wrapped up in all their furs and huddled together out of the wind under their low slung tarp, it was merely a little uncomfortable, rather than being any threat to their lives.

Over this unforgiving landscape bristling with harsh jagged-bedrock they travelled to the north-east for another long day, but were halted on reaching an abrupt ridge of bleak-peaks ponderously curving round, running to the east then turning back south in the distance. In a gap between two high peaks they progressed as far north as they could and met a sheer drop formed of high cliffs running roughly to the east and west. From there they could just see hints of the sea on the far horizon and the river Rhuø leading to it across the wide flat plains. The drop below them fell sharply to vast conifer-strewn slopes high above the plains, the stunted trees dotted amongst the base of the cliffs between the multitude of colossal blocky fallen rocks and huge splays of scree. There were some smaller chains of hills running off to the north, but nothing which provided access up to the high ridge on which they now stood. It was a bitter and very exposed position to remain but they made an inspection as best they could from their high vantage point but quickly became satisfied that the near vertical cliffs contained no route up. Moving away from this exposed edge they spent another night in a far from ideal spot, tucked underneath the overhang of a cantilevered rock, cold, but well fed from their extensive supplies.

Making a start well before dawn they travelled to the east for about a half day, though progress was slow over the unforgiving terrain. It was here they met the western edge of the very top-end of their valley, which they knew to be impassable, except for the pass to the far south. From this high vantage point, they could just make out where The Steading laid to the south-east, discernible just as a cleared patch in the forest. At a rough guess it was only twenty some or so miles as the crow flies, but out of reach nonetheless. It was a bittersweet moment as they knew they had a good deal of travel left, south, then back north once down into the valley. It was at least welcome to note that if they could find no way down, neither could any other.

With another two days hard and convoluted travel to the south, they reached the pass that led down to their valley, just as the sun was setting, with no little relief as the way had been hard, and better left forgotten. Seeing no reason to do otherwise they camped out in the same spot they had previously, welcoming the more plentiful supplies of dry wood which would keep them warm that night. They rested that evening considering their arduous journey, essentially some hundred and seventy odd miles or so covered in a vast meandering-loop, but they reflected on the welcome fact that their perimeter was as secure as could reasonably be hoped for. It was also welcome that there was the possibility they may one day mount a hunting expedition to seek out the reindeer to harvest their pelts and meat. They calculated that it may only be thirty miles in a straight line to edge of the lower plateau; with a decent semi-permanent camp to harvest and process a number of pelts, it would be well worth the journey with the aid of the hardy ponies.

They awoke early the next morning to a thin layer of fresh snow, crunchy underfoot and indicative of plunging temperatures on its way. They spent the morning carefully picking their way down the pass, thankfully still dry, but there were still a few hairy moments as they descended past the thin snow-line into icy slush. Sindri was however as sure-footed as always and helped provide them with an anchor as he zig-zagged down, avoiding any mishaps. From the base of the pass they relished the relative warmth, and once they had stripped off some layers and stowed them away, they made ready for a brisk trot back down the valley to The Steading. As they travelled the increasingly well-worn paths they marvelled at the forest, almost a little claustrophobic after so long in the open expanse of the upland tundra, but still very glad to be home.

It was towards dusk that they arrived back at The Steading, being welcomed by the dogs once their initial wariness had eased as they realised who had returned. Everyone was elated to see them, most a little worried about their now extended trip, though knowing it was a possibility when they left. Merrick and Arwyn made presents of the exotic reindeer meat, a treat for the kids with the still-soft jerky, a very different flavour and a novelty. The remaining hunks of reindeer meat were unloaded, a little frozen but soon were being chopped up for vast pots of stew and a small roasting-joint set by the fire in the main hall.

As they sat in comfortable chairs that night, following a good scrub and a welcome change into fresh clothes, they recounted their tale and showed them the fine reindeer pelt, stiff as it was frozen still, but clearly it would make some wonderfully warm clothing. As they finished up their tale all were satisfied that there would almost certainly be no unexpected surprises from the west, a great feeling of security knowing the difficult northern valley entrance was the only way into the valley.

Merrick and Arwyn were unsurprisingly exhausted from their trip and with the unaccustomed warmth of the hall and the comfort of the cushioned chairs, they soon dozed off, contented light snores accompanying the soft conversation of the rest of the group. They let them slumber, happy to have them back and spoke of their admiration for the pair, knowing that the trip would have been incredibly strenuous, though they wouldn't admit any such hardship. They later gently woke the pair who were groggily led to their beds where they laid down and quickly fell still, bundled up in their fresh bedding, heads sinking into their soft feather pillows, content and soon falling into the deepest of sleeps.

23 - Deep winter

As they approached mid-winter the frost was their near-constant companion, the days all too short. The winter thrushes had now arrived in force, including massive flocks of 'seeping' redwings and nosily 'tsaking' fieldfares which took to stripping berries from the innumerable rowans, service trees and hawthorns that filled the steep valley sides, the narrow zone of ffridd habitat between the uplands proper and the ancient woodlands below. It was a beautiful time in its own stark way, the hoar frosts particularly stunning when they coated every surface in sparkling crystals of ice, jewel-like in the weak winter-sun. Increasingly though this meant there was little left to forage for their animals so they stabled them and retreated to the house, venturing out less and less, reflecting the habits of many animals ready for hibernation. Their stores had however been further supplemented by trapping and hunting and were full to bursting, so they did not range far unless there was specific need.

On a particularly bone-chilling day, quiet but for the occasional metallic rhythmic-clang of Bolin's forge, there came the first substantial snows. Gentle at first but soon covering the land in amorphous white and drifting in the wind. This was no winter storm as they had first encountered on arriving at the valley, but it did mean that travel was now less simple, with snowshoes a permanent fixture in the porch. It was however an ideal time to teach the children the way of winter subsistence, so Merrick proposed to take them camping to absorb the ways of survival and cold-weather hunting.

Sioned would have been the ideal companion on this trip but her pregnancy was now very advanced and likely due any time soon. It was really best to get the children out of The Steading, to give her some peace and to stop them getting underfoot when the day of birthing came. Sioned had created a private space in the smallest of the bedrooms that she and Shulvan would now use. It was in the quietest part of the house, furnished with a wicker cradle and large double-bed freshly finished and wonderfully carved. The children had been put into a new room, with their sleeping pallets made into cabin-type bunkbeds, with simple woven-wool curtains, blankets and new feather-pillows giving them their own cosy space; they were all old enough now to want a little privacy.

Merrick could not hope to properly manage the group of children on his own without unnecessary risk, though they were all competent from about five years old in the ways of camp, and could carry fair loads; he would need another adult to assist. Bolin was perhaps a surprising choice, but they all thought it would do him good to get away from his precious forge, which he hardly left it sometimes seemed. Merrick knew that Bolin had been teaching some of the children the ways of the forge, and behind his gruff exterior he had a special place in his heart for them all and so agreed, though with seeming reluctance that was akin to asking him to destroy a less favoured hammer.

The children were a motley crew, many being orphans they had found on their travels, though all considered old enough to assume various jobs of the homestead. Bolin's fledgling apprentice was a quiet and wiry older girl named Aderyn, though she much preferred Eryn. She was perhaps to some a surprising choice given her diminutive stature and somewhat shy demeanour, but she had stamina beyond her years, recently honed by hours pumping the bellows and hammering on the anvil. As it was with Bolin, Eryn hated leaving the forge; she had grown accustomed to spending her days learning to the exclusion of all else, but had sense to know that the lessons could continue, with the spoken lore of the blacksmith as important as smashing hammer to glowing metal.

Merrick was a favourite of the children; he had a playful side that delighted them with games and silly riddles, a wry smile not often far from his lips. Being a leader meant he sometimes had to chastise, but he did so in a quiet way that left you feeling disappointed with yourself rather than generating any fear. He found it very hard though to be upset with the spirited children for long and it was often left to Arwyn to deal with some matters, her calm and even temperament being better-suited to more complex problems.

Merrick and Arwyn were a couple, but they had never formally made their relationship one of marriage, that being unusual in these times when things were more fluid and less formal. Like many adults they had tried to have a child, but it was not to be. As a consequence of fewer babies there tended to be less lifelong-bonding of couples for the sake of the children and so relationships tended to form and reform, it being entirely unremarkable to change partners. It was not altogether clear why so few children were born, those that were carried to full term not normally surviving more than a few hours. In any relationship most saw it as a duty to at least try until their fertility had been verified either way, even if this temporarily meant another partner in the equation. It was desperately sad that children were so scarce and often died so young, and was why Sioned's pregnancy was seldom directly discussed, but the hope was there in everyone's' thoughts. Arwyn however was a confidant to Sioned, being one of those people who rarely said any more than was needed, being dependable, intelligent and a rare beauty in a stark unorthodox way. She was always in the background, making occasional small suggestions, observing, coaxing and binding the group together, rarely bossy except when circumstances warranted. Arwyn may in other circumstances have joined them on the trip, but she felt she could be useful in the coming days to support Sioned, whichever way it turned out.

The expedition would number seven with the adults included, the children ranging from eight to Eryn's near seventeen summers. Eryn hated sometimes being lumped in with the children, but she would very soon come of age and then be considered an adult proper, though it was really an arbitrary milestone of pure tradition. All of the group were more than competent in the ways of the woods, though it was with some trepidation that their parents let some of them go, albeit that they would never be many miles away. Although most of the children were adopted, they were an intrinsic and accepted part of the extended family group looked-after by all, and fiercely treasured for the rare gift they were in this era.

Preparations were soon underway, the children keen to get out of the house after being cooped-up and excited to go on an adventure with Merrick. Eryn was happy to be out with her master to learn his lore, and quietly glad to give her aching muscles a break from Bolin's tireless instruction, as much as she relished the work.

Merrick hoped that he would teach the children some advanced winter trapping and hunting skills, though they were more than capable in easier times, they had to be prepared for the long winter as well. Crafting of life-saving emergency snow shelters, building of long-log fires and all the many other winter skills would form the foundation for their potential survival if there came a need.

They all had effective snowshoes, made to measure, being flexible yet tough. These were a great improvement on the temporary affairs they had used on their initial arrival at the valley, the upgrades being formed of steam-bent ash, cross webbed in cords of rawhide with custom toe-holds for their boots, then bound and buckled in strong thick leather of the aurochs, beautifully supple from its prolonged tanning in a tannic acid-rich oak-bark solution for several weeks. For the winter they had already substantially upgraded their cold weather gear with the fine but

191

fantastically-insulating wool of the long-haired goats, having a superb combination of long outer-hairs and thick soft-hairs close to their skin. It could be used for knitting with minimal spinning, which left it relatively soft and a brilliant insulator, but tough once it bound together. This wool also gave them new felt-liners for their boots, along with under garments of thin but sweat-wicking long-johns and mid-layers. Over these were layered soft but wind and water-resistant waxed buckskins, forming pliable but tough trousers and jerkins. Their fur-lined overcoats were similarly made, though these were only really needed when they stopped for extra warmth. The thick woollen-jumpers of sheep's wool they had brought with them from before their time in the valley were still serviceable, being heavily darned and patched but essential in the deep cold. The largest of the youngsters had new jumpers of goat's wool, with theirs progressively handed down as the children rapidly grew, nothing wasted and constantly repaired, the oldest jumpers being painstakingly unpicked and re-spun to form new. Hats, various gloves and mittens completed the main gear, again layered to help cope with changing conditions and activity levels, excess sweat and damp clothes surprisingly being among the biggest of issues when it came to heat loss. Wool was their friend in this respect, managing to keep them warm even when fairly saturated with sweat and great for wicking-away moisture.

The soft brain-tanned hides taken from the deer would provide bedrolls and extra covers, with their dense winter-hair providing for excellent insulation against the cold ground, tightly woven wool ponchos also acting as their bedding blankets to trap warm air. Between them they took enough tarpaulin to form two large tents, of stretched waterproofed leather hides stitched together. A frame would need to be fashioned to hang this, made from cut greenwood-poles, but their staffs would provide the majority of the structure if needed. The front of these shelters was designed to be left partially-open for the winter, the principle being to allow the radiant heat from a special long-log fire to keep them warm through the night.

Weapons and tools were the next items to be made ready. All of the children were skilled in the use of their slings, but they also now had their freshly-made bows which they constantly practiced with, mainly taking smaller game such as squirrels and larger birds. They would however be concentrating on trapping skills this trip so left their bows, with some reluctance, in preference to the easily-packable slings. Knives were a necessity and children had these from a very young age, being no strangers to gutting carcasses and meat preparation. Their knives had tended to be multipurpose 'jack of all trades', but Bolin had since created a range for specialised jobs. They all had a general purpose solid full-tang knife, capable of being used to baton thick wood for the fire, but which could also be used for the finer processing of carcasses or woodcarving. The blacksmith had now supplied them all with specialised knifes, being thinner, with a flat grind rather than the multi-purpose robust scandi-grinds of their main everyday knives. These would be better for finer work of skinning, but still capable of gralloching and processing the carcass. The new knives also had natural-antler handles to avoid slipping, with great grip superior to that of wood provided by the ridged and bumpy form of the unworked material. They were mounted in strong hard-wearing leather sheaths, decorated in simple scrollwork, hung from their necks. These knives should, with care, last them into adulthood and beyond. In addition to these knives, they tended to carry at least one flint-scraper in their belt pouches, ideal for de-fleshing hides and pelts, also good as a back-up striker for creating sparks with their steel knife in a pinch.

The kit that would be required on the trip would be quite considerable, and they intended to over-pack for the sake of safety. Rather than load everything onto their backs, they would take a pulk, essentially a long sled pulled along with them, mainly constructed of birch, which was in itself very lightweight, with long waxed-runners for longevity and decreased friction. Though functional it was a handsome piece of equipment, light carvings adorning the curved front pieces to resemble a pair of mythical dragon-like beasts. In addition to the plentiful food and consumables, it would mean if they took any large game, any meat they didn't eat while out, could be brought back home. Despite taking the pulk, they were careful to ensure the essentials were also about their person in on-belt pouches, for fire lighting and emergency rations. Less critical kit was in their bentwood-framed packs, with the remainder on the pulk. Though the trip was unlikely to be hazardous Merrick always drilled it into the children that preparing for the worst was best until it became second nature.

With various trail-food packed including nuts, dried meat and emergency pemmican, along with numerous special treats provided by Nineveh secreted away, they made ready for an early start. The children were excited, but serious in their own way, eager to get going on what was seen as a great adventure.

They took it slow to begin with, conscious they had some way to go to the area intended for their camp near the head of the valley, normally taking most of the day. The children were fairly used to snowshoes, but there was a difference when hiking in them for some miles, different types of snow also necessitating different technique. When snow was particularly powdery, in extreme cold, it more or less sieved straight through the snowshoes, rendering them much less effective and a chore to use. Merrick and Bolin took it in turns to demonstrate the knack, essentially with exaggerated movement and keeping legs apart to a degree, feeling quite unnatural to start. Each of the party had with them two stout-staffs on this journey, acting a little bit like ski-poles. Skis were in theory a mode of travel they could use, but the valley tended to boulder-strewn ground and fallen trunks, so weren't ideal until the snow got pretty thick and compacted. Initially the adults and Eryn took turns to pull the pulk sled using padded harnesses, but they encouraged the children to have a go, two at a time. They did manage, but in fairness it was cumbersome due to its bulk and they ideally needed made-to-measure harnesses, though on the way back, with reduced weight and being downhill, it would be easier.

With Bolin making light work of trail blazing, they trekked slowly in each other's trail, progressively compacting down the snow, making the way easier, initially over the home pastures, then through the woods. The group then followed the river up the valley, though mostly now frozen and partially snowed over; it could be heard in the relative stillness, tinkling and faintly rumbling beneath the entombing ice. They continued up the valley for some miles, and with a likely place in mind, crossed where an ice-bridge had formed over what was normally rapids. Given that the glaciers were accumulating this time of year, the water level was much lower, and easily passable where the river was strewn with exposed boulders and choked up with debris and now solid ice. Here was an opportune moment to discuss the effects of hypothermia and cold water immersion. It was stressed by Merrick that the young and old were especially susceptible to the cold, given their propensity to lose heat more quickly from the core, with less thermal mass and fat reserves. A buddy system was adopted to look out for signs of early hypothermia, including loss of fine motor-function, shivering, blueness in the lips, confusion and general lethargy. At the same time all were reminded to check themselves and their buddies for frostnip and more serious frostbite at regular intervals, as it was not always obvious but treatable if caught early enough. Key was their feet which should never feel completely numb, that indicating potential freezing of the flesh, resulting in classic blackening and need for possible amputation to stave off gangrene. It was drilled into the young

195

ones that early detection was paramount, but to always raise the alarm with the group, to ensure the affected person was warmed, but slowly, to avoid shock. They would later show them the art of fire lighting in the snow and emergency shelter making which might one day save their lives.

They kept up a better pace now the children were adapting to the cumbersome snow shoes, and all started to develop a steady, though somewhat ungainly rhythm. Through the course of the day the group gained altitude up the valley and started to come to a thinning of the woods. Merrick wanted them to have an easier first night, so they made their base camp there, where they would still have plenty of wood for fires, but with easy access to the deeper snow to practice making shelters. The site they ultimately selected sat in the lee of a series of holly bushes, which helped cut down on the wind with their dense waxy-foliage.

Tonight, they would set up their waxed-leather tarps, but first they cut down stout greenwood poles and lashed them together to form two basic A-frames with a pole across the apex. The tents had three sides with some overhang to the front, but otherwise open to allow the warmth of the fire to penetrate and reflect around the shelter. With little fuss they had the shelters set up opposite each other and were then processing medium-sized seasoned trunks for the fire. The technique was to create long-log fires of seasoned hardwood, two trunks resting on the ground by digging away the snow if possible. Onto these two logs they filled the crevice with stacks of kindling and thick branches on top, the third log left to one side to add on, once it was well underway. Built in this fashion the fire should last most of the night, with only minimal attention. With the two shelters set-up and the fire ready to go, they all took the opportunity to practice their fire-lighting skills. On route the children had collected various bracket-type fungi,

196

including the birch polypore of which the inner could be usefully used for plasters for small cuts, or also as a strop for sharpening their knives, always useful to have in their belt pouches. Other useful fungi collected included the horse hoof variety for fire-lighting found on beech and birch trees, best collected from under sheltered overhanging-branches or similar so they were as dry as possible and not starting to rot. These they harvested for processing down at camp to get at the dry central-core which was made into strips, roughed up with their knife edge to form a fluffy nest then kept in a warm pocket to dry further and to avoid any moisture in the air allowing damp to be absorbed. Into this they could later throw sparks from their flint and steel, creating the ignition source for the fire. The children were all aware of this method and the alternative combination of iron pyrites and flint, but those were seldom used and much more difficult in the snow. Normally they would use the much simpler King Alfred's cake fungus from their dry tinder-bundles, typically found on fallen ash-trees hereabouts, best thoroughly dried, but it was good to have practice with alternatives. Once they all had this achieved in a capable fashion, they added the glowing embers to piles of oil-rich scraped birch-bark, which soon leapt into a bright flame with a coaxing series of firm but controlled blows and by adding lumps of pine resin. This they quickly laid onto a brace of dry split-logs and first added fine birch-twigs and long curled feathersticks, then some thinner split branches from the ancient gnarled-pines that dotted the upper reaches of the valley, their pungent resin-impregnated wood soon catching despite the deep cold. Adding onto this blazing pile they stacked chopped logs with their exposed dry-core and soon had a decent blaze. Once this was established, they added the final third long-log atop, with a gap created with cross-laid branches to allow the oxygen to get in. Bolin would teach them tomorrow the way of the bow drill to create an ember by friction alone, as it was a hard skill to master, especially in the cold, but important if flint and steel or iron pyrites were not an option. They were very conscious that flint particularly was not common in this area so needed to be conserved, but potentially may be found closer to the coast on the lowlands.

Though the dark came early this time of year there was still ample daylight left so they set off in two groups to scout the area and lay snares, which should potentially yield hares and perhaps willow grouse, otherwise almost invisible in their white winter-coats. The snares were set in various locations where there seemed to be established game-trails, though often faint and intermittent in the wind-blown snow. The children were taught about the subtle gaps in vegetation known as smeuses and the more obvious lines of travel know as snickets, some eyes being better at picking these up, little Seren especially, but all more than capable. All were proficient in setting snares, just less-so in the winter which required a particular knack. Often these tracks would be accompanied by hairs caught up in briars and subtle prints which could be examined to give an indication of particular animals present. The snares were made of thin sinew and finely-woven plant fibres, some static and placed across the snickets and smeuses, with others of a more ingenious type utilising a clever highly-sensitive trigger formed of a bent sapling under tension which would spring-up tightening the noose of the snare and hopefully trapping the animal as it passed. A benefit of these traps was the raising of the trapped animal up off the ground avoiding the prize being snatched by a hungry fox. These traps were perhaps more effective in the summer with the saplings being less prone to snapping in the cold, but it was possible to achieve if temperatures hadn't dipped too low. Bolin was considered a decent trapper, though Merrick was the acknowledged expert and well on the way to making a fine winter fur-coat from the pelts harvested so far. They set a large number of these snares, the children taking the lead and soon getting the idea, despite a fair few triggers accidently, or perhaps otherwise, set off to their great delight.

Though they had plenty of food to make their late afternoon meal, Merrick wanted to take advantage of the last hour or so of fading daylight to see if they could get some fresh meat. Leaving behind two to watch the long fire and split more wood, the remainder of the party divided-up and they created a line of beaters, to scare up whatever grouse and hares that might be about above the treeline. The beaters drove any animals they found to the other team armed with slings, who were downslope and had hidden themselves as best they could. This initially only put up one willow grouse which flew off at an angle too difficult to hit, but as the evening was starting to come to a close, they located a small covey of the birds which flew up and were hit in quick succession by the hunters, resulting in three good-sized birds for the pot. These would nicely supplement their meal and were quickly plucked of their feathers, the skin broken and the chest meat removed with their thumbs slid up the breast bone. The wings were then twisted off and the remains of the carcasses given to the dogs, but resulting in a decent amount of fine breast meat. They took the meat back to camp and busied themselves lightly seasoning each breast with salt and herbs, then wrapped them in some of the cured boar-bacon they had taken from the cold store back at base. As Merrick explained, the key with grouse was to cook them briefly to keep them tender, browning them off first, ideally with a little butter. They had a frying pan with them, but to show them another method, he found a suitable flat rock, taking care to ensure it wasn't full of moisture. Rock cooking was a little hazardous if the slab was saturated with water as it could crack with some explosive force, so care was exercised. The flat slab needed to be warmed first by the fire, then heated slowly, reducing the chance of cracking. Once it was hot and sizzling with a little fat, it was ready for cooking on. Within fifteen minutes of adding the bacon-wrapped breasts to the scorching stone, they were cooked to perfection, the bacon crunchy and the grouse tender and most. Accompanied by acorn-flour bannock bread with dried fruit, it made for a fine first course of the evening.

With the grouse polished off they started prep of the first of the trip's stews that would form a hearty late supper, adding plenty of herbs and lard to the pot with some cubed venison to brown off, then allowing it to simmer in plenty of water. Later they added some potatoes, onions, carrots and some salt; this was allowed to cook slowly, resulting in tender meat and a lovely rich gravy which would help warm them through, keeping them in energy for the long night ahead. While they were waiting Merrick took out some lengths of woody elderflower shoots about a hand-width's long, and started showing the children how to form some basic whistles. These were simple but fun to make, the pith being soft and easily hollowed out, with the knack being the carving of the upper air notch and the fitting of a small plug with a tiny gap on the mouthpiece, to create the high pitched sound. After a few attempts most of the kids had functional whistles, though the adults quickly started to regret the lesson with the resulting cacophony of discordant noise; still though they would make excellent distress whistles if nothing else.

Earlier on, while cutting the tent poles and fire wood, they had gathered a pile of feathery pine boughs which they had shaken loose of snow and stacked to one side. Before the last of the light fled they stacked these in their shelters, forming a thick insulating layer onto which their bedrolls, hides and blankets could lie. Before turning in they would first re-check their feet for any early signs of frostnip then hang any damp clothes and their boot liners from the internal ridge of the tent, the small apex at the top trapping considerable heat once the front overhanging flap had been partially lowered. At night they would wear their spare woollens and rotate them as needed to dry, any moisture otherwise being a chilling heat sink. The adults and Eryn would take it in turns through the night keeping an eye on the fire and building it up as needed, but generally the long-log style should keep going for most of the night with minimal attention. On rotation of shifts they would greet each other with steaming pine-needle tea dosed with honey, with the last of the shift making a start on an early breakfast for first light.

It wasn't long before most retired to bed for the night, tired, though excited. For some the journey had been hard, unused as they were to trekking for miles in the snow with cumbersome snow shoes and dragging the pulk. To help them settle Bolin told them stories of brave adventurers and heroes of ages past, and soon they were all more or less asleep, exhausted but happy wrapped up warm in their furs. Eryn then managed to get Bolin to herself to discuss smithing, and they did so until late into the night.

Merrick woke first the next morning, and was glad to see that Bolin on last watch had gotten the kettle boiled and tea made. The remnants of last night's stew had been bulked out and the frying pan was on the go with the honey cured bacon making a wonderful smell, which rapidly woke all the others. Merrick made the morning bread, essentially thin flatbreads cooked on a rock by the fire, but with dried fruit for sweetness and calories. Breakfast was devoured in short order and they all made ready for the day, rotating into dry woollens and adding extra layers to stave off the cold. The first job was to check the snares, and they were pleased to find a brace of hares and a plump grouse in the traps. These were quickly dispatched, where still alive, and prepared for their later meals. The grouse would do to bulk out lunch and the hares would make an excellent hearty stew for later with some additional venison. Given the cold all they needed to do was to string them up in a bag in the trees, to discourage any theft by larger predators, not that many were likely to be about, most being in hibernation and not otherwise seen in the valley so far.

The main aim of the day was teaching the kids advanced survival techniques, of snow shelters and cold weather bow drill fire lighting. The youngsters were split into two groups, with Bolin to teach the bow drill, and Merrick the art of the snow shelter, swopping at about mid-day. It was quite amusing watching the kids trying to split themselves up, most wanting to go and play making shelters rather than the hard work they knew the bow-drill could be, but in short order Eryn had them sorted out, wryly separating the known mischief makers.

The snow shelters would be initially formed of a mound of piled-up snow, the top layer to be tamped down to create a more compact layer. This was then left to harden in the deep cold while they hunted again and collected more firewood, keeping moving to stay warm. On returning they began to hollow-out the mounded structure from two sides, meeting in the middle, then blocking one up. This was completed with a ventilation hole and a small candle placed in an alcove in the side wall. Merrick explained that the major problem with this type of shelter was the build-up of bad air which could make them groggy and was possibly fatal if missed. This could be avoided with a small beeswax candle being lit, which if it started to flicker and gutter would indicate the need to reopen a possibly snowed-over ventilation hole or add another. Perhaps surprisingly the combination of the candle and body heat could add a fair few degrees of warmth to the air inside the structure, the difference between life and death in a survival scenario. Merrick also highlighted how the shelter deadened sound, and that it was possible to miss a storm building-up snow and burying them, so it required constant vigilance. He also demonstrated a similar principle on the mountain side with a snow-cave configuration, though he recommended the quinze hollowed-mound, if there was a choice, as there was less chance of snow slipping on the valley bottom. A true igloo was possible to construct with blocks cut to form a dome, but snow type and consistency was critical, unusual at this latitude but being the preference in the far frozen north.

After a good lunch of grouse, bannock, sweet jams and hot tea, the groups swopped teachers for the afternoon. Bolin was an acknowledged expert of the bow drill, and the first group were now already quite capable adding to their previous basic competence. As explained to the afternoon group the key was selection of materials, but often it was a matter of trial and error and personal preference. He demonstrated the manufacture of the flat base-board and the strung bow, then proceeded to show them the proper way to mount the stick into the string of the bow, using a smooth shell as a bearing block on top of the rotating drill, to reduce friction in the hand. He soon had them making the implements and having their first go, stressing the need to keep rewarming hands in their gloves to aid dexterity. As expected, there were a lot of frustrated faces and aching arms within no time at all, the cold making the job much harder than it was on a dry sunny day, when most had previously practiced the art. Bolin then showed them again the technique, calm and steady, expecting them to watch and absorb. The next time they tried, there was much better success, with a good deal of smoke created. That done and the charred hole in the board primed, he demonstrated how to notch the hole on the side cutting into the side of the board to collect the black dust and let an ember build on another smaller piece of wood below. With easy long movements of his bow, he seemed to create tiny embers with ease and the students took heart. This was short lived though as this was the hardest element to perfect. Bolin told them not to lose heart and stated, with some pride, that only Eryn had managed to create a fire from an ember that morning. He explained that though much was indeed technique, a good amount had to do with stamina and it was not something he expected them to pick up straight away. With a break to drink some tea and a re-warming in front of the fires allowing deadened arms and numb fingertips to come back to life, they all began to feel less disheartened. Coming back to the bow drill with added vigour they were before long all creating much smoke and, with surprise to all, the littlest of them, Aeron, managed an ember which he quickly transferred to some fluffy reedmace seed from his tinder pouch and achieved a brief flash of flame. This was met with much congratulations and only a little jealousy. Aeron's success soon had them all attacking the drills with venom, but as Bolin explained, with a small twinkle in his eye, it was skill rather than raw power that was key. This did little to dissuade, but the smoke created was prodigious and little Seren managed a short-lived ember. Bolin was more than happy with their effort and said that he was confident, with more practice, that they would all have the knack soon enough.

Later that day Merrick pronounced, with just a little devilry, that the students were to spend the night out in their quinzes. This was met with no small hesitancy by most of the children, but they fancied the adventure and no one wanted to be the first to refuse. So that night, after hearty meals and reminders to watch out for hypothermia and frostbite, the children were installed in the snow structures. With surprise, it was a good few hours before the first children came back to the long fires, and Bolin and Merrick gave them hearty slaps on the back for doing so well, not expecting more than an hour or two. The children soon realised they had done well, beating expectations, and were settled into the warm camp, appreciating just how effective the long fires were. Only two stuck with the quinzes through the night, little Aeron and Eryn. The two had wisely doubled up and shared body heat, combining and layering their boughs of fine spruce, sheepskin bedrolls and blankets, thus spending the night in relative comfort. Bolin and Merrick were very impressed, especially when it turned out this was at little Aeron's suggestion. They commended the pair to the group as an example of how thinking laterally, and looking out for others besides just yourself, could save lives.

They spent the rest of the third day honing their skills and becoming comfortable out in the snow. Over the few days trapping they had caught a good number of the abundant snow hares, and so Merrick was happy in the knowledge he now had enough raw material for the fur overcoat he wanted to complete. As they returned back to The Steading on the fourth day, Merrick was confident that all could look after themselves in an emergency, but Aeron was one to watch out for, being bright beyond his young years.

The parents welcomed their respective children home with some relief, especially with the events of the past days they had endured at the Steading lodged in the forefront of their minds. They knew the young ones had been in good hands, but they were all so treasured, it was hard to let them go. The experience though had clearly given the children pause for thought, and all seemed to have grown beyond the mere few days of a single trip.

24 - New life

While the children had been away from The Steading on their camping trip, a relative peace had descended over the house not seen since the height of summer when the little ones spent most of the day out adventuring and assisting with chores. Nonetheless, the peace was uneasy as Sioned's unborn baby was at the forefront of their minds; by their calculations, she was past due.

Preparations had been made, with all available spare cloths, towels and absorbent pads gathered, thoroughly cleaned and disinfected. Various herbs had been prepared to several strengths for pain relief, but otherwise they used simple mild teas to help her stay hydrated, relax and sleep. They had encouraged Sioned to walk about the house as much as possible during the day, though she was by now very heavy and carrying low; keeping mobile was though one of the ways that seemed to help.

Early one morning Sioned awoke to fairly mild pains, though these soon subsided and she managed to sleep for some hours more, in a dozing-like state. Later that morning she began to experience the mild but now quite regular pains which to her and the others indicated the baby was possibly on the way. Nineveh and Shuldan were soon on hand, with others close by to assist as they could. Shulvan would of course be there, partly to learn the way of midwifery, though as an anxious father, he would be there mainly for Sioned's comfort, such as it was.

The pains lasted for most of that day, though they had come further apart as the day was gloaming, and this allowed her the brief respite of some light sleep, though with dreams that were best left forgotten. The house had an eerie quiet, the snow outside deadening sound, but all took care not to disturb Sioned; even the dogs knew something unusual was happening and so were uncharacteristically still.

Towards midnight, the pains started again, in increasing frequency and for longer periods; it seemed the time may have come. As the pains progressed further and reached a new crest of agony, Nineveh and Shuldan gave Sioned comforting words that all was as it should be, gently massaged her and bathed her with damp cloths. They also gave her a mild poppy-based narcotic with her tea to reduce some of the pain, though it took just the smallest edge off, as she needed to keep the process going as naturally as possible.

As the night wore on, nobody could sleep for worrying, the sounds of Sioned's pained cries making that respite a near impossibility in any event. All were anxious for her as the labour continued through the night, the only other sound being the creaking of the roof as the snow settled and the random low-crackles of the fires.

The morning came with Sioned bathed in sweat, but still battling with the fiercest of will; they had managed to keep her hydrated, but with difficulty as it was making her feel bloated and sick. Nineveh and Shuldan then considered the time was nearing and started to get Sioned into a position to let gravity assist the birth. They positioned her upon the side of the bed with her pelvis lowered, with support from a cushioned wooden-seat which had padded boards angling out to each side, keeping her legs relatively comfortable. As this was Sioned's first pregnancy, they knew it would not be easy, but hoped it would not be her last.

As the day wore on Sioned made to push as instructed on the peak of the wave of pain, using the breathing exercises she had been employing throughout the day. She took a larger dose of the pain medication, though at this stage that barely took the edge off the increasing agony.

The long hours went on, the house ever silent, but for Sioned's distressing screams of pain. As it was proving a difficult birth Nineveh and Shuldan took the decision to intervene and assist the baby's passage. Using a very fine knife crafted from razor-sharp obsidian, thoroughly boiled, with hands cleaned and disinfected, they made a small incision. This immediately helped and the baby's head was then more easily able to pass, though with no small amount of blood. With a final series of pushes the baby was finally delivered and the cord cut, the placenta more easily following.

Nineveh and Shuldan quickly assessed the baby, it was surprisingly whole, though completely silent and ashen. They cleared his airways and gently massaged, then clapped his back to release any mucus. All was silent for many unbearable seconds, but then a croak, and a small cry was released with a sudden pink flush to his skin. This was the sweetest sound they could hope for, but they knew the first few minutes and coming hours would seal the baby's fate.

While introducing the baby to Sioned, they took pains to clean her as much as possible and gave her another painkiller while she was stitched. They had left the protective waxy-coating on the skin of the baby, and then had wrapped the little one in fresh cloths, but first letting them have the important skin-to-skin contact. The small bedroom window was then cracked open a little for fresh air and the fire was stoked to provide a comfortable warming glow. They then took the time to make sure that Sioned was hydrated with a nourishing light-broth.

Now all that could be done was to wait and see if the baby would survive the crucial first hours; there was little aid they could offer beyond emotional support and making them as comfortable as possible. A key milestone was trying a feed, but first the pair rested a little.

Having given the pair a short time to rest, Shulvan gently awoke Sioned from her light doze. Nineveh and Shuldan explained that although the baby was sleeping, they needed to try and get him latched on for a first feed, that being a very important first step, getting the essential initial protective nutrients into the new-born. With some coaxing the baby awakened, but was very groggy, with his pulse slightly erratic. This was very worrying, but with a little massaging and movement the child became more awake. With that improvement they encouraged the child to try and take some milk. Despite persevering they could not get him to suckle, and while Sioned may have gotten a few drops onto his lips, he was soon lethargic again. They were all desperately worried and it seemed this would be another case of a child who would be tragically lost. A decision was taken to allow the child a short rest, while continuing to gently massage him and to monitor his heart and breathing. In a last ditch attempt they exposed the infant to some colder air near the open window, which perked him somewhat and improved his colour, then quickly took him to his warm mother. With coaxing, and at first with the smallest of drops upon his lips, the infant started to suckle. With quiet joy the group watched as he grew stronger in his attention and some minutes later was satiated with a contented soft burp.

From then on all went well, with baby taking more milk and soon being greedy for more, sucking his fingers and murmuring when he felt it was time. Given that most pregnancies ended before full term, and that most new-borns tragically passed within the first few hours, the household felt blessed beyond measure at this very promising beginning. For Sioned the experience was life changing in a way she could not have imagined. She found in herself a new introspection from that day on that would never leave her, her youthful exuberance tempered by the fact that she now had a precious life who would depend upon her.

It was on this basis, with great relief, that the children returned from their trip, the house filled with the joy of a new arrival. With everyone home and plenty to celebrate they held their Yule midwinter feast, and named the baby Ianto. As was their tradition from deep in the past, its origins unknown, the feast called for a tree to be brought indoors and decorated. In anticipation of the event Bolin had located a fourteen-foot spruce tree which they harvested and brought into the great hall; the fresh citrusy-smell wonderful. This they festooned with small decorated biscuits in various shapes, twig-made stars, pine cones, mistletoe sprigs, holly and all manner of crafts they had been busy making over the long winter evenings. Following a gargantuan feast all exchanged small hand-crafted gifts, mostly practical items, including new knife sheaths, belts and clothes but all personalised and decorated as suited the recipient. The children also received various sweet treats and new gaming sets to their great delight, which they played until late into the night. The festivities were illuminated by a host of their precious beeswax candles, bright-burning ash wood on the fire, accompanied by singing and fuelled by more food with generous amounts of drink toasting the new arrival. It was a time of great happiness, a house of children, where such numbers would now only grace a large village in this era of otherwise ever ageing and declining population; they all felt blessed beyond measure.

25 - Spring

The spring brought with it a welcome early thaw, though the days were still chilly and all too short. No longer being housebound meant the group could get on with jobs around the homestead, left until much later last year with the prolonged snowstorms. The warmth soon brought the streams and rivers to life, engorged with meltwater and roaring through the day and night. Before long the sap was rising in the trees and green shoots started their tentative emergence from the bare ground, pushing up towards the light then exploding with growth as the days further warmed banishing the frosts. There was a fecundity in the air that could almost be tasted but certainly smelled, the organic rich odour of awakening life accelerating as each day passed; it promised to be a very good year.

In the coming season they hoped to harvest some of the oats for actual consumption; the last crop had been replanted in early winter purely as seed. It would again be harvested in another few months, but then replanted back out as soon as they could, in another section of the ploughed field. Given the crop would deplete nutrient levels, they would likely leave the initial planted area fallow, then manure this as much as possible. Though supplies were limited at present the area was then planted out with various collected seed, scattered to encourage plants which acted as a green fertiliser by fixing nitrogen back into the soil; clover and borage being their main source. Oats were however a great crop for the newly turned soil, as it should suppress most weeds fairly quickly and grow prodigiously in even relatively low temperatures, as was now the case. The healthy and filling oats they should hopefully have by late autumn would be great for a number of foods, including to make a flour, with goat's milk and honey as a wholesome breakfast porridge, to make biscuits, cakes and a plethora of other foodstuffs.

The vegetable beds would need to be rotated to move the previous year's nutrient-hungry tomatoes and suchlike to another patch, to give the soil a chance to recover. Even with the significant amount of soil improvers and fertiliser added over the autumn, field rotation was they knew critical, for allowing nutrient replenishment and avoiding establishment of pests and disease. At best it was a laborious task of picking off the pests and washing down the leaves in soapy liquid and suchlike, but at worst with depleted soils and unseen pests this could decimate their crop and leave them with limited seed for the following years. As a safety-net emergency supplies of seed were kept back each year, but they could well do without having to grow those on, just to replant as seed in order to increase their supply again to sustainable levels.

In terms of other substantial plans and projects, they hoped this year to expand the range of outbuildings, first with a substantial timber-framed barn, which would need a large number of joists, poles, beams and boards. In addition, to protect from heavy snow, the roof would be strengthened with sarking, essentially cross-laid planks, over the new rafters. This would require a large amount of timber processing, but they proposed to form the uprights from simply debarked, rounded trunks sunk into the ground, scorched on the bottom butt ends for longevity. Where possible they would square off just the ends of the cross beams and joint and peg them together for speed. The roof covering would be formed of green-oak shingles rather than slate, but which would have inherent durability and resilience.

All being-well in completing that project, they also hoped to commence a modest log cabin for Bolin and Eryn. Strictly still master and apprentice, there was something beyond respect growing between them, though all knew Bolin would have the greatest of regard for her coming of age as a time for any union. Even though Bolin seemed to be older, he was in fact somewhere in his early twenties, his bulk and heavy beard doing much to give the impression of near middle age, especially when added to his weather beaten and deeply lined face. Appearances though were of little concern and everyone approved of the match, though it seemed Bolin and Eryn were the only ones unaware of their relationship developing beyond mere respect.

The other project they had at least hoped to prepare for was a long house to be constructed separate to the main house, to house Sioned, Shulvan and Ianto, to form a sizeable cottage hospital building and treatment room. This would be a major undertaking, not least because it would ideally need slates and a large quantity of stone to be hauled not inconsiderable distances. They would need more ponies to be captured and tamed for this project and others, so that would come first, once the valley passes were safe again.

It was an ambitious series of projects, but they knew that with the forge producing a steady amount of tools, many jobs would be made much easier. The ponies were also worth their weight in gold and cut down on the endless and tiring tasks. First though were the many essential tasks of spring, but with those completed they could move onto the various projects.

Despite the pressing need to be outside and getting on with the various necessary tasks of spring, there was only so much light in the day, the fairly northerly latitude meaning night came early. However, a massive bonus was the ample time it gave for projects indoors, lit with the bright fire of the hall, various beeswax candles and oil lamps where needed. Over winter the large great hall and kitchen had been a hive of crafts and projects, keeping hands and minds busy during the long dark days. Most would be engaged with repetitive and fairly mindless tasks like spinning and knitting, keeping the need for precious candles to a minimum, but perfect for retelling of the sagas, singing and teaching the children all they needed to know. Others could be found perfecting the tillering of a new bow, or happily carving a new spoon right up next to the light of the fire, functional or decorative as the fancy took them, simply taking pleasure in the craft.

Now that spring was here and sap was freely running into their collecting buckets, it was a perfect time to harvest birch bark, which had a multitude of uses. With a deep knife score around the tree at the top and bottom of the bark section to be harvested, a long slit could then be made up between them, then the section peeled away by teasing fingers and blunt wedges between the bark and the inner trunk, eventually coming away in great rubber-like sheets. If just the right tree and section was chosen it was possible to get a complete sheet of many feet in length with just a few small holes where branches may once have been. It was with a near perfect sheet of bark some fifteen feet long that they started construction of their first one man canoe. In theory they could have made do with smaller sheets stitched together, but a single piece was preferable if possible. The smaller children were incredibly sceptical that the bark of the tree could do the job, used as they were to more solid craft of simple hollowed-out trunks, but as the bark was brought indoors and laid out, they began to appreciate the tough yet supple skin it would provide, almost leather-like. The elders Amaethon and Rhian took great pains to show the children every step of the process, ensuring they could complete each element themselves, the expectation they would be able to replicate the majority of this on the next build. In theory much of the process was similar to other tasks they all knew well, but in practice there was a great deal to learn and it was a good refresher for all to get involved with.

For the project they had cleared a good area of the main hall furthest from the fire and set up a production line between them for finalising the component parts. Many of these parts they had harvested last year and worked on over the last few months, four leaf-shaped paddles already completed and hung on the wall, glossy with multiple coats of oil and wax. With the skin of the craft laid out on the stone slabbed floor, cushioned with some wide planks laid at right angles to its length, they flexed and coaxed the bark into a flat sheet in the warm provided by the fire, using hot water to soften it up as needed. They were very careful not to let the bark get too hot or dry as it could otherwise crack. Over the next few days the bark was further coaxed to form a U-shape, the outer bark now forming the inside of the canoe. To keep the shape, long upright stakes were fitted into holes bored into the planks running each side of the freshly formed U, tied together with cord across the top of the canoe, then gradually tightened as necessary, with the inside weighted down with smooth rocks from the river. Giving the bark a day to rest into its new shape, while keeping it moist, the pre-prepared timber frame section of the canoe was laid out and roughly assembled together, tweaking as needed. This was a critical stage as the width particularly would limit who could use the craft, too wide and it would be hard to reach each alternating side to paddle, too narrow affecting its stability and handling. In the end they had made sure the craft could be handled by the oldest of the children as a minimum, the younger being potentially able to use the craft in pairs with a small paddle each.

The ribs of the craft, as with most of the timber components, were formed of sweet-scented cedar, tough and flexible, capable of being bent to shape with steam or hot water. Over winter many of the U-shaped ribs had already been roughly formed and steam bent by Amaethon and Rhian, but required much tweaking to suit the shape now dictated by the sheet of birch bark. First though they installed the top frame into which they could fit the ribs. Before fitting the ribs it was

215

necessary to add in long lengths of thin cedar which would sit between the ribs and the outer skin, the longitudinal lengths providing stiffening in conjunction with other elements of the frame, as well as providing some protection of the bark from the canoe's occupants. Making all these sections had been time consuming, but was perfectly possible by simply splitting and smoothing with just axes and knifes, though use of new draw knives from the forge made life simpler. It was in fact beneficial to minimise the use of tools, splitting or more accurately cleaving allowing natural grains to be exploited, increasing strength, compared to cross-cutting the grain with a saw which introduced weaknesses.

Amaethon and Rhian began the process of finalising the ribs, arguably the most time consuming aspect, being carefully steamed, trimmed and tightly fitted to suit each section. The tapered ends of each rib would be wedged between the skin and the top of the frame known as the gunnels, skirting the outer top lip of the canoe. However, before final fitting of the ribs, they needed to complete a few more tasks. The gunnels would of course naturally press in toward each other with the pressure of water on the sides, but were kept apart by cross beams called thwarts, formed of strong ash, the central piece also forming the cross piece or yoke for carrying the canoe upside down, balanced on the shoulders. Before they could finally secure the ribs, the front and rear of the canoe needed to be formed around the laminated timber bow pieces, in an upward sweep at both ends. Again this was another aspect that required experience, Amaethon explaining that if the ends were too high, it would risk catching the wind like a small sail and make handling of the craft difficult, too low and it could dip under waves and rapids potentially engulfing the craft. As with all the build this was done purely by eye, no two canoes ever being the same, the natural materials dictating much of the final form.

With the prow and stern cut to its final shape, the two edges of the bark were then held together with a multitude of eager hands and basic clamps, like large clothes-pegs, then pierced with bone awls and double stitched with thin split spruce root. That done the outer skin of the canoe was lashed to the gunnels, bound with the spruce root through holes pierced in the bark and wound around the spruce frame, stiffening it together along its length. This was a big job and even with all hands on deck, making the holes and stitching the root, it took a couple of long evenings. Though everyone's hands were used to this kind of work, and blisters were unusual with the benefit of thick calluses, it was repetitive and fiddly, requiring strength but precision. Nineveh made sure anyone who needed it iced their hands before going to bed, no one wanting to be incapable of work the next day, a special salve of beeswax and yarrow then applied helping with softening and treating the inevitable nicks and cuts. Finally, with the bulk of the craft now complete, the last of the ribs could at last be knocked into place with firm application of a timber mallet, tightening and allowing the canoe its final shape. This was quite an unnerving experience as they had to be tight and so some force was needed. It was with no small sigh of release from all, that the final and tightest rib was knocked home.

With the final form of the canoe complete, they could stop damping down the bark and allow it to slowly dry and settle, the various spruce root stitching also drying and tightening up the various bindings and stitches. This process inevitably resulted in some small cracks, and with the tears and holes they had already stitched, a final waterproofing to seal them up was essential with pitch, the tarry resin formed from spruce gum and pine resin mixed with charcoal and fat. It was a messy job with the pitch sticking to already sore fingers and taking some weeks to remove, but it was amazingly effective, waterproof and flexible once dried. It would take a few test trips on the

217

river to find all of the canoe's leaks and weak points, but surprisingly few came to light, illustrating that the birch tree providing its skin had been chosen well.

They had a good amount of the slender spruce roots left over, along with the tar pitch which could be stored in dried blocks and reheated as needed for repairs. A patch kit would be stowed in the canoe, along with some spare ribs, with the rest of the left over materials being kept in the stores for more major repairs. A huge advantage of the canoe was that it could be constructed with the simplest of materials and repaired in the field to give years of service. In the months that followed, to increase longevity of the canoe and save carrying the craft to the river, they created a store nearby up off the floodplain, a basic frame with a roof of birch bark, with spare parts and various paddles close to hand. In time this developed into a small shack for storage and overnight stays, a favourite place for many to spend a day or two if solitude was needed, peacefully fishing and paddling on the river.

The craft was a remarkable achievement, light and nimble on the water, skating across the rapids and shallows with the minimum of fuss. It was of course of great practical use, though for many the pure joy of using the canoe was its true calling. The craft was an undoubted work of art and the culmination of many hours work, the skills thus passed down to the next generation. It was near perfect, the first of many they would make and treasured even once it was finally beyond repair some years later. It would eventually be hung in the rafters of the main hall, admired for its simplicity and gorgeous organic form, triggering numerous tales told around the fire of simple days just messing about on the river, for many a year to come.

26 - Expansion

As soon as the passes opened an expedition was mounted to find new ponies to add to their invaluable pair. This time they were located with some ease, being on the lower plateau this early in the season, forced down from nearer the glacier-topped mountains by the still present thick winter-snow. They took their tamed ponies with them and that persuaded in another couple of the curious herd. It still took about a week, but they managed to halter another pair and with the calming presence of the other two, along with copious amounts of precious root vegetables, they had them off the hills and acclimatising to their new life in the valley. Initially the new ponies would be left to get used to their new surroundings, letting them observe the trained pair, Sindri quickly becoming their leader. It didn't however take long for Nineveh to show them the basics and the pair were soon useful pack animals, though a great deal more unruly than their more domesticated brethren. With three mares and one stallion now tamed it was hoped there may be foals in the not too distant future to supplement their herd.

With most of the fields planted out, preparation of timber was the next major job, the trees mostly felled the previous year and brought back to The Steading. In shifts they set to work in the huge saw pit, cutting the timber they wouldn't split and cleave. It was back breaking, dusty and repetitive work, but over some weeks they had churned out enough beams and boards for the barn, and before long enough for the much lesser roofs of the cabin and cottage hospital. The timber was fairly dry, though it would season for some years even once incorporated into the buildings as it continued to adjust to the internal temperature and humidity. The oak frames were prepared on the ground, jointed and then temporarily pegged. The frames being deemed satisfactory, these were then numbered at the corresponding joints, broken down and stacked to dry under cover. The tannins in the air from all this drying lumber, oak bark, offcuts and sawdust often caught the throat when passing the stacks and the pit, most unconsciously learning to give the area wide berth before long.

The next massive job was producing the oak shingles, this was a fairly simple process once you had the knack, essentially splitting down pre-cut lengths of log with a number of newly made froes, like thick wedged knives on a right-angled handle. To get at the best material, straight, ideally knot-free lengths of oak trunk were selected, split into half with an axe, then further radially cleaved into shallow wedge shapes with the froes. The centre heart part of the trunk was cut away as it tended to split off, along with the soft outer sap wood, the remainder then used to cleave down into the shingles. The wedge-shaped shingles were finished off with an axe to even them up as needed and to bevel the sharp bottom-edge to increase longevity. The tannins in the oak would help preserve the shingles for many years, and should resist too much warping. They would however need to overlap them to a considerable degree, ideally three deep, which further increased the amount needed. With various rotating teams working on the shingles off and on, they formed the many thousand needed for the barn and cabin over some weeks, each person managing up to two hundred a day when up to speed, the by-product keeping them in kindling for several months to come. They knew though that with care the roof could last a century, especially if they could contrive to make a preserving oil of some form to maintain water repellency.

The hospital building would be a more formidable challenge; though relatively modest in size, it would likely need wide foundation trenches down at least a few feet, to be then filled with compacted rubble, sand and clay. Forming the foundations back up to existing ground level that year would be an achievement, but was something they could work on in most weather conditions.

When it came to collecting the stone, the ponies led by Sindri were an amazing team, collecting some tonnes of material a day from the nearest scree slope, on a near mile round-trip. The trenches were surprisingly quickly filled and so they then started the collection of more angular rectangular lumps for the main walls. With shifts, led by Merrick, working flat out for some weeks, a good store was collected and piled up, a faintly sulphurous smell emitted as they stuck each other indicating their volcanic origin.

Though shingle roofs were excellent, the hospital called for a more substantive and long-lived roof, this meant slate. Slate was not available in the valley, but the scree-ridden hills to the south-west high above the valley were riddled with a decent slaty shale-type rock which would be more than adequate. Previous scouting had rather fortuitously located an old path along a side feeder river leading up to a small quarry, where slate must have once been previously mined and processed. It was partially open cast, but the way the seam of best quality slate ran meant that whomever had mined it in the past had opened up a long tunnel into the hill and brought out great quantities of stone for processing. There was the remnants of an old timber rail system, now mostly rotted out, but with what their predecessors had mined previously there was little need to rebuild this for their purposes. In any event the mine shaft was very precarious looking, most of the support posts having long since rotted away. With some solid buildings still existing at the mine, though in need of repair, it became a camp where they could set up a workshop. The production of slates was a job for a skilled and experienced hand, but none of the group could claim to be that. It was in some ways akin to producing oak shingles and required a good eye to note the natural seams in the rock, or cleaving lines, which could yield a good split. It was however a very dusty job, though the nearby river meant they could easily wash up at need. After a few expeditions they had a more than adequate workshop and bothy camp; then before long had created a production line which soon produced the thousand odd required and more.

During these processes the forge ran at full tilt, producing nails, picks and spades, horseshoes, froes, drills and chisels, amongst all manner of other useful things. Between the master and apprentice, they kept up the steady supply, the ringing of the forge often heard well into the night. In terms of raw materials, a single supply run could bring back a great deal with the help of the four ponies. The pony team obtained a more varied supply this time around, including softer copper alloys for roofing nails, flashing for roof joints around the chimney stacks and suchlike. They had to range a little further than before but they found these more exotic materials in semi buried lines of thick wire in the soil, in parallel lines of three, mostly intact except where it was permanently wet. They had little idea what these may once have been, but were treasure troves once found, often extending for great lengths. They were simple enough to process into wire type copper nails with a mould created from a small steel header to form the large domed ends. These could be produced fairly quickly, a few a minute, whereas steel forged ones would have taken minutes each with much greater expenditure of energy. In addition the copper was ideal as it should react less with the tannins in the wood shingles compared to ferrous iron which would quickly corrode. They made a good number of the roofing nails, anticipating the need, but it was a laborious job. Bolin quite wryly and conveniently discovered making nails was Eryn's 'speciality', much to her thinly-veiled annoyance. It was though a pleasant life for the pair in the forge with intermingled projects of a more challenging nature, constantly busy hands honing their art, though Nineveh often despaired at their sooty appearance in the kitchen, hounding them out for a good scrub on many occasions before letting them have their evening meal. With all the work Eryn progressed quickly from apprentice to the status of a journeyman in Bolin's estimation, very seldom now needing to offer instruction. They often had at least one of the children on the bellows and shovelling charcoal while the pair of blacksmiths worked side-by-side, all the while acquiring a deepening bond of fellowship and respect.

With various jobs in progress, the task of finding a good source of clay was next, though this would be left in situ until they needed it. What they were looking for was a sticky soil where water tended to pool rather than drain. There were such soils on the valley bottom near slower feeder streams which had brought these clays off the fields and woods. In places these areas were eroded back to some extent to expose the less-vegetated layers beneath. They weren't significant deposits, but would do for what they had in mind, mainly just to pack out the central stone infill of the long house walls and to provide bonding as it dried and hardened. Hopefully it would also be of good enough quality for lining the chimney stack, but they would need to test that first. In theory they could build the chimney with fired clay forming a terracotta pipe as the main liner, but for safety this would be supplemented with clay packed around the pipe all encased in a thick wall of stone.

It was a hard spring and early summer period with these backbreaking preparations, mostly monotonous and having of course to be fitted in around everything else that needing doing around the homestead. However, they achieved a great deal simply by putting in the effort and working as a well-oiled team, the four ponies of massive benefit. The group still found time to enjoy themselves though, whether that be out hunting, fishing or just a lazy day in the canoe exploring and watching kingfishers, all knowing that a productive break was vital for their

223

mental wellbeing. Before long though there came the day they could at last make a start on the first new building, an important step in consolidation of their place in the valley.

27 - Barn raising

Raising the new barn would be the culmination of many months of preparation, but it would also be quite the festival occasion, with everyone involved and all treating it like a holiday they justly deserved. Various delicious food and drink would be provided throughout the day to keep everyone going, with the work done at a fairly relaxed pace, with singing of the old sagas very likely. The glorious weather certainly helped, the odd fluffy cloud passing across an idyllic blue sky, with a pleasant cooling breeze and the warm sun on their backs, perfect for the work ahead.

To start they finished digging the last of the post holes into which the upright main supports would be positioned, the bottom ends of the straight larch trunks having previously been burnt and carbonised to increase longevity by way of increasing water repellency. The bark had been previously stripped off as this would encourage insects and rot if left on the trunks. Using round wood poles was ideal in many ways, not least avoiding massive amounts of milling to make them square, but also because by avoiding cutting into the wood fibres, they were much stronger and so less timber was needed. The post holes were then backfilled around the new uprights with compacted fine stone for good drainage and then overlain with compacted clay which would repel water. The clay was then capped with slabs of drystone angled to shed water away. The foundations would also be protected by the large eaves overhang of the eventual roof and further shielded behind the building's walls, which were to be feather-boarded shiplap-type. These measures ensured that the posts could, with care and maintenance, last for many decades at least without rotting, but even then, in theory they could be cut short with a new section spliced in or just propped up on slab-like stones.

With the uprights installed and temporarily propped up, the more intrepid of the group tentatively climbed these on ladders and installed the header beams linking the tops of the poles down each side of the building and at each gable end. With ready-made squared-off mortise and tenon joints, they soon had some of the desired rigidity, further increasing once wooden pegs were firmly pounded in, tightly locking the joints together. Across the centre of the building they added the tie beams linking the poles across the internal space; these were also braced up against the main upright poles with supporting diagonal buttresses forming a triangle. The tie beams were incredibly important, literally tying the walls together and stopping the load of the roof pushing and splaying them out. This required some ingenious jointing and fixing of the upright poles, headers and tie beams, but with only a minimum of fettling they slotted into place, with the wooden locking-pegs hammered home. With those elements in place they could then see the plan and scope of the barn to greater effect. Though they knew the building would be large, it was quite a sight to see the pre-made frame together at last, providing many thousands of square feet of useable space with the intended upper storey.

Next were the tall king-posts, positioned to the centre of each gable end linked by crossing tie beams, with further supporting and bracing triangular trusses. These posts would be full height at each gable end and secured in deep holes, but not in the central part of the building, to provide for an unencumbered square work space on the ground floor reaching up to the roof. The tall king posts provided the maximum height to the ridge and across which was placed the long ridge-beam fixed with a huge mortise and tenon joint, linking up at the one third and two third points across the building with additional centre-support posts mounted on the cross-tie beams. To each side of the central king-posts were positioned shorter queen-posts which would provide for the principal cross beams called the purlin, supporting the roof mid-way up its diagonal and further braced to help tie the roof together. Given the heights involved this had to be done with a basic crane, a very long larch trunk supported at the base on a wide moveable frame and pegged out with tight guy-ropes. With a boom arm that could be rotated across the top, they could place the massive beams forming the ridge and purlins with some precision, but still it was a worrying point of the build with the heights involved, many a thumping-heart hammering away as they watched the nimbler of the group shimmying-up the skeletal frame to peg the beams firm across the joints.

With the ridge beam secured in place they could conduct the topping-out tradition of mounting a yew branch to the ridge, supposedly to appease the tree spirits and thank them for the gift of the trees which made the timber frame. Few harboured anything you might call superstition or were of a religious persuasion, but it did no harm to have respect for the forest and all it provided. With the topping-out complete, they were then very much ready for a break, including a small celebratory tot of honey-sweetened elderberry wine, which was much savoured. All then made themselves comfortable for a while and surveyed what they had achieved, while good-naturedly debating their next move, with a late lunch being a hot topic. There was a huge spread brought out from the pantry, with many cold meats, salads, pickles and light breads along with an excellent fish-chowder spiced with garlic-mustard leaves for those who wanted something warm. They kept the meal relatively modest though, conscious that a lazy afternoon stuffed like suckling-piglets was not going to get the job done. That evening they could indulge, though it would be a long day yet, the light likely to hold out until well into the evening.

Anchored across the top ridge, the bottom headers and the purlin supports they started laying the long diagonal rafters, which held themselves to some extent under their own weight with interlocking

227

notches on the underside, but were jointed and pegged together where they crossed each other at the ridge as well for security. To further help tie them together and stop them splaying out under the load, cross ties were installed high up in the roof space forming a series of tall A-shapes. Across the rafters were laid sarking boards secured with further wooden pegs, ending up with what looked like a weirdly angled floor. Across all of this were nailed-in thin roof baton strips to mount the oak shingles and allow a little air gap beneath. These cross running batons also usefully provided temporary purchase for the workers' feet on the otherwise smooth roof, making the job a whole lot less precarious.

The shingles would need to be installed another day, but the main superstructure was now in place and looking mightily impressive, the sarking already providing a substantial roof of sorts and enclosing a huge space. There would need to be feather boarding added to the outside walls, the primary purpose being to cut prevailing winds driving in the rain, but that could wait for now. The principle use of the barn was to be as a covered area for storage, including on the upper floor and in the roof space, but also as a large workspace out of the elements. Basically they now had that, being more than useable as it stood and a massive asset to the developing farm.

The barn was an imposing two-storey structure, the highest at the homestead by some margin, a good two times as large as the original stone-built barn. It had been a huge undertaking to make ready all of the materials and pre-prepare the frame and all the complex joints, but in the end, the building went up with only a few setbacks, mainly tweaking and fettling of the mortise and tenons due to anticipated drying and shrinkage of the timber. They had all learnt many useful skills which would be put into further practice with the other buildings; it was especially important that the children at least watched and learned, as this process of barn building might be seen perhaps only once or twice in their lifetimes. The barn was however far from the children's mind at this stage, their stomachs rumbling in anticipation of the feast.

All that day Shuldan had been keeping an eye on a turf-covered fire pit containing a large boar taken from the expanding herd that was now semi domesticated, allowed to roam the woods and given supplementary feed. The carcass had been left to slow cook and smoke in apple chips for a delicate flavour and was impregnated with honey into deep cuts in the skin, with the body cavity stuffed with soaked apples, rehydrated after long storage from the year before. The meat had been left to slow cook all day, with the juices of the apples providing a moist succulence and a wonderful sauce. It was an incredible smell that emanated from the pit, the dogs especially found it quite irresistible and spent much of the day close-by carefully 'guarding' the food. With the uncovering of the pit and the removal of the meat, everyone was salivating in anticipation, keen eyes keeping a watch as it was pulled apart into succulent shreds, the moreish crackling finished off over a hot fire then devoured.

Accompanying the pork were great vats of creamy coleslaw, lightly salted and spiced, being another speciality of Shuldan, made the day before to let it marinade. With this there were a host of crisp salads, hard-boiled wild-bird eggs, quiches, fresh pizzas, vegetables, pickles, oat cakes, cheeses and sweet sauces. There were also some breads, made of nutty acorn-flour; tasty though they were, they could not wait for the finer flour of the oat harvest currently maturing. Nineveh had made a wonderful display of these breads in elaborate browned weaves, topped with various seeds and chopped hazelnuts, all delicious. Shuldan then produced a series of other excellent dishes including batches of griddled rosti-potatoes, finely chopped with onions and bound with egg, all decadently fried in butter producing wonderfully spiced and hearty fare to refuel the workers. To finish were pancakes made to Nineveh's secret recipe, and bowls of tiny summer-strawberries picked wild from the meadows and woods; these were agreed to be delicious with a little honey and goat's milk cream. To wash down all the food there was large amount of tart cider, blackberry wine, beer and sweet lingonberry liqueur to finish, imbibed while they listened to Shuldan play his recently completed flute, a massive improvement on the children's basic elderflower whistles. He had painstakingly fashioned the instrument from a hollow vulture bone found on the plains, and had just finished the final decorative carving of its surface. The sound produced was almost eerie at times, the old melodies echoing the flickering flames and deep dark around them as night fell. As he played most joined in, some with improvised drums, and others adding their range of voices with mellow bass of the men, the melodic sopranos of the women and the trembling reedy voices of the children and their whistles. They knew this as a jøik, an ancient oral tradition recounting tales of their ancestors and the natural world. The effect was at once beautiful, mournful and uplifting. They sang together late into the evening, intermittently taking a break to nibble their favourite titbits and to lubricate their throats with their chosen tipples, all the while the sound of laughter ringing out into the night. Some had rather sore heads and bleary eyes as a result come next morning, but nothing that a bracing swim in the river and a swig of birch tonic could not more or less cure.

In the days that followed they fitted out the barn at first-floor level with its internal planked floors to each end, leaving the central area to its full height, creating a wonderful airy space, aiding good ventilation. In due course they would add carvings to the great beams and posts, but that would be a project for the long winters. Once all the infill studwork and strengthening noggins were eventually completed, the sides were feather boarded with fire-scorched planks of more irregular trunk edges, but leaving doors at first-floor level at each gable, with ropes and pulley systems to lift up the stores inside and out. The main double barn doors faced out onto the fields to the south, with great strap-hinges fashioned from oak. These doors were replicated as great shutters on the opposite north wall and could be demounted to create a breeze through for tasks such as drying, threshing and winnowing of the oats. Within one side of the main barn doors was a smaller portal for general use in the winter, but generally they would remain fully open, to aid ventilation.

The roof of oak shingles was the next task completed over the coming days, with pre-drilled holes in each, and a great number of copper clout-nails, a job deemed laborious, but therapeutic and satisfying in its own way. To the edge of the large overhanging-eaves they created a series of timber gutters from rot-resistant cedar, essentially two fire-treated boards in a V, sealed with pine pitch at the pegged joint, the downpipe being made in a similar way, but as a box shape. The fire scorching was a very old technique which should prolong the life of the wood, making it more resistant to rot and pests. Ideally they would form cast-iron gutters, but the amount of metal required was beyond their means and in any case the scorched wood could last a surprisingly long time once further protected with a good amount of oily birch tar, being easily repaired as needed. To reduce the speed of the water hitting these comparatively fragile wooden gutters they had made sure to decrease the pitch of the roof at the outer edge, forming a pleasingly characterful shallow-curve. The water collected would be kept in a system of stone-lined tanks below ground, bedded into a thick layer of clay. They wouldn't be leak free, but covered over would allow for a good water supply to be kept close-by year round. To retrieve the water they had a system a bit like a short well, with buckets and a nearby trough made of elm which was very water resistant when kept wet. A further bonus of the underground tank was that it shouldn't freeze quite as quick as other sources, making things easier come winter.

On completion of the barn, they then took a week or so to catch up on jobs around the ever expanding farm. Though it was a fairly slack time of the year, the start of the autumn harvest was just around the corner. In the days and weeks that followed they eventually got used to this large building they had created, a relative behemoth. It was hard to believe they had managed it, but it went to show that with preparation and team work, they could achieve a great deal and this spurred them on to think about completing one more building that year.

28 - Creating a hamlet

The next project was a relatively simple job compared to the barn, a cabin for Bolin and Eryn. They had already debarked and pre-cut the logs for the walls and sawed the beams and planks for the roof; it being a simple affair, construction was soon underway. The foundations comprised a shallow trench through the thin soil, down to the bedrock, and a base of free-draining gravel and pads of stone, onto which the timbers could be laid. They were fortunate that the nearby woods contained some larch, ideal for the foundation logs, being rot-resistant and generally very straight and easy to work, avoiding the need for excessive packing-out of gaps with moss and clay. Scribing the logs to create the corner interlocking half-moon cuts with saws and adzes was the most time-consuming aspect of the work, but they found that working in teams, two logs at a time, was efficient and speedy once in the flow of the task. These were built-up in a long rectangle, to a height of one-and-a-half stories at the triangular gables, the ends and ridge supported by central posts which ran floor to ceiling internally. The two bedrooms would be in the roof space, with a simple steep stair up, separated with a timber screen. Once the main rectangle of the log walls was complete, window openings were cut out and frames installed to help fix and support the logs. The front door was crafted from a lovely set of cherry-wood boards, rich with interesting grain, which was later covered in a layer of birch bark inside to provide some further wind proofing. Over the front gable would be an extended overhanging roof to provide a covered area over the door, with a simple wooden deck to help stop mud being tracked straight into the cabin.

The roof was next to be installed, a simple inverted V-frame of rafters secured with a bridle joint at the apex, resting atop the long central ridge pole, itself sat atop the two log-built gable ends. This left the interior space open and unencumbered by supports excepting some high internal cross ties providing a tall A-shape. Across the rafters they laid reinforcing sarking boards, then thin batons for mounting the shingles. They had kept the best of the oak shingles for the cabin, which would be overlapped up to three deep. The shingles would be oiled every few years to aid water repellency; this oil being created from heating the bark of the birch tree, resulting in a tarry preservative which should waterproof and repel insects. It would need topping up as the shingles dried to a light grey, but should ensure the roof lasted for many decades. For the stone chimney-stack they used some of the precious copper to flash around it to seal against the roof. The fireplace and stack was a quite bulbous affair as they had no mortar, lime being scarce, but it would be bound together and lined with clay, which would harden in the heat of the fire. They may end up needing to re-line this with some form of metal flue, but that was for another time; at worst they would need to patch-up gaps with further clay. It ended up an odd looking cabin, the oversized chimney almost looking like the furnace in the forge in some respects, but that suited the occupants just fine.

Next were the final finishes, the internal floors, basic kitchen, storage and so on. It was a rustic affair but that was to the blacksmiths' taste, who would spend most of their time in their forge in any event, and would still take most meals with the group in the main house. The only convenience they requested, or rather Nineveh and Arwyn had insisted on, was a separate tepee-like timber hut nearby to serve as a sweat lodge to dislodge the grime of the forge from their pores. This combined with a stream nearby and a decent plunge pool below a small set of waterfalls would be excellent for the pair to bathe without turning the bathhouse black on a daily basis.

With heavy oak-shutters installed for the windows, the final delicate process was fitting the small glass panes, bedded in with a light putty made from linseed oil and animal fat, to fix it in place, with thin wooden strips to further secure the pane. The production of glass was a great recent achievement by Eryn assisted by Arwyn, who had both been experimenting in the forge. It was far from perfect, but with fine sand gathered from the beach, repeatedly sieved, then heated to burn away impurities, they could make a basic small glass pane in a flat mould of sand, though opaque and quite thick; four pieces being enough for each small window with glazing bars. They were fine for letting some light in and would be left propped open most of the time in any case. Eryn had also attempted making some basic glass jars, but for now then were beyond her fledgling skills, though she would persevere.

It was amazing to see the cabin go up over that week, but they all knew the hard work that had gone into its preparation; the final assembly was therefore relatively quick with all hands on deck. Before long Bolin and Eryn had moved in and had installed their belongings and personal effects, giving the rest of the group a chance to spread out more in the main house.

Though they hadn't anticipated that they would make much headway on the new hospital building, working off and on that year they had already completed the foundations and were on the third course of stone for the thick walls. The clay had worked beautifully in the warm weather and set solid, with occasional wetting down and covering in wet moss to avoid cracking. A key had been the incorporation of manure, wood ash and straw for binding the clay which had been rammed into the rubble core to consolidate and key it together. The external part of the wall was fairly tightly-jointed drystone, but with an angle to drain any water out. With the large roof overhang, penetration of the wall with direct rain and splashback off the ground should be minimal, and would only get so far as the clay core.

With everyone now available, all hands were put to work to gather the clay as it was needed, to make the mix and bed-in the next several courses. It was a messy job, and a bit pungent but of course the youngest children loved it, stripping naked, pounding the mixture with their feet, then simply washing down in the nearby streams afterwards. A near constant stream of stone was brought on the strong backs of the four ponies, with some of the group at the scree slopes on the valley side selecting the best, most angular stones, which naturally cleaved into blocks if necessary. With continued good weather they quickly had the next several courses complete, then the gables and chimneys, and were able to then concentrate on the roof. Even in the intense sun the clay would need at least a few days to set but ideally weeks to allow for the loading from the weight of the roof. They decided that rather than add the complete load of the roof to the walls, it would be prudent to internally add extra upright beams firmly bedded into the ground to support the crossing tie beams and the ridge. In time it would all settle and by then the walls should be completely dry and set solid. If they wished the support posts could then be removed, but may as well remain.

With the main walls in place, the basic form of the building became apparent, being in a well-chosen position in a fairly secluded part of the meadow, sheltered and often bathed in sun. Essentially it comprised a traditional long house with a large cooking and living area to one end, with a bedroom to the other and a small internal hall and porch. An additional central room would act as a consultation room and hospital bed. There would be some limited loft space for storage and a child's bedroom, but the main living area was left exposed to the full height of the roof, leaving a great area for drying clothes, herbs and suchlike.

The slates for the roof had been made over the course of the year in a few expeditions to the mine. It was initially a very laborious process as they learnt the skill of selecting the stone, cleaving and squaring off, but it was something the older children could also help with and became a regular adventure. With a steady increase in output as they mastered the technique and acquired purpose-made tools from the forge, the slates were all now ready, but needed to be transported back to the valley. With all other jobs complete, all hands were made ready for what would prove to be a major task.

The movement of the slates from the mine, to the head of the valley was relatively simple, being downhill mostly; it was the boulder strewn stretch down the steep valley-side that was dangerous, and great care had to be taken. Even the ponies had issues with this section, despite their sure footedness, and so they created a human chain over the worst parts. This all took the best part of a week and was perhaps the most exhausting task any of them had undertaken, but excepting some minor cuts and bruises, it went well. Once down the worst of the rocky valley side, the ponies were again able to take the full loads, and in this way they transported the some thousand-odd slates back to the building site.

With the slates stacked for use, Arwen proposed and all heartily agreed to take a day to rest and catch up on light chores; they then made ready for the last effort of weatherproofing the building. The roof timbers had been pre-made and numbered at corresponding joints, and so once the internal support beams were in place, they added a frame to the top of the wall then tied these together with beams across the width of the building atop the internal upright posts. The ridge then was added, with a purlin for mid-way support up the pitch, and finally the rafters. It was a relatively simple job to then sark board the roof, add the batons and install the slates. The slates were pre-punched with a specialised pointed hammer to form the fixing hole and they used more of the copper nails. The apex was finished with fire-hardened clay ridge-tiles, and the joins around the chimneys at each end flashed with the last of the copper.

With the outside pretty much complete, the windows, doors and internals were fitted. It would take some considerable time to complete the job internally, but it was habitable and this could be completed at their leisure through the winter now it was watertight and capable of being heated.

With Shulvan, Sioned and Ianto moved out, in addition to the blacksmith's recent move to their new residence, the main house felt substantially less crowded and so the bedrooms were rearranged and furniture added to create hidey-holes for those who wished some relative solitude. Everyone now had a little more privacy and comfort, very welcome for the long winter ahead when they could be housebound for weeks at a time.

With the efforts of the last few weeks they all agreed it would be great to enjoy a period of enforced rest after the long year; the amount they had achieved had exhausted them all. It was quite extraordinary what they had accomplished in forming what was now a small hamlet, but they were aware there would need to be one last push for the harvest. With light chores completed each morning, they all spent the rest of the day doing whatever relaxed them the most, though nearly all kept busy, with crafts sat out in the sun, working in the smithy, riding the ponies, canoeing, playing with the dogs, rambles in the woods and overnight excursions up to the waterfall cave and pools. It was a gorgeous time of the year, summer turning to autumn, but still long warm days, near perfect, including for ripening the harvest.

29 - The harvest

Compared to previous year, there was an absolute glut of fruit and vegetables with an added bonus of an oat crop; however, given their growing herds of goats, pigs and ponies, it may be needed in part for supplementary fodder if there was a harsh winter. The meadows would however provide for an abundant hay crop, the newly-completed barn offering plenty of room for it to be piled up to keep dry, which should more than tide them over. An added bonus for the children was that it made for a fun place to play, jumping from the first floor of the barn into the great soft-mounds of hay and straw with squeals of delight.

The oats had done exceptionally well through the year, and would now be a substantial but very late harvest on the second crop, the first having been planted early in the winter last year and grown just to produce seed to replant. They had been extremely fortunate with the mild weather, and it had been a risk to plant quite late this year expecting it to be ready, but the crop had matured beautifully with the long summer days and occasional warm showers.

The main harvest began just as the stalks had reached a golden yellow, with the oat heads being firm and quite dry, though some extra drying would certainly be needed. The trick was to ensure that they were not too dry otherwise in harvesting much would shake loose and fall to the ground where it would soon be lost to the ever-present flocks of birds. To start they scythed the oats at their base, as close to the ground as they could to obtain all the valuable straw. They used a modified cradle-type scythe for this job, which had a number of timber ribs parallel to the bottom metal cutting-blade, acting as a guide and scoop to lay the crop flat to one side. This was then bundled and made into upright stacks sat up on rocks to aid ventilation and allow the crop to further dry in the sun. With two people taking turns scything and everyone else stacking it was, once the knack was found, a therapeutic task, though very tiring. The resulting stacks then stood in the fields for a time, drying in the light breeze and warm days, regularly turned over and inspected until agreed they were nearing perfection.

With the oats cut and dried, the now dusty stacks were transported to the barn, by hand and pony back. With the great demountable shutters removed from the rear of the barn it created excellent airflow through the centre space, which aided the drying, threshing and winnowing process by blowing away the chaff. To say this process was a laborious task was a great understatement, and required four adults at a time with great wooden flails working in a rotating pattern, literally beating the oats off the stalks against the ground, which would then fall to the freshly-completed stone-slabbed floor. These oats were then repeatedly thrown into the air by the children and the wind blew away the outer husks. It was a very dusty job and made all involved itchy and grouchy, but that was soon solved with a refreshing dunk in the nearest stream. As the oats were processed, they were taken to large wooden storage bins on the first floor of the barn, lifted up in sacks they had made of woven natural plant-fibres, mostly nettle. The straw was kept and stacked to one side of the ground floor, for the animals' bedding and for some for the vegetable beds next year, where it would be used as a mulch.

The harvesting of the oat crop was a massive achievement and ended with a small celebration, though it was a weary one indeed. About one quarter of the oats would be kept back for seed and some in reserve; they had harvested about forty-five bushels in all, nearly three quarters of a tonne, which should last them some considerable time. Much of the crop would be laboriously milled down to a flour as required, using a large two-person rotary hand-milling quern, a seemingly basic looking device, but which effectively pulverised the oats between the rotating action of the thick granite discs. This impressive harvest could not have been achieved without the workspace in the barn, and the great fortune with the weather, with a light winter, great growing conditions and a dry autumn. They would not run this risk again; fate should not be tempted too often.

The industrious bees were now spread over three sites of about a half-dozen large hives each, located around the meadow. New colonies had been found in the valley and transferred to new skeps, where they had settled in well. Most of the existing colonies had been split early in the year where well-established and the most productive provided with further abutting hives for overflow honey-storage. Some of the colonies had been taken to the nearby heather-rich valley sides, increasing production, but all had gorged on the rejuvenated fruit-tree blossom in the orchards, productive in fruit despite their heavy prune a year ago. The latest timber hives mostly replaced the woven skeps of the year previous, being double walled for insulation, slatted externally to shed rain, with a large protective lid. Internally they contained open boards which dropped into the frame inside the hive, and could be taken in and out to check on the bees' progress in filling these with waxy comb and honey. With about ten large frames to each hive, they had harvested about forty-odd pounds of honey from each over the year, but still leaving plenty for the colony to make it through winter. In terms of wax, this had to be scraped from each frame to uncap the comb and release the honey; with this they gained about a pound-per-hive each year, totalling about twenty pounds altogether. This made a fair few dozen candles of various sizes, but they would still be a scarce resource, with a decent amount of wax needed for jar sealing and medicinal use. For special occasions like midwinter, they would supplement the light of the fire and create a lovely atmosphere and smell, much superior to the smoky tallow-based candles and oily wick-lanterns they otherwise used. Really though it was only winter they tended to use candles and lanterns, otherwise being outside until near sunset and rising with the sun.

The vegetable beds had been rotated with varying crops, and with the huge amounts of fertiliser dug in the previous autumn and winter, including the accumulations of the long drops the year before, they had been super productive. As a result there had been more than enough crop surplus to supplement the animals' feed; this meant over that year the pigs had multiplied and become a lot less feral with being fed and the piglets partially hand reared. As a result they had managed to harvest two of the oldest and a few young boars; much of that meat had been cured and stored for the winter. To the satisfaction of the group Shuldan made a good batch of bacon, the loin joints being salted and cured, then partially dried. After about two weeks, with massaging of the meat every couple of days, it was ready to be smoked over fruit-wood chips for several hours, then thickly sliced. Everyone agreed the taste was amazing, salty sweet and smoky, simply served with flatbread and goat milk butter. In addition to this meat they kept one of the younger boars in a pen near the stables, and once fattened it would be harvested for the mid-winter feast. With so much pork there was also a good amount of fat for making a decent supply of soap. The rendered pig-lard had particularly good quantities of glycerine which made a wonderfully moisturising soap, very much needed to keep their skin in good condition over the harsh winter. They had massive amounts of wood ash, so making the necessary lye was easily accomplished by boiling a vat of watery ash and skimming the resulting lye off the top. Nineveh and Shuldan made one of the soap batches with some charcoal from the kilns this time round, which helped absorb and mask the scent of the hunters, and in any event resulted in excellent cleansing, as well as treating minor skin-conditions that sometimes arose. Some was also made with lavender, yarrow and beeswax, which gave a less abrasive soap and left a wonderful scent.

As the household now had a decent supply of soap it meant they could always afford to stay clean and importantly reduce chance of skin infections and catching stomach bugs, though some of the more feral children were less than impressed with this new regimen.

The tomato crop this year was tremendously abundant, the excess having been boiled down to a rich puree for storage within sterilised sealed-jars. It represented a wonderful source of vitamins and made the base of a tasty sauce for many dishes, including a number of different soups. A good deal of tomatoes were also sliced and sun-dried on long strings, then kept in airtight containers; this helped preserve more of the nutrients than through boiling and were wonderful reminders of summer, excellent on pizzas with Nineveh's spicy pork-salami. These were an especial favourite of the children, who loved using the new pizza oven in the herb garden, a massive clay construction roofed over with an oak-shingled roof which they had completed for the summer and used on many an evening for a simple but delicious meal.

Through their careful management last year, with much of the crop given over to the building up of seeds, their potato crop was phenomenal. With the cellar already busting, they built great drying-racks and storage bins in the barn, where at first-floor level they should last for many months, in the relatively cool, dry atmosphere. Rodents may well be an issue, but with careful checking and fixing of holes in the double-layered oak bins, they should not lose too much, the dogs also being excellent deterrents though in reality poor rat-catchers. There was still some hope that they might manage to track down some wildcats in the forest and tempt them to become resident farm cats, to further help keep rodents under control. The wild cats were however incredibly secretive and the only sign so far had been scat found in the more remote western-part of their valley, but the hope was there for the future.

With the last of the vegetable beds and fields harvested, they were all liberally fertilised as they had the previous year, with wood ash, compost, and so on, but that year they could also use their abundant supply of well-rotted animal manure to dress the surface as well. It made for a wonderfully rich organic-soil, pungent and dark which should, with crop rotation, help provide for good harvests in the years to come. Now the beds were up and running and largely weed-free, there was little need to dig them over, being energy intensive, but also damaging to the delicate soil-microbiome which was best left undisturbed and allowed to develop.

Next year they hoped to grow much more flax, or linseed as it was also known. They had a small amount of seed collected on their travels, but had started growing that purely for seed since they arrived and now had some twenty-odd pounds surplus, with some having been recently used to make oily putty for the window-pane fitting in the cabin and longhouse. They had been painstakingly splitting the growing plants as well to increase productivity, which had been successful, but it was a laborious process. Next year they hoped to increase production to use the crop to a much greater extent, as the plant was very useful for pressing out nutritious cooking-oil and making linen from its fibres. Though far from essential, it would be good to have another source of vitamin-rich fat from the oil, and a lighter cloth than the spun goat's wool, as versatile as it was. It would unlikely result in masses of linen and it would be far from finely spun and woven on their basic loom, but it would be great for bandages, sheets and suchlike.

With the harvest in and all happy that it would see them comfortably through the winter, they turned their thoughts to the final hunting-trips of the year, but at last feeling they could start to relax, the bulk of the work done.

30 - Trapping and fishing

This year it was agreed that there would be a concerted effort to hunt the verdant plains to the north-east of their valley, to help conserve convenient resources nearer to home and upon the adjoining high plateaus. The lowland plains to the north, sandwiched between the mountains and the sea were largely unexplored, but based on their travels to collect metals, and to gather resources at the coast, those lands were clearly abundant, especially with auroch, being a highly desired meat for their flavoursome beef and thick supple-hides. The group would also try this year to catch the peak of the salmon run up the river, before the fish had been out of the salt water of the sea too long and started putting all their energy into making eggs and degrading their muscle. They also hoped to take some capercaillie, the large turkey-like grouse of the ancient pine woods, with a few individuals heard on previous trips in the spring. The plains would also be abundant in other animals, many deer, hares, rabbits, various large ground-dwelling birds, possibly some sheep and suchlike. If the opportunity presented itself, they also aimed to trap a number of animals for furs, to improve the thermal efficiencies of their cold-weather gear, including beaver, fox, mink and possibly wolf. Bear was also a possibility, the meat being flavoursome and their fur excellent for winter clothing, but it was a significant risk to hunt.

This trip would be aided by taking the dogs to assist in the hunts, who could corral certain prey for ease of shooting with the bows, or to be taken with spears. The dogs were also excellent at forcing birds and other small game to break cover, the pack animals being able to cover huge areas with relative ease. Lastly the dogs would also offer some protection from predators, such as the wolf, lynx and bear, by way of passive deterrent with their scent and loyally defending them to their deaths if necessary, though in all likelihood they wouldn't encounter any such danger.

The trip should see a large amount of meat, fish and pelts harvested, and so Nineveh and Shuldan volunteered to act as a shuttle between the fishing area and home, then the plains and home, to move the harvested game. With the four ponies they should be able to bring back home large quantities of valuable resources, as well as being able to resupply the hunting party with provisions from The Steading. There was some risk in shuttling the resources, but the ponies were far from being defenceless, able at need to apply a swift kick which would disable most predators. In any event Nineveh and Shuldan were more than competent with their bows and spears. A further trade off was that a smaller group would attract less attention, their tracks being easily mistaken just as a small group of ponies, so overall much less likely to reveal the valley and their home.

Shulvan and Sioned had volunteered to stay at The Steading, to look after the homestead and the animals, baby Ianto also being a little young still for extensive travelling. This time all of the children would join the party, every hand needed for the hunting and meat preparation, as well as to develop the skills they would need themselves for the future. Sioned was of course one of their best hunters, Shulvan being more than competent, so none doubted their safety in the secure homestead.

The kit they would take was much the same as previous trips, with an added number of light barbed-spears for the salmon fishing and hunting of game on the plains. The weather would likely stay warm and was always much milder down away from the mountains, so they could afford to pack lighter gear. The tents would be their standard tarps which had been freshly re-waxed in case of any storms. They would probably have one fixed-camp for fishing, but the hunting on the plains would likely necessitate a number of camps, depending upon where the herds were and their mobility. They would however keep their plans loose and see what came their way given much was simply unknown.

Bolin and Eryn were happy to come and join in the hunt, though they would also be keeping an eye out for scrap metals they could take from any wrecks encountered. The beauty of the animals being used to go back-and-forth was that there would likely be spare capacity in the ponies' packs, if not the gathered material could be stashed and picked up on another trip. As always it would be good for the two blacksmiths to get away from the forge; that year had been incredibly busy for them, though they savoured the work.

With final preparations, the group departed The Steading with light hearts and looking forward to a few weeks at a different pace of life, exploring a new area, no doubt eating well and testing their skills. They set out early one dewy morning, stealthily making their way down the west-side of the rocky entrance-gorge and passing out through the valley mouth, soon heading north along the river, navigating the vast conifer forest of the mountain slopes. The river Rhuø eventually spread out from the tight confines of its gorge and became generally more placid and sinuous, joined by the odd feeder stream every now and then. The river was often hemmed in and overhung with trees, except where it passed over any protrusions of harder rock, often then forming rapids and small waterfalls with sparser vegetation thereabouts. It was these areas that would be ideal for fishing, with the earliest of the migrating salmon already congregating on their way upstream in the pools below the waterfalls and rapids. They had found many likely spots on their past travels, but one had stuck in their minds as a prime position, being more open than usual and less wooded, so hopefully reducing chance of bears who would likely also be attracted to the same prime positions, but in more densely wooded spots.

On arriving, they flattened an area of tall grass for their camp, and set to erecting their tarpaulins into tent-like lavvu configurations. They then created one large central area where seating logs and a large stone-lined fire pit was positioned to create a communal space for meals. The fireplaces were fashioned of rocks to create windbreaks and flat areas for food preparation; over them Shuldan quickly had large tripods erected to hang their kettles and spits to roast fish and meats. Food would be kept in bags which would be strung high-up in trees away from the camp, hopefully out of the way of inquisitive animals. Anything which needed to be kept cool was bagged up and submerged in a calm pool by the side of the river, then weighed down with stones. Buckets and skins of water were then filled, being sure to soak them thoroughly on the outside to aid evaporative cooling of the contents. These were then strung-up on tripods and further covered over with a makeshift shelter of leafy branches to keep them out of the sun. So far from its source the river water could well have picked up a variety of pathogens so anything they would drink would ideally need to be boiled but the big camp kettle was nearly always simmering, being topped up as needed. If the water source was more suspect, or turbid with sediment, they could employ a tightly-woven cloth bag to filter the worst, then run it through fine sand and charcoal, though this was seldom really necessary. The reality was that through exposure to pathogens in the past they rarely had any major stomach upsets, but it was not ideal to end up with even a minor illness when they were aiming to travel a good distance on this trip.

With camp substantially set up, they further investigated the fishing area, which they could see was teeming with the salmon they hoped to catch. There was no obvious sign of bear in the area, which normally was abundantly clear with fish remains scattered on the banks. Often just the brains of the salmon were eaten in a gorging frenzy of calorific fats, making ready for hibernation in the not too-distant future. There were a good number of rocky vantage points for spearing the fish; they could afford to be choosy with those they selected, any not quite up to scratch would be fine for their meals in camp.

Before long the children were trying their hand with the spears, tied at the end with a strong thin-cord and looped around the wrist to avoid losing them as they practised. There was a little skill required, but such were the numbers within easy reach, bunched-up beneath the waterfall, it was difficult to miss once your eye was in and adjusted to the refraction of the water. With instruction the children spent a glorious afternoon fishing and ended up with a good number which would be perfect for their supper. Some of the fish would be stuffed with ground ivy with its mildly minty and sage-like taste, quite excellent cooked in the embers of the fire, which once removed, fell apart into succulent juicy-flakes. The prime specimens of the salmon would be more simply cooked, gutted and the exposed flesh pegged to a rough plank of green wood, then propped by the fire. This was a lovely way of cooking, being easy to control and giving a slightly-crunchy top, sealing in and concentrating the lovely juices and flavour. Where possible the salmon's eggs were harvested as well, the roe having a lovely slightly-silty taste of the ocean with a subtle moreish-sweetness, though it was not to the taste of everyone. The fish and roe was served with traveling bannock bread, loaded with juicy dried fruits, and various wild greens including the clover-like lemony wood sorrel, tiny wild onions and chervil, complementing the fish superbly with a pinch of salt. They had brought with them a few root vegetables for any leaner times, along with some freshly-milled oat flour, but they expected to mostly live off the land, and tonight was no exception. To finish they baked some of the early wild-apples found hereabouts, wrapped in leaves and buried in the coals. They had with them a good supply of honey which they drizzled over the resulting flavoursome and slightly gooey fruit, dusted over with crumbled oat-biscuits. It was a splendid wild feast; all slept that night the contented slumber of those outdoors and looking forward to many such meals to come.

The following day was a little overcast, but this made for excellent fishing, with the glare of the sun off the water minimal and making picking out the choicest salmon a simple task. The group had split that day to form a fishing party and another to start making the smokers. Much as they had done now many a time, they made large tripods covered in wide sheets of stripped bark, over the coals of a hardwood fire, then added soaked oak woodchips. This started the process of creating a slow burning smoker, which they loaded with filleted salmon, hung on simple racks. The smell was amazing, with a smoky sweet crust formed, permeated through with the preserving smoke. After about a day the fish were removed and kept in a shaded area for further drying, concentrating the meaty fish and getting rid of any last residues of moisture the heat of the smoker had not driven out.

It was on the third day that they saw their first bear, initially very cautious, investigating from the far side of the wide river. Once the beast was sure that the group was no threat, it started its own fishing, scooping the fish from the head of the tumbling waterfall as they leaped up, with a hunter's consummate ease. This was no youngster, but an experienced bear, strong and skilled, in the prime of its life. It gorged on just the most calorific parts of the fish, mostly the brains, leaving the rest scattered haphazardly along the shore. It was at first unnerving sharing the wide river with the bear, but they kept out of each other's way and there was plenty of fish to go around. Soon various birds were attracted in by the easy pickings; corvids, gulls and osprey all making an appearance and cleaning up. As the bear finished its feasting, then sauntered off, some of the older children riskily swam over through the shallows and took a number of feathers left over from the squabbles between the scavenging birds, the osprey's being particularly coveted prizes. They were chastised by the adults for their recklessness, but the risk of attack by the bear was very low, it being far from hungry enough to have an interest in some scrawny humans.

With the first big-batch of smoked and preserved salmon now ready some days later, Nineveh and Shuldan took the first load back to The Steading, it would be a few days before they returned, and so production was reduced, giving the others time to explore. They hoped to find feeder streams to the river which could in theory lead them to water meadows ripe with beaver. Their pelts were excellent for making water-repellent clothing and their meat was much like a rich pork, quite excellent marinated and slowly cooked. If they had the opportunity, they would consider harvesting a bear, for its meat and hide, but they would need to ensure they took little risk. Mink would also be a prize they would set traps for, the pelt being superbly soft and insulating. This relative of the weasel was likely to be found along the rivers and streams where wooded, but they would initially set out bait on apparent trails and assess where the traps would be best. The pine woods hereabout should also contain capercaillie, the turkey of the woods, being still relatively far from the more lowland plains. Though the birds were secretive and difficult to track down, it would make a wonderful change to their diet. The dogs were ideal for tracking down their scent, where this time of the year they would spend most time feeding within the undergrowth on heather tips and early lingonberries. In winter they would be mostly in the tree-tops eating the young tips of pine boughs; very much harder to hunt, as-well-as much less tasty to eat, the pines thought by some to give them a slightly-astringent taint.

With all of these opportunities, their main aim was of exploration and assessing the relevant habitats. With the abundance of salmon they could afford to use the excess to bait certain areas, the mink being the main target. The beaver could be tracked down by their lodges and flooded meadows, with snare traps set over obvious runs and baited with fresh green-shoots of alder and suchlike. This scouting would take some time but fitted into their current downtime from fishing and preserving.

The first successful hunt was in the pine woods with the dogs, a group of capercaillie being startled and taken down in mid-flight with blunt-tipped arrows and slings. Three plump females made for an excellent meal that night, spit roasted over the fire, basted in butter and herbs. They ate the birds with a plethora of mushrooms, fried in a little butter and accompanied by sweet roasted wild-garlic stems. It was another superb meal, all the better for being wonderfully fresh and simple; a glorious taste of the woods.

Shuldan and Nineveh were back later on the next morning and so the work of harvesting and preserving the salmon continued with renewed vigour. Progress was swift and many salmon were soon landed, enough to fill the smokers for days to come. With only minimal attention needed on the smokers, the majority of the group went back out to trapping, pleased to see that beaver had been caught at three sites out of four, the dozens of snares they had laid having done their jobs. These were taken and then skinned, the hides de-fleshed, washed, stretched and left out to dry. They would be fine for transport back with the next load of fish, ready to be tanned in due course. The beaver meat was quite excellent and a welcome novelty, being left to marinade over night, then slow cooked in their big stew pots. With Shuldan's excellent all-purpose spice mix, it provided wonderfully succulent and hearty stews, with potatoes, onions and carrots added from the stores.

During their camp they had seen the odd lone bear using their fishing spot from the opposite bank; after initially checking out the humans the beasts rarely then took much notice of them, focussed as they were upon their fishing. It was really a less than prime spot for bears, being so exposed, but it was not surprising they tried their luck at the inviting waterfall, being on an obvious pinch-point for the migrating fish. The previous day though had seen an older bear, which seemingly had trouble trying to catch the leaping salmon, going to scoop the fish just too late the majority of the time. Those it did manage to catch were wolfed down in their entirety, a marked difference to the bears they had seen before taking just the choicest parts. They noticed the animal left that night with its nose towards their camp, but thought little of it. The next day the bear tried again at the waterfall, but somewhat half-heartedly and with very little success. Again it sniffed the camp when it left, but with increased interest that had the hunters concerned. That night what they presumed to be the same bear was nosing around the far reaches of camp at the smokers and had taken some of the fish harvested that day. The morning after, surveying the damage, the group decided it was too risky to leave the animal to try its luck again, perhaps closer to camp. The bear was clearly sick or getting too old to feed itself if it was resorting to partly-smoked fish when they were so plentiful in the river. If they were just to leave the area, they ran the risk it would follow either the group, or more likely, the caravan of ponies with the last batch of fish, now it had a taste for them. With only a little debate it was decided that the bear should be tracked back to its resting place and an ambush made ready, though all were under no illusions as to the danger posed in the hunt.

Late morning, with heavy spears prepared, and arrows with broad points and hazel shafts freshly straightened over the fire, Merrick led the hunting party out, with the excited dogs under close control. The bear was simple enough the follow and as they saw more of its tracks they noted an abnormal pattern to its gait, clearly favouring one side with minimal weight on one paw evidenced by the consistently shallow print. Any wound likely causing the limp would make the bear more dangerous and unpredictable, but it did at least help explain its unusual behaviour in approaching the camp to steal food.

They followed the tracks for some distance, using the dogs to pick up the trail when it went cold, though this was rare in the soft alluvial-soil of the wooded hinterland the bear had kept to. The party came in time to an area which made the dogs nervous and so it was assumed the bear must be nearby, perhaps the spot it had slept overnight. With hindsight it proved very fortuitous they decided to stop, and within just a minute all could clearly hear the soft disturbance of undergrowth less than eighty feet to the south of their position. Having already agreed a plan of action, they set this in motion and the hunters broke into two teams, picking their way silently through the wooded understorey, the dogs spread out between them, but under control with a system of low whistles. In this way they stealthily came upon the bear, evidently quite lethargic and stumbling here and there, a subtle sickly-smell assaulting their highly sensitive nostrils as it did. With great caution they approached and made ready their bows, all making sure their best heavy broadhead arrows were readily to hand, knocked to their strings and partially drawn. The dogs were then instructed to start barking to create a distraction in the centre, the two groups of hunters then approaching obliquely on each side. With a signal from Merrick the archers let their arrows fly, striking the bear about its flanks. This caused the bear to rear up in pain, the scent of its blood soon heavy in the air, but no arrow had made a killing blow. The hulking black bear may be malnourished, but clearly it was a magnificent beast in the prime of its life until recently, and still had thick muscle which was hard to fully penetrate by arrows alone. The dogs were instructed to press their harassment of the animal, keeping its attention focussed; this gave the hunters opportunity to approach and ready their spears.

However, despite best-laid plans and before they were properly in position the bear suddenly cantered forward at speed which was quite unexpected, almost carelessly swiping a massive paw at one of the harassing dogs, which crumpled without even a whimper. At this the hunters ran forward, some throwing their spears and others running forward to close in. On seeing this approach, the bear started a lumbering run towards the group led by Merrick, arrows and a spear hanging from its side and rump, hot crimson-blood dripping profusely as it ran. As it approached the hunters, Merrick instinctively rammed the butt of his spear into the ground and braced his foot behind it, just as the bear turned its murderous charge towards him. Merrick's heart was thundering as the bear came at him, now seemingly in slow motion, but he kept his nerve, knowing that to turn-and-run would likely result in his being mauled to death, or simply swatted-aside like the dog. As the bear approached, Merricks' perception of time further slowed; he felt the thudding vibration of the ground, while noticing it's slightly off-gait run, the spittle flicking from its slathering maw and the raw ferocity in its hypnotic eyes. Merrick nonetheless held his nerve, and with near-perfect timing tilted the braced spear and it took the bear full in its massive chest, the inertia of the beast's bulk driving itself onto the heavy shaft, though striking Merrick with a glancing blow as it did. With the abrupt halt it briefly shuddered then fell, the spear had evidently taken the bear full in the heart; with a last few rasping pants and convulsive gushes of sticky hot-blood drenching Merrick in an arterial spray, it fell to one side, and lay still.

Though glancing the force of the blow Merrick received was considerable, leaving him dazed and near unconscious; he lay besides the bear, prone on the forest floor, breathing laboured and covered in it's blood. Rushing to him the hunters noted their leader's obvious head-wound caused as he had hit the floor, oozing profusely, but which Arwyn soon had cleaned and staunched, then bandaged. After some minutes he started moving, to everyone's relief, though his breathing was wheezy and hard won; on examining his chest there were some abrasions along with much bruising and perhaps a broken rib or two, but thankfully nothing obviously serious. After washing him down in the river they strapped his injuries up as best they could and applied some salve to stop festering and swelling, but they were impressed it was not more serious given the force of the blow, his strong muscled-frame and quick reactions no doubt saving him from more serious injury. It would however be some considerable time before his ribs fully-healed and he once again regained complete lung-capacity without inducing pain.

With Merrick's wounds triaged, and the adrenaline of the kill starting to subside, they next examined the impressive musky-hulk of the black bear, a good deal bigger than any they had seen before, potentially a grizzly hybrid. At once they saw an ugly-looking wound to its side, clearly the reason for its gait noted on the initial tracking. It didn't take long to explore the rank puss-filled wound and in it they found a knapped flint spearhead lodged deep within the muscle of the shoulder, partially healed-over but festering. It was far from the large leaf-shaped steel spearheads they carried, and was not a weapon designed for hunting a bear, perhaps a deer at best. The embedded flint spearhead and short length of snapped wooden-haft would clearly have caused the bear immense pain, and despite the loss of a dog, the hunters felt glad they had brought the magnificent beast to the end of its life, shortening its undoubted suffering.

257

The fallen dog had clearly suffered a broken neck and crushed spine, a quick death at least, though all were sorry to lose any of the pack. They respectfully buried the animal under a low cairn of rocks on a high point near the river with honour deserved to a member of the hunting party, as well as a pet who would be much missed. The other dogs laid around the grave and remained a while, pining and whimpering in soft unison as they lamented their loss, until reluctantly they left with the hunters at their gentle but firm command.

Besides Merrick's injuries, the most worrying aspect of the situation was that the spearhead found lodged in the bear indicated human presence, perhaps not too far distant. However, with the age of the wound and the condition of the bear, indicating it had been wounded some weeks ago at least, it was far from clear proof of an imminent threat or close proximity of another settlement. Given the lack of any other sign of human presence since their arrival, and that the bear seemingly had only moved to their side of the river to take their food, they decided that the others very likely originated from the east side of the river Rhuø and perhaps some several days travel at least, given the distance bears could quickly travel. It was more than likely that the wound had hampered the bear's ability to hunt and defend its territory, likely resulting in its displacement by another dominant bear. Nonetheless, their vigilance increased and it made them resolve to break camp soon and move some way west into the plains, where they should be further removed from any threat.

Returning to the camp they decided to dispose of the remainder of the unsmoked fish they couldn't eat and take the near complete load back to The Steading using the ponies the very next day. Nineveh and Shuldan would be accompanied by some of the dogs, along with Bolin and Eryn for added security, with repeated requests made to them by everyone to be very careful. Bolin was an accomplished tracker by way of his eye for detail and he promised he and Eryn would pay special attention to the muddy banks of the river, examining the ground for any sign of other humans.

The bear carcass was quickly skinned and roughly de-fleshed, with its massive head and claws also taken to be preserved. They left the meat, fearing the likely blood-poisoning that had resulted from the long-festering wound, evidenced by its jaundiced eyes; it was a shame to leave the large amount of ordinarily excellent meat, but it was just not worth the risk. The carcass would soon be broken up by scavengers, all evidence of the kill being removed in just a few days.

That evening they made preparations to break camp and with the morning they were ready, the pony train already on its way at first light. Given the lighter-than-expected load on the ponies going back to the Steading, one of the four was kept for the group to transport some of the heavier camp goods and to let the injured Merrick ride on occasion, but everyone was laden beyond their comfort zones; nevertheless they all understood the need to be gone before the ponies could return back from The Steading. The camp was left as near 'no trace' as possible, though it would be some time before all sign and scent had been erased.

31 - The plains

The group cautiously made their way further north downriver where they picked up the crumbling remains of the old road of their ancestors, though barely recognisable as such, comprising an indistinct linear mound mostly subsumed by vegetation. From there, if they went west, they knew from previous exploration that they would gradually leave the lush deciduous-woodlands surrounding the river, and encounter the grassland plains previously partially-explored. On-route to pick up the old road, they had carefully monitored the ground around them and the banks of the river, for any sign of other humans, as well as keeping an eye to the sky for campfire plumes; thankfully they saw none.

They had agreed with the pony team to follow the old roadway west for a steady two days, then to head north at that point, leaving a subtle way-marker. The turning point would be wherever most conveniently masked their trail, ideally being in an area of hard ground with a shallow stony-watercourse they could travel through for some distance. After about a day's hard march in this direction, they would halt, make camp in a hidden spot and wait for the others to catch up, watchers set to bring them in safely and to monitor that they weren't being trailed.

Travelling in the plains would be in single file as much as possible, to hide their true numbers from all but the most skilled of trackers, though it had the trade-off by making their combined track more readily apparent. While walking the line of the road they hadn't noted any sign of other humans, and they began to relax as they left the river Rhuø further behind. Anyone travelling to the west would very likely have used the fragmentary remains of the roadway as a convenient guide, no sign meaning either complete absence, or very infrequent travel by humans. There was some trade-off in this approach, as they would leave obvious sign of their passage, but given the lack of any sign of humans on all previous travel this way, the risk was considered minimal.

Describing the area as plains was perhaps somewhat of a misnomer, being more scrubby rolling-grasslands than wide-open prairie, with various small-copses of deciduous trees filled with birds, which loudly protested as the travellers invaded their respective territories. Almost at once on entering the plains they encountered herds of wary deer, a few of the mighty auroch in loose groups, and various birds spooked up as they came too near. No doubt there were good numbers of apex predators present, though these would mostly stay out-of-sight, fear of humans still strongly engrained in their psyche. The rolling landscape had continued for much of their journey two days west, though on entering a more elevated area, the ground became hard and stony, with much less vegetation, various stunted scrubby-grasses and herbs being more common. They agreed this would be an ideal place to leave the remnants of the old road, so they left their way-marker, comprising the traditional setting of a smaller stone atop a larger with another small stone on the south-side. Usually this would mean turn south at that point, but they had agreed with the pony team to set the marker backwards to the norm and additionally to turn north in five hundred footsteps instead, taking every effort to minimise their trail. The precaution was likely unnecessary and the way marker would soon be removed on the pony team's arrival, but it did no harm to be cautious.

On leaving the road they took great pains to ensure their way was not easily detectable, despite the compacted ground being unlikely to show any obvious foot or hoof prints. Their pony could do this without any effort, being very careful where it placed their feet at the best of times, so they had little worry there, but the odd scuff mark or crushed plant was all but inevitable. The stony, scarcely-vegetated soil eventually gave way again to lower ground, which evidently held more moisture, being verdant knee-high grass and dotted with scrubby bushes. The grass parted easily as they walked through it and little evidence of their trail was readily apparent, the gently swaying sea of vegetation soon settling back and subsuming signs of their passage. It was a beautiful landscape, varying little but hypnotic and almost feeling as though they travelled across an ocean of grass, the copses like small islands providing convenient features to aim for.

After about half-a-day's hard march, the keen eyes of Durian noted in the far distance a substantial linear wooded-area running roughly east-west; this could potentially provide some decent cover and mask a little of the smoke from their camp fires, so they made their way there. By this point of the journey, the youngest children were clearly starting to flag a little, though they would not be the first to admit it; Arwyn therefore got them to take turns to ride the pony and all received sweet treats to fuel up on, soon revitalising them for another few miles. On finally arriving at the tree-line some hours later, they found the ground below the trees seemingly retained more moisture than the surrounding grasslands, hence the lush vegetation. Not far beyond the belt of trees they encountered a limestone escarpment, a ridge of more sparsely vegetated rock which protruded maybe forty feet or so above the rest of the plains hereabout. It was likely this rock formation that acted as an area which rain ran-off and saturated the soil around it, creating some small ponds and boggy areas, but fairly dry itself. The whole ridge was only about half a mile long and about four hundred feet or so wide at a maximum, but this had resulted in a small oasis around it, when compared to the grasslands. It was an excellent place for a camp, providing water, wood and a highpoint from which they could survey much of the plains, being more open to the north where it dropped-off more steeply. They would however move slightly-further west before they made camp, as the area was a little boggy, with insects already creating a nuisance. Following the escarpment, they came in time to a stretch which further reared up, and at its base were a series of small cave-openings a little up the slope. Within a hundred yards was a large spring which gurgled out of a natural bedding-plane in the rock down into a series of pools, one almost like a large natural-bowl, before flowing away via a small stream to meet the soil of the plains; here it formed some shallow ponds and quickly spread out. Otherwise the area was relatively dry and hopefully free from too many biting insects. Following investigation of the pools they set about exploring the area further, being wary of the openings in the escarpment which could lead to a cave system; bears were unlikely, out in what was the plains, but could potentially harbour wolves and possibly lynx, though they likely would have left the area long before their actual arrival. Cautiously they investigated the spaces and found some remnants of desiccated animal scat, but nothing recent. The caves were all relatively dry, if a little musky, though only one was big enough for them to stand within. It was soon decided to use the larger cave to sleep in, saving them the bother of putting up all the tarp shelters.

Following a good check over of each other and the dogs for ticks inevitably picked up from the trek in the long grass, they spent the rest of the day collecting dead-standing wood, of which there was an abundance in the belt of trees. A good supply was stacked and put undercover in one of the smaller caves, the other being given over to their pony, with room for the other three, when they arrived. They gathered various dry grasses to line the floor of the temporary stable, and soon had the animal installed in its new home, letting it have a much-needed rest. Next, they got a small fire going and boiled water to make tea; the pungent smoke was minimal with the dry wood and had soon dissipated by the time it reached the tops of the trees. In any event with the coming evening it mattered little, as it would soon be dark which would veil the visual presence of any smoke plume.

On their journey here they had spooked various birds, including partridge, corncrake and quail. Always on the lookout the ever vigilant Arwyn had managed to take down a great bustard, a substantial bird of about thirty pounds or so of useable meat, like an oversized turkey, though tasting more gamey, similar to partridge. They were incredibly quick-running on the ground, but this one had taken off into its ungainly slow-flight, and so was easily taken down. Being such a big bird, it would take considerable time to cook, so tonight they would eat some of their travelling stores and make a proper fire pit the next day. The dressed bird would be stored overnight, wrapped up in leaves and tied up in a sack to shield it from flies, hung up in a cool shaded-tree away from scavengers.

Next morning they started the day by digging a fire pit to cook the bustard, this they did away from the limestone which would crack and potentially explode, in a cleared area of soil. The hole was then lined with rounded igneous-type stones found dotted on the plains, loaded with wood, lit and allowed to burn down to a thick bed of coals. The bustard was stuffed with some onions and cloves of garlic from home, then wrapped in various wild cabbage-type leaves to help keep it moist. The bird was then laid on some wet woodchips to keep it off the coals, allowing it to stay moist. The pit and bird was then covered over with some of the super-heated rocks, then a layer of soil and sod which would allow it to slow cook in the makeshift oven, to be uncovered later that day.

While the party waited for the pony team to catch up, which might be two days at least, they started to further scout the area, noting already that it was absolutely teeming with wildlife. As they had initially thought likely on arriving, the smoothed apex of the ridge was a great vantage point, as they could see some distance around them in a wide arc to the north, also being much less vegetated that way. It was clear that the ridge would cut much of the prevailing northerly-wind and allow the trees to grow in its lee, but to the north there was no such break in the plains until the more coastal dunes, being many miles distant, and only just visible to the keenest eyed of the group in the clear autumn air as a hazy smudge on the horizon.

It was settled over a leisurely breakfast that the party would split into three, with one to tend to the camp, and the other two to range out to scout for good hunting spots and to monitor any herds. They would take enough supplies with them for one night, but would be back if they could help it to enjoy the slowly-cooking bird, which would be an unusual treat, already causing everyone to salivate in anticipation.

The group staying at the camp had decided it would be prudent to set up their tarps outside of the caves, to provide for some shade and additional shelter. Being south-facing the area turned into a sun trap come midday with the rocks radiating back heat, and while this was welcome in the autumnal mornings and evenings, by the time the sun was at its full height, it could be uncomfortable. Being unsafe to build a fire onto the limestone itself, they found more of the so-called erratic volcanic-rocks, which could be dug from the soil of the plains with only a little trouble. There were also a good number of flint nodules on the plains, presumably associated with the chalky limestone of the area; these they were careful to avoid using for the fireplace given their propensity to crack in the heat. The igneous-type rocks helped them form a decent base for the camp fire, and allowed them to build up a small edging wall to act as a wind break to also absorb some of the heat, to be gently radiated back. With that done, they collected more wood and processed it down to useable pieces with their collapsible wood-framed bow saws and then split it with their axes. It was hard work, the sweat soon rolling down their faces and stinging their eyes, but between them they processed enough for some several days at least in one session.

These jobs had gotten them pretty dirty and sweaty, so they took the opportunity to take refreshing baths in the spring-fed pools, the lower ones being relatively warm, with the water having flowed over the now warmed-up rocks absorbed from the hot sun. They agreed to keep the small top-pool clean for drinking water, while using the lower ones for washing. The small group were soon contentedly splashing about and cleaning themselves down in the largest bottom most of the pools. It was a great deal more pleasant than the pools by the waterfall at home, which were cool at the best of times, the water being not long off the mountains and glaciers. They felt they could get used to these wonderfully-warmed pools and lazed much of the morning contentedly washing themselves and their clothes, then sun-bathing on the adjoining warm smooth-rocks. Before long though they wanted to eat, breakfast now a distant memory, so they left the pools and made a light lunch from their supplies and lazed about while that digested, feeding titbits to the cheeky robins and numerous tits that frequented the area. Soon though they had to move, as it was nearly time to dig up the bird from the fire pit, to let it rest and cool. To complement the meat they would have some of the wild sweet-potatoes they had tracked down not far from the ponds, along with various mushrooms from the woods, including field and penny-bun type, which would be excellent simply sliced and fried in some fat and wild garlic. The sweet potatoes would be slow-cooked in the cooler coals of the fire with some fresh herbs, wrapped in leaves to stop them burning; the moreish carbohydrate would form a delicious accompaniment to the bustard, with the mushrooms and a salad of wild greens. The sweet-potatoes were a rare treat, only growing in temperate climes normally, showing how warm it must be hereabouts year-round, the radiative effect of the limestone outcrop potentially being key in creating a heat island.

The scouting parties returned late afternoon, reporting good numbers of potential prey to the north-west and north-east, certainly enough that this would be an ideal place for a semi-permanent camp, being shielded away from those herds. This was great news to all, who had quickly grown fond of the spot, especially the children who loved the warm pools in which they could play in the sun. The hunters explained that they had not gone near the herds, being content to observe them and get a feel for their movements and habits; but on their return they had fully scouted the woods, and one party had come across some pheasants, taking two with quick stones from their slings mid-flight. These were quickly plucked, then gutted and would be roasted over the fire. Cooked whole the skin kept the tasty fat close to the leaner meat of the birds, and with occasional turning on a green-hazel spit, was soon browned off. As with the bustard preparation they took care to wash down their tools and hands, using a little soap, then pouring boiling water over the metal of their knifes and a small butchering axe. Once the pheasants were well-cooked, it was eaten warm as a starter straight from the fire, the slightly-burnt skin and outer layer of fat being wonderfully crunchy, the flesh juicy and full of wonderful flavour. The remains were given to the dogs, once the small bones had been removed, who hungrily wolfed down their share.

With that appetiser the group were hungry for more and with the potatoes now ready and mushrooms fried off, the bustard was brought out from its resting place at the back of the cool cave for their supper. All received a very generous portion, and the dogs lapped up the many morsels thrown their way. The breast meat was a little like chicken, but the delicacy was the thighs and legs, being more like hare or golden plover. The onion and garlic stuffing added good flavour to all parts of the meat, but with the smoky-sweet taste of the woodchips especially, it was quite superb. All slept well that night, some slightly sun-burned from the long days on the open plains, but clean, well-fed and happy in the knowledge this would be their home for some time to come.

It was in this way that the next two days passed, the hunters out observing the herds, and bringing back various smaller game. The larger hunt would await the return of the pony team to help transport the meat back to the camp for further processing, being also conscious that they would be tired with the days of travelling and not wanting an immediate homeward return. While they were waiting Amaethon took the chance to show everyone who was interested how to form flint arrowheads, scrapers and small axes. Their steel versions were superior in many ways, but it did no harm to have an alternative source of tools, metal arrowheads in particular being wasteful when razor-sharp knapped heads could be formed with relative ease. All were conscious that although they could scavenge for scrap metals, these were becoming harder to find. Mining for ores was they knew of little use as they were rarely any untapped resources close to the surface, these seemingly have been mined out ages ago.

The start of that day was spent in selecting the best flint nodules, looking for those lumps which were most consistent with a fine grain with few inclusions, which made working them much more difficult. A similar approach was possible with other forms of rock, including obsidian and the volcanic rocks close to home, so was something they could practice further on their return. Having chosen a good few nodules, Amaethon set up an area for working the flint, well-away from camp, the detritus that would soon accumulate a giveaway to others of their presence, and less than ideal if trodden upon, much being razor-sharp. With a thick piece of leather sat across his thigh, Amaethon gathered everyone around to demonstrate the art of knapping. First, he showed the knack of only moving the nodule, while bringing down a harder rounded-rock in a consistent motion, avoiding too much strain on the wrist, by using the whole arm in the early stages. With the easy grace of an expert, Amaethon proceeded to strike the flint, forming level platforms where he could then take off chunks by striking just inside the fresh edge, resulting in sharp slithers of flint, many of which would be perfectly adequate as scrapers for de-fleshing and makeshift knifes with a little more working. The key was getting a feel for the flint, which took experience, and so he quickly had others trying out the process for themselves, to varying degrees of success.

As the day wore-on the more intricate skills of the flint knapper were explored, using different materials, including antler for removing finer flakes then moving onto production of fine arrowheads and spear points with pressure-flaking techniques. By the end of the day, most of the group were proficient in production of a basic toolkit and arrowheads, some positively enjoying their new-found-skill and keen to do more. Amaethon was pleased with everyone's progress, confident that in a pinch they all had the skill to make tools to help keep themselves alive. A couple of the younger children showed particular promise and in time absorbed much of their teacher's skill, producing useful tools and passing on their knowledge in due course to the next generation. As with many crafts some simply enjoyed the practice of knapping for its own sake, relaxing in its own way with a by-product of creating useful items and keeping the old skills alive for the next generation.

The pony team arrived as predicted, bringing good news that they had not seen any sign of other people on the western riverbank. It was therefore assumed that the wounded bear must have been travelling for some time from further east, while gradually weakening, perhaps picking up the odour of the harvested fish and ultimately crossing their path in desperation. The team explained that they would have made better time, as they were taking turns to ride the lightly-laden ponies, but Bolin and Eryn had been distracted by the wrecks on the highway, finding many good bits of scrap metal that they had stashed for their return visit. The team were quickly shown the pools, the caves and lookout, all being very proud of the spot, with much agreement from the blacksmiths and Nineveh and Shuldan, as to the excellence of the camp. They in turn gave the news from home, reporting that all was well with the homestead and that all the fish had been successfully stowed-away in the recently expanded cold-stores. They advised that they would need to be careful not to harvest excessive amounts of meat, as the stores were already pretty full. With less need for meat to store, this left room for transporting numerous skins, which would come in very useful, especially that of the auroch. This should still leave a little room for some of the scrap metals on the ponies, much to a certain pairs' clear delight.

Given that the hunting would be much less of a significant undertaking than originally thought, they could afford to give the travellers a good break and treated them to all manner of delightful meals, with another bustard, pheasant, hares, the last of a small auroch and the subtly differently-tasting deer of the plains. The sweet potatoes and plethora of mushrooms were also a delight, and with Nineveh's and Shudan's expert eye for cooking, their fresh supplies of herbs, honey and slabs of butter and cheese, they soon had everyone salivating in anticipation of each delicious meal.

While the final preparations were made for supper, they all took it in turns to take a bath, and the pony team agreed they were a great treat, the warm waters relaxing tired muscles. Fresh supplies of newly-made soap crafted by Shulvan were used, including one smelling of lavender, but full of a blend of moisturising and cleansing ingredients including yarrow oil, which deep cleaned without leaving anyone sore. Their clothes also received a thorough scrubbing, ridding them of the dust of the plains and the general grime of travel, and then were placed over various thick bushes of rosemary and lavender to dry in the sun and absorb their cleansing scent.

The next day the travellers took it easy while the hunters checked on the latest movements of the herds. They had pretty much decided to take two auroch and had therefore selected a pair of second-year smaller females, which should be less challenging to hunt than the great males, but still provide for excellent meat and useful thick hides. The animals would need to be taken by wearing them down over a chase with the assistance of the dogs, but they hoped it would be possible to spear them several times about the chest from a safe distance, with the blood loss leaving them open to final thrusts with their heavy spears to finish them off. While it might be possible to use their heavier bows, they had no wish to simply wound the animals and cause suffering if they managed to escape, so chose the more difficult stalk.

With their plans in place they started out the next morning, then split into two groups to tackle each of the beasts. Shuldan and Nineveh would stay with the ponies and the younger children, not wanting to risk them in this fairly dangerous hunt. Being trampled or gored by the auroch would be a horrible end for anyone, but they could not afford to risk the children, much to their disgust at being left out. The children were however mollified to some extent by being given the important job of using their keen eyes to monitor the hunter's progress from the ridge, and to await the signal fires if they went out of view.

In the end their careful preparations made simple work of approaching the targets, and one team had theirs down relatively quick, after a short

271

chase with the target panicking and breaking a leg, thus making short work of then finishing it off. The other group though ended up some distance from the camp after a long exhausting-chase, though safely concluded. The children watched the hunters and noted the final resting places of the aurochs, confirmed with small signal-fires. With two keeping an eye on the situation, the others excitedly ran down from the ridge to Nineveh and Shuldan shouting the good news.

The ponies were soon readied, with the smallest children getting rides. Nineveh and Shuldan then split the party, with two of the four ponies going to each kill, carrying the tools needed for the skinning and butchering. On arriving the hunters had already made some progress, each party having bled out the animals with a cut to the arteries in its neck. After leaving them about twenty minutes to drain, they starting the skinning to first expose the chest cavity, though it would be a long job, taking great pains to keep the hide intact, as much as was possible. The carcass was then gutted and the heart, liver, tongue and kidneys put to one side in protective waxed cloths, out of the way of flies and in the shade. Between them, and aided by the ponies, they would then roll the huge auroch to complete the skinning and rough de-fleshing, then start cutting up the carcass into large sections, using their bow saws and axes. It would take some hours, though they would take all of each animal back to the camp on ponies and their backs between them, hopefully in just two trips. They were conscious the kills and discarded guts would likely attract scavengers soon, with birds, including some of the plains numerous vultures, already starting to circle high overhead.

Transporting the meat back to camp was an exhausting affair, even with the ponies taking the bulk, and on their second return trip they were sweaty and sticky with gore, being constantly pestered by flies. It would however be a long day still, with their needing to cook and preserve the meat and complete the de-fleshing of the hides. They had made great fire pits and spits during the past few days over which the meat would be slow cooked and deeply smoked, preserving much as strips of jerky. This would take much of the night and into the morning, following which they would set the meat over the fairly cool smokers for at least another two days, to preserve it further for the trip home. First though they would take it in turns to bathe and scrub themselves and the ponies clean; before long the pools were tinged with a scarlet hue, though soon washed away by the constant flow of fresh water from the spring.

The hunters were treated to hearty stews and baked root-vegetables, with freshly-baked camp bread. With what little stew was left they added more water and piled in the best bits of the aurochs' spine and neck meat to boil down for further tasty meals the next day. Mushrooms stuffed with butter, garlic and breadcrumbs were also on the menu, roasted in leaf-wrapped bundles in the fire. While all this was cooking they had fried off slices of the auroch liver and snacked on that delicacy, feeding chunks to the dogs who ravenously gobbled up the morsels. The tongue meat would be boiled, then smoked and would make an excellent trail food with chunks of bread, tomato chutney and foraged greens. As a special treat the dogs were also given the heart and kidneys, along with some of the bones cracked open for the marrow.

The four great auroch-horns were taken as drinking vessels, excellent for quaffing the beer, cider and mead currently brewing at home. The brain was extracted to be used for tanning the thick hides, but some would also be eaten, being extremely nutritious, about a third fat, ideal in a curry-type meal, but great for bulking-out stews as well. The skulls were then discarded, having been cracked apart to remove the horns, tongue and brain. The skulls, along with just a few other parts deemed not usable, were taken some distance from the camp and left out for scavengers, though there would be slim pickings, with very little wasted.

The two mighty aurochs would yield at least five-hundred pounds of useable meat each, though once this was cooked and smoked, it would be a good third less being partially dehydrated. While at camp they would also eat the meat less simple to preserve, but even with that, they foresaw that the two aurochs would yield a few hundred pounds each of excellent quality meat to take home. Though that would greatly add to their stores, one of the main bonuses of the trip was of course that having been away from The Steading, feasting off the land for many weeks, they would be a good deal better off than if they had stayed at home and depleted their stores and local supplies of game.

The meat was tended through the night in shifts as it cooked, though mainly to guard it from inquisitive scavengers attracted by the tempting aromas. These animals would mostly be dissuaded by the bright perimeter fires they had set, but the group's general presence and unfamiliar human and canine scent would also assist. As the evening came the whole scene was intensely primeval, the smoke swirling around the hunters, lit up by the flickering fires in hues of red and yellow, the darkness of the night encircling them with the innumerable stars above, the wash of the Milky Way particularly prominent that night. They gave thanks to the animals they had taken, imitating their lives and the hunt in dances around the fire, while they loudly sang and feasted through the night.

The warm dry days that came followed a comfortable routine of hunting the herds of deer, processing, preserving and relaxing in the spring-fed pools. Despite their feasting virtually every day, the huge stocks of meat they had amassed would help keep them going through the winter with ease, and as planned would reduce the pressure on their more local stocks of deer, pigs and other game. In addition to the meat, they also spent time preserving, then tanning the numerous hides they had harvested, producing supple leathers. First the hides were soaked in lye from soaked wood-ash to aid de-hairing, then scraped of any residual fat and flesh using their newly-made flint scrapers, which were surprisingly effective to those used to steel implements. This left a hide which could be tightly strung onto a frame and then liberally worked with a mush of brains to tan and soften the skin to form a quality leather. A messy and tiring job but which produced some beautifully soft material, some of which was used immediately replacing simpler items of clothing and equipment straight away, but much was kept to take back to The Steading. At the limits of what they could transport between them and the ponies, they decided it was time to travel home, though at a leisurely pace. Bolin and Eryn were however quite worried that they would not be able to pick up all their scrap metals, but they were determined to have a good supply for winter projects, so elected to make another trip before the icy weather returned, if needs be.

The camp would be left much as they found it, leaving no trace as far as was possible, with the campfire stones taken away and randomly hidden in the woods for future reuse. On removing the stones they noted that where the scorched and burnt bedrock of limestone had mixed with ash, it had created patches of a crude lime paste-like substance where the dowsing water had quenched the final embers of the fire. It was good to find that the limestone was suitable for making a quicklime, as it was a useful material for making mortar and lime wash, though it was some considerable distance to transport it back home. They would however think on the possibility of creating a small batch of dried lime on future trips, as The Steading would need some of its mortar tending to in the not too distant future. Padded out with coarse sand and ash from the valley, they may get away with quite a

275

small fresh-lime proportion, and could reuse any crumbled pointing from the walls of the dwelling, by crushing it back into the mortar mix. Another project for the future, but an important resource added to their mental map of the area.

The remainder of the camp was given a final going-over and the caves thoroughly swept out. It was clear that the area had been occupied, but in a month or two the wind and rain would re-naturalise the area to a great extent. They planned to return to this camp early next summer, looking forward to it already, and all were sad to leave, having had a relaxing time, despite the hard work. However, all were conscious of the often-plunging night-time temperatures, despite being on the temperate plains, and knew that getting home to prepare for the winter was now their priority.

Travelling home and slowly gaining altitude, it was plain to see the change in the landscape, with autumn proper now upon them, the plains having faded to less vibrant greens, though still abundant in forage for the many grazing animals. There was a cornucopia of early autumn berries on offer as they walked, easily plucked and popped in their mouths, the sweet and sour hits taking their minds off their heavy packs and their relatively rotund bellies built-up from their constant feasting of late. They were as a result moving quite slowly compared to their inbound journey, but eventually reached the old road and followed it east, with the blacksmiths collecting the odd treasure of precious scrap on the way, any stash left causing no end of groans.

The great river Rhuø eventually came into sight, though often obscured by the enveloping mass of trees which followed it as it flowed across the plains. They had little need to follow the river on their homeward journey, and chose instead to cut across the plains to reduce their journey time, all too aware of their seemingly ever-burdensome loads. After some miles they came upon the more coniferous woods skirting the low hills, but still a good day's travel from home with even a brisk pace. They took the decision to camp at that point, not wishing to do so too-close to the valley entrance and act as any sort of beacon signposting the way. Discrete sub-surface fire holes were employed with small secondary feeder-tunnels for ventilation, dramatically reducing down any smoke. Once the boiling of water and suchlike had been completed, they extinguished the fires and kept a cold camp until nightfall, reducing the risk of smoke being seen from afar. Come night they created a small perimeter of fires to ward off any animals nearby, conscious that the smell of so much meat, even if dried and heavily smoked, would potentially interest scavengers, though unlikely.

The next day the travellers awoke before first light and continued at a renewed pace, eager to be home and safe. The mixed deciduous forest bordering the plains gave way to fully coniferous-woodlands as they gained altitude, generally open with a thick carpet of bilberries and heathers with the odd large-mound of duff created by the wood ants. In time this further changed to just stunted pine on the upper slopes of the steep mountainous slopes each side of the valley entrance, from which spewed the river Rhuø down its self-carved rock strewn gorge. Autumn was noticeably further advanced as they gained altitude upon the north-facing slopes, with little green now left in the odd deciduous tree, but supplanted by a beautiful hue of rich browns, golden yellows and vivid reds. Distracted by the beauty of the season they ascended the incline reaching up to the steep-cut ravine at the valley entrance with little mind of their burdens, being eager to be home.

Following the river, it often went out of sight as it cut-through deep gorges, though small waterfalls and rapids were sometimes glimpsed, but always heard. They took care to choose different paths each time they ascended into their valley, to avoid any game trail becoming more obviously man-made. With difficulty they picked their way through and eventually left the steep-sided rock-strewn gorge area and came to their valley proper. It was always a revelation how different the valley was, sheltered and noticeably milder in the sun, its moderating microclimate providing an oasis totally unexpected from the climb up. Within just a couple of hours they had passed through the oak, ash and thorn woodland predominating at the valley bottom and came to the coppiced hazel-woods, with the various low mounds of the charcoal-making pits. The excitedly barking dogs and gleeful children then ran on ahead, feet crunching the carpet of leaves underfoot, the adults taking their smaller backpacks. They were warmly met by Shulvan, Sioned and Ianto whom had heard the noise and come down to welcome them. It was a joyful reunion, with most of the group having been gone now for many weeks. They all remarked how baby Ianto had grown and how well the family looked, though all were keen to quickly stow away the meat, skins and furs then unpack their things so they could relax their weary bodies.

The meat was the first item to be sorted, the bulk taken down to the cold store, and with some effort they managed to squeeze it in. The not insubstantial remainder was left in the larders upstairs for more immediate use. A few of the party were left to set fires in the cold hearths to drive out the slight damp, the main house having been mostly empty, with the family living up in their longhouse on the meadow. Divested of their packs the rest of the group went back outside, Nineveh and Shuldan splitting off with three of the younger ones to untack and brush down the tired ponies, then get them stabled away on some fresh straw. The ponies had done a terrific job over the past few weeks, but now needed a long well-deserved rest with lots of treats. They would be taken out for brief walks around the meadow to stop them getting stiff and allowed to wander the pasture the next day, but for now needed rest. Amaethon and Rhian were also keen to see to their domain, and quickly made their way to the potting shed to pack away the various seeds they had harvested, including a number of precious sweet-potato tubers, set with pride of place on special storage racks to grow on next year from the early rooting shoots. They would need to be coddled indoors initially, then in beds situated within the sheltered herb-garden under cover until summer, given their comparatively tender nature, but if they could grow them on successfully, it would be a welcome addition to their diet, though a luxury for the effort.

Bolin and Eryn were soon up to their cabin to drop off their packs, then straight to the forge, eager to relight it after so long away. They had a multitude of ideas to try out, including how they could improve the glassmaking process with purer charcoal and moving away from the idea of moulds to potentially trying to force air into a glob of glass to create a thin bubble, at Arwyn's suggestion. There was much to work out, but the hope was that this would lead to better jars to help increase their storage capacity in the pantries. Despite their exhaustion from the trip, the sounds of the forge quickly started to emanate from their domain, a welcome and familiar sound which made the group feel at home.

Some went to greet the pigs and goats, now considered pets as much as sources of food. It was good to see both herds' young were growing-up fast, the second brood of the year for some of the animals. They did however note that one of the goats not scheduled for the pot was missing, Sioned advising that they would explain later once the little ones had settled into bed. Those that checked on the fields noted the last of the autumn vegetables were nearing their peak, with various late tubers and squashes which would soon need to be harvested and stored. They were impressed to see that Shulvan and Sioned had been very busy, with various repairs to fences and buildings, another mulching of the vegetable beds, manuring to the fields and all manner of completed chores ready for the winter. They had also been busy in their long house, the consulting room of the hospital now fully ready, pristine and fully stocked. A huge number of herbs, fungi and medicinal barks and leaves had been harvested as well and were drying on racks in the main room of the new house, with some neatly suspended from the ceiling. The smell was quite something, wholesome and medicinal, a true apothecary in the making.

With dusk quickly coming, they all went to their respective houses and rooms to finish unpacking and wash up for a late supper. While they were doing so, Shulvan and Sioned made ready a large vat of venison and mushroom stroganoff and put some bread and roast potatoes in the oven. This they then left in Shuldan's and Nineveh's capable hands, once they were washed and ready. With extra herbs, tomatoes, cream and large range of vegetables, they soon had the house filled with wonderful smells, the butter roast-potatoes particularly mouth-watering with their rich aroma. While this was cooking Shulvan and Sioned proceeded to sort out great vats of boiling water so everyone could wash up and bathe.

That night, their bellies once again full and their bodies scrubbed, they sat in comfortable feather-cushioned chairs in front of the great fire in the hall, and told each other their tales. One-by-one the younger ones were put to bed, tired after their long journey home and sleepy with the now unaccustomed warmth of being indoors with blazing fires. With the little ones tucked up in their soft beds, and at everyone's repeated insistence, Sioned somewhat reluctantly started to tell them the tale of the missing goat.

She explained that some days after the pony team had come to drop off the second batch of fish, pelts and the bearskin, they had started to hear howls in the night of distant wolves. They assumed that the much-reduced human presence and the temptation of the goats and pigs must have led them to the valley, perhaps back to one of their natural hunting grounds from which they might have been displaced. At first they thought the wolves would keep their distance, but they soon saw them skulking one evening around the pastures, some thin and quite scrawny-looking, so decided that action may need to be taken. Though in all likelihood the wolves would stay clear once everyone came back with the dogs, it was a risk. The next day Sioned had lain wait with her bow in one of the elevated hunting-blinds high up in a tree at the edge of the pasture where the wolves had been seen; she stayed there from early morning to late into the night, but with no sign. The engrossed listeners knew that simply staying still that long was no mean feat, albeit the blind allowed for some limited adjustment to stave off cramps and to take on food and drink. However, the next morning Sioned explained that she had come across various tracks indicating the wolves had approached from the opposite side of the homestead and had been brazenly nosing around the stables and pens, indicating they must be hungry. Thankfully the buildings had been doubly secured so the wolves couldn't get to the goats and pigs, but the experience had clearly shaken them badly. One visit from the pack they could perhaps tolerate, but two nights running was concerning, seemingly their human scent of little concern. Typically wolves kept to themselves and it was unusual to see them, normally keeping to the plains and uplands where rich pickings could be had. It may perhaps have been that they had been temporarily displaced by their arrival in the valley and with what might appeared to have been a new competing pack with their dogs. That there were so few of the wolves, no youngsters and that they seemed undernourished, indicated they had perhaps been forced into sub-optimal hunting grounds in competition with other packs, but had returned now to potentially reclaim their territory. The cause of the wolves' arrival was unclear but could not be allowed, as magnificent as they were.

Shulvan and Sioned decided that though they were unlikely in direct danger, there was unacceptable risk to their livestock, and potentially themselves and Ianto. They had planned to take one of the old goats for meat mid-winter, so this they did that day, bleeding it and gutting it in the pasture, near Sioned's hunting blind. They left behind the guts, parts of the scraggy legs and head mounted on poles, then with Shulvan and Ianto safely in the longhouse, Sioned took up her position with her bow and wickedly barbed arrows to hand. Bar a few carrion feeders, which she chased off with stones from her sling, it was quiet, but she knew the potent smell of the fresh kill would be carrying ever further, providing irresistible attraction to the wolves if they were still around and hungry. Just before dusk, she heard, then saw the small pack arrive, spread-out, and approach with great interest, cautiously sniffing the area, but seemingly with little obvious fear. She let them approach and allowed them to start pulling down the remains of the goat. While they were distracted, she notched an arrow and let it fly at the closest; almost before that had reached its target, she had a second arrow in-flight, both taking a wolf each with a solid thunk to the base of their skulls which dropped with barely a sound. The other four were face-deep in the remains of the goat, not noticing the loss of two of their pack. With the same deadly and almost supernatural precision, Sioned took two more wolves in their chest and shoulders, the others finally noticing something was gravely amiss with the muffled thumps as the heavy arrows struck. On seeing their fallen pack members, the other two leapt away from their meal, one just avoiding another arrow arriving a split second too-late. They needed no confirmation that a superior hunter had them in their sights and started to make a run for it. Sioned watched the wolves loping away at speed, carefully took aim and let fly, taking a further wolf in its side, not clean, but a killing wound all the same. The last wolf, continuing to run, made for the trees, a sharp angle to Sioned's position. With another arrow notched and following the line of the beast's flight she let fly; this arrow was not so true but did pierce the wolf's rear leg, though it passed right through, causing it to stumble and howl in pain, but unfortunately not a killing blow. It picked itself up and ran with a great limp, hot blood dripping from the nasty wound. Sioned quickly gathered her weapons, climbed down from the platform in the tree and gave chase. Her quarry was not hard to follow, the heavy blood-loss leaving an easy trail, detectable by sight as-well-as by the sharp metallic tang in the air. Nonetheless, the animal had a head start and the last thing they needed was a lone wounded-wolf about the homestead. In the failing light Sioned was starting to lose the trail, but she could hear the occasional crash of the animal in the undergrowth, not far ahead. With an alarming suddenness she came on the wolf, who had turned to face its pursuer. It was a hefty beast, potentially the alpha male, though young, with a glorious shaggy mane of silvery grey. Though clearly in pain, it was a dangerous foe, cornered and ready to fight to its last breath. Sioned took her first light throwing spear and let loose, but the wolf dodged, clearly still in the fight. With her second spear at the ready she attempted to flank and close on the animal, but it mirrored her action, keeping head on, presenting less of a target and keenly watching her in the way wolves do, as if looking straight through you. Then with an unexpected lunge it tried to jump at her, though with limited power given its wounded leg. Sioned managed to get her spear forward and strike it with a glancing glow to its side, a bloody gash causing it to leap away in a yelp of pain. They continued to circle each other, the wolf clearly tiring as its life blood drained away from the two wounds, stumbling every now and then in a listless way that indicated its life was soon to end. Sioned decided that there were no need for heroics

283

and backed off, the wolf following but more and more slowly. With a final low growl, the wolf's back-end collapsed, and then it fell to its side. As the animal's panting became shallow Sioned watched as its end came, then as it became still, she approached and speared the wolf through its ear and into its brain to make sure that the danger had gone, and to ensure it suffered no more.

As Sioned finished telling her tale, she looked around to see wonder on the group's faces, awe that she has managed to take a pack all by herself, no matter her known skill with the bow. She played down their admiration, saying it was just something that needed doing and that Merrick could have easily managed it too. Merrick's face was one of subtly expressed awe then a small smile; he knew he could not have managed the feat with the bow, the pair of head shots particularly near impossible, but he guessed Sioned would not want the attention. Looking up in the rafters of the hall he at once saw the processed and tanned pelts of the wolves, surprised he hadn't seen them before for what they were, assuming initially they were the normal deer in the gloom.

The soft pelts were taken down and admired by all, fine but dense medium-length hair, freshly moulted into their winter coats. The pack leader's pelt was though without doubt the most impressive, an unusual silvery grey, though that was overshadowed by its size, almost akin to one of their ponies, a truly impressive brute. Merrick could see it in Sioned's face that she had seriously underplayed the threat and the feat she had achieved, he was sure the tale would grow in the telling by others, her modesty only enhancing the tale. Merrick knew however that she would have regretted having to cull the pack, her admiration for the animals' grace and skill as fellow hunters shared by all.

With the bear pelt and the wolf skins, they had between them the makings of some rather impressive winter cloaks which they would likely line with the soft goat's wool for added warmth and protection of the skins. Bolin said that he would be able to make some strong clasps in a fine polished silvery steel, and set to discussing the design with Eryn. The group agreed that Merrick should take the bear, as befitted him as their leader; he found this a little uncomfortable, but he knew the group would not take no for an answer. He accepted the honour with good grace and soon had the thick pelt cast about his shoulders, and all agreed he looked fine indeed, cutting a rather imposing appearance.

The wolf-pack leader's pelt went with no discussion to Sioned of course; she too was uncomfortable with the honour, but all knew she more than justified that and more with her song-worthy feat of hunting the pack and its fearsome leader. She took it and put it about her shoulders, the soft silvery grey fur contrasting and enhancing the unusual bright blue of her eyes and dark brown hair. She was without doubt the image of a hunter, confident in her skills, but without a hint of youthful arrogance that she had shed over the past year. Merrick thought on how she had matured and was proud, a silent barely perceptible nod to her saying all that needed to be said.

The other very-fine wolf pelts would be used for various projects but including as insulating hood liners and trims, keeping in the warmth and breaking the profile of the face for hunting, being good additional camouflage. All would receive a deep hood of wolf pelt, with an outer layer of softened auroch hide, dyed to a dark brown and waxed to repel water. The rest of the auroch-hides would be used mainly to make new boots over winter, with most now needing a new pair. The luxurious beaver pelts would make excellent oversized winter mittens, though currently they only had enough for five pairs, so they would be held for

285

communal use, though likely most often by whomever went out hunting in the colder weather.

They spent the rest of the evening telling each other tales of the eventful past several weeks, the bear hunt, the alarm of possible human presence, the abundance of the plains, the caves with their wonderful pools, and so it continued deep into the night. As they recounted their tales the horns of the auroch were passed around with the first of the mead, and an excellent early cider. With a number of the still precious, but now more plentiful beeswax candles lit, the stories continued until well past midnight, but then one-by-one, following a cup of relaxing chamomile-tea, they made their way to their beds happy and content.

32 - Autumn

Late autumn, turning to early winter, was a time of plenty in the valley with a superb harvest and their productive fishing, trapping and hunting expedition. It gave time for everyone to relax and enjoy the glorious season and abundant golden light, before the deep winter arrived. There were still numerous daily chores to complete, including tending to the animals, preserving foods, hunting for fresh meat and fishing trips if they fancied it, but generally there was much more free time to pursue various projects at their leisure.

Of course the blacksmiths spent much of their time refining their art and making two quick trips to stock up on scavenged metals, to tide them over the long winter. Of great success had been their trials with glass blowing, a fine art, but they had now mastered the basics. The key was having manufactured a thin metal blowing tube to expand a blob of molten glass into a thin bubble, the use of various moulds to form desired shapes and fine precision tools for cutting and aiding handling. They produced a range of useful glassware, mainly for food and drink storage, but became adept at creating glass sheets of better quality for windows, eventually replacing their earlier opaque efforts in the new dwellings and fixing those in The Steading. Though modest, they also made enough for some small cold-frames and cloches for giving seedlings a good head start come spring, and might possibly look to make a basic greenhouse in due course. However, that would involve the need for a great deal more high-quality sand and to collect any broken glass they could find for raw materials. In theory sea glass washed up on the shore, and shifting through old middens, was a great source of raw material to melt down and reuse, but may take time to accumulate in sufficient quantities; nonetheless there was no great rush. However, of particular success in the glass making was a near perfect thin sheet which was used to provide a picture frame for the vellum map which had led them to the Steading. With a beautiful burred oak surround the map was mounted in pride of place in the hall, the frame and glass protecting it for generations to come.

Given the success in the glass making Shulvan put in an order for a number of glass beakers, flasks and suchlike which helped enormously with his experiments, being ideal for precise diluting, distilling, measuring, and boiling. His research led to some fairly potent pain killers, effective anti-festering poultices for wounds and other useful medicines. It was during these discoveries that he noted the effectiveness of boiling and soaps for killing off pathogens and other nasties, leading him to reinforce the need for regular hand washing and general cleanliness, reducing incidences of stomach upsets and infections to an impressive degree across the group.

Trips up to the waterfalls to further explore the caves were also top of many peoples' to-do lists. The store of firewood was increased and various improvements made, including raised log beds, storage bins, basic shutters for the openings, installing a stout oak door to the top of the tunnel entrance, and all manner of other useful improvements. It formed an excellent place to get away from The Steading if anyone wanted a change, and if ever necessary would be a superb refuge. A few supplies tended to be left after each trip, safely away from rodents in thick oak-crates suspended from the ceiling. These provisions, along with some of their older furs and blankets, provided for a comfortable existence and much reduced the amount of kit needed for subsequent trips.

With time to spare the fields were further expanded, turned-over with the plough and left for the large clods to break down over winter with the hard frosts. There would be an excess of planting area in the year to come, but the plan was to rotate the crops and leave an area fallow for each year, to recover nutrients and increase productivity. All four of the ponies were now adept at pulling the plough and it didn't take many days to have the new area turned, expanding the fields to several acres. While they were creating these new fields they also took the time to create a few furrows in the less-productive damp areas, to create several rows of willow coppice. It was easy enough to plant whips with the furrow pre-made, simply pressing in a small stick of willow, then firming the soil around the cutting with the heel of a firm boot. In a few years this would form a productive stand of long thin whips, ideal for basket making especially, but also for items like soil sieving frames, trugs, chairs and hurdles. As a side benefit the copse would be massively productive in spring nectar for the bees and other insects, as well as providing a decent hedge and windbreak.

Arwyn had started basic afternoon lessons for the children that year, mostly taking place outside and being predominately practical. She had also started a log of their time at The Steading, mostly for fairly mundane purposes, including keeping a log of stores, a calendar of sorts for planting and harvests, observations on the weather, and suchlike. Producing the paper from pulp wasn't simple, but it was possible with effort, and was another project that they now had the time for. Ink was relatively simple, being most often made from the galls found on oak trees, mixed with vinegar and small bits of iron. The concoction was gently dipped into with a trimmed goose-feather quill and Arwyn's flowing hand was often heard scratching away into the late evenings, recording the doings of the settlement and some of their stories. The children were taught to read and write to a basic level, but for most it wouldn't be a skill often employed. There were however one or two of the children who became interested and helped out Arwyn with her record keeping.

One of the many success stories of that autumn was the capture of some migrating wild geese, who had been caught on the waterlogged pasture with the lightest of the fishing nets ingeniously rigged up to a fast pulley system. With a massive fuss of honks and hisses their flight feathers were clipped and they were penned to enable their slow domestication. This provided for a much more reliable source of eggs in due course for the spring and summer, supplementing those they found in the wild, most often from duck nests. To protect the geese through the winter they were kept in the barn in a purpose-built pen, with stout wooden walls to keep out the foxes and badgers, though they were fearsome birds when roused and didn't really need to be coddled. In addition to the dogs, they made excellent intruder alarms with their loud honking calls, though once they were part domesticated, this was only in relation to foxes, badgers and suchlike. They became relatively tame in due course; this only required some handling of their chicks, who quickly latched onto their human masters as being their adoptive family. Again like the goats, they were almost seen as pets, and it was a sad day for some of the children when they took a bird for the pot, but such was the way of life on the homestead.

Sioned and Merrick held regular classes on bushcraft and advanced tracking, not just for the children, but for any adults who held an interest. It would do no harm to have more of the group being superbly well-trained hunters, notwithstanding that all were more than capable of hunting at need. The sessions centred just as much on making the best of their senses than anything else, teaching greater reliance on smell and touch, often as not sitting in the woods with eyes closed and gradually expanding awareness of the small noises and often barely detectable scents. Once senses were better tuned, sessions were conducted by way of tracking plumes of scent, ranging from mushrooms to hidden deer and otherwise unseen apex-predators that were ordinarily rarely come across. Some had the aptitude, being able with the training to use this new found skill to practically walk blindfolded, touch and smell guiding them on even the blackest of nights. Sioned and Merrick also led further camping trips, mainly for the young ones, but Bolin was a regular feature, imparting his lore to any who were interested. He also taught the way of the fighting staff and spear, being arguably the most skilled of the group, most certainly in terms of throwing distance and brute power. Bolin was also a fine story teller with an imagination that quickly ran to fantastical tales of vast cities with soaring buildings of glass, countless self-propelled wheeled metal-carts that transported goods and people, great metal boats as big as islands that plied the oceans and other equally fanciful tales, the most outrageous being a tale of metal birds. Bolin would insist that most of what he said was likely true, having for example seen the skeletal remains of now overgrown, near unbelievably high buildings in his youth. Most of the children however, found this hard to accept as true, but still enjoyed the tales, perfect for engaging their young minds when sat around the camp fire.

The autumn carried on in this way with fine clear blue skies, all enjoying life in this most glorious season. Nonetheless, as the days rolled on there was a noticeable change in the air, with frosty mornings and shortening days heralding the winter to come. The tempo of life on the homestead picked up as a result, final preparations becoming more pressing, though there was really little left to do but make their lives more comfortable.

33 - Stranger

The mild autumn vanished and a harsh winter suddenly arrived, early and unrelenting, the snow soon covering the valley with drifts several feet deep. It was a stunning, yet harsh, landscape with the wind plastering the trees in snow on their northward side and often leaving trailing icicles on the leeward side. The houses were similarly covered at times, though the heat that leached-out tended to keep this mostly at bay. Navigating the valley could be blinding on occasion, with whiteouts fairly common; even the steepest cliffs being covered in ice and snow at times, softening all hard edges. Snow blindness was a real problem on some days, but was countered to an extent with goggles created by making an eye mask of thin smoothed bone with just a thin horizontal-slit, massively reducing down light, but allowing for some awareness of their surroundings. For those who managed it the waterfall at the valley head was stunning, a massive multi-pillared column of blue and shadowed ice reaching up hundreds of feet, much wider than a dozen great tree-trunks combined. Air bubbles and water droplets were suspended in places within, forming opaque and clear sections, with a multitude of icicles now frozen solid for some months to come. The multi-tiered waterfall reaching high up-and-out of the valley was a truly awesome sight, inspiring them to poems, songs and carvings of any unadorned surfaces in the great barn of The Steading.

The animals were kept in their stables for now, there being little point in allowing them out to try and graze; the hay in the barn would keep them very well-fed for several weeks at least, and they could supplement this with oats and root vegetables if needs be. Despite being often cooped up they didn't seem to care and were quite content to stay out of the warmth-sapping wind, being fed, watered and groomed by the children.

Food was plentiful with their bursting stores; a hearty full-flavoured stew or soup always seemed to be on the go, with fresh-baked bread made each morning, producing mouth-watering smells which permeated the main house. There was plenty of filling oats, honey and creamy goat's milk, which made for very filling breakfasts, with bacon and pancakes as a treat for as long as the eggs held out. They tended to roast a large haunch of venison early in the week, which then supplied their meat for the next few days, with potatoes and other vegetables bulking out these meals and providing essential vitamins. With the various pickles, preserves, jams, tomato purees for sauces, dried herbs, cheeses, butter, and all the many other provisions, they would be well-fed for many long months. The forced time inside also meant all had plenty of free time to pursue their hobbies, though nearly always this meant something useful being crafted, including embroidery of new clothes with the numerous cowries and other tiny shells from their trips to the sea. The forge was kept going in all but the worst of storms, the partially open front being shuttered up at need, but generally providing a still constant stream of useful items, including increasingly fine glassware.

Despite the weather, Sioned and Merrick were nearly always out and about on their snowshoes, and with some modifications to the design of the basic pulk sleds, they had created increasingly sophisticated sleds which their powerful dogs could pull in teams of three or more. These were amazingly efficient on even the deeper snow once it had hardened, the increasingly thick blanket smoothing out the lumps and bumps of the valley floor. It took some training, started the year before with practice pulling of the general-purpose pulk sleds, but the dogs soon had the knack, loving the exercise after being cooped up for days at a time. With the training complete, the group had free reign of much of the valley and could easily get to its head and back in just a few hours, with a hard run on the packed trail. There had been various

293

improvements made to the sleds, basically making them as small and as light as possible, with rounded upright handles to the rear to hold onto and a braking system which was essentially a friction pad you stood on at the bottom rear when needed, which when used lightly also helped gain traction in the corners to stop the sled sliding and skidding out. The dogs had been fitted with soft leather sock-like booties, which dramatically decreased ice build-up and soreness in their feet. All of the group were keen to come out for rides, being exhilarating to go at such speed, often fifteen or twenty miles an hour or so with six dogs attached. The short-legged mountain ponies could at best manage a slow bouncing trot, but it was a fairly uncomfortable ride and nothing beat the experience of the dogs pulling a sled full-pelt over the smooth snow.

The sleds made winter hunting trips a fantastically enjoyable experience, enabling them to traverse the valley to the herds with ease, and taking with them full camping gear as they wished, though they often used the refuge of the caves. There really was little need for more meat given the overflowing stores, but it did make a welcome change to eat the rich-tasting winter grouse and snow hares. They would often eat this game on thick rounds of rye bread with just a little salt, the simple fresh flavour of the succulent meat being enough after the full-blown taste of the smoke preserved meat and salty fish in the stores.

In this way they became proficient at travelling in the snow, which seemed set in for some months to come this year Amaethon had confidently announced. It was agreed that they would take advantage of this new-found mode of travel and a clear spell of weak wintry sun, to venture out onto the plains to the north-east of the river, and further establish if there were other humans present in the area. It was a nagging issue and they could do without the worry. Though unlikely to be the case, it was possible the river Rhuø represented the westward extent of another group's hunting ground, and if so, they would be better placed knowing this and keeping to the western side as much as possible. The added benefit of the snow would be that any tracks left by others would be easily visible at some speed, presuming no fresh falls and continued light winds. Mounted on the fast sleds, a great deal of the plains could potentially be explored and checked out.

Though the river Rhuø below the valley was a considerable obstacle all the way to the sea, it was swimmable with care in the wider slower sections, even for the older children, as they had shown on their last fishing trip a few months previous. It was however very difficult to cross with provisions of a substantive nature, especially in the freezing winter and was very dangerous in the spring floods, so likely was a formidable barrier to any groups considered migrating, or hunting the other side. However in the valley they could cross the river with relative ease in places, including at wider shallower sections by simply fording through, when the river was not in spate. However, there were also boulder-strewn sections which allowed them to virtually step-across with care, following some deft rearrangement of the boulders each year, but in placing planks pegged into holes laboriously drilled into the rocks and erecting a rope hand-rail, it was passable with great ease. This time of year of course these were de-mounted as they were liable to be washed away, but with the river icing over in places it was easily passable. This was seldom the case with the river on the plains where the climate was milder and the Rhuø wider due to additional feeder streams and rivers.

In any event, the homestead was on the eastern side of the valley and they could get down on that side of the gorge-like entrance, though with a great deal more difficulty that the west, which was their normal route out. The eastern route had been very rarely used, there being no particular need to go that way, especially when it was so difficult. However, with the deep snow smoothing the way, and the use of the sleds, it was much less of an impediment if tackled with care, particularly on the way down.

The more they thought about it the more they came to agree that it really was an ideal time to scout east of the river; especially as they could move with great speed, eating up many miles a day. If there came a need to avoid others, they could get away very quickly, their more obvious tracks being somewhat obscured at need by dragging a branch behind them, with what was left being quickly covered over in the regular snowfall or driving wind. Even if by some unlikely chance their tracks were discovered, they would be impossible to catch by anyone on foot. At full speed they could be fifteen miles or more away from danger in just an hour, and could lead any pursuers a merry dance over the plains with false trails. In light of these facts, they considered the benefits of scouting out any potential threat overcame the small risk.

Merrick and Sioned prepared with the efficiency of a pair well-used to each other's company on their numerous hunting trips, and so were ready to be off within the hour. Merrick said his goodbyes to Arwyn, embracing her then tenderly touching foreheads; most were unaware of the strength of their bond, one of mutual love and deep respect. Sioned embraced then kissed Shulvan and little Ianto, sad to leave them, the first time of any length since his birth, but he was now fully weaned and Shulvan could more than cope, with plenty of help to call on if needed.

As the pair departed all thought they cut rather impressive figures, Merrick, tall, bearded and broad, carrying off his black bear-cloak with unconscious ease, Sioned with her lovely soft wolf-cloak, her svelte but athletic figure almost equally tall. Riding on the sleds they looked like something from one of the great sagas; a pair of heroes setting off on an adventure, their great wolf-like dogs eagerly leading them. Any doubts some of the group had once had about Merrick as their leader had long since evaporated over their time at the Steading. It was more than likely that without his leadership in bringing them to The Steading, they would have long since perished.

The pair made their way down their wide valley, past the hazel coppice and the oak woodland, coming to the head of the steep gorge. Unlike normal the rocky gorge was relatively smoothed out by the snow, and by taking most of the weight off the sleds and carrying the loads on their backs for any tricky sections, the dogs could more or less skim across much of the compacted surface, with the sled gliding behind them, controlled through judicious use of the brake and ropes. Merrick and Sioned picked their way down the slope on their snowshoes, a hand on their sleds and giving commands to the dogs, though they could judge the best way pretty much on their own. It was not an easy task, but made easier by going downhill, with just a few sections where they had to detach the dogs and lift the sleds over particularly large boulders which had been blown clear of snow. Looking back they were hesitant about getting back up the steep drops, but knew it was achievable, despite its foreboding appearance.

On reaching the bottom of the gorge they repacked their sleds, and with the dogs full of boundless enthusiasm had soon picked their way down through the sparse stunted-conifers on the exposed north-facing upper slopes. The way was simple enough as they quickly descended, the area beneath the mature pines on the lower slopes being wide and open with various fairly obvious trails created by game, and further smoothed-out by the thick and compacted snow. It was however pretty slow going, with most trails meandering here and there. They followed the river downstream as much as they could, keeping an eye out for sign of game and any indication of other humans. They noted various hoof prints and places where deer had scraped down to the underlying vegetation to graze, along with the odd area they had compacted when sleeping, but not much else in the way of wildlife. This was more than expected, with many animals well into their hibernation cycle, some several weeks away from waking and most having migrated nearer the milder coastline. There were however plenty of birds going about their business, including large flocks of mixed finches, crossbills and crested-tits abounding, perfectly happy in their wintry home.

They continued to an ever-lower altitude while keeping parallel with the river, picking up the pace as the trees began to open up in the transition to the plains, increasing wind-chill causing them to wrap their faces ever more tightly. Given dusk would be coming within the hour, they made a wide circle then came back into the tree line, and located a spot for camp out of the wind. Next to the river they scouted an area which may once have been an old waterfall, but had eroded back to create a horseshoe-shaped sunken area at an angle to the current northerly-course of the shifting river. The more east-west configuration provided for some relief from the biting north wind and should help contain the dogs to a smaller area, also deadening their occasional noises. There was a small overhang forming a shelter where the horizontal slabs of a denser rock jutted out, the softer beneath having being undercut by the dried-up waterfall. With the addition of an angled front with their tarps and the sleds turned on their side for partial side walls, completed with blocks of snow, this provided an ideal camp. They swiftly had most of the snow cleared out, right down to the gravelly bedrock and then formed thick raised beds of green spruce and pine boughs, insulating themselves from the warmth sapping rock and snow. With some flattened stones they created a high-backed fire place and soon had a fire boiling some water for sweet tea. They would need substantial amounts of wood to see them through the deep cold of the night and so they both set to chopping and splitting the abundant dead-standing wood thereabouts, seeking hardwoods where they could for long-lasting coals.

With the dogs situated at the back of the overhang on their own spruce-bough bed covered over in wool blankets, Merrick prepared and gave them their supper while Sioned started making the pairs' evening meal. They had snacked on dried meat, honey cakes and apples on the trail, keeping up their energy, so weren't very hungry just yet, but looked forward to something hot to warm them and fuel up for the long night. Brought along with them was an excellent mini cast iron pot, ideal for slow cooked stews; though somewhat of a luxury with the bulk, but with the sleds it meant they could afford the extra weight. With the pot half-filled with water, they added partially dried onions, carrots, potatoes and venison which they let rehydrate, then simmer for an hour or so, adding a little salt and other herbs. They had brought some flour, so could make bread with some dried fruit, but they still had some baked fresh that morning, negating the need for this meal. Instead, Merrick made a few high-energy flour and suet dumplings, flavoured with some herbs, to drop into the pot when the stew was nearly ready.

With the pot simmering away and smelling wonderfully moreish after a long tiring-day in the cold, they left the bundle of contently-full dogs dozing on their bed in front of the fire and walked the outskirts of the camp, noting various spots where deer and winter hares had been grazing through the thinner spots of snow. With luck they may see the hares come morning and take a few for the pot and the dogs; ideally though a small doe would be perfect. While out they also collected more wood, ensuring that they had plenty stacked-up to keep a blazing fire going all night in shifts.

The pair rarely spoke, not seeing the need for chit-chat, silent gestures most often being enough, getting on with the camp tasks with efficiency born of many hours in each other's company. By unspoken agreement they finished the wood collection and came back to camp, the slowly-simmering stew now nearly ready and being kept a close eye on by the dogs in their dozing rest. As was usual the stew was most excellent, being simple, tasty and filling, the gravy mopped-up with some bread. On finishing the food they rinsed out the pot then added a little more water to heat and used this to clean the bowls and spoons with a little abrasive-sand. The small camp kettle was then put on to boil and then left to cool a little, following which small lumps of chaga fungus were added to gently roil and steep for an hour or so. As always the key was to boil their drinking water to kill any pathogens, but not to destroy the nutrients of the tea, a long slow-steep being best. The chaga tea had an unusual taste, being earthy, mildly sweet and a little bitter, but pleasantly so, being a calming brew perfect for winding down after the exertions of the day. With the tea eventually deemed ready for the first cups, they stuck a sprig of spruce into the kettle spout to filter any lumps of the chaga and poured the steaming brew into their kuksas. They passed the next few hours in companionable quiet with just the odd few words, drinking the wholesome tea, watching the fire greedily consume its fuel, listening to the near-hypnotic silence of the snow-laden woods and the soft snores of the dogs.

Next morning they awoke before dawn, making ready a calorific breakfast of fried bacon, cheese with a little mustard-seed melted onto a fruit loaf, topped off with a sweetened tomato-sauce. They then sipped some dried lemon-balm tea with a touch of honey while warming themselves by the fire and made plans for the day as the dawn came. It was agreed that the camp was ideal as a base for ranging north down-river and back for that day at least, and perhaps for the next after that in skirting the edge of the plains to the east and back. They were conscious travelling across the middle of the plains would leave them very exposed to view and the harsh elements, but that skirting the plains from within the edge of the woods would at least give them some cover, while being able to see across the more open expanses. It was a loose plan, but it gave them structure to the days ahead, hoping to cover perhaps dozens of miles at a steady pace while tracking.

The dogs were soon quietly yipping and ready to go, excited at the prospect of another day cantering through the snow. They were in their element, being at least partially husky-type dogs, solid but wiry beasts at about fifty-five pounds each with wide powerful-chests. The dogs' coats were perhaps a little short than was ideal in the winter conditions, but this did mean they didn't easily overheat in the warmer summers. They were in many ways similar to the wolves of the area, though of very different temperament, happy to accept the humans as their pack, with Merrick their leader. With the sleds in place, the dogs were clipped to a central line and attached to this via thick wool-padded leather harnesses to spread the load evenly across their well-muscled chests. They would take all their gear even though they hoped to return to this camp, better in case a change of plans was needed or they became stuck elsewhere.

Before long the two sled-teams were making their way down river, edging the wooded areas which gave a view across the plains but hid them from sight. As the ground opened up they were able to go with some speed, but chose to keep it to a steady trot to monitor the ground for any tracks and so as not to exhaust the dogs. Ideally the teams would be much larger, perhaps at least six dogs to a sled, but the others of the pack that had not come were just pups and feeding mothers. There were limits to how many animals they could feed and reasonably sustain year-round at The Steading, though for the future, that might change. The three dogs to each sledge worked hard, despite the steady speed, and at around midday they decided to rest.

The dogs were left to cool, then watered once their panting had abated, then given a very small meal of rehydrated venison. While the dogs were resting, Merrick and Sioned made a small near-smokeless fire under the trees, brewed tea and ate a meal of cured auroch-tongue, hard cheese and bread. With the party rested they made their way back out again, planning another hour's travel northward at the same steady pace. This they did, and with the hour up, they had a short break to water the dogs and to check them and the sleds over. With all deemed well they made the trip back to the camp travelling at an exhilarating pace now they had no need to carefully check for tracks. It was welcome that they had only seen animal tracks and no sign of humans over the plains, though really they had little expected such activity.

On route back to camp they came across a large herd of deer, though they were too exposed to attempt a hunt, and they soon bounded off further onto the plains. Thinking of the signs of animals feeding the night before in the thin snow of the clearing adjoining camp, Sioned suggested they approach with stealth to see if they could bag some of the hares or possibly a small doe. Agreed it was worth a try, they pulled up the dogs a good half mile before the campsite and Merrick took charge of both teams and leading them at a walk to the east to cool down, their breath forming plumes of misty vapour as it combined with the rapidly-plunging air temperature. They agreed to meet up in about an hour-or-so, giving Sioned time to approach with care and see what might be taken.

Sioned approached the camp with the skill of a hunter who was well-used to stalking such prey; she took a wide detour from the tracks they had left on the way out that morning and approached from the south-east, ensuring her scent was not carried on the wind coming from the north. Her plan was to approach the top of the overhang with great care, where the vegetation and treeline still gave her cover, then check on the clearing below, if possible taking a shot from that point. Coming to the overhang she went on hands and knees for the last thirty yards through the powdery snow, then with great patience peered over the rim of the depression, her wolf mane trimmed hood breaking her silhouette with trees behind her. They were in luck, several deer had come back for the easy pickings of the partially uncovered freeze dried grass and were concentrating on grazing before nightfall. Having already silently pulled an arrow from her fur-lined quiver on the approach, she nocked it to the bowstring and pulled back, smoothly releasing almost at once as she rose. The arrow flew and solidly thunked into her target, a first winter doe, quite small, but it would yield the perfect amount of tender meat for the two hunters and their dogs.

It was a clean kill, centre chest, ending its life with just a short jerk of shock and falling still to the snow. The other deer of the small herd had leaped off almost as soon as the arrow had struck and were now nowhere to be seen. Sioned stood, dusted off the accumulated powdery snow and made her way around the top of the small cliff, down the sloping side and came to the deer. She retrieved and cleaned the bloodied arrow, replacing it in her quiver with satisfaction that it was still whole, it being one of her better steel-headed arrows. She then set about skinning and butchering the carcass with quiet efficiency. It wouldn't need to be a pretty job as the hide would be disposed of along with any other parts left over, at some distance from the camp. The legs, shanks and neck, along with the heart, liver and other edible organs would be kept back for the dogs. The main carcass she would mount onto a heavy spit and, with a long log fire, would slow roast it for some hours; that should keep them going for some days at least, including sharing with the dogs once they had finished the raw meat, bones and offal.

With the carcass partially butchered, she started moving the meat to the overhang, wondering where Merrick had gotten to, though only mildly concerned. On arriving at the overhang she turned from dragging the carcass and was a little shocked to see a bundle of ragged blankets on top of one of the raised beds they had made. Dropping the meat she had her belt knife out in one fluid motion, crouched and ready to deal with any potential threat. With no movement from the bundle she cautiously moved forward, taking a long stick from the woodpile and reaching with it towards the mound. She prodded it tentatively, to no effect, then pushed harder, the result being a small moan, but which quickly subsided. Sioned's first reaction was to quickly move forward, the cry was one of a small girl or young woman, clearly unwell. The lack of a fire in such conditions, with their stacked wood so close to hand, meant the girl must be in a bad way indeed as the source of heat could save her life come nightfall. Now with calm quick-efficiency she approached the ragged bundle, carefully peeling back the grimy covers. She uncovered a slight girl beneath the rags, a young woman in fact, not far from her age, but horribly thin and dirty, frostnip evident on her nose. Sioned soon had the unconscious girl checked over, no obvious broken bones or other wounds, but clearly very malnourished and weak, her fingers close to frostbite. As she was doing this she heard Merrick approach with the dogs, and she signalled to him to come. Merrick came upon the two with the young girl just starting to come around in Sioned's arms. As she awoke there came over her face a look of shock, then fear, but no sound. She weakly tried to move away, but Sioned held her still with little effort and she soon fell back again, exhausted but petrified.

Merrick and Sioned quickly had a warming fire burning and the sleds forming a wind break. They carefully piled their blankets and furs around the girl and gave her a little water, which revived her somewhat, enough to open her eyes more fully and stare at them both, but she remained still. The girl was clearly in shock at seeing them, but they supposed they did make imposing figures in their bear and wolf cloaks with a team of wolf-like dogs at their command. They shortly had some water on the boil and added small bits of meat and dehydrated vegetables to make a thin plain broth; the girl's attention was unwavering from that moment on. While it was cooking they offered her some of their bread, soaked in a little water to soften it. With some hesitancy she took the bread, smelled it and nodded quick thanks and devoured most of it in an instant, coughing a little afterwards. In a while the broth was ready and they offered it all to the girl, she took it in wide-eyed wonder, initially pushing it back to them as if to offer them their share, but she soon understood it was all hers. With alarming speed she practically inhaled the broth, wiping the pot clean with the last of the bread. They then offered her a wrinkled apple, much to her clear astonishment. They were worried the girl might consume this with the same speed as the broth and choke, so used a knife to slice it for her. The look of alarm when Merrick first took out his knife was soon replaced by the look of hunger at the apple slices which she silently took. They indicated she eat slowly and explained with gestures their concern she might be sick if she ate too quickly, but assured her the apple was all hers. Merrick then gave the girl the rest of the apple, handing her his eating knife, handle first. She took the apple with a small nod of her head, and reached to her belt for her own knife, which they saw was a long flint shard with a wrapped leather handle, functional and deadly sharp, but much inferior to their more robust, forged-steel blades they all carried at The Steading.

They left her then so that they could tend to the dogs, which the girl had only just fully registered, having previously been focussed on the fire and food to the exclusion of all else. Her first reaction was one of alarm, but within just a few minutes she saw that the dogs were simply curious about her, rather than showing any sign of aggression. In fact she saw how they nuzzled up against Sioned and Merrick, clearly friendly to them, and she relaxed a little, her hands and feet pulled close to the blazing fire, attempting to thaw them out.

Sioned had moved back to the deer carcass and started dressing the bulk of the meat for the spit, feeding much of the rest to the dogs. The girl's face at seeing so much meat was a sight to behold, a mixture of surprise, astonishment and then great hunger at the meat now sitting over the fire, starting to produce the most wonderful smell as the outside seared and sizzled. She sat and watched the meat while it cooked, with quick glances at the dogs and Merrick and Sioned every now and then. The dogs were later brought into the shelter where they laid upon their blankets and dozed. This gave the girl another place for her gaze to dart until she realised they would do her no harm and her attention went back to the meat.

While the meat cooked and was encrusted with salt, herbs and basted its own dripping juices, they tried to communicate with the girl, to ask her name and where she had come from, but she remained silent. Clearly they would not make much headway tonight given her nervous state, so they let her be while they sorted out their camp and made another raised bed. In time she nodded off, clearly exhausted despite her fear, though she awoke within a short time.

As the girl warmed from within as she digested her meal she emerged from her cocoon of blankets, revealing her very tangled hair beneath a well-worn cap of ragged wool, a crudely-cut jerkin and basic wrap-type boots. She was clearly layered in many skins, but most were just swathed and tied around her and were only basically tanned, being quite stiff and unyielding, though no-doubt effective. They noted she only had a small travelling satchel and a staff, with no sign of any bow or additional clothing. Sioned reached for her bags to pull out her extra hooded overcoat and offered it to the girl. She slowly took the shell embroidered coat with great reverence and fingered the soft wool and fur trim as though it was the finest thing she had ever seen. With some considerable coaxing the girl simply placed it over her shoulders and put up the hood, looking a little less wild as a result.

With some hours passing in silence the meat was then deemed ready and the first slices given to the girl. She seemed to understand their wish for her to eat slowly and so she did. Her face was a sight to behold as she ate each mouthful of the tender well-seasoned venison, as though she had not eaten properly in many days, if not weeks, and certainly not anything akin to the feast she now had before her. It wasn't long before she was satiated, though having not eaten that much due to her stomach having shrunk from near starvation; with a brief nodding of her head, she fell asleep and remained so for the night.

Merrick and Sioned withdrew from the overhang to talk, not wanting to disturb the girl and eager to see what each other thought. Clearly she was little threat but they agreed it would be best if they took turns watching over her that night. It was unclear from what direction she had come and she could have been there since they left that morning; it was perhaps even likely given the presence of the nearby deer indicating they hadn't been disturbed in some time. They would in the morning check to see where her tracks came from and perhaps consider one of them taking a sled and following them to see where they led.

The next morning came with Merrick making a breakfast of bacon, sliced venison, cheese and freshly-made bread with dried fruit. The girl started suddenly awake, seemingly at the smell, with Sioned soon after slowly coming to with a yawn. Though the girl was less frightened, she was clearly hesitant and didn't wish to leave the perceived security of her bed, but that was no matter. Giving the girl her breakfast with a soft reminder to eat slowly, she did so with delight soon obvious on her face, especially at the sweet tomato-sauce she was offered to smear on the meal. They tried talking to her some more, to little effect, so they did not press her further. She seemed content to sit and rest, so they let her be to recover her strength, taking care of the camp around her. They were however pleased to note that she appeared to have regained full dexterity in her hands with no sign of any harm, bar a little frostnip.

Sioned suggested that she stay at the camp with the girl as she seemed more comfortable with her, and that Merrick take all six of the dogs and strip down a sled to the essentials for speed. This would allow for a scouting trip to follow the girl's trail as far as he could by about midday, then return. Merrick agreed and was soon off, moving at a great pace with the six dogs.

The exhilaration of the expanded team of dogs and the stripped-back sled was quite incredible, at times he was touching twenty miles an hour, though averaging about ten to keep the dogs fresh. He was following a clear trail of often deep footprints, consistently keeping just within the treeline at the edge of the plain. There had very fortunately been a slight thaw overnight but which had refrozen, accentuating each of the girl's small footprints. With no fresh snow and only a little wind since the trail was left, it should hopefully keep the trail clear for some considerable time. With each passing mile, Merrick was more-and-more impressed at the girl's stamina; despite her clear exhaustion and malnutrition, she had evidently been walking for several hours at least before getting to their camp and without the benefit of snow shoes. At about mid-morning and some twenty miles east, he came to what must have been her last camp, a poor affair of snow piled up against a fallen tree and scraped back to the ground beneath. Checking the area he could see no sign of any fire; seemingly she had spent a cold and hungry camp here before walking some twenty miles through thick snow overnight; that she had survived was quite incredible given the freezing temperatures. Seeing no reason to stay he cleared evidence of the camp as best he could, remounted the sled, and set off further east.

Some thirty miles later and having crossed a frozen river, he came upon another camp, with signs of a small fire this time and the remains of the fur of a small hare nearby. Beyond the camp fainter footprints continued off into the distance beyond the outliers of treeline across the more open plain. Merrick knew he was at the extreme limits of making a safe return to camp by nightfall, and reluctantly he decided the mystery would have to remain. Perhaps they could get the girl to talk in time, but clearly she had not come from any settlement which was close by, travelling an extraordinary distance each day for a poorly-provisioned and minimally-equipped hike.

Having fed the dogs a small amount of well-chopped meat and given them plenty of water when they had first stopped, Merrick let them rest a while in anticipation of the long journey back. He made himself a small fire, brewed hot tea with honey and chewed on some spiced-venison jerky. He faced east while he ate, scanning the crystal clear horizon and the plains for any sign of other humans and settlements, but saw nothing, not even any distant smoke plumes. Finishing his meal he cleared away all evidence of his fire and did the same with the few remnants of the girl's camp. Walking out on her tracks for a hundred yards east he came to an area of thin snow cover where the footprints were indistinct, working back he started brushing over the trail with a branch, obscuring it somewhat, but ensuring that come the next snowfall or with the benefit of a drifting wind there would be next to no sign, certainly little detail. Getting ready to depart he did the same around the camp and then attached the branches to the back of the sled, obscuring the trail again for about a mile. At that he launched the branches into the undergrowth and came back around on himself a few times, looping to confuse the trail. It certainly wouldn't fool any tracker worth calling themselves such, but it was better than leaving a trail a child just out of swaddling clothes could follow.

With the trail obscured, he surveyed the sky and saw he had about two or three hours to dusk. He would be travelling in the light of the moon for a good way, but he would make the most of the light that would reflect back off the snow and confident knowing the route back was clear of any obstacles. He let the dogs take the lead, thus setting a cantering pace they were comfortable with, but eating up the miles. It was an exhilarating way to travel, the cold breeze keeping Merrick awake and leaving a frost in his beard from the moisture in his exhaling breath. Towards the end of the journey back the dogs started to flag a little and he let them trot as they wished and ran alongside at times to ease the load and keep him warm, easy enough where the snow was thin. Some two hours after dusk the team made it back to camp, completing some hundred or so miles in the round trip within astonishing time for dogs not born to the sled.

Sioned was pleased to see him, some slight worry playing around her eyes that most would not detect. They would discuss the trip later, first the dogs needed to be checked over, fed and watered, then settled onto their beds near a warm fire. They would likely need to let them rest the next day, being completely unused to such long and strenuous journeys, but having done themselves proud.

As the dogs settled and had their legs massaged and paws treated with a soothing balm, they all came around the campfire for a late supper. Merrick was pleased to see that the girl had clearly been helping out, and was currently stirring the stew and making ready to serve it up. Sioned explained that she had left her bed late-morning and had assisted in light camp-tasks, then washed herself in the frigid river, though needing to rest again mid-afternoon. With good food and a change into some of Sioned's spare clothes, she was making an extraordinary recovery, and on waking from her nap had been kneading bread and making the meal, which Merrick found was delicious. It was clear from Sioned's looks that she had been unable to get much out of the girl, but she had managed to confirm, through a series of gestures and soft words, that physically she was okay bar being severely malnourished and exhausted. Sioned also explained that she had taken to calling the girl Ithryn, for want of any name the girl could tell them. Merrick then told of his journey, directing praise to the girl for her extraordinary stamina, but she merely looked frightened at mention of this and shied away from looking to the east.

In time it may be possible to get the girl to speak, but for now they let her be, there was little point in forcing the issue. They did however explain that after a rest day tomorrow they would be going home, and asked if she wanted to come. Not wanting to scare the girl they didn't tell her the size of the group, but told her all about the safety and security of the valley homestead, its many resources, and how she was very welcome to stay. She looked slightly bewildered at the mention of the house and farm, but seemed interested. Sioned and Merrick knew they were taking some risk in giving her such detail, but they were also conscious that really the girl had little choice, and in reality she would unlikely be able to find the homestead, not giving her any specifics on its location and distance. With some reluctance on her part, they eventually received a nod and accepted that as her agreement. With their food digested and the fire built-up it wasn't long after before all three were tucked up and warm in their sleep rolls and furs, tired after the long and unusual day, soon joining the dogs in soft slumber.

They awoke next morning to find Ithryn making bread and in the process of frying-off the last of the venison as small steaks. As they awoke she handed them some lemon-balm tea with a little honey and went back to the meal preparation. With the meal finished Merrick made to clean the dishes, though Ithryn protested, but he firmly made it clear that they did not expect her to be their servant, but were more than happy that she share in the chores. They thought she looked a little relieved, though perhaps slightly disbelieving.

They decided that morning to take the dogs for a walk to stretch off what must be very sore legs and shoulders, and to see if they could track down more deer, preferably a small doe to see them through to the next day and their journey home. They did see a small herd on the plains but they were too exposed to stalk. On walking back to camp they were keeping among the trees and suddenly realised Ithryn had stopped and was pointing to the trees. She evidently had a sharp eye as she had spotted a group of capercaillie roosting near the tree tops, virtually invisible to even Merrick and Sioned's eye. Sioned quickly pulled off her mittens, had her bow out, strung, and arrow nocked, with Merrick following suit. Motioning Ithryn to stay with the dogs, and instructing the animals to stay, the two stalked towards the roosting birds, coming at them apart and on an offset route to the tree, intending to look as though they would pass each side at some distance, being of little perceived threat to their quarry. On reaching an optimum angle they made a subtle signal to each other that they had a shot, and as one, turned and took aim at a bird at opposite ends of the roost. The blunt-tipped flu-flu arrows almost struck each of the selected birds as one, and both fell to the ground, with the others rapidly disappearing with a brief frantic flight deeper into the trees.

They returned to the camp with the pair of large birds, likely some thirty-or-so pounds of good meat, ideal to feed the small band. The hunters started on the plucking and gutting while Ithryn brought the fire back to life and started loading a good pile of hardwood to burn down to a bed of cooking coals. She then started making two spits to each side of the fire, and began selecting suitable herbs to mix with some wetted breadcrumbs, along with a few salted oats to make a moist stuffing with the last of their dried onions. Sioned and Merrick both noted with satisfaction that the girl was clearly more than capable of looking after herself and being of use around camp; she would be a welcome addition to the group, if she chose to stay.

The birds were slow-roasted that afternoon, being basted in nearly the last of the butter and their own juices as they dripped. They all took it in turns to turn the birds, and after some hours the skin had developed into a dark golden brown. While they waited, Sioned had taken Ithryn to see if they could find some hares and see how she did with a sling. Sioned managed to bag two, and Ithryn one, so these joined the birds and were quickly roasted on the fire, an excellent starter which the dogs also enjoyed.

As dusk came the birds were deemed ready; the dogs had been given a good amount, along with much of the rehydrated meat chunks that had been brought for them. Ithryn has overcome her initial fear of the dogs and had been hand-feeding them various morsels, much to their delight; they had clearly adopted her as one of their own, two of the animals now sleeping each side of her with their heads on each leg and the others close by.

The birds were delicious, though the meat a little tinged with the taste of pine from their winter diet; accompanied by another loaf of sweet bread loaded with dried fruit, it filled them to bursting. With copious amounts of steeped chaga-tea to wash it down, they sat back contented and sleepy. They congratulated Ithryn on her sharp eyes, thanking her for the fine meal. She sheepishly accepted the praise and even seemed to manage a brief smile, which for a moment lit up her face, but disappeared as quickly as it came. Merrick tried to draw more out of the girl with tales of their home and adventures, and he thought she seemed interested, though she wouldn't do much more than nod at appropriate points. With their food digesting and the fire loaded-up for the night, they all settled down, Ithryn surrounded by a pile of dogs who were contentedly snoring and occasionally chasing rabbits in their dreams.

34 - Home

Early the next morning the trio arose refreshed despite their shifts tending the fire; the dogs had also recovered and were eagerly stretching, yipping and ready to be off to enjoy the simple delight of pulling the sleds. The last of the capercaillie was finished, excellent with a pinch of salt, on a buttered slab of bread with the last of the tomato sauce. While this was washed down with lots of hot sweet tea, the dogs picked over the few morsels that remained of the birds, the last scraps of the venison and then started nuzzling their masters, clearly eager to be away.

Between the three of them they made short work of putting out the remains of the fire and sweeping away the ashes. There was some scorching which couldn't be helped, but was minimal with the bed of flat rocks they had placed beneath and then hidden in the woods. The boughs used in their beds were then cast into the centre of the free running river and the last of the firewood scattered back into the forest. The camp was therefore left with little sign of their coming and would fully return to nature before too long, likely overnight given the look of the heavy snow-laden clouds pushing in from the north.

The dogs were harnessed and carefully hitched to the two sleds, Ithryn and Sioned to take one mounted side by side, with Merrick to the other, the weight being about equal with more of the baggage stowed on his. On the way out of camp they left a series of confusing loops in both the north and easterly directions, then on crossing a particularly complex set of tracks on thin snow, started dragging a bough behind each of them to obscure details of their trail. It wasn't perfect, but with the next snow fall and some wind, it would certainly add confusion as to their eventual direction of travel if anyone happened to come by, though it seemed extremely unlikely based upon their exploration.

The party then continued south towards home, making good progress uphill, on a switchback-like course up the slope to save tiring the dogs with the long steep-incline. It would be a solid day's travel, especially with the added weight of their additional passenger and the indirect passage up the slope, but they were in no great rush. In any event they made good time, the dogs now being used to the hard work, with their masters jogging at times alongside the sleds on the thinner snow beneath the trees. Towards the end of the day they came to the bottom of the canyon entrance to the valley, pleased to see that even with no snow since they left, their outward tracks were barely perceptible, having been covered over by loose windblown-snow. Merrick and Sioned put on their snowshoes and took their packs off the sleds, with Ithryn staying as much as she could on the two sleds, not having any to wear. Notwithstanding this disadvantage, she had limited trouble in the snow with her light frame causing little extra strain to the animals. Coming to the trickier boulder-strewn sections, the three took most of the load off the sleds, then helped the dogs by lifting them up and finally hauling the sleds up and over. It was difficult work for several sections, but they took it slow, not wanting to sweat too much, as it soon gave you a numbing chill when you were forced to stop.

While they were making the climb dusk had come and gone, and it was with a final effort they gained the head of the gorge. From the top they were on home ground and even in the dark, with just a half-moon's light, the dogs found their way with ease, quietly yipping in excitement. Moving through the dense oak forest, then the coppiced-hazel stands, they came to The Steading, though the house was dark with the shutters closed, but its bulk was evident in the moonlight with wisps of smoke visible from both chimneys. With Ithryn very hesitant and sticking close to Sioned and Merrick, they moved their packs into the porch and unhitched the dogs. The sleds were simply turned-over and laid-up against the side of the house, the eaves would protect them for the night. During all this the dogs had been eager to get inside, to eat supper and lounge in front of the warm fire and so had been softly scratching at the front door, quietly whining, but didn't bark in-line with their training. The door opened to the rest of the dogs, along with Bolin and Eryn, staffs in hand, seemingly half-expecting trouble, but not surprised to see it was their dogs, who would often make such noise after being let out before bed and wanting to come back in. With his eyes adjusting to the gloom Bolin then saw Merrick and cheerfully embraced him in a warm bear-hug, saying they had given up expecting them that night given the lateness, but that there was plenty of stew on the go and fresh bread when they were ready. Before Eryn had chance to greet them, Merrick had turned to beckon forward Ithryn who was timidly looking-up at them from Sioned's side. Merrick introduced her to the blacksmiths, saying that they had found a new friend, but that the story would need to wait a little while for them to get warm and eat.

After divesting themselves of their cloaks, gloves and furs onto spare pegs in the hall, Sioned showed Ithryn into the warm kitchen and introduced her to Nineveh, who was busy putting the finishing touches to a delicious-smelling supper. With barely a second look, Nineveh had bent down and embraced the thin girl in a long motherly-hug and then bodily picked her up and gently sat her down in a comfortable corner seat, quickly ladling out a big bowl of stew and plating-up fresh bread, seeming to sense that the last thing the girl needed was questions. Not long after saw Sioned with a hearty bowlful sat in front of her too, and the two started wolfing down their food, incredibly hungry after the taxing day. Merrick, Bolin and Eryn came in a few minutes later, closely followed by Shulvan, who all sat, warmly welcomed Ithryn with little fuss and started eating. There was shortly a buzz of conversation with questions as to where the others of the group were; Nineveh explained that some had already eaten and were in the main hall, with Shulvan

317

and the baby at the cottage, the various younger children settling down for bed. Ithryn's face was one of astonishment, first at the mention of a baby, then the children; to her new friends it seemed as if this was the most normal thing in the world to be speaking of. Seeming to forget her recent muteness, she falteringly spoke up to ask how it was possible there were so many young ones, saying that she had been the youngest in her village by far, then trailed off, as if she didn't want to remember more. Merrick quickly made to continue the conversation and explained that most of the children were found on their travels and had been welcomed to the group and adopted by some of those she saw at the table, the baby simply being a rare blessing, gesturing to Sioned as he spoke and explaining she was the mother. Ithryn heard all this in half disbelief, then suddenly broke down in quiet tears, but through her gentle sobs they heard her tentatively ask if she could join them too. Merrick took her gently in his strong arms, formally stating in the old speech, with a tight throat and tears in his eyes: *"natürlig Ithryn, du ist hjertelig welkømmen, alltid"*. All of the group were in tears of joy after that, sensing that hers was a story much like most of the group and knowing how much this would mean, having a safe place to belong.

Later, with a huge supper starting its slow digestion, they took Ithryn to the hall and settled her in front of the fire in one of the new bentwood lounging chairs padded-out with cushions and thick blankets and furs. With a hum of conversation mingled with soft singing, she was quickly lulled into a deep sleep, and not much later, tenderly carried upstairs by Sioned, where she was tucked up in Nineveh and Shuldan's warm bed; tomorrow they would find her a place of her own, but for that night Sioned would be her companion.

The rest of the group continued their excited discussion late into the night, eager to learn more of the new addition to their close-knit group.

Merrick spoke of what little he had learnt, but stressing how impressed he was with what she had achieved in her long trek in deep winter and surviving on her own for what must have been weeks given her state. They were all relieved to learn of the lack of any other human presence nearby, and agreed that they were extremely lucky to have been favoured with such a capable young adult as an addition to their extended family. Sitting back in their favourite rocking chairs and laid-out on comfortable loungers, sipping on a warming mulled blackberry-wine, they all felt content, happy and grateful for all that they had achieved and carved out for themselves. The Steading had and would provide.

Epilogue

Ithryn, for that was the name she kept, was soon introduced to the rest of the inhabitants at The Steading, becoming an indispensable part of the household, and some years later, their next leader. She never did say what had driven her to come so far with little hope, but all knew it would a story similar to many heard before and felt no need to press her.

The New Year came, spring arrived and thus the cycle of life at The Steading continued, much as it would for decades to come. They made regular expeditions out of the valley, but never came across any other settlements or groups, despite extensively travelling to the east and west. They eventually came to accept that theirs might be the only enclave for a thousand miles, but they always kept look out for any that might need help, as they had with Ithryn and the children.

Little did they suspect that theirs was actually the last human settlement for perhaps thousands of miles, with only a few tiny-pockets of humanity such as theirs now existing across the world. Those communities that hadn't simply fizzled-out for want of the next generation, had often broken apart and withered away, decimated by conflict, disease and famine. Though they didn't know it their valley was one of the few places that could sustain a human population, the glacier-fed river supplying water which was relatively free of contamination that fell from skies.

In time, as the insidious and unseen poisons of the air and water finally dissipated to levels more conducive to human life, The Steading would form the nucleus of a new society that began anew, slowly growing, but always within the limits of what the land could provide. Babies were still an event to treasure, and it was unusual for a couple to have more than two children surviving to adulthood, but this was enough, and kept an equilibrium with the environment that could be sustained. Peace, contentment and joy in the simple life were their treasures; they needed no more.

Printed in Great Britain
by Amazon

84652860R00189